A Place to Belong

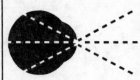

This Large Print Book carries the
Seal of Approval of N.A.V.H.

A PLACE TO BELONG

LAURAINE SNELLING

THORNDIKE PRESS

A part of Gale, Cengage Learning

GALE
CENGAGE Learning·

Detroit • New York • San Francisco • New Haven, Conn • Waterville, Maine • London

Copyright © 2013 by Lauraine Snelling.
Scripture quotations are from the King James Version of the Bible.
Thorndike Press, a part of Gale, Cengage Learning.

Thorndike Press® Large Print Christian Fiction.
The text of this Large Print edition is unabridged.
Other aspects of the book may vary from the original edition.
Set in 16 pt. Plantin.

LIBRARY OF CONGRESS CATALOGING-IN-PUBLICATION DATA

Snelling, Lauraine.
 A place to belong / by Lauraine Snelling.
  pages ; cm. — (Thorndike Press large print Christian fiction) (Wild west wind ; book 3)
  ISBN 978-1-4104-5536-9 (hardcover) — ISBN 1-4104-5536-X (hardcover)
 1. Women ranchers—Fiction. 2. Brothers—Fiction. 3. Black Hills (S.D. and Wyo.)—Fiction. 4. Large type books. I. Title.
 PS3569.N39P57 2013b
 813'.54—dc23   2013003396

Published in 2013 by arrangement with Bethany House Publishers, a division of Baker Publishing Group

Every writer has to be gifted with friends who play a behind-the-scenes role of encouragement and support. One of my special friends is my assistant Cecile. We have worked together for more than ten years, and besides all her office skills, she has developed a marvelous gift of reading my mind. Amazing how much easier it is to communicate that way. I thank God for her. What a gift she is to me.

1

December 1906
Argus, South Dakota
Just get out of the wagon. Cassie Lockwood swallowed — hard.

"Are you all right?" Mavis Engstrom was smiling up at her. "No hurry."

I'll have to see them again. Look at them again. Only this time it will be daylight and close up. If the judge asks me to identify any of them, I won't be able to. I never saw their faces. How to explain this to someone else? Her stomach clenched and she felt like two hands were squeezing her throat. *Breathe. And get down. One thing at a time.*

When she thought back to that night, she started to shake all over again. Gunshots in the night, voices hollering horrible things, grabbing her rifle and returning fire, the searing pain of a bullet in her arm, the wagon burning so brightly she could see men on horseback circling the cabin, the Engstroms

7

coming over the hill but too late to do much more than scare off the intruders and pull the burning wagon away from the cabin. Then passing out from loss of blood and agony.

All that was left from her lifetime of years in the Wild West Show had burned up that night, along with the wagon she'd traveled in and lived in. The scenes of churning, crackling chaos and loss had branded on her memory. But mostly the fear and the anger. Who would do such a thing and why? All because of Chief and Runs Like a Deer. How? Who? Why hate Indians like that? What difference did it make to those men if Indians lived at the Bar E Ranch?

The men had been caught and confined in the local jail in Argus, South Dakota, awaiting a circuit judge to try and sentence them. And she had been forced to shoot a man, winging one of the perpetrators. Nightmares of that night had plagued her for weeks while she recuperated down at the ranch house, with the Engstrom family taking care of her.

All because some troublemakers got liquored up and decided to frighten away the Indians. Chief and Runs Like a Deer were certainly no threat to anyone. But the officials had not demanded that they testify, only she and the Engstrom brothers, Ransom and Lucas. She'd lost a shooting match because of the injury, but what good would it do to send these men to prison? Other than to keep them from inflicting such fury on someone else. That would certainly be a good thing.

Cassie let Lucas Engstrom, the younger brother, help her down. Lucas insisted he was in love with her, and he was certainly playing the part of the gentle, strong young swain today. She shook out the folds in her dark serge skirt and straightened her shoulders, wrapped in a dark shawl to keep out the cold of the December day. She should have worn her black wool coat, but it had grown to look shabby from the long years of use. When she had looked in the mirror, she'd perched her black hat with the fine veil on the top of her head, hoping to give her an appearance of proper fashion.

Her mother would have been proud of her, she knew. The approval in Mavis's eyes had stilled the rampaging butterflies, but on the wagon trip to town they'd taken to cavorting again. What kind of questions would the judge ask her? What if she didn't know the answers? She hated to remember that night but now she was being forced to. One more strike against the three men.

One more strike that fanned the no-longer-sleeping embers of anger that the memories caused. She'd lost the shooting match in Hill City due to the injury to her arm, lost the purse that would have kept them in winter supplies, including the critically needed cattle and horse feed. She who could drive nails into a log with her sharpshooting had been shot in the arm in a midnight raid on her new home. That act of injury had severely damaged everything — her arm, her livelihood, her reputation as a sharpshooter, and so many dreams. She straightened her shoulders, narrowed her eyes, and gave a curt nod.

Was she ready? She most certainly was. May they rot in prison for all she cared.

The large room over JD McKittrick's mercantile was used for community meetings and, when needed, as the courtroom. The only places larger were the churches and the school building. Mavis had told her that they hadn't had a visit from the circuit judge in years, since most cases, what few there had been, went to Hill City for court.

With Mavis in the lead and Lucas and Ransom behind her, Cassie gathered up her skirts and climbed the creaky wooden stairs to the courtroom. Dormers with windows, along with wide windows at each end of the room gave enough light to see, but up at the table where a black-robed man waited, kerosene lamps added illumination. Several other men in black suits and ties were gathered around his table, and the only one she recognized, Sheriff Edgar McDougal, beckoned them over.

"Since Judge Cranston already dealt with the other case, we're about ready for you all. Have a seat." He motioned to the straight-backed chairs lined up in front of the table. One chair sat to the right side and the others to the left of the judge.

Mavis nodded. "Good morning, Judge Cranston, gentlemen. I've a question, if you please. Will the three be tried at the same time?"

"We're debating that right now. Won't be long."

Cassie forced herself to take deep breaths. At least this wasn't as formal as some pictures she'd seen. Formal enough, though. The judge sat at a plain old table rather than an imposing bench, but it and his chair had been set up on a platform at least two feet high. He looked down on everyone else. That was imposing enough for Cassie.

Never having been in such a situation before, she really had no idea what to expect. She turned to Mavis and whispered,

11

"Will there be a jury?"

"Doesn't look like it."

They turned at the sound of more feet on the stairs. Three women came up together and nodded to those gathered.

"Those are the wives of the men on trial," Mavis whispered to Cassie. "The first of them in the blue cape is Case's wife, Molly. The lady in the black coat is Joe Jones's wife; I forget her first name. They live out a ways."

"You may sit over there." The sheriff pointed to seats off to the right. A few more townspeople came in, and gradually the rows of chairs filled.

The judge said something and the sheriff left the room while another man moved two more chairs next to the lone one. It looked like they would try the three together.

"At least that will speed things up," Mavis said to Cassie from behind her gloved hand. They took the straight-backed seats the sheriff had indicated, and the four of them sat down.

After greeting the Engstroms and Cassie, the reverend Brandenburg settled himself into the fifth seat.

Mavis leaned forward to nod a greeting. "Thank you for coming."

Cassie tried to smile politely but failed.

Whenever she moved her mouth, her whole face started to quiver. *Lord, please get this over quickly.* No, that was wrong, her whole body quivered like the golden aspen leaves she'd so admired. Shaking like this in public was not admirable. Why was it she could perform in front of hundreds of spectators but this trial was turning her into a mass of jelly?

The stairs creaked loudly. The sheriff and two other men came in escorting the three prisoners. Together they made their way to the front of the room and faced the judge's table. The deputies transferred the handcuffs to the arms of the chairs and stepped back.

"All ready?" the judge asked the sheriff.

"Yes, sir, everyone is here that needs to be." At the judge's nod, he announced, "All rise. Court is in session, the honorable magistrate Homer Cranston presiding."

They all stood and then sat down again after the judge sat.

Cassie studied the man who would most likely change several lives this day. The silver-haired judge looked to be in need of a haircut and an extra night's sleep. Deep creases in his face, from nose to chin, deepened further when the lines in his forehead flattened out. He didn't look like

13

he smiled much.

He scowled, looking around the room. "Ladies and gentlemen, I want to make several things clear before this trial begins. First, there will be no histrionics in my courtroom. We will hear all the evidence, and then I will make a decision. If necessary, we will postpone this trial until January, when I will be able to circuit through here again. But I do not believe that will be necessary." He looked to the sheriff.

Sheriff McDougal nodded and then picked up a sheet of paper, stood, and cleared his throat. "Our case today concerns a nighttime raid on the cabin at the Bar E, the Engstrom ranch, on November" — he glanced at the paper in his hand — "November 13." He looked directly at the prisoners. "I present to the court the defendants: Case Svenson Beckwith. Joseph Clarence Jones. Judson Hercules Dooger."

Hercules? A quiet little titter washed across the room. Cassie smiled in spite of herself.

"The charging papers regarding said raid state that these three suspects rode up the hill above the main ranch complex on the Engstrom spread in the middle of the night. Their covert entry constituted trespass. While screaming and discharging firearms,

14

they circled the cabin. Someone fired a shot that wounded Miss Cassandra Lockwood, who, with her men, was protecting the cabin and their lives. The state contends that during said raid, the suspects set Miss Lockwood's Wild West Show wagon, parked next to the cabin, on fire, and it burned completely. Thus the charge of arson."

Of course. Arson. Why had Cassie not even thought of that? No doubt because she was still mourning the loss of that last link with her past.

"Mr. Dooger was wounded in the exchange of gunfire, and the Engstroms brought him, along with Miss Lockwood, to Dr. Barnett here in Argus for treatment. Later that same night Mr. Beckwith and Mr. Jones were apprehended when they tried to sneak back into town. The three have remained incarcerated pending trial because of the extreme likelihood that they would leave the area if released. The charges include trespass, arson, willful destruction of property, harassment, drunk and disorderly conduct, and discharge of firearms with intent to kill."

The judge looked to one of the black-suited men who stood along with the three accused. "Do you understand the charges?"

"Yeah, but we didn't —" Mr. Jones burst out.

The judge silenced him by slamming the gavel on the table. Cassie jumped. "You will be given your turn to talk."

"But —"

The gavel slammed again and the judge glared at the lawyer. "Mr. Jenski, if you, as their lawyer, can't keep your clients quiet, they will be barred from the courtroom."

"Understood. Yes, sir." The lawyer glared at the leader of the three and barked in a hoarse stage whisper, "You heard the man."

Sheriff McDougal ignored the dirty looks from the obvious leader of the three accused men. He glanced back down at his paper. "The state calls Miss Cassandra Lockwood to the stand." He motioned to the empty chair beside the judge's table.

Cassie ignored the shaking in her knees and stood. Mavis squeezed the hand that she'd been holding. *One step at a time,* Cassie ordered herself. She kept from looking at the men, but she could feel them drilling her with their eyes. She turned at the chair and faced the sheriff.

"Put your hand on this Bible."

She did.

"State your full name."

"Cassandra Marie Lockwood." Her voice

16

gained strength with each sound.

"Do you swear to tell the truth, the whole truth, and nothing but the truth?"

"I do."

"Please be seated." He set the Bible on the corner of the judge's table and nodded to him as well.

"Miss Lockwood, I would like you to tell me what happened that night. Can you do that?" Judge Cranston had considerably softened his tone.

She nodded. "We had all gone to bed like usual. My friend Runs Like a Deer and I slept in the cabin and the two men, John Birdwing and Micah, slept in the show wagon that was parked right beside the cabin."

"And Micah's last name?"

"I don't know, sir — Your Honor. He might not have a last name. I've never in all the years I've known him heard him give one."

"I see. How long have you known him?"

Cassie squinted, thinking back. "Close to ten years, I guess. He came to the show and asked for work and my father hired him."

"And what did he do at the show?"

"Took care of all the animals and did whatever else was needed."

"And John Birdwing? I take it he is an

Indian?"

"Yes, a Sioux Indian from the Rosebud Reservation. We always knew him as Chief."

"How long have you known him?"

"Since I was a baby. He came to the show when my father took half control of it."

"I see."

"You said another woman sleeps in the cabin?"

"Yes. Runs Like a Deer. We found her with a broken leg on our trip south from Dickinson, North Dakota. Dickinson is where the show was declared bankrupt and disbanded."

The judge nodded. "Back to the night in question. You were all sleeping when what happened?"

"My dog, Othello, set up a furious barking. By the time I got to the door to see what he was barking at, we heard shots and men yelling and horses running. Chief and Micah were yelling too."

"So what did you do?"

"I grabbed my rifle from the pegs by the door and stepped out to return fire."

"Were the two men with you shooting?"

"Yes, Your Honor. They had at least one rifle and a shotgun. It sounded like a 20-gauge."

"Did you aim at anyone?"

"I did when one of them came around again. They were circling the cabin."

"Did you see him fall?"

Cassie shrugged. "I'm not sure. Then I could smell smoke, and someone yelled, 'Fire.' I kept shooting and then I was slammed against the cabin wall and realized I'd been hit. I think the Engstroms rode up the hill then, and the other men rode off. They — the Engstroms, I mean — pulled the wagon, now on fire, away from the cabin so the cabin wouldn't burn, but the wagon was burning so fiercely and the water barrels were on the side of the wagon . . ."

She closed her eyes to think better. "By that time I was fighting to keep from passing out. I don't remember any more, other than I think I was on a horse, and then at the ranch house, and then on a horse again, and then I woke up at the doctor's house the next day."

"Do you recognize those men over there as the ones circling the cabin?"

What should she say? *When in doubt, always tell the truth. Even if those three win?* Cassie shook her head. "I couldn't see anyone that well. Just horses and riders and guns firing."

"I see. Do you have anything else to tell me?"

19

Again she shook her head but then paused. "I learned that getting shot is a terribly painful thing, and my arm still has not regained all the strength I had before. It's hard to be a professional shooter when you have a weak arm."

"I can understand that. You are truly a professional shooter?"

"Yes, sir. I mean, Your Honor. Besides being a trick rider. I have shot in matches all over the country."

"You usually win?"

"Yes, sir." Cassie wondered at his interest. Did she sound prideful? She decided to add a bit more. "That's about the only way I know to make a living."

"Thank you, Miss Lockwood. Cross?" The judge looked toward the three suspects' lawyer. The man thought a moment and shook his head.

"You may stand down," he said to Cassie and motioned to the row of chairs.

Cassie did as he said, but by the time she got there, her knees quit on her and she sank into her chair. Mavis picked up her hand again with gentle pressure. Cassie blinked back the moisture that threatened to flow down her face.

"You did good." Lucas spoke from her left side.

"Ransom Lockwood to the stand," the sheriff called.

She watched as Ransom repeated the vow and took his seat. He didn't appear scared or shaky at all. He told of the dogs barking, their ride up to see flames, hearing the shots and all the yelling. "We rode in, firing in the air and yelling back. We saw two of the men ride off and a horse with no rider circling around. The wagon had flames coming out the door and the sides, so we pulled that away from the cabin.

"Chief and Micah came out of hiding, and then we found Miss Lockwood sitting against the cabin wall, covered in blood. She was bleeding from being shot in the arm. Chief discovered Jud there." He indicated the fellow with Hercules as a middle name. "A bullet had grazed his head, a pretty deep one, and we put him back on his horse and told him to hang on. With Cassie in front of Lucas, we headed back down the hill to where Mor waited. Sorry, I mean my mother. She put a tourniquet on Cassie's arm and told us to get her to the doctor as fast as we could. We rode in on horseback because that was faster than hitching up. I was sure she was going to die before we could get to town."

"And Mr. Dooger?"

"He looked a lot worse'n he was."

"That was your medical opinion?" An arched brow accompanied the question.

"No, sir. But to be truthful, I had a hard time feeling any sympathy for a man who could take part in such a thing."

"Thank you, Mr. Engstrom."

Lucas was called next, but he didn't have any new information, so his time was shorter. The sheriff testified that he'd thrown Jud in jail after his wound was bandaged, and that the other two were caught later.

"I think we'll break for dinner, folks, and hear from the accused afterward. Court is dismissed." Judge Cranston banged his gavel and stood up even as the sheriff was calling, "All rise."

Reverend Brandenburg smiled at the Engstroms. "The missus and I figured this is what would happen, so she has dinner waiting for us. We can walk or, of course, take your wagon."

"Oh, a walk would feel so good." Mavis gathered up her coat and slipped into it while Ransom held it for her. Lucas helped Cassie into her shawl, patting her shoulders before stepping back.

Cassie stopped a sigh. Lucas had vowed he would make her fall in love with him.

Surely this was another bit of his plan. But she had to admit, right now a touch from anyone helped dilute the fear that seemed to flow along with her bloodstream. What if these men got off scot-free because she, the witness, could not identify them? It would have been so easy to simply say they were the ones.

What if their next attempt, now with thoughts of revenge, was many times worse? Was she being fair to Chief and Runs Like a Deer to keep them in harm's way? But then, what else could she do? They no longer had a wagon to live in if they decided to move someplace else, and she had no idea where someplace else could be. With winter hard upon them, they would have to have dependable shelter if they traveled. The wagon had provided that.

Gone now.

And I don't want to leave here. I want to live here, especially since, thanks to my father, I own half of the Bar E. Not sure whether this was a plea or a promise, she kept pace with the others as they walked for what seemed like a thousand miles to the parsonage next door to the church.

2

Mrs. Brandenburg greeted them at the door, and Lucas helped Cassie with her shawl. They filed into the dining room to sit, Lucas at Cassie's elbow. Her knees thanked her as she dropped into her chair and Lucas scooted it in.

Mrs. Brandenburg dished up bowls of steaming soup as soon as they sat down. "There is bread in one basket and crackers in the other. Mavis, I tried a new cracker recipe. You'll have to be honest and tell me what you think of it. I put dill seed in it, of all things. Ran the seeds through the coffee mill. Now we're probably going to have dill-flavored coffee for a while."

Reverend Brandenburg offered up the grace along with a plea for justice and nodded to the others. "We need to be back at the court by one thirty. Judge Cranston is a stickler for time, and I know he wants this wrapped up today."

Lucas snorted. "I don't see any need for a hearing at all. We caught Jud red-handed, or redheaded as was the case for him, and the others never said they didn't do it."

"But they have the right to a trial. I'm just glad there is no jury to make it take longer. Although everyone here knows Case's bigotry, he's never been one to keep his mouth shut." Brandenburg dunked one of the crackers in his soup. "Delicious." He smiled at his wife.

She looked not at him but to Mavis.

"What do you think?"

"I want the recipe."

Cassie could have been eating sawdust for all she knew. She could not pay attention. *I don't want to leave here, Lord. What's wrong with wanting a home? Here I think I have one, and now this.*

"Don't worry about this, Cassie." Mrs. Brandenburg laid a hand on her arm. "All will be well."

Cassie sent her what she could manage of a smile. A nod would have to suffice. Both Mavis and Mrs. Brandenburg knew how to trust God, no matter what. She, however, was still trying to learn that.

She did have enough curiosity to ask, "What does *cross* mean? The judge said it when he was looking at the lawyer."

"Cross examination," Reverend Brandenburg replied. "The defense declined, because they didn't want the court to hear that damaging testimony twice. Not too important when it's only a judge, but it's very important when a jury is hearing the case."

"Thank you." She managed a smile this time. So the reverend knew quite a bit about law as well as faith.

Cassie and the Engstroms arrived back in the courtroom with ten minutes to spare. Here came Sheriff McDougal with his charges; his deputies again handcuffed the three prisoners to their chairs. Loud enough to be heard easily, Case grumbled something about being bound to the chair like a common criminal.

"Shut up," hissed one of the others. "You want to make this even worse?"

"You tell me to shut up and —" Case's ugly face grew even more so.

The judge entered, the sheriff called, "All rise," and the afternoon was under way.

The sheriff called Dr. Barnett to testify. He described the wounds and his treatment. "That young lady could have lost the use of her arm had things gone only a tiny bit differently. Even worse, she could have died from loss of blood." He shook his head. "I left the South to get away from the Ku Klux Klan and to find that same kind of hatred here . . . Heartbreaking, that's what it is."

Judge Cranston looked up. "Cross?"

Again the lawyer shook his head.

The sheriff announced, "The state rests."

"Defense?"

Reluctantly, it would appear, the lawyer called, "Case Beckwith to the stand, please."

A deputy unlocked the chair half of his handcuffs, and Case bolted upright. He plopped down into the witness chair.

The sheriff glared at him. "Up."

He stood.

The sheriff waved the Bible. "This is a Bible, in case you've never seen one before. Put your left hand on it and raise your right. Your other right."

Case repeated the familiar promise to tell the truth, the whole truth, and nothing but the truth. Was he capable of that?

Mr. Jenski, the lawyer, stepped in next to him. "You've been identified as one of the miscreants. Do you dispute that, Mr. Beckwith?"

Case growled, "We didn't go there to do any arson or murder. We just wanted to scare 'em a little so they'd move on. We didn't set fire to nothing. We didn't mean to shoot anybody. She just got in the way. Maybe she even did it on purpose to get us in trouble."

Cassie gaped. Her stomach felt as if she'd just been punched.

The judge asked the sheriff, "Cross?"

He was smirking. "No need. No, Your Honor."

Mr. Jenski looked pained. "You may stand down, Mr. Beckwith."

"But I ain't done testifying! We didn't really hurt anything, except some too-big-for-her-britches stranger. We didn't start no fire, so *they* musta. They did it to get us in trouble, I tell you. We're innocent!"

The judge roared, "Stand down!"

And Case did so.

The judge glared at all three. "Anyone else have anything to say?"

Case howled one more time, "We're innocent!"

The lawyer was covering his face with one hand, his head drooping sadly.

"Very well. We already have the confession of Mr. Dooger that you three were all in on the raid, and now you, Mr. Beckwith, established that you were there. Does anyone here present have any proof or credible witness that might change any of that?" The judge looked at Mr. Jenski, then rather imperiously around at everyone else in the room.

Mr. Jenski shook his head. His face was, to Cassie, exactly what defeat looked like.

The judge picked up a piece of paper. "Then I declare the defendants guilty as charged. The defendants will approach the bench for sentencing."

Sheriff McDougal cleared his throat and then poked Case to make them stand. The deputies unlocked their handcuffs from their chairs but, Cassie noted, cuffed the men's hands behind their backs. Reluctantly, the three shuffled over and stood before the platform.

The judge leaned forward, his elbows on the table. "I feel constrained to point out that if you three had the brains God gave a goose, you wouldn't be standing before me today. You acted despicably and brought shame to this town.

"Case Beckwith, I hereby sentence you to five years for each count, to be served in the state penitentiary at Sioux Falls, the sentences to run concurrently." Eyes narrowed, he stared at the big man. "Possible parole at three years if you behave yourself."

Case glared back at him, but for a change he kept his mouth shut.

"Judson Dooger, I sentence you to one

year on each count, your sentences to run concurrently. I hope you can learn to think for yourself and not just follow a bad leader. Joseph Jones, you receive the same sentence as Mr. Dooger, and the same advice. Are there any questions?"

"Who's going to take care of my family?" Mr. Jones muttered, shaking his head.

"You should have thought of that before you went off carousing with Mr. Beckwith. Case closed. Court dismissed." The judge brought his gavel down — not so loudly this time.

"All rise." The sheriff did not look particularly excited or happy. Was he pleased he had won?

With a great deal of noise, chairs all over the room rattled as people stood to leave. The volume of many voices grew. Cassie could not bear to look toward the three wives. What now? How must it feel to hear and see your man taken away?

Judge Cranston stepped down off his platform and started to remove his black robe.

Cassie said to no one in particular, "I don't understand. Why didn't he just sentence those three without the trial, if the evidence was so cut and dried?"

Reverend Brandenburg shrugged into his

coat. "We may be a ways out from civilization, but we maintain the civil law. The trial followed the letter of the law. Those three can never say they did not receive a fair trial." He went up to the judge and stuck out his hand. "Good to see you again, Homer. You want to come by for supper? You know there is always a room for you too."

"Thanks. Wish I could, but I need to be on that five o'clock train. You come on down to Rapid City one of these days. 'Bout time for a real visit." He stepped in closer. "If I could have justified it, I would've sent him off forever. You can bet that Case Beckwith hasn't learned any lesson. He'll be trouble in prison too. Count on it."

" 'Fraid you might be right, but you never know. The Holy Ghost might get ahold of him and make him a new man. That's what we've been praying for." They shook hands, clapped each other's arms, and walked off together.

"Are you all right?" Mavis asked Cassie.

"Can you beat that?" Cassie nodded toward the men. "They know each other."

Mavis seemed downright lighthearted. "To quote a good pastor friend of mine, God works in mysterious ways His wonders to perform."

31

"Did you know who the judge would be?"

"No, and I didn't know that Reverend Brandenburg and Judge Cranston were friends. But then, there are a lot of things I know nothing about. I do know that we can rest easy now and go on with our lives. Let's go home." She hooked her arm through Cassie's on one side and Ransom's on the other.

Cassie glanced over to see two of the women comforting the third, Mrs. Dooger, the one whose husband had been the one with the wound to his head.

She heard the woman cry, "But my Jud isn't a bad man, he was just —"

"Stupid!" interrupted Mrs. Jones. "To go to the saloon and get mixed up with the likes of Case Beckwith, and my Joe was just as stupid. I'm sorry, Molly, but that's just the way it is. And now we all get to pay for their stupidity."

Who will help them out? Cassie wondered as they left the courtroom. *For that matter, how will the rest of us manage? We're paying too. Nothing is for certain, that is for sure.* After all, what if she could never shoot again professionally or do her trick riding routine, thanks to a stupid man who put a bullet in her arm?

3

Another day of putting off getting those timbers up to the mine. Granted, it was Sunday tomorrow, but surely God would understand that Ransom needed to work when the weather permitted. After all, this was South Dakota in December. Snow, deep snow, was imminent. Woolly caterpillars and animals' dense coats predicted a bad winter, and the signs never lied. At least not that he knew of. But so far, the killing winter had held off, allowing them to cut and mill the pine trees. He needed to remember to be thankful for that.

But Ransom wisely kept his thoughts to himself as he continued with the evening chores — milking, since Gretchen was spending the night with Jenna. Lucas had left before twilight to get set up for the evening elk run. Sometimes they came down the hill, and sometimes he needed to go looking for them. Since there had been

no rifle shots, Ransom figured tonight would be the latter. Still, Lucas would most likely get his elk. As a hunter, he was superb. Tonight he had taken Micah and Chief with him. Maybe they would come back with two.

He finished the milking, tossed more hay in Rosy's manger, and checked on the hogs. Since they had plenty of milk again, he poured soured skimmed milk from the cream can beside the hog gate into the trough and added cracked oats. Didn't he see a grinder over to Dan Arnett's house that would let them turn that steam engine into a grinding machine too? Probably was all rusted up, but they could remedy that.

He whistled his way to the house, stopping by the springhouse to strain the milk and set it in pans for the cream to rise. One thing he'd love to buy was one of those new cream separators, but it didn't make sense for the one or two cows they had. As best as he could remember, Rosy was due to calve in February. He needed to check the calendar.

Taking a jug of cold milk with him, he tramped on up to the house. For a change he didn't have to go throw wood on the smoker. Since the light was still on in the bunkhouse, he rapped on the door to re-

mind Arnett it was time for supper.

"Come in, come in." Did his voice sound even more gravelly than usual?

Ransom stepped into the bunkhouse, now meticulously clean with a stack of books on the table and a rocking chair in front of the stove. From a utilitarian bunkhouse, this place had been rendered quite homey. Arnett sat with his wool-stockinged feet up on the fender, book in his lap.

"Surely can't be suppertime already," the old man said with a chuckle. "But then I get to readin' and the time just drifts on by."

"Mor will be ringing the bell any minute now. Hey, I was thinking. You got an old grain grinder out by your machine shed?"

Arnett slit his eyes, gazing into some distant place. "Why, by jerky, I think you're right. Hey, that might to be another cash machine for you. Let folks know you can grind grain and they'll be bringing their cattle feed over. You know, we might keep that old steam sister going after all." He slapped his thigh, making the book bounce and slide to the floor with a *thunk*.

He stood and stretched before limping over to his boots and jacket by the door. "We'd best get that Monday afore the snow buries it again. We'll take it all apart, get the rust off it, and put it back together. Be good as new." He shrugged into his sheepskin jacket and clapped Ransom on the shoulder. "Good for you, boy. You got a memory like an old bear trap. Why, think I got one of them too, up on the barn wall."

Ransom closed the door behind them, and they headed on up to the house just as Cassie came out to ring the iron triangle, the song of which echoed across the valley. As they stepped up on the back porch, two rifle shots answered the supper bell.

Ransom heaved a sigh. "Guess I better get the wagon out there. Tell Mor to go ahead."

"You need another pair of hands?"

"No, thanks. There are three of them already." He turned and headed back for the barn. Good thing he'd not let the team loose like he'd thought to do. One of the horses nickered when he opened the door. Stepping into the quiet warmth of the barn, he lit the lantern hanging on the hook by the door and, using the dim light, lifted the harnesses off the wall and hauled them over to the stalls where the team waited, ears pricked as if they'd heard the shot too and knew that meant a trip out of the barn.

"Guess you two don't like staying in here after all, eh?" He slung the harnesses in place, buckling and snapping everything together, and then backed the horses out one at a time. As he led them outside, one on each side of him, Ransom stopped at the wagon tongue set on a chunk of log, and they backed into place so he could snap on to the whippletrees and the wagon tongue. They stamped their feet and blew steam into the air. The temperature had dropped noticeably since sunset.

After checking to make sure nothing was rubbing or loose, Ransom climbed up onto the wagon seat, gathered the long lines, and flicked his wrists to send the *go* message to his team. They trotted smartly out of the yard and through the gate to the long pasture. He'd have several more gates to open and close before reaching the hunters. If they had come down a different way, Lucas would let him know. A quick bark behind him and he stopped the team to let Benny ride up on top with him. It was a shame he didn't let Arnett come along; company was always nice. And he knew the old man liked to be useful.

"Sorry, I just didn't think. So used to doing it all myself."

The dog whined beside him and wriggled all over when Ransom thumped him on the ribs and rubbed his ears.

Instead of two elk, they had an elk and a deer.

"Micah's first deer," Lucas bragged. "Those shooting lessons are paying off, for sure."

Ransom nodded. "Looks good and heavy. How'd you see those little prongs in the dim light?"

"Lucas said shoot when it breaks through the brush, and I did."

"Right through heart," Chief added. "Like he's been shooting for years. He run the rabbit snares now too."

"Thanks to all of you, I have good teachers," Micah said.

Ransom stopped his eyebrows from rising in surprise. Micah didn't usually say a whole lot. In fact, Micah had been talking more lately, up at the sawmill, asking questions. This was a good thing. He was certainly one fine worker. You only had to show him something once. Just the other day Micah offered a suggestion that was a better way to do something. He might have been just an animal handler at that Wild West Show, but there was far more to be discovered in that young man.

Arnett had commented on Micah too. Maybe between the three of them, they could get a lot more done on the ranch this winter and into the spring than Ransom had ever dreamed. And with Arnett's experience and machinery, maybe they'd even bring in some cash money.

After hanging and gutting the two carcasses, Ransom invited them all to eat at the house, but Micah and Chief said Runs Like a Deer would be expecting them. They took the heart, liver, and tongue from the deer and rode up the hill.

"I was thinking you'd not found any, late as it was," Ransom told his brother as Lucas pulled the tall doors together and dropped the hasp in the lock.

"Micah got his deer way up on the hill at the aspen grove, and I thought sure the rifle shot would spook the elk herd, but they must have been way up back. We slung that buck up across behind Micah and headed on down. We settled in under the trees, and they finally made their way down. Good thing we had a bit of moon so I could see enough to shoot. Almost shot a cow and then this young buck stepped in front of her. That was close." One did not shoot the cows if they wanted the herd to continue. "You'd think by now they'd not come down that same trail all the time."

They scraped their boots and, once in the kitchen, set the bucket with the innards up on the counter. They hung their coats on the tree. A kerosene lamp on the table spread enough light to welcome them, so Lucas paused to turn it up.

"Your plates are in the warming oven," Mavis called from the big room. "Let me finish this and I'll be right there."

"I'll take care of it," Cassie said over her shoulder as she wandered into the kitchen. "How'd it go?"

"Micah shot his first deer." Lucas turned from washing his hands at the sink.

"Good, then maybe I won't have to go hunting anymore." She opened the flue, then set the stove lids back to the side and added a couple of chunks to the coals already flaring from the draft. "Coffee will be hot in a jiffy." Fetching the loaf of bread from the bread box, she sliced off several thick hunks and set those on a plate on the table. Mor and Cassie had left the hunters' place settings on the table after they ate and cleaned up, so all was ready for the men. As soon as they sat down, she set their plates in front of them. "Would you like beet pickles?"

"Always," Lucas replied with that special smile he reserved for her.

Ransom kept an eye on his brother without seeming to make the effort. Perhaps what he'd thought was infatuation really wasn't. Had he misjudged his brother's feelings for Cassie? Based on Lucas's quick declarations of undying love in the past which, unsurprisingly, died after all, this was something new. As Ransom thought about it, the only woman Lucas had ever continued a relationship with was Betsy Hudson. What to do about that mess plagued them all. So when Lucas arrived back at the ranch a couple of months ago and said he'd found the woman of his dreams but he'd not met her yet, what was a brother supposed to think? Common sense had never been one of Lucas's strong suits.

When he'd learned that *the woman of my dreams* was a trick rider and shooter in Wild West shows and held a paper that said she owned half of their ranch, well, Ransom had never claimed to be anything but a common ordinary rancher — with a slow-fused temper.

Snatches of the conversation between the two tickled his consciousness, but he had learned he was better off if he tuned them out. He could go easier on the judgmental side that way. No need for him and Lucas to get into another so-called discussion, which was really a polite name for brotherly fighting.

Ransom finished his meal, cut himself a large slab of the leftover gingerbread, buried it in applesauce, and with a refill on the coffee, took cup and plate to his desk in a corner of the big room. He settled into his cushioned chair with a sigh. Of all his many favorite places on the ranch, this was tops. Unless he included being stretched out on the leather-cushioned couch a few steps away. His father sure did know how to make comfortable and substantial furniture.

Ransom pulled out the drawings he'd made of a possible furniture line, based on some of the things his father had made and others he'd thought of himself. He studied the schematics. He planned on using the lumber long dried out in the barn for a couple of end tables, incorporating cottonwood branches for the legs, like his father had. That was a distinctive touch. All the pieces proclaimed western ranch design. Where would they find a market?

Mavis stopped beside his desk. "Dreaming?"

"I am. Think I'll start with these." He pointed at the pair of tables. "I can work on them here in the evenings."

"True, once you get all the pieces cut." She glanced around the room with a smile. "Ah, the stories these walls could tell."

"What are you working on?"

"I'll never tell. Christmas is coming, and you know better than to ask questions."

He made a face. "Right, sorry." Christmas and, as always, there was no money to buy gifts and he'd not started making anything. At the moment, he didn't even have any ideas of what to make. He needed some time with his mother without all the others around. Lucas and Cassie laughed their way into the room, and Lucas settled into working on the buttons he made from antlers and bones to send to his buyer in Chicago. Cassie picked up the knitting needles Mavis had given her, along with the yarn, and resumed her painful progress. She seemed to be ripping out more stitches than she was putting in.

Good thing she was a better shooter than a knitter. The thought made him smile. One had to give her credit for sheer determination and stick-to-itiveness.

After chores the next morning, they gathered on the front porch as Lucas brought up the wagon. Usually by now they'd changed out the wheels for the sledge runners, but no snow, so no runners. Ransom helped the women into the back of the wagon, along with Dan Arnett up on the seat with him, and got everyone bundled warm with elk robes and quilts.

"Why don't you join us?" he asked Lucas, who was mounting his saddle horse.

"I have some errands to run after church, so I'll ride."

"As you wish." What kind of errands could he be referring to? But Ransom put a guard on his tongue. After all, Christmas was coming and no questions allowed. If only his curiosity could be stilled as easily.

"I need to talk with Reverend Brandenburg after church, if that is all right," Cassie said as Ransom helped her to the ground in the churchyard. "I need to see if he can come out to the ranch to marry Micah and Runs Like a Deer."

"We're not in any rush."

"Thank you."

Gretchen met them inside the church, and thanks to some unseen machinations, Lucas ended up on the end of the pew, obviously not next to Cassie, where he wanted to be. He glared at Ransom, but Ransom made a slight motion to the Hudson family four pews behind theirs. Betsy had returned from her trip, and the family could see no sense in throwing fuel on the fire. Mavis sat on one side of Cassie and Gretchen on the other. Ransom made sure the grin of pride he was feeling did not show on his face. What a family he had.

But then, the Hudsons had just as interesting a family. For years, Lucas had considered Betsy his girl, and everyone assumed that one day, when he was financially stable, he'd propose. Now here he was courting Miss Lockwood. Betsy had disappeared suddenly, mysteriously, and now she had reappeared. Where had she gone? What did she do while she was away? Ransom really ought to ask, but he couldn't quite bring himself to do it. Frankly, he didn't care enough to ask. That was Lucas's job. He's the one who had courted her, sort of.

The glow lasted through the service as he and Gretchen shared a hymnal and Mavis looked out for Cassie. Arnett sat next to Mavis, leaving Lucas on the wall side. Afterwards, Mavis made a point to greet the Hudson family as if no hard feelings had ever transpired. Ransom admired that in her, especially because he knew that her openness was no act.

Betsy's little sister, Sarah, scowled smoldering coals at Lucas, but Mrs. Hudson took her cue from Mavis and returned a cheerful greeting.

"Have you heard anything more on the

rustlers?" Ransom asked Mr. Hudson.

The rancher shook his head. "Strangest thing, no one has. Like they fell off the face of the earth. Took two head from us. Two from Jay Slatfield, and Arnett said he wasn't sure but maybe several. He don't run his herd as carefully as he used to, you know."

"Not surprising, I doubt he can see far enough to count heads. He does all right reading, however, so don't count him out yet."

"Oh no, I'm not, just trying to figure out what is happening."

"Nothing. Looks like the sheriff got the right men in jail after all."

"Well, if that don't beat all. From what I heard, that was some fracas at your place."

"That would surely be one way to describe it." Ransom glanced over and realized Cassie was back beside the wagon with his mother and Gretchen, so he excused himself and stopped at the tailgate to help them into the wagon. Lucas was nowhere to be seen and his horse was gone, so he must have left immediately after church. Perhaps he'd told their mother where he was going.

"Lucas said he'd meet you all at the ranch," Arnett informed him when he picked up the lines.

"Did he say where he was going?"

"Nope. And I didn't ask. Sure was good to be back in church like that. Thanks to you, Mavis. You folks are real friends." His voice cracked on the last word.

Ransom backed the team and swung the wagon around to head for home. "Thanks, Arnett. We've been neighbors for a long time. Glad we can help each other out. Kinda fits in with his sermon today, didn't it?"

"Ya ever get the feeling like Reverend Brandenburg's been listening over your shoulder at times, or can see into your mind? I mean, it's uncanny."

"Mor would say that is the Holy Ghost at work."

"She sure would" came from the wagon bed.

Ransom and Arnett swapped a glance. Maybe taking this time to be with his family was more important than setting posts and supports in the collapsed part of the mine after all. Somehow it would all get done. At least he sure hoped so.

4

Mavis listened with one ear to Gretchen and Cassie and with the other to the conversation between the two men. While Ransom was usually the silent one, he was obviously making an effort to talk with Dan Arnett. And Dan, who once had thrived on conversation, was just as obviously realizing he'd missed too much and wanted to get back into living again. He'd always been a storyteller, but she wondered at times if he remembered the early days of ranching in the Black Hills area, since he didn't bring that up much. He and his wife had come to their ranch maybe three or four years after she and Ivar moved into the cabin.

That cabin. Who would have guessed that that "temporary" structure would still be finding good use? The first year Ivar and Adam Lockwood had lived in it. And then after Adam left for the Wild West show circuit, taking John Birdwing with him, Ivar lived there alone until they were married. Then it was home to the newlyweds until Ivar could complete the main ranch house. And now, Cassie's dear friends lived there, and it was still in good shape. Who would live there next?

As did all the ranchers in this area, Arnett and Ivar had traded off work. House raisings and barn raisings, fencing and haying. I'll help you and you help me. As more cattle arrived, there were roundups and brandings and a great deal of sorting during those years when the range was open and livestock roamed, before barbed-wire fences started crisscrossing the valleys. When Arnett bought the sawmill, life became easier for all of them.

Maybe this afternoon they could get the old man telling stories in front of the fireplace. She'd suggest it to Ransom. The two of them got along real well. Arnett did not need to spend the afternoon alone in the bunkhouse, though he kept saying he didn't want to impose on their hospitality. Mavis didn't mention to him that this was far easier than one of them going to his ranch every day to check on him. When they moved the dog and chickens over, Arnett came to live in their bunkhouse — for the rest of his life, as far as she was concerned, if he'd only listen to her.

Ransom drew the team to a halt beside the house. Their off gelding shook his head impatiently. He knew where his feed was, and it wasn't here. Ransom stayed in the box. "How about taking charge of keeping that front fireplace going today, Arnett? Most likely that'll be where we all end up."

"If'n you want, a'course I will. Besides, I got something I want to talk over with all of you. Any idea when Lucas will be home?"

Mavis smiled. "He said in time for dinner, and you know Lucas, he doesn't like to miss out on apple pie."

Arnett cackled as he stepped to the ground and came around the wagon to help the womenfolk out.

"I don't suppose you'd like to give me a hint?" Mavis shuffled her skirts back into order as she waited for Cassie and Gretchen. She loved to hear the old man laugh; one could never stay too somber with Dan Arnett around. That was one of the things she'd missed after his wife died, because she used to egg him on until they were all panting from laughter.

"You did remember to tell Micah and the others that we expect them to join us for dinner?" she asked Ransom when he came into the kitchen from unhitching the team.

"I did. They said they'd watch for the wagon to come back." He hung his long jacket on the coat-tree by the back door. He automatically checked the woodbox to see if it needed filling.

"Lucas took care of that this morning."

Ransom nodded.

Mavis loved seeing all the faces around her table as they bowed their heads for Ransom to ask the blessing. This room, this whole house, was designed for lots of people to share meals and the work of ranch living. She paused long enough in the serving to catch a comment from Micah. A grin split her face. He'd actually said something funny and set Arnett into a laughing spell. Even Runs Like a Deer smiled and nodded. Cassie and Mavis exchanged a look of pure delight. From the looks and sounds of it, they were all starting to become a family. Lucas tossed his coat aside and slid into his chair just as the meat platter got to him.

While Mavis kept all her thanking and praising inside, she felt like her feet didn't touch the floor and she might burst into song at any moment. Now, that would be a shocker.

"Hey, Chief, you remember the time that bear chased us all up on top of the cabin?" Arnett slapped his thigh. "Never laughed so hard in my life, seeing that old sow start up the ladder. She was one determined mama."

Chief nodded. "You could laugh — you were already on the roof."

"What happened?" Cassie's eyes were as big as the rim of the cup in front of her.

"We was roofing that cabin. Ivar and Chief was splittin' shakes, and Adam came running out of the woods like a bear was on his tail."

"Only because one was." Mavis tried to keep a straight face and let Arnett get them all laughing.

"Mor?"

"He's telling the truth, Lucas. I wasn't there, thank the good Lord. I might have keeled right over."

Arnett continued, "Well, Adam was a-hollerin' to get on the roof. Doors wasn't in place yet. And we scampered up that ladder without touchin' a rung."

Ransom chuckled. Micah chuckled and then snorted. That made Cassie laugh outright. Runs Like a Deer near to choked. Lucas belly-laughed and Arnett could hardly continue. He shook his head and wheezed. "Adam hit the roof and that mad mama started up the ladder. She was a-huffin' and a-gruntin'. I thought sure we was done for."

"Was the tree there to climb?"

"Not near as big as now. But Ivar and Chief, there, grabbed that ladder and gave it a mighty heave out and away. That old bear went down with the ladder, head over teakettle. She done quit rollin' and shook her head like she had a mighty goose egg on it. She staggered around some and then headed back up to the woods. Adam said he'd made a big mistake and got between her and her cubs."

"Greenhorn!" Chief shook his head. "Almost got us all killed more'n once."

With everyone still chuckling and snorting and wiping their eyes, Mavis finally got to her feet. "Anyone for more coffee?"

For some crazy reason, that set everyone to laughing again, and she poured the round of refills with the coffeepot shaking.

"How come we never heard this story before?" Lucas asked.

Mavis shrugged. "Guess Dan wasn't here to tell it."

The old man smiled inside that grizzled beard. "Oh, I got lotsa stories about your pa. Fine man. He just lacked a little bit on the laughter side of life."

Deep inside but not on the surface, Mavis had to agree. Lacked laughter. Ivar did that.

Lucas asked, "Is that bear rug up at the

cabin the hide of that bear?"

Arnett wagged his head. "Nope. That was a big boar that got into the barn one night. Your pa shot that one just before the bear got to the cow. He killed one of the pigs first. He musta been some mad to be on a rampage like that. It was late in the year, and he should've already been hibernating, but for some reason, he wasn't. Ivar always thought maybe somethin' had gone wrong in that old boar's head that set him on a rampage like that. Good thing he didn't attack the house."

"That was after we left?" Chief asked.

Mavis replied, "Ja, just before Ivar and I moved down from the cabin. The barns and one of the sheds were up, but the house wasn't quite ready. Ransom was just a little fellow, and Lucas wasn't born yet."

Lucas frowned. "How did Far manage to get down the hill from the cabin in time?"

The memory washed over Mavis as if it were yesterday. "The dog set to barking, really fiercely barking. Ivar tore out of that cabin like the bear was after him. When the door opened, we could hear the pigs screaming. Nothing raises the hair on the back of your neck like an animal screaming in terror. I was praying so hard and clutching little Ransom to me. . . ." She shook her head. "Thought it was the end of our dreams for sure." Mavis pushed back her chair. "And on that cheerful note, you men go on into the other room, and we'll clean up here and bring the pie in there."

Cassie's eyes were still huge as she scraped plates and carried them to the dishpan, steaming on the reservoir. "None of that was made up?"

"No need to make up stories when real life hands you things like that."

"I suppose you're right." She scraped another plate. "Oh, I just remembered — I forgot to tell Micah about the plans for his wedding."

"We'll bring that news in with the pie. We need to plan a wedding dinner at least, something for them. I don't think the Indians make much fuss for weddings like white people do."

Runs Like a Deer looked up from the dishpan. "When?"

"Reverend Brandenburg said he'll come out Tuesday after dinner, and if that's not all right, to let him know."

She nodded. "Good." The young woman was hard to read, but Mavis thought she could see that Runs Like a Deer was pleased.

The men were gathered around the low

table in front of the sofa, looking at some drawings that Ransom had spread out for them to see.

Mavis recognized his plans for furniture building. One thing was certain, Ransom knew how to dream. Mining and ranching and building furniture. Like his pa, he never lacked for future things to do. If only they could come up with money to buy what they needed. Lucas dreamed too, but his was more to homesteading in Montana, and she'd put her foot down there. She was not leaving this ranch. She'd done all the home building she'd ever cared to do. Now she wanted to enjoy the fruits of all that labor.

She'd never told Lucas he couldn't go. She even offered to send cattle with him. It wouldn't really hurt to have more grazing land, especially now that Cassie owned half of this ranch, not that she'd mentioned anything about that again. It appeared that Cassie was happy just having a warm, comfortable home. Other than wanting to earn money to pay her share. The thought of that always made Mavis shake her head. Cassie did not understand the ways of family, that was all. Of course, if she and Lucas were married, something Mavis still wasn't too sure was the best thing, a lot of these questions would be moot.

Ransom gathered up his papers and smiled up at his mother. "Smells wonderful, as always."

"Heating the pie up releases the good fragrances all over again." She set the tray on the table and motioned Runs Like a Deer to do the same with her tray. Cassie handed out pie plates and forks while Gretchen brought in the coffeepot. With everyone all served, Mavis took to her rocking chair and smiled around at the others.

"So what do you think of Ransom's ideas?"

Dan Arnett nodded around a mouthful of pie. "Big question is, where to sell the furniture."

Lucas waved his fork in the air. "I have an idea. What if I contact Wheeler and ask him for suggestions. He resells the buttons he buys from me. Maybe he'd be interested in furniture too."

Ransom stared at his brother, a smile widening his eyes. "Why, Lucas, I think you hit the nail on the head. That could indeed be a door opening."

Arnett chuckled, a bit softer than his cackle. "This be some good day for ideas. Let me tell you what I've been thinkin' on."

All eyes swung to him.

He took another bite of pie, scraping the

last of the juice from the plate, and set the plate down. He wiped his mouth with the napkin, glanced at his coffee cup, shook his head, and settled his shoulders. "Now, I been thinkin' . . ."

Mavis bit her lip. Talk about a showman. This was a side of her neighbor that she had seen long ago but had only seen a hint of lately.

Lucas started to say something, but she hushed him with a look. Gretchen, sitting on the stool at her mother's feet, looked up into her face. Mavis answered with a slight shrug and shake of her head. She had no idea what was coming either.

Arnett turned to Ransom. "Now, you know I been after you to buy my sawmill." When Ransom started to respond, the older man raised his hand. "Hear me out." He sucked in a deep breath and heaved it out on a sigh with a nod. "I say we run these two ranches together. I'd just as soon deed you the land outright, but I have a feelin' you wouldn't accept that."

"You can be sure —" Mavis stopped at his raised hand and headshake.

"Just wait a minute. You'll get your turn."

Mavis rolled her lips together. This was indeed Arnett's show. She caught a look between her two sons that told her they had a lot to say too.

"We could use that barn of mine for dryin' the lumber we mill and turn it into the furniture-makin' place. Lucas gets married and he can move into that house, not have to build a new one or leave for Montana. Micah has a good head for mechanical stuff. I can teach him to keep that old steam engine runnin' and use it for powerin' all kinds of machinery. If Ransom finds some gold in that there mine, all the better. You might be needin' to look for more help, all this begins to pan out.

"I'm perfectly content livin' in that bunk-house — build a little house for my pup there on the porch, and we'll be right as rain. I can take care of the hogs and chickens and keep that smokehouse goin' when the rest of you are too busy. Still some good left in these old bones, but like Mavis knew, living alone was killin' me. Now I think of it, that Mr. Porter in Hill City might be a good one to talk with about all that furniture we'll make. He might have some ideas about marketin' it. You know, sellin' it."

He raised his cup. "Think I'll take a refill on that now, missy." Gretchen surged to her feet and pulled the coffeepot from the stand on the edge of the fire in the fireplace. She made the rounds refilling all the cups and still no one said a word.

"About that wedding . . ." Cassie said softly.

"After a pronouncement like that, why not talk about a wedding." Ransom heaved a pent-up breath and shook his head again. "What did Reverend Brandenburg have to say?"

"He'll be out here Tuesday after dinner to perform the ceremony." She looked to Micah. "If that is all right with you. And Runs Like a Deer."

Micah nodded. "That will be good." He looked to his soon-to-be wife, and she nodded also and then quickly ducked her chin, staring down at her lap.

Ransom looked to his mother and brother, then at Arnett. "You sure gave us a lot to think about, my friend."

"No more thinkin' necessary. Let's just go ahead with the plannin'."

"Arnett, you can't just —"

He raised his hand, palm out. "Don't go tellin' me what I can and can't do. I'm an old man, and I can do what I want with what I own."

"But what if your daughter comes back?"

"I'll send her a letter if'n I can figure where to send it. Seems like I don't have too good a luck with my family folks.

Something musta happened to her too, or you think I woulda heard from her by now."

Mavis and the others knew how his sons had either died or left and not returned. His wife died, and years earlier two of his little girls had died of some strange illness. Children often died young. And here he was, soldiering on.

"Now, before you go to thinkin' on all the reasons not to do this, you think on this. What else can I do with what I got? Sell it all? And to who? I don't wanna give you no bad neighbors, you know. And besides, I'm not real good at takin' care of myself anymore, as you know." He paused, squinted his eyes a bit, and raised one finger in the air. "I got it. I'll sell it all to you — lock, stock, and barrel. Give me a piece of that paper, Ransom, and I'll draw up the deed right now. From me to you for one dollar and lifetime care. There!" He grabbed a blank piece of paper and reached for the pencil.

5

Dumbfounded was now a figure of speech Cassie understood.

Glancing around, looking from under her eyelashes, she could see the others felt much the same. Ransom had shifted to his granite look; Lucas's eyes were wide and he was shaking his head slightly; Mavis wore straight-lined eyebrows, a sure sign she was thinking hard on how best to deal with this shock. Gretchen caught Cassie's glance and covered a giggle. Runs Like a Deer was studying her hands in her lap. Micah kept looking from Ransom to Mavis and back, as if he expected one of them to blow at any minute.

"I know. I dumped a big heap of my longtime thoughts in your laps, all sudden like. But I'm gettin' up there in years and if I wake up some morning in heaven next to my dear departed wife, I don't wanna be wishin' I'd taken care of this sooner." He looked to Mavis for help. "Mayhap I should have come to you first."

Mavis shook her head. "Dan, you've had time to think on this, and you just caught us all by surprise, shock rather. I mean, we've been trying to figure out how to buy the sawmill, and you come up with all this."

"I ain't just givin' it to you, ya know. It's a trade-off. You give me a home — only God knows how long that might be — and I get to have the time of my life, workin' with these fine young men, dreamin' big dreams and runnin' more cattle on that spread of mine . . . er . . . ours. I couldn' do all that without you all. Don't you see? You'd be doin' me the biggest favor of my later life."

Was this the way business was done in the West? A pencil and paper deed and a hand-shake? From the looks on the faces of those around the room, she had an idea this wasn't the usual way for any of them. Cassie tried to wrap her mind around all that was going on, but she had enough trouble trying to piece together enough cash money to cover the necessities for those living in the cabin. Not that they were asking for anything, but they were her responsibility. She took that on when they left the Wild West Show behind.

She glanced at Mavis again and realized

she was praying. She kept telling Cassie that God was indeed in control and had a plan for her life. A plan that showed how much He loved her and all the rest of them.

Ransom cleared his throat. "Okay, Arnett, let's chew on this a while. I don't want you signing anything over to us yet."

"How long, son? You know I'm living on borrowed time as it is."

"How do you figure that? You're healthy as that mule in our back corral. I know you've slowed down some, but that is to be expected." He held up a hand when Arnett started to say something. From the look on his face, Cassie was pretty sure he was all set to argue. "Let me finish. You know it takes me a while to get the words all together."

The old man nodded and rolled his eyes. "You saying I'm old and you're slow of speech? Mayhap you're wrong on both counts."

"Maybe." Ransom looked to his mother, who gave a slight nod.

Lucas caught Cassie's gaze but she couldn't figure out what he wanted. Arnett's comment about Lucas getting married. She'd not said yes. And she no more felt like saying yes now than ever. Why couldn't she just agree? He would make a good husband. She was learning to be a good wife. He made her laugh. He wanted her to keep shooting and promised he would help make that possible.

And now there was even the possibility of a real house. But she loved the cabin up there, even for the short time she had lived in it. But Micah and Runs Like a Deer needed a home too, and the cabin had been home to newlyweds before — Mavis and her Ivar. And what about Chief? Perhaps . . . Perhaps what?

She realized that silence took up the room. It was so quiet that the popping of a log just thrown on the fire sounded gunshot loud. What had she missed? Why was Ransom looking at her and what did he want? He dropped his gaze back to the drawings in front of him. Arnett still had the pencil and paper.

A funny feeling tickled the back of her neck. What had she seen in Ransom's eyes?

Mavis stood and headed for the coffeepot. "Anyone want more pie?"

Runs Like a Deer rose too. "I'll take care of it." At the nods from those around the room, she took the tray, but Mavis shook her head.

"Just bring the pie in here. Much easier."

Eating pie seemed to break the conversation barrier, but it left everyone carefully not mentioning Arnett's offer. Something like if George were standing in the middle of the room and no one wanted to talk about the bull buffalo standing in there. Strange how people could be like that.

When they were seated again, Mavis picked up a thread of conversation that must have been going through her mind. Or she was grasping at anything to bridge the gap. "So if you don't mind, Micah and Runs Like a Deer, we will have the ceremony right here as soon as Reverend Brandenburg arrives. I think his missus is coming too. I will bake a cake and we can celebrate with coffee and cake. Is there anything you need?"

Micah shook his head and smiled at his soon-to-be wife. "I haven't seen too many folks get married. The one time was at the show, and after the ceremony, there was a big party with music and dancing, and some people brought presents like it was Christmas. We have everything we need, thanks to all of you already." Runs Like a Deer nodded her agreement.

"Do you have a ring for your bride?" Lucas asked.

Micah shook his head. "We need one?"

"No, probably not, but I've made you one.

Let's hope it fits. It'll be ready for the ceremony."

"Well, we need to get going on the chores," Ransom announced when he'd drained his coffee cup. He tightened the thong holding back his long hair. "I'll take care of feeding the pigs and chickens. Gretchen, you milk and —"

"I'll milk and do the barn chores if you and Micah will pitch down a load of hay for the morning," Lucas interrupted.

Ransom and Gretchen both stared at their brother, their mouths hanging open. Lucas was volunteering to milk and do chores?

"Are you sick — in the head, I mean?" Gretchen asked.

Lucas tried to look innocent but failed miserably. "Just take it for what it's worth. This way you can help Mor get the supper ready."

"Right. It'll take four of us to warm up the soup." Mavis smiled at her female forces. "I think this calls for a celebration. Come on, I have an idea."

"What about me?" Arnett looked about from face to face.

Lucas cackled. "You keep the fires burning, and perhaps you and Chief can come up with more stories for the rest of us to enjoy."

Arnett glanced over at Chief, who shrugged. He seemed as confused as Cassie.

"And maybe we'll let you be the taste testers."

"Hey, not fair. I'm the best taste tester." Lucas winked at Arnett. "Taking my job away, eh?"

Cassie followed the others to the kitchen, each of them picking up cups and plates on the way. She could at least wash dishes. That she knew how to do.

Ransom opened the back door and turned to his mother. "There are three mighty sad-looking hounds out here. I know they'd like a chance to warm up at the fire."

"Well, let them in."

Othello came and sat in front of Cassie, staring up at her with adoring eyes. She bent to smooth back the thick coat he'd grown, now that he was outside most of the time. He and Ransom's Benny shared the spacious doghouse on the front porch, and Arnett's dog stayed as close to him at the bunkhouse as possible.

"You know, Arnett, if you want your dog in the bunkhouse with you, I don't mind a bit."

"You mean that?"

"Of course. That is your house now, and

you do what you want. The door is always open to this house for you too. I don't want you holing up over there, and yet I know you are enjoying the reading time."

Runs Like a Deer brought the soup kettle up from the cellar and set it on the back of the stove as Mavis asked her.

"Do you know how to make dumplings?"

Runs Like a Deer shook her head. "Like biscuits?"

"Sort of, but we drop the spoonfuls of dough into the boiling soup, or at times on stew."

"Here, we'll have a cooking lesson for Cassie too. Dumplings are just biscuits with less flour. In fact, you can just beat an egg, add salt and flour, and drop it into the soup. That works too. This time we'll put in some baking powder to make them lighter."

Runs Like a Deer asked, "Is it like fry bread? My grandma made fry bread."

"No. These dumplings will be steam cooked in boiling broth. Fry bread is cooked in hot oil. They are both very good, but they taste a little different."

With the dumpling dough ready for the soup to heat to boiling, Mavis took out another bowl. "Now we'll make chocolate pudding. If we had a baked pie crust we'd turn this into chocolate cream pie, but pudding sounds mighty good tonight."

After they'd finished supper and were passing the dishes of pudding around the table along with a plate of sour-cream cookies, Gretchen announced, "Cassie made the pudding." Cassie felt her cheeks flush.

"And both Cassie and Runs Like a Deer made the dumplings," Mavis added.

Later, when they were all arranged around the big room, Cassie picked up her knitting again and glared at what should have been neat rows. There was a hole two rows back — again. She sighed and started returning the stitches to the opposite needle to go back and pick up the dropped stitch. At least she was getting good at the tearing-back part. She understood the principle that practice makes perfect, but she also knew that practicing something wrong never made it right.

Why did she have such a hard time concentrating on what others made look so simple? Gretchen had learned to knit when she was five. Her fingers flew with the yarn and needles much like her mother's did. Cassie's mother had taught her how to sew and mend and stitch beautiful embroidery. She'd been thinking of creating a sampler for Mavis, but it would take a long time and wouldn't be done for Christmas, at least not this Christmas. She picked up the dropped stitch, making sure the yarn was turned the correct way on the needle, and went back to finishing the knit row. Then she would do the purl row. And then the knit row.

She felt someone's gaze on her and looked up to catch Lucas's smile. She returned the smile, and her thoughts scampered back to his proposal, or rather to his vow to make her love him. Was there any reason for her not to love him? He was certainly good-looking, with his boyish face and short curly hair. Many marriages started on friendship and some with just a letter in the mail — mail-order brides. Of course some of them were never happy, yet others were. But then, marriages based on love alone sometimes turned out happily, when others did not. So confusing, life. In the Wild West Show, she'd had few choices to make. Now it seemed that everything involved making a choice — every single thing.

Oh no! Do not think on anything but knitting. She rammed the needles into the ball of yarn and bit her bottom lip. What a waste of time this was. She could be filling shells for her practice shooting. At least she could do that right. Maybe she wasn't cut out for all this homemaking stuff, although she did enjoy the cooking and learning new things in the kitchen.

After the others went on up the hill to the cabin and the brothers headed down the hallway to their rooms, she joined Mavis in the kitchen. "What are you doing now?"

"I decided to make sourdough pancakes for breakfast, so I am feeding the sourdough."

" 'Night, Mor," Gretchen said after a yawn. " 'Night, Cassie."

With just the two of them left in the kitchen, Cassie stirred the milk and flour as Mavis told her. They measured out two cups of sourdough starter for the pancakes and added two of the fresh mix into the dough and set the crock back up on the shelf behind the stove. Then Mavis beat the starter into the dough that was left and set that on the warming shelf of the stove.

Mavis wiped off her hands. "This is what we used all the years before we could buy soda and baking powder at the store. Sourdough was good yeast. Leavening. I got my original starter from an old woman who came out here with her son and his wife. She died several years later, but she made sure that her starter lived on. She told me then that it was already fifty years old. So when my family starts homes of their own, this starter will go with them."

Cassie inhaled the faint perfume of her dough. She knew it would be stronger by morning when she'd add the beaten eggs and bacon grease and more flour. Somehow the thought of passing on dough like this made her feel like crying. Was having starter passed on part of becoming a member of the family?

The next morning they were just sitting down for breakfast when a knock on the back door caught them by surprise. Ransom answered the door.

"Come in, Chief! You're just in time for Mor's sourdough pancakes."

Cassie smiled at her longtime friend. "Please sit down."

Chief sat, but he waved away the plate she set in front of him. "I come to say good-bye, like I say before."

"Good-bye? What . . . ?"

He glanced around the table at all the looks of shock. "I go back to reservation now, before snow starts. I told you from beginning I would do that."

Cassie had trouble finding words. "I know. But . . . I thought you liked it here. I was hoping and trusting that you had changed your mind."

73

"Chief, John, w-we . . ." Mavis stuttered to a stop. "I hoped you would make your home here. You are part of our family."

He shook his head. "Thank you, but I need to go home."

"Home on the reservation is not what it used to be." Ransom too was shaking his head. "You know we have plenty here for you to do, and by spring, perhaps we'll even be able to pay wages."

"I know all that. I thought about this a long time."

"I'm sure you did." Mavis heaved a sigh. "You know you will always have a home here, should you decide to visit or return."

Cassie tried to talk around the lump in her throat, but she couldn't. She tried not to cry, but tears trickled down her cheeks in spite of her. Chief was part of her life, all of her life, like a piece of her mother and father, the sole remaining piece.

"This does not have to be good-bye. You know we want Indians to be part of the Wild West show, the rodeo, next summer." Lucas leaned forward. "We'll be coming to look for you and hope you will bring us others to be part of the show. Especially those who know the old ways of doing things, some good riders, some who want a job, not for a long time, though who knows where this one show will lead."

"You sound like Adam Lockwood, so long ago," Chief said. "I went along for one season and look what happened."

Mavis wiped her eyes too. "I'm so glad you brought Cassie to us. We will never be able to thank you enough for that." She blew out a breath. "No matter what you say, this ranch is your homestead too. Both Adam and Ivar would say the same thing. You are the only one left, and if nothing else, we need to hear the rest of your stories of those early days. I know Cassie wants to know more too."

Stop this, Cassie ordered herself. *Stop sniveling! You will see Chief again. This is not the good-bye he says it is. The reservation isn't across the country, only somewhere out beyond Rapid City.*

A short time later she stood on the front porch and watched her friend and teacher ride off. Another piece of her heart gone. How she hated the idea of his leaving!

Her whisper to herself accompanied her waving hand. "Thank you."

6

Tuesday morning the clouds hung low.

Cassie woke from a restless sleep in which she kept dreaming that Chief was in trouble. She was never sure what had been the problem, but the urge to go to him tore at her.

He had made the choice, but what if no one wanted him to be there? True, the townspeople here didn't want Indians around either, or at least some of them didn't. What difference did it make that Chief was a Sioux Indian? He was just like any of her other friends, only closer because they'd been together a long time, thanks to their years in the show. Since he'd been her father's good friend, she'd known him since she was born. And what about his eyesight? How would he hunt? Where would he live? Did he still have relatives there? What was life like on the reservation?

She fought the tears again. Today was supposed to be a happy day, a wedding day.

But some people would castigate Micah for marrying an Indian woman. All this bigotry made her angry deep inside. She pulled on her woolen petticoats and waist, slipped her wool skirt on over her head, and pulled on her long wool stockings. With a sweater added for good measure, she jerked the hairbrush through the ripples left by her nighttime braid.

Life just wasn't fair. That was all there was to it. If God loved everyone like the Bible said, how come the Indians didn't have that love too? Maybe one of these days she'd sit down with Reverend Brandenburg and ask him. He was a pastor, and she knew he and his wife didn't hold anything against the Indians. After all, they'd invited them all for supper at their house and made sure they had more food for the next days.

And he was coming out here to perform the wedding ceremony that afternoon. She bundled her hair into a snood, hearing the rattle of stove lids that said Mavis was up and preparing breakfast. Cassie had gone to sleep thinking maybe she should learn to milk the cow and take care of the barn chores. After all, if she was indeed a member of the family as Mavis said, then she needed to do more of the day-to-day work. She made her bed and headed for the kitchen. She knew Mavis had a lot planned. Not often did one host a wedding at their house.

"Are you warm enough?" Mavis asked. "The temperature really dropped last night, but Ransom said it was warming, which possibly meant snow. And here we are this morning with new snow."

"You think Chief made it to the reservation yesterday?"

"I doubt it, but then I don't know how far it actually is. Sure wish he had stayed a few more days at least."

"How about until spring, and then I'd say, 'Oh, please stay through the summer,' and . . ."

"I know." Mavis chuckled. "How about slicing that ham and getting it fried up. I'm mixing cornmeal mush today. Then we can have it fried tomorrow."

Cassie stepped into the pantry and brought the ham in from the meat safe. This time of year, outside cold took the place of the ice that kept the icebox cool during the summer, and the pantry, because it was warmed indirectly off the kitchen, kept things from freezing solid in the long winter. What a delicate balance. Much of what Cassie must learn about this place was logical in its own way, but still it must be learned.

She savaged the ham more than slicing it neatly like she'd seen Mavis or Ransom do. She couldn't even slice ham right. Where was Chief, and more important, how was he? Her mind screamed that he was buried in the snow. Another picture flashed of him on his horse, plodding through the snow, his elk robe over his head. Where was all this coming from? He'd been the one to know what to do when they'd been stopped by the blizzard in October.

"Cassie, what is it?" Mavis laid a hand on her shoulder.

"I'm worried about Chief. Would someone take him in?"

"Most likely he would not ask. This isn't a blizzard, just snow falling and cold. He knows how to take care of himself."

They turned at the stamping of boots on the back porch, and Mr. Arnett pushed open the door. "Sure is pretty out there."

Cassie stared at the old man. All she could see was danger, and he saw how beautiful it was.

"That ham smells mighty good. You want me to turn it? I can do that, you know."

Cassie handed him the long-handled fork. "I'll set the table."

"Makes ya think of Christmas, don't it?" He moved the pan off the hotter part of the stove and looked around.

"What do you need, Mr. Arnett?" Cassie studied his grizzled beard and wondered if he'd trimmed it last night. Somehow it seemed less scraggly.

"No 'Mr.' I'm Arnett. There's lotsa Dans out there. Only one Arnett. How about a platter to put in the warming oven?"

Cassie dug one out from under the counter where the kettles and baking things were kept and handed it to him.

He set it down on the back of the stove. "Ya need to warm it up first."

Cassie and Mavis shared a smile. Obviously something had happened to make him decide that this was really home now and he wasn't a mere guest any longer.

"So, we're havin' a wedding here today. Right?"

"This afternoon, when the Brandenburgs get here." Mavis turned at the boot stomping again, two pairs this time. "I'm setting the mush on the table. Cassie, bring that cream pitcher — oh, and the milk too." She slid the platter of pancakes into the oven to keep warm.

Gretchen blew in from down the hall, where she had been getting ready for school. "Thanks, Cassie, for helping in my place. Mor, I can't find my school notebook."

80

"Did you look under my knitting basket?"

"How did it get there?"

"You're asking me?"

"Nope, anyone in general." She flew into the big room and came back waving her notebook in the air, triumphant.

With everyone seated at the table and grace said, Cassie returned to the stove and began breaking eggs into the skillet as the men ate their cornmeal mush. Mavis had turned the job of frying eggs over to her. She slid the fried eggs onto another warmed platter, retrieved the platter of ham from the warming oven, the pancakes from the oven, and set them all on the table. Arnett waved Mavis to stay seated and brought around the coffeepot.

"You sure there will be school today?" Ransom asked.

"I'm riding over to Jenna's house, and her brother is driving. Biscuit will stay in their barn all day."

Cassie knew that Biscuit had become Gretchen's horse after she graduated from the pony. They had then passed the pony along to a family with small children. Gretchen kissed her mother's cheek, waved at the rest of them, and bounded out the door to where Ransom had tied her horse. Another part of family life Cassie must firmly plant in mind: Ransom got Gretchen's horse ready for her each school day before he came in from chores.

Looking out the window over the sink, Cassie realized the snow had let up to just a flake here and there. And it wasn't knee-deep, as she'd first thought.

"George acted like my best friend this morning," Lucas said when the conversation lagged. "That old bull sure has a mind of his own."

"He grew up that way," Cassie told him. "Chief said buffalo are like that but never to trust them. He didn't trust George until he'd known him for years. But then George will do things with Wind Dancer and me that he won't do for anyone else. After all, he has to remind people he is a wild bull buffalo. That's the way they billed him at the show."

Lucas grinned. "Well, the others aren't tame, that's for sure. There was quite a rattling of horns out there when we opened the fence around the haystack. That's long-horn talk for 'Stay out of my way.' "

Ransom rolled his eyes. "Even those young ones you brought didn't argue with the buffs this morning. That is the greatest thing to see, the piles of snow on the buffalo backs, like they're wearing a white robe on top."

Cassie had seen that on the trip south. The show had never wintered in snow country, and so much of this was new to her. Chief had explained it all to her, as part of her training.

Chief. She already missed him.

When they were done eating, Cassie cleared the table, tossed the three round ham bones to the dogs lying by the back door, and listened while Mavis gave out the instructions for the day. She and Mavis would do the baking first while the Engstrom men shoveled paths to the door. Arnett said he'd take care of the woodboxes.

Cassie's hands broke up bread for stuffing, but her thoughts wandered elsewhere. Then she got an idea. "Mavis, I've been thinking. Not only do I not have Christmas presents, I don't have a wedding gift for Micah and Runs Like a Deer either. But then I thought, Micah likes that rifle, and he really knows how to use it. I can give him that. What do you think?"

"I think that would be perfect."

Grinning, Cassie tackled the stuffing with renewed vigor. One problem solved.

The smoked geese and a wild turkey that Lucas, the adept hunter, had brought home were stuffed and ready for the oven when the cake came out. The rolls would bake last and the bread would go in, in between.

"Dan, if you'd like, peel the potatoes. Lucas, take an ax to that big squash in the cellar. We'll send pieces home with both —" She stopped and stared at Cassie. "What is Micah's last name?"

Cassie shrugged and sort of snorted. "I have no idea. He's always been Micah. You'll have to ask him."

"Well, he'll need one for the wedding certificate, I'm sure. I know you want this to be all legal and such." Mavis frowned. "And Runs Like a Deer?"

Again Cassie shrugged. Why had she never asked this question? She thought Runs Like a Deer had been married before, or maybe not. How did one know? "Well, Micah can sure use the name Lockwood if he wants to. I'd be proud to have him share my name. I always wanted a brother." She glanced at Lucas. That's what she felt like when she was with him. His little sister. Or maybe not so little but younger, at least. If she felt that way with him, why did she not feel the same way about Ransom?

This would take some thinking on, but later. Right now they had to get ready for a wedding.

Sun diamonds spangled the white fields and the puffy hats on the fence posts and railings. Around noon the clouds started to break up, separated, and finally disappeared, leaving behind a clear blue sky. By the time the buggy arrived with the Brandenburgs, icicles coming off the roof were dripping and singing of sunshine. Micah and Runs Like a Deer rode in double on his horse. Micah turned him loose in the corral at the barn. Lucas unhitched the Brandenburgs' team. Because they were pretty warm, he took them to the barn to wait out of the cold. Cassie did not doubt they would spend much of the day munching contentedly on hay.

"Welcome, Reverend! Hello, Elouisa!" Mavis greeted her friends and held the door open wide.

"Sure is beautiful out here," Reverend Brandenburg said, turning to look out over the valley. "Seeing buffalo in your pastures just tickles my funny bone. Nothing boring about the Bar E, you can bank on that."

Elouisa was smiling dreamily. "Ah, Mavis, I could sit here and watch out your windows, take my knitting and a cup of coffee, and —"

"You come out anytime. We can do that together. Cassie is learning to knit too."

"Cassie is failing at learning to knit, you mean." Cassie helped Mrs. Brandenburg off with her coat. "I'll hang these up for you." She smiled at the pastor too. "Thank you for coming."

"Is our about-to-be-wed pair here?"

Cassie grinned. They were hiding in the kitchen, but she wasn't about to tell the pastor that.

"We thought to have the ceremony right here in front of the fireplace." Mavis nodded to the roaring fire. "Do you need anything?"

"No." He held up his Bible. "I'm all set. This looks fine. Who will be standing up with them?"

"Cassie and Ransom will, if that is all right with you."

He nodded. "And where is Ransom?"

"He will be right in. Dan Arnett is here too. So we'll have a bit of a party."

"And Chief?"

Cassie's heart did another little plop. "He left for the reservation."

Reverend Brandenburg frowned. "Why would he do that?"

She shrugged. "That had been his plan all along. I was hoping he had changed his mind."

"I think he knows he can come back if he

wants to. At least I hope he believes that," Mavis said. "We told him so. He left yesterday, just as we were sitting down for breakfast. I pray he made it all right."

"Do you have a way of contacting him?"

"We will find a way."

"I know the Indian agent quite well. I'll contact him."

Cassie breathed a sigh of relief. "Thank you." She heard Ransom and Lucas come in the back door. "If you are ready, I'll go get the others."

Entering the kitchen, she smiled at her friends. "We're ready for you."

"Are you sure you want me to stand up with you?" Ransom asked Micah.

"Please." Micah looked to Cassie.

His nervousness made her catch her bottom lip between her teeth. "It'll be okay."

Runs Like a Deer shot a glance at the back door, as if she wanted to vanish out of it. Instead, she squared her shoulders and tried to smile at Cassie. She was only able to nod, a very brief nod. Lucas and Arnett went ahead and Ransom guided the others ahead of him.

Reverend Brandenburg had his back to the fire and a smile wide as the Black Hills to greet his party. "Thank you for asking me to do this for you, Micah, Runs Like a

Deer. I am honored. And I know our Lord is shining His pleasure down on this group too. I need one more thing: your complete names, to enter into our church records and to fill in the marriage certificate." He looked to Micah. "Micah?"

Micah swallowed and looked to Cassie. "Lockwood." The word nearly broke in his mouth.

Cassie nodded, her smile rivaling that of the pastor. "My father would be very proud to share our name with you. Thank you." *I will have a brother and sister after this.* Her heart sang out. *Thank you, heavenly Father! Tell my mother and father about this, if you will.*

"And you, Runs Like a Deer?"

"Cranston." She stared at the floor then looked to the pastor with a swift glance before her gaze again riveted itself to the floor.

"Good. Then let us begin." He motioned for the two of them to stand in front of him, and Cassie took her place beside the woman with Ransom on the other side of Micah.

"Dearly beloved, we are gathered here in the presence of God and this company to join these two people in holy matrimony. Let us pray."

Cassie felt the rich words flow over and

around her. She knew she had done the right thing in asking this man to perform the ceremony rather than a justice of the peace or following an Indian tradition that might or might not even be the correct tradition for Runs Like a Deer's heritage.

"Do you, Micah Lockwood, take this woman, Runs Like a Deer Cranston, for your lawfully wedded wife?"

Micah Lockwood. Cassie couldn't quit smiling. She listened to the remainder of the short service with half a mind while the other half jumped up and down for joy. Now Reverend Brandenburg was saying, "I now pronounce you husband and wife."

Micah gave his bride a quick kiss on the cheek and blushed red. His bride looked no less nonplussed. Surely they both knew this was coming! Deep inside, Cassie giggled, but she didn't let it show.

Everyone applauded, and congratulations flowed like honey on a hot day.

"Congratulations." Ransom shook Micah's hand. "Guess this makes you officially part of the family now that your name is Lockwood."

"Micah, did you never have a last name?" Cassie asked a question that she'd wondered about for years. Her father had thought the scraggly young man that came asking for a job one day was ashamed of his last name, and Cassie had never wanted to hurt his feelings by asking. Now, at last, curiosity overcame her.

"I don't know. Don't remember much about when I was young. I know I was real sick for a long time, and when I finally got better, I didn't remember much from my life before. Then my mom got sick and died and an old lady took care of me. She told me to call her Gramma, and I did. When she died, I was on my own, and all I knew was taking care of her animals."

Cassie stared at him. "How long before you came to the Wild West Show?"

"It came to town about the same time, and an old man who was a neighbor said I should go ask for a job, and I did. And your father hired me. A mighty good thing."

"All these years you never said anything."

"You never asked." He smiled at her, about the biggest smile she'd ever seen. "When your pa was dying, he asked me and Chief to take care of his little girl. And so we did our best."

"But now Chief left."

"Said he figured you was now where you needed to be and weren't nothing more he could do for you."

Cassie sniffed back tears that she refused

to allow to fall and perhaps sadden this day. All these years her father had provided for her after all.

"I always knew Adam Lockwood was a fine man." Mavis nodded as she spoke, a smile playing with the edges of her eyes and mouth. "And this just goes to prove it. Goes to prove our heavenly Father makes it all work together for good. Every time I see that verse in action, I get goose bumps."

Reverend Brandenburg shook Micah's hand. "Thank you for such a fine story on such a fine day. Makes my heart about bubble over with joy. And now, I was told there would be cake, and I think coffee and cake is another fine idea." He rubbed his hands together.

His wife elbowed him in the side. "You always think coffee and cake is a fine idea, especially when Mavis is doing the baking."

"Now, Ellie, you make fine cakes too."

Mavis was beaming. "You all sit down and visit, and we'll bring it in here. I made a layer cake for this special occasion."

When everyone was served, Reverend Brandenburg blessed the food and the newly married couple. His eyes lit up at the first bite of frosted cake. "Sure makes the drive out here worthwhile, not that we didn't have a dandy mission on top of that."

Runs Like a Deer sat slightly behind Micah, and when Cassie saw her look at him, she had to smile too. Runs Like a Deer loved her husband. You could see the love, actually see it. It glowed from her dark eyes. It vibrated through her body. And while she didn't smile much, she did when he said something or turned and looked at her.

Arnett dug a package out from behind him in the chair and handed it to her. "I thought you might like to have this. Belonged to my wife."

Runs Like a Deer stared at him, then down to the proffered box, shaking her head.

"Take it," Micah said softly.

She did and unwrapped a small cameo on a black ribbon. "Oh my." She draped the pendant over her hand. Shaking her head, she tried to hand it back. "Too fine."

"Thank you from both of us," Micah said, his hand cupping the one holding the cameo. "We will treasure this."

Runs Like a Deer swallowed hard. "Yes, thank you." With both hands she clutched the piece of jewelry to her chest. "Thank you."

When the two rode back up the hill, they had buttons from Lucas, an ax from Ransom, ownership of the rifle he'd been using from Cassie, a box of kitchen things from the Brandenburgs, and two cooking pans from Mavis that Cassie knew were Runs Like a Deer's favorite pans to use.

"We better be heading back to town," Brandenburg said. "Get your coat, Ellie, and we'll be on our way."

"Getting coolish out there again," Ransom said. "We'll bring up your team. You stay in here where it is warm." He and Lucas shrugged into their sheepskin coats and headed for the barn.

Cassie began gathering up the dishes. She scooped up some cake crumbs from the edge of the cake plate and closed her eyes, the better to appreciate the delicious treat. Maybe she should just tell Lucas that she'd marry him. Get all this yes-and-no stuff taken care of. Uncertainty was never a comfortable shirt.

Just tell him.

Ransom's orders to himself sounded faintly like some of his memories of his father. He stared up at the ceiling but couldn't see it in the darkness. He could usually fall into bed and immediately into the deep well of sleep, but not tonight. Was it the wedding this afternoon in the big room that was causing him to doubt his actions? Micah and Runs Like a Deer both looked happy, and while neither one of them showed their emotions much, today had indeed been a special day for them.

And Ransom had caught his brother watching Cassie. Why had she not accepted his proposal? Surely marrying Lucas would solve a lot of her problems. And if he really allowed the rather unchristian thought to take life, all the ranch would be back in the family. So why didn't he just tell Lucas that he now believed that Lucas was truly in love with Cassie and all his shenanigans with Betsy were the actions of — of what? An irresponsible boy? One who indeed trifled with a fine young woman's affections, like Betsy's brother had said? And he was Lucas's best friend. Was Betsy so brokenhearted, as her family had said, that she would go off somewhere to pine?

His thoughts tumbled over and around one another, each hollering for attention, like a schoolyard full of children playing blind man's bluff.

What about Cassie? As always there were two sides to every coin. She still maintained she did not want to marry Lucas. And she treated him like a brother, which is what his mother said Cassie had said more than once. How would she know what she felt if she'd never had a brother or ever before been in love? But then, had anyone asked her if she was in love with someone from her past? She'd never mentioned a man in her life, other than her father, of course, and that despicable Jason Talbot.

Ransom thumped his pillow and turned over for the third time. Maybe he should just get up, light a lamp, and work on some of the things on his desk. While the accounts were all current, he never had enough time to draw his dreams of furniture to build. Or to look through the catalogs that came in the mail. He huffed out a sigh. His mother would tell him to quit stewing and start praying. But why should he expect God to work this out? After all — after all, what? Now he was even questioning his questioning. And what about the offer Arnett made? He needed to think that through and come up with something they could all be comfortable with.

Having the old man living at the bunkhouse was not payment enough for a ranch, not in any kind of deals he'd ever seen. Actually, he'd thought that if Lucas and Cassie were to marry, they could move into that ranch house rather than up to the cabin like Cassie had mentioned.

How could life get so complicated? All he wanted was to get the mine restored and spend wintertime up there, digging, searching for another vein of gold. Something kept prompting him to do that. Was God truly talking to him, as his mother said might be the case, or was it his ego, wanting to prove his father wrong? Why did he have the feeling that there was a secret in that mine? Did his mother know the secret and just refused to tell, or . . . Mor was certainly a good one for keeping secrets. She had even kept secret that the Lockwoods were half owners of this ranch. His eyes finally felt heavy enough to close, and he exhaled another deep breath. Maybe he wouldn't have to go work at his desk after all.

Ransom woke to a frost-rimed window, the early shards of morning setting the intricate patterns painted on the window to spearing his eyes with shafts of yellow brilliance. Stove lids rattled from the kitchen. His mother was up. Maybe he should talk over some of his late-night musings and see what she thought.

But the sight of Cassie starting the fire in the cookstove instead of his mother stopped him in the doorway. With her hair bundled into a snood and one of his mother's aprons nearly covering her from neck to foot, she rattled the grate just like Mavis taught her.

"Would you like me to do that?" he asked.

She jerked around, one hand to her throat. "Goodness, you have to go and scare a body like that?"

"Sorry, I didn't mean to."

"Thank you, but no thanks. I need to learn to do all these things, and the only way to learn them is to do them. I'm thinking I need to learn how to milk the cow too. Oh, and Lucas has already gone to the barn."

Without bellyaching? Ransom made sure his shock didn't show on his face. With Cassie in the kitchen, he would've thought his brother would be there offering to start the fire. "Is Mor ill?"

"Not that I know of."

"No, she is not ill" came a voice from behind him. "But I can't believe I slept in like that." She lifted an apron off the hook on the wall and, after sliding her arms through the crossed straps, tipped it over her head and fastened the ties at the waist. "Now, Cassie, how do you want me to help?"

"If you'd like to start the coffee, I'll get the cornmeal mush out and slice it. We fry it in the saved bacon grease, right?"

Mavis nodded and walked to the sink to pump the handle for water to flow and filled the coffeepot.

The fire crackled in the stove and perfumed the air with the fragrance of pine from the pitchy kindling Cassie had started it with. Ransom made a mental note to check the chimney for tar buildup. He hadn't done that lately. Most people just let it burn out now and then. That sort of wild and roaring fire made him too nervous. He'd sweep, thank you.

Mavis set the coffee water on the hottest

part of the stove and fetched the ground coffee from the cupboard. Instead of grinding coffee every day like many people did, she usually ground a quart jar full and kept it in the cupboard.

"Looks like we're about due for some grinding here." She emptied the last of the coffee into the pot.

Ransom looked at the clock over the kitchen sink. "Is Gretchen up yet?"

"Yes. She's getting ready for school. She said she feels like she's on vacation, not having to milk in the morning. You going to pitch hay down?"

"Thought I'd hitch up the team. We filled the wagon last night." Once a day they hauled a wagonload of hay from the haymow and fed it to the herd. As soon as the snow got deep, they would open the fence around a haystack and feed the cattle that way in order to keep them up closer to the barns. So far there had not been enough snow to even put the wagon bed on the sledge runners.

He stopped at the kitchen window. "Those clouds are hanging mighty low. Bet we get snow again today, and from the looks of it, more than we've had."

Cassie paused as she was slicing the cornmeal that had set up firmly in a bread pan. "How do you know that?"

"Ranchers learn to read the weather signs. Black clouds like those to the north mean snow at this time of year, and in the summer you would most likely see lightning forking against the black. We are long overdue for a heavy snowstorm."

"Do you think Chief made it to the reservation by now?"

"I'm sure he did," Mavis answered. "That other snow wasn't really enough to slow down a horse."

"I sure hope he writes and lets us know he is all right." Cassie's voice sounded mighty worried.

"Reverend Brandenburg said he'd make inquiries." Mor's voice sounded soft and reassuring.

Ransom shrugged into his sheepskin coat and clamped his hat down on his head. "If the wind kicks up and builds drifts, we'll be in it for sure." He stopped on the back porch and pulled his leather gloves on. Usually by now he was wearing the gloves his mother knit to go inside the leather. When it really got cold, he had fur-lined mittens that he pulled on.

He stared up the hill to where the rising light set the frost-coated trees on fire as the sun hit them. Smoke rose from the chimney of the cabin and from the bunkhouse too. One of the cows bellowed, to be answered by another. A horse whinnied. Lucas came out of the barn with the milk bucket on his arm and shut the door behind him, dropping the bar into place.

"Breakfast will be ready in a few minutes, so we'll haul hay afterward. I'll get Gretchen's horse saddled," Ransom announced, as if Lucas didn't already know all that.

Lucas nodded and headed for the well house, where he would strain the milk and set it in pans for the cream to rise. "I'll ask Mor if she wants the cream in to churn. We have quite a bit. I took a bucket of skimmed milk down to the hogs and the chickens."

"You already fed them?" Another shock. What was happening to his brother? Maybe, just maybe, he'd decided to grow up and begin to accept more of the responsibilities around here without being asked. Maybe the thought of marriage was encouraging that decision. Maybe this could be a good thing, after all.

He saddled Biscuit and led the horse up to the house, tying it out of the rising wind. When he entered the kitchen, he found Cassie frying the mush as fast as Gretchen and Lucas could devour it. With the churn sitting by the stove, he figured they'd have fresh butter for dinner.

"Why didn't you have the wagon come by and pick you up here?" he asked his little sister.

"They'd have to leave earlier. Hudsons ride over too. I think John doesn't really want to drive the box."

In a way, Ransom admired that his little sister was thoughtful toward her schoolmates. "But he's the oldest now that his brother is gone. I'd say he's stuck with the job."

She nodded. "I don't mind riding over. I'd rather ride all the way in, but this is warmer and easier on Biscuit." She looked to Lucas. "Did you guys ever ride in the box?"

"Didn't have the choice. They built the box after we were out of school. Jenna's pa came up with the idea." Lucas nodded when Cassie asked if he wanted a refill on his coffee.

Arnett chimed in, "My wife taught our children when they was real small. Then they built the school in Argus."

"Why don't you come drive the wagon while I pitch the hay out?" Ransom suggested to Arnett after they finished breakfast. "Then we can take a load of wood and supplies up to the mine. You have something else planned, Lucas?"

"Nope, but if we're going to work up there, we do need plenty of supplies. Long as that storm holds off."

The three men dressed for the cold and headed to the barn.

Can animals be obviously eager when they're just standing there looking? It sure seems like they can. Every eye watched and every ear pricked forward as the hay wagon approached the gate. Every hoof hurried over, the shaggy animals surrounding the wagon as the men forked out all the hay. Ransom felt something deeply satisfying about meeting such primal needs in the animals under his care. George swung his massive head toward one of the longhorns. She quickly found another place to eat.

The three drove back to the house and started loading firewood. The wind kicked up, but they ignored the cold and drove on up to the mine, where they tossed the wood into a somewhat haphazard pile inside the mouth of the mine. On the way over to the sawmill, they swung by the cabin to ask Micah if he would come help load the timbers.

With four of them working, the job went fast. That Micah certainly didn't sit around exploring his fingernails. He was a fine worker. They took two loads of the cut timbers and, backing the wagon in as far as it would go, stacked the timbers in piles, ready for restoring the mine. On their way back for another load, the snow swirled and dipped, but still the main storm held off.

"You must be holding your mouth just right or something, because those clouds haven't opened up and dumped all over us," Lucas teased his brother.

"I guess. Thought sure it would hit before now." They unloaded the third load before the snow grew thick enough to cut visibility. "It's dinnertime, so Micah, you want to come eat at the house or — ?"

"Thanks, but I'll go back to the cabin. If you decide to continue —"

"I doubt it. Once this starts it'll probably snow all night. You got all you need up there?"

"Plenty of wood, more that I could split if we need it. Thanks for asking." Micah strode off to the cabin, and the others drove down to back the wagon into the barn again and unharness the horses. When the three entered the kitchen, the smell of fresh bread and cinnamon rolls greeted them.

Ransom inhaled deeply, savored the scent for a moment, and smiled at his mother. "Now, that is a smell worth driving miles for. Surprised we didn't get it clear out to the barn." He hung his coat, muffler, and hat on the tree by the door.

"Dinner will be ready shortly. Lucas, before you take your coat off, could you bring in some more firewood?" Mavis asked.

"Thought the woodboxes were my job," Arnett said, pulling on his jacket. "You need more for the fireplace too?"

"I don't know. We've not been in there today." Mavis opened the oven door to pull out a pan of cookies. "Cassie, do you want to take care of these while I check on the dumplings?"

Arnett was a just as willing a worker as Micah, be it a tad slower. And just as eager to help, Ransom noted. The old fellow slipped into his coat without buttoning it, popped into the front room, and came popping back out, then slammed out the back door. He soon returned with two carriers of wood stacked deep. He was obviously nearly as strong as he used to be.

"Mavis, is that chicken and dumplings I smell?" Arnett dumped the split wood from one carrier into the kitchen box and carried the second to the big room fireplace.

"It is. That old hen who figured she didn't need to lay any more eggs is now our dinner. Better we eat her than she dies of old age."

Ransom watched as Cassie slid the cookies off the sheet and filled the cookie jar with the cooled ones. She and his mother seemed to work together like they'd been doing so for years. He stepped up behind her and snatched one of the still-warm cookies. "Thanks."

She rolled her eyes. "I suppose now Lucas will want one too." She offered him a cookie on the end of the pancake turner. Lucas did not refuse it.

"What about me?" Arnett hung his coat up and grinned at her when she handed him a cookie. "Did you bake these, girl?"

She nodded. "Applesauce and raisins in them. I thought to frost them too, but we didn't get that far. Today I learned how to churn and wash butter. That old churn takes some arm strength to get the butter to turn."

"Good for your arm?" Lucas asked.

"I guess." Cassie rubbed her upper arm. "Maybe I should be the one hauling in the wood."

"Then what would I do?" Arnett grinned at her as he sneaked another cookie.

Ransom watched the interchange, contentment somewhere down in his middle. He caught the way Lucas smiled at Cassie.

Perhaps this really was the way things should go. The thought had been floating in and out of his mind all day. He needed to talk with Lucas.

After dinner, with the snow beginning to pile up, he got into his coat and gloves. "Come on, Lucas, we better get the rope strung to the barn in case this turns into a blizzard. I think we'll milk early too, just in case."

Arnett stood. "Mavis, you got anything for the chickens?"

"There by the back door. I'd give them some of that sour milk by the pigs too. They really go for that."

"No wonder Pa used to do this before the snow hit," Lucas grumbled.

Ransom nodded. They should have done this before the ground froze so hard, he thought as the wind buffeted them, pelting the snow against their faces so hard it stung. He and Lucas took turns pounding in the posts with the sledgehammer. The old rope they always used for this was fraying a little. He cut out and reknotted one length that had nearly parted. By the time the rope was strung, they were both sweating under their jackets.

At last they stepped into the barn and together pulled against the door to get it closed. Immediately the roar of the wind subdued to a rumble. Inside, the barn was just as cold as the outside air, but without wind it seemed beckoningly warm. Ransom lit one of the lanterns and, hanging it on a post, climbed the ladder into the haymow. They forked the hay down and filled the wagon for the next morning's feeding. Lucas milked the cow. Ransom cleaned the manure from the gutter and tossed straw down for bedding. He fed the horses and cleaned their stalls too.

Gretchen brought her horse in to unsaddle him. "You already milked?"

"I did. You take this on up to the well house while we finish up here." Lucas handed her the bucket. "You want Biscuit kept in the barn or let out?"

"Up to you." She pushed open the door. "In the barn. It's getting bad out here."

The storm raged on through supper and screamed around the eaves after they moved into the big room. The fire snapped and danced its defiance against the storm, creating its own music. The dogs lay in front of the fire, Othello and Benny by now fast friends.

"We need to run a rope to the bunkhouse too," Lucas said as he got out his button-making supplies. "And to the well house."

Ransom nodded. This was the kind of thing their pa had always been ready with. Ransom should have attended to the safety ropes long before this. But when he thought about the day, he felt a smile inside. They had actually hauled supplies and wood up to the mine, and no one had complained. It was a shame they weren't already up there. A storm like this couldn't make any difference to the work underground.

He wanted to talk to Lucas, but he couldn't say what he had to say with the others around, especially Cassie. So what could he do?

"Lucas."

His brother looked up.

Ransom nodded toward the kitchen. "Come on."

"What do you need?" Lucas asked once they stood over by the sink.

"I've got something I've been wanting to tell you." Ransom sucked in a breath. This was harder than when he'd rehearsed it in his head. "I want to make an apology."

Lucas started to say something, and Ransom held up his hand. "Let me finish please. I've got to tell you that I think I made a mistake."

Lucas's eyebrows rose. He stared.

"I know, it's probably not the first or the

last, but I want you to know that I give you my blessing to marry Cassie. Looks to me like you really do love her, and I do want you to be happy. Her too. So whatever you need me to do, you let me know. All right?" He stuck out his hand.

Lucas shook his brother's hand, that inscrutable gaze remaining on his face. "Thank you. This means a lot to me. I'm . . . uh, I'm surprised."

"I know, me too." Ransom didn't quite understand. Lucas ought to be real happy. Instead, he just stood there looking . . . looking how? Overawed. Dumbstruck. Confused. Why not happy? "Let's take a plate of cookies back in with us. Maybe someone wants a cup of coffee. I know I do."

"Forget the cookies, let's take cinnamon rolls."

That night as he waited for sleep, Ransom found himself thinking too much again. *Sure hope I made the right decision. Lucas better take real good care of her!*

His eyes popped open. Now, where did that come from?

8

"Don't worry about it, Cassie. No one expects presents. We all make most of ours."

"I know, but I've never had people like this to give presents to. In years past, I bought something for the few people I exchanged with. My father used to give something to everyone in the show." Cassie shrugged. "I've not had family before . . . well, not for a long time."

Mavis reached out and hugged the girl who had already taken a daughter's place in her heart. "Ah, Cassie. We live simply here, and we love sharing all that we have. I understand wanting to do something, so let's think what you can do."

"Knitting isn't one." Cassie rolled her eyes.

Mavis chuckled. "I can see that you have difficulties with that, but those last rows are looking better and better." She paused. "It really concerns you, doesn't it?"

"Yes."

"Then let's set you up with some projects. I have all sorts of fabric scraps and a lifetime supply of embroidery floss. We'll think of some nice things."

"Thank you, Mavis!"

Mavis checked the ham that was roasting for dinner. "I think I'll put some rhubarb jelly on that ham. For some reason that sounds mighty good about now."

"Rhubarb jelly?"

"I know, it sounds strange but it's good. If you want to start peeling the potatoes, Cassie, we'll mash them for dinner."

"The men will be here for dinner?"

"Ransom said so. He figured they'd be done hauling the hay and that other load of wood by then. They switched the wagon bed from wheels to runners." She glanced out the window above the sink. "That snow sure makes a glorious vista out there."

The storm had dumped nearly a foot of snow before it left to snow somewhere else, leaving a pristine world that now glittered in the sunshine.

"When the boys were young they would take the toboggan up on the hill in front of the cabin, and we'd slide down. Lucas brought out one of the horses one year to pull the toboggan back up the hill and then we let the horse pull us up into the woods. I'll never forget that day. It was the winter after their father died, and while they thought they were pretty grown up to be sledding, they wanted to make sure Gretchen got to do all the things they had done when younger. All of us know how to ski too. Have you ever skied?"

Cassie shook her head. "We never wintered where there was snow. I guess that is why I am so enthralled with seeing the world so different. Look how the branches on that pine tree bend down. Is snow that heavy?"

"You can be sure it is. If the snow gets really deep, we've had to shovel off the roof so it doesn't damage it."

"But it looks so fluffy and light."

"Let's get the dinner ready, and then I'll give you your first lesson in skiing. That gentle slope between the house and the barn is ideal for a beginner."

"You think I can learn how?"

"As graceful as you are on horseback, you'll be a natural. We'll set the potatoes to simmer and green beans with bacon and onions the same. When we see them coming we can rush back in and finish up. You'll be schussing down the big hill before you know it."

Half an hour later, Mavis was waxing the two pairs of skis she'd taken down from under the eaves on the front porch.

"Why are you doing that?"

"So they glide better, and it keeps the snow from sticking to them. Usually Ransom does this one evening in front of the fire. He does a better job than I am doing." She leaned the pair against the wall and started on the next. "This is one of those things that make wearing pants a great idea. Getting up after you fall down in skirts is much more difficult." When she finished, she set the skis on top of the snow at the bottom of the steps.

Othello bounded across the snow, his doggy grin making both of the women smile. He just about wagged his tail off and tossed snow like a shovel with his nose. When Cassie picked up a handful and tossed it at him, he leaped to catch it and then looked bewildered when he had nothing. He looked around, searching for his catch.

Cassie laughed and threw more, to have the same thing happen again.

Mavis laughed with her. "Okay, hang on to me and step onto the skis with your feet in the marked places." She bent down and buckled the ski straps over Cassie's boots and then handed her two sticks. "One for each hand, these are ski poles to help with your balance. Let me show you." She strapped on the other pair and, digging the poles into the snow, strode or rather slid off. She looked over her shoulder. "See how easy it is? Just like walking, but you push with your feet."

Cassie copied what Mavis had done and laughed with delight when the skis slid smoothly forward.

"Now keep your balance forward over the tops of the skis, or they'll slide away and leave you on your fanny in the snow."

Cassie slid up beside her.

"Good. Now we'll be going down this slope, and you can get dumped easily because skis don't know when to slow down. You can be flying after just a few feet." Mavis pushed off and picked up speed, demonstrating. "You can slow your skis by pointing your toes in. Like this. Tips close together, tails wide apart. It's called the snowplow. The skis do what your feet tell them. You will have more control if you stay slow. But if the skis cross, you'll fall." She slid to a halt.

She started downhill again. "Once you get used to your skis, you can stop like this."

She flipped both tails to one side, and immediately she was parallel to the slope.

"So much to think about," Cassie muttered. She gingerly pushed her right foot forward.

"Keep your feet together."

"Oh." She slid the left up and then pushed off like she'd seen Mavis do. The ski went forward and she fell back, flailing arms and poles and down with an *oof*! Othello ran over, tail bannering, tongue lolling, licked her face, pressed his cold nose to her cheek, and licked again. Then he planted both front feet on her chest and barked at her.

"Get away, you big goof!" She pushed at him, laughing and trying to sit up at the same time.

Mavis used a wide-angled step to move back up the hill and slid to a stop beside her. "That's why you learn to snowplow like I told you and keep your weight forward." She extended a hand to help her up, but when Cassie tried to stand, her skis took off again.

"Okay." Mavis dropped her hand and stood parallel in front of her. "I'm blocking the motion now. See if you can use your poles to stand up, and we'll start again."

After finally making it to the bottom, Cassie learned how to sidestep back up the hill and snowplow down, this time without falling. She let out a shout when she made it to the bottom still standing. "Wouldn't it be easier to take off the skis and walk back up the hill?"

"Here it would, but when the snow is deeper and the hill steeper, you need to be able to get up and down the slopes without walking, since skis keep you on top of the snow and feet will break through, up to your knees or deeper. Snow is beautiful but snow is also dangerous."

Mavis shaded her eyes with her mittened hand. "Here they come. Your first lesson is finished, and you did very well. I thought you would be a natural skier." They side-stepped back up to the porch, leaned their skis against the wall, and with Cassie wearing a grin as wide as her face, returned to getting dinner on the table.

"From the looks of those ski tracks, someone took a fall or two," Ransom said as he hung up his jacket.

"Cassie's first time on skis. She did very well."

Lucas turned to look at her. "You've never skied before?"

"I've never seen snow like this before. The worst I've seen was the blizzard in October. Here, the snow goes on forever. And look at the trees; they are so beautiful."

Nodding, Lucas hung up his hat. "Snow does make the world look all new. Covers up the bad stuff, the drab, the worn-out look of fall ending."

Mavis looked at her son. "Lucas, that was lovely. You never cease to amaze me."

"Amuse me is more like it," Arnett added. "Had me laughing all the way down the hill."

"Any time you want to go skiing on the big slopes, let me know. Skiing is a great way to get around in the winter. Do you think Micah skis?"

Cassie shrugged. "Micah continues to surprise me." She smiled on the inside. *Because he now has the same last name I do, does that make him my brother?* "I'm sure that if you suggest he learn to ski, he will do just that." She set the plate of sliced bread on the table and smiled at the old man. "Can I get you anything, Mr. Arnett?"

"Are you mad at me?"

"No. Why?"

"You keep calling me Mr. Arnett. Everyone else calls me Arnett. I'd rather you did too." He sat down at the table. "A cup of that hot coffee might just warm me up on the insides."

"Gladly." She fetched the cream pitcher

from the icebox and the coffeepot from the stove. "Anyone else?" At their nods, she filled the other two cups and returned the coffeepot to the stove. After Ransom said grace and all the plates were full, conversation lulled while they ate.

Ransom broke the silence. "Looks like we have all we need up there at the mine. Guess we'll stay up there tomorrow and see how it is to camp through the night."

Arnett shook his head. "I'll sleep in my bed, thank you. These bones are gettin' too old for a bed on the hard ground."

"That's why we brought that hay up there, to cushion the beds."

"I know, but you two or three youngsters can go camping in the mine. I'll do your chores down here both night and morning, if I need to."

"I thought you would only do that in emergencies." Mavis passed the meat platter around again.

"I'm just wanting to make sure we have all that we need. Might never need to do that, but we'll be prepared."

"He wants us to work through the night, Mor. You know how he is about the mine." Lucas shot his brother a raised-eyebrow look.

"No, I . . ." Ransom realized his brother

was teasing. "Maybe that's not a bad idea. We can work there at night and on the ranch during the day. We'd get a lot more done that way."

"I often wish I could do that. Work all day at one thing and do something else during the night, like sewing or knitting, with a big fire in the other room and the quiet of the night."

"Sometimes seems like you do that already," Ransom said. "What time did you go to bed last night?"

"I have no idea. I got going on my project and didn't want to stop. Cassie is spoiling me by starting the stove and the breakfast. It's kind of nice waking up to the smell of coffee. I just followed my nose to the kitchen."

Cassie smiled. "I like starting the breakfast in the morning, but if we are to have pancakes tomorrow, you need to tell me how to do that with the sourdough starter. I thought I'd make extra so I can do the biscuits like you did."

"You can start a separate batch, you know, just for the biscuits."

"I know. Just seems like a good use of time and supplies. One of these days I am going to learn how to make cinnamon rolls like you do."

"Teach her how to make apple pie too." Lucas nodded to his mother.

When he smiled at Cassie, Mavis watched the action. It appeared to her that her younger son was indeed falling more in love with Cassie Lockwood all the time. He touched her hand when she served, he had a special smile just for her, and he encouraged her in all she was learning to do. Mavis knew how much her son loved apple pie, and here he wanted to make sure his wife knew how.

It all depended on Cassie now. Would she give in and allow herself to fall in love with this very appealing young man? Not that Mavis was prejudiced or anything, but she wanted Cassie in the family perhaps even more than Lucas did. It looked like he was finally settling down and would assume his full responsibilities of the ranch.

"You know, Lucas, I think when you and Cassie get married, you ought to move into my old house," Arnett said with a piece of meat on his fork. "It's all furnished and everything. We'll get all the stuff cleaned out of it, you know, like I mentioned before. Seems like such a good idea to me."

"You know, Arnett, we need to do some talking yet about your proposal." Ransom shook his head. "I just —"

"Now, don't you go ruining a perfectly good meal. We'll talk about that another day. I got me some ideas too." He looked to Mavis. "I think every meal is better than the one before it. Can't begin to tell you how much it means to me to be part of this family."

"Dan, you are welcome, but we do need to talk about your proposal. Ransom . . . well, each of us, is giving this a lot of thought, and I'm sure we'll come up with something that works for all of us."

"I already have what works for me. Far as I'm concerned, it's a done deal."

Mavis shook her head. "Stubborn old coot."

"That's right and don't you be forgetting it." The twinkle in his fading eyes belied any sternness he tried to convey.

That evening, when they all gathered in the big room, each busy with his or her project, Ransom turned to Lucas. "I have something I've been thinking on and I'd like to talk to you and get it off my chest."

"In here or the kitchen?"

Ransom narrowed his eyes, thinking. "I guess in here because the others have heard me blast you with my other thoughts."

Mavis watched her two sons. Lucas appeared to be relaxed, but the tension line in his jaw was tight. And Ransom shifted in his seat, not really comfortable either. *Lord, keep this pleasant, please,* she entreated. These two had gone at it before, many times with less incentive than this. She'd prayed then too.

"What?"

Ransom heaved a sigh. "I just want to ask your forgiveness again for insisting that you didn't really love Cassie but were doing your usual flirting around."

"Thanks, brother." Lucas narrowed his eyes and leaned back in his chair.

"No, please, I really mean this. If you still plan to marry Cassie —"

"I do." He smiled at Cassie. "As soon as she agrees."

"Then you have my blessing, like I said before. And I wish you all God's blessings." He took another breath and smiled at both of them.

Mavis watched Cassie shake her head. It appeared she was still not ready to accept Lucas's proposal. Would she ever? Pride in her eldest son made her smile. He had come a long way when he could ask for forgiveness like this. He'd always had a hard time admitting when he might be wrong. *Please, Lord, lay your hand of blessing upon this union. She's like my daughter already, and this would just make it perfect. And if they lived over on the other ranch, what more could I ask for?* She smiled at her eldest son. Other than a good wife for him too. A woman who would think he was the greatest man that walked on this earth or at least in this valley.

Wherever she is, O Lord, bring her to us.

9

Maybe I should just agree, Cassie thought.

Everyone had gone to bed, but when she couldn't sleep she had returned to Mavis's chair by the fireplace, a light shawl wrapped around her shoulders. After stirring the coals, she'd added wood to the fire and now sat staring into the flames. If only she had been watching Lucas's face when Ransom announced his blessing. Why couldn't she just accept that and make this final? What would be wrong with marrying Lucas? He said he loved her, and she knew she loved him, but the problem was the way she loved him. As a brother, not as a husband. And that was a huge problem. Surely that would come with time. She remembered a Romanian couple that performed with the show for several years. It had been an arranged marriage. They had not even met before the wedding, and they were doing all right. Surely so could she.

She and Lucas could live in Arnett's house, and that way the brothers could run both spreads effectively.

All the family would benefit if she would only say yes.

God, Mavis says to ask you and I have, but I don't hear any answers. But then, I don't think I've ever *heard you answer.* As she thought about this, she observed that there were people in the Bible who married because it was the best thing, not necessarily for the kind of love she had seen between her mother and father. God had blessed those marriages. *Dear God, would you bless this one?*

Would she regret it later?

She'd not thought about that before. Marriage was forever, but was her assumption true that she could learn to love Lucas forever?

The look on Ransom's face when he gave his brother the blessing floated through her mind. Was he doing that out of duty, or did he wholeheartedly believe it? *Think, Cassie,* or would it be better to stop thinking? Leaning back in the chair with a heavy sigh, she watched the dancing flames. Pictures of her mother and father flashed through her mind. While her parents had always included her in whatever they were doing, she knew they'd rather be together than with anyone else. Close together, touching . . .

She paused. They had hated to be apart. How many times had she heard her mother say, *"Your father will be back in a minute"*? Or an hour. And if longer than that, she touched the locket she always wore with their pictures in it. The treasured locket. Gone now.

Cassie's mind would not shut down, so she used a coal from the fireplace to light one of the kerosene lamps. She drew the handkerchief she was hemming from under her failure at knitting and continued the tiny stitches. She had embroidered a mono-grammed LE in one corner. Fancy stitching she could do, so these would be her gift to the men on her list — the two Engstroms, Micah, and Mr. Arnett. No, just Arnett. She'd designed — in her mind at least — a reticule for Gretchen and a bookmark with "The joy of the Lord is your strength" on it for Mavis. Something for Runs Like a Deer still eluded her. She should have started months ago.

A pang of longing ripped into her heart. How her father would have loved bringing his wife and daughter to this place! What a shame that he had never left the show dur-ing the off-season and come here, at least for a visit.

That led to thoughts of the future. What if she joined a show or made guest appearances at shows during the season to make enough money to add to the ranch, not just pay for her own supplies? She'd heard Ransom talk of adding more cattle, and with the joining of the two ranches, there was now enough land to do that. How many acres that meant, she had no idea, but he'd also talked of Appaloosa horses like her father had dreamed of and new machinery — breakdowns were hard on everyone, or so Mavis said.

Money. So much of life revolved around money, mostly never having enough. Or any at all, in her case. The yard of linen she had purchased to make her Christmas gifts had taken her last cash, but Mavis's scrap bag did not have what she needed. She knew she could put it on the ranch credit or on her own, but the totals owed were so horrifying already that she couldn't do it.

If she were to agree to marry Lucas, would he go along with her ideas? He'd already said he would travel with her and manage her affairs. But would he? Could he? Mavis had stated unequivocally that Lucas would not travel with her unless they were married. She said she would come along when needed. That meant they'd need money for more railway fares, hotel rooms, meals. The list not only seemed unending, it kept lengthening.

"Go to bed." The sound of her voice made Othello, who was sleeping at her feet, raise his head. "It's all right, fella, just talking to myself." She reached down and stroked his head and then, setting her needlework aside, got up to add wood to the fire. She'd never reacted to things like this before — not able to sleep so staying up, dressed and awake. She folded the finished handkerchief and laid it on top of another in her sewing basket, another gift from Mavis.

Receiving gifts and never having anything to give in return ate at her. Here at the ranch she was doing all the receiving from all of them. That had to change!

Mavis found her in the morning sound asleep in the chair, the fire burned to embers but nowhere near out. She shook Cassie's shoulder. "Cassie, child, wake up and go to bed."

"No, I can't." Cassie blinked and, sitting up, blinked again before rubbing her eyes. Where was she? The fireplace, Mavis, Othello whining and nudging her with his nose. "Oh, I'm at the ranch."

"Yes. Where else would you be?" Mavis peered into her eyes. "Cassie, are you all right?"

"I think so. I . . . I guess it was a dream."

"A dream? Why are you sleeping out here?"

"I dreamed I was . . ." Cassie paused. "I couldn't sleep, so I decided to work on my Christmas gifts. I guess I finally did fall asleep." She stretched her neck from side to side and shivered. She shivered so hard her teeth chattered. Guess she really was cold. How come she'd not awakened?

Mavis pulled her own shawl off the back of the chair and wrapped it around Cassie. "I'll get this fire roaring. It is already warming up in the kitchen. You dear child, a body could freeze out here when the fire goes down." She stirred the lively embers and added kindling, seeing the flames lick it joyfully. "Although from the looks of this, you've not been asleep long." After adding more wood, she turned again to Cassie. "I think you should go to bed for a while. Good way to warm up. And get some sleep."

Cassie stretched her arms over her head, shivered and yawned, stretched some more and then yawned again while shaking her head. "I must have slept long enough. I better get going on the pancakes."

Mavis grumbled as she let the dogs out through the front door, but Cassie ignored it. She truly did not feel like going to bed. She had too much to do, and it felt like she had an answer. She needed to talk with Lucas — and soon.

The kitchen was indeed warmer, and standing next to the stove, beating eggs into the risen sourdough, she became even more certain. She had to tell Lucas. Should she do this first, or should she make a general announcement like Ransom had last night? What was best? How come she felt so certain now and had dithered before? Had God really spoken to her in that dream that had already faded from her memory, leaving only a feeling of certainty? If that was what this was.

She moved the now-solid can of saved grease down from the warming shelf onto the stove so she could add melted lard to the batter.

"I found Cassie asleep in the chair," Mavis announced to the men as they headed for the barn and the chores.

Cassie shrugged off their comments, not willing to let go of her train of thought. They could have the wedding on or around the New Year. That would give them a little time to get ready, not that she could see much need to get ready. Her mind leaped back to the package she had stored in the now burned wagon. The locket of her mother's to wear during the wedding. A treasure beyond measure, almost all that was left to her except memories. The thought brought tears to burn her eyes again, tears from a well she'd thought had long ago drained dry.

"Cassie, what is it?" Mavis asked softly.

"I just remembered the locket of my mother's that burned in the fire. It had a picture of my father in it and when he was off on one of his trips, my mother would stroke the locket." Because he wasn't there to be touched.

She'd tell Lucas when the men came in for breakfast.

She'd stopped shivering, but now she felt her hand shake. This was a rather momentous decision. Was she doing the right thing? Surely if this was God's message to her, it was the right thing. The breath she sucked clear to her toes didn't help a whole lot.

"Cassie, are you all right?"

"I will be." Cassie could feel Mavis studying her. "Should I start frying these now or wait until they . . ." The sound of boots being scraped on the back porch made her smile. Guess that was an answer. She dipped batter out of the bowl held in the crook of her arm and poured circles on the griddle. She'd already tested the heat of it by dripping water on it and seeing the drops dance and jump.

Mavis turned the ham steaks and stirred the browned potatoes before transferring the food to serving platters and bowls. Dishes of applesauce already sat on the plates around the table.

"Sure smells good in here," Arnett said as he hung his muffler on the tree. "I could smell breakfast clear to the bunkhouse. Made me rise from my bed and follow my nose right here."

"Good. Now figure a way to bottle that, and we'll all be rich." She set the platters on the table while Cassie watched for the rising bubbles in the frying batter and flipped the first batch over to cook on the other side. By the time Gretchen slid into her chair and the men sat down, she had the first platter ready. Mavis took that and Cassie poured the next batch. Only by counting the circles could she keep her mind from screaming off to the coming pronouncement.

When they'd all had enough, she set the remaining batter aside, moved the griddle to the top of the reservoir, and took her chair. Before she could even butter her pancakes, she said, "I have an announcement to make."

Get this over with. Do it now. She nodded to the voices in her head and looked at Lucas. "I will marry you like you asked, and I was thinking the wedding could be sometime around the first of the year."

Lucas didn't smile or nod or anything. "Are you sure?" he asked softly.

Cassie paused only to draw a breath. "Yes."

Gretchen let out a whoop, Ransom nodded, Arnett slapped his palms on the table, Mavis instantly looked incredibly happy, and Lucas . . .

Cassie waited, her heart thundering, holding her breath. Maybe this wasn't right. Had she made a mistake after all? Why, oh why?

The smile started at the corners of his mouth and moved up his face. "Good. That is wonderful."

Cassie let out her breath, dizzy from the holding. Her muscles unclenched, making her aware she'd not realized she was holding all of herself in abeyance of his answer. Why had he hesitated? Did he own a streak of cruelty she'd not realized?

"I just had to be sure," he said, rising to come around the table. He kissed her cheek and the top of her head. "Thank you. Your

134

wish is my command."

Cassie felt a giggle rising but swallowed it. Gretchen reached over and squeezed her fingers. "Now I'll have a real sister. Oh, Cassie, this is so absolutely perfect. I was hoping and praying, and then I was afraid you would say no and leave, and I . . ."

Mavis put an arm around both Cassie's and Lucas's shoulders. *"Lord God, thank you, and I pray you bless these children of mine."* She sniffed and licked her lips. "Right now I am about as happy as I know how to be. Not sure that even hearing the vows could make me happier. What a way to start this new day. Oh my word, we have so much to do."

Ransom groaned. "There goes the work on the mine." He wore a sort of smile, but it was nowhere near the happy smile that glowed on his mother's face.

Cassie checked. The last thing she wanted to do was make anyone unhappy.

10

Did I do the right thing?

The thought bedeviled Cassie all that night, making her sleep full of nightmares and restless turning.

When she staggered out of bed in the morning to start the fire, the idea of marriage to Lucas seemed impossible. But as she started the coffee she blew out a deep breath. *Cassie Marie Lockwood, you have agreed to this marriage and you do not go back on your word. Not ever. You know better. If this isn't God's will, He would have closed the door like Mavis said. So give yourself a chance. Lucas will be a loving, charming, and generous husband. He wants you to succeed in shooting as well as in being his wife. You will make a good home, and the two of you will be very happy.*

Now she just had to say those things often enough that she could begin to believe them. Believing that God loved her and wanted the best for her worked, most of the time. Well, maybe not most but a good part of the time. As she read more in her Bible, she had to believe it was true, and if it was true and God never lied, then He loved her, even her. Last night she'd read the verses about loving one another. God surely wouldn't tell her to do something if He wouldn't make it possible to happen.

That's not the problem took up the other part of her mind. Of course she loved Lucas. She loved Gretchen and Mavis too. But surely love that led to marriage was far different than loving one's brother or sister or friend or even mother or father.

She stiffened her elbows and, planting both hands on the edge of the sink, peered out the kitchen window. All she could see was the light from the window forming a square pattern on the back porch, a snow-covered back porch. It must have snowed again during the night.

Lucas and Ransom had stayed up at the mine as they'd planned, reminding their mother that the deeper they went into the mine, the less the temperature changed. Only in the mouth of the mine did they feel the weather.

I need to go up to the mine, she thought. But she never had been good in dark, closed places. However, her father had been there. Might there be something left up there to remind her of him? She heard getting-dressed noises coming from the bedrooms. Mavis and Gretchen were up. When she scraped enough frost off the pantry window to look out, she saw a man with a lantern heading for the barn. Arnett was living up to his word to do the ranch chores.

Surely this would have been a good time for her to learn to milk the cow. She'd fed the chickens and gathered the eggs a few times but had yet to feed the hogs or milk the cow. Or drive the team, let alone harness and hitch up the team. Always there had been men around to do those chores. She'd never even had to fill the woodbox.

As a rancher's wife, she'd have a whole world of things to learn. Like the gardening, putting up all those jars and crocks she saw in the cellar. If she allowed herself to think on it, she might just go running for her life.

"Good morning." Mavis's smile lit the room. "Oh, it is so nice to come in here to a hot stove. Lots of times, Ransom or Lucas start it if they get up before I do, but they don't start the breakfast or the coffee."

"Coffee should be ready in a couple of minutes."

"I thought today we would make dough-nuts."

"Doughnuts?"

Gretchen wandered into the room, stretch-ing and yawning. "Doughnuts. We haven't made doughnuts in forever. I want to help." She turned back and went to get dressed.

Cassie poured two cups of coffee and set them on the table. "I have some questions."

"Sure. Since we don't have to make break-fast for the boys, we can take a coffee break. I'll make French toast for Gretchen and us. Oh, and for Arnett. I almost forgot him."

Cassie sat down. "I saw him head for the barn with a lighted lantern."

"So what is bothering you?"

"Lots, but I've been thinking of the mem-bers of the show troupe I left behind. I wish there were some way we could find them, and if they are not working, maybe we could hire them for the show next summer. They would at least know what to do."

"What a great idea. You ought to suggest that to Lucas. He's the one working with Mr. Porter."

"But how do we go about finding them?" Cassie asked.

"Well, the Indians might have returned to the reservation, most likely did."

"Unless they went with another show."

"But you said most shows laid everyone off over the winter. We can write to the man in charge of the reservation or the Indian agent and ask him. I know Revered Brandenburg has some contacts there. We can ask him on Sunday."

"Thank you." Cassie sipped her coffee, enjoying the feeling of warmth radiating from her middle. "Do you want me to slice the bread for the French toast? I'll get the eggs and milk first."

"Good. You take care of the eggs and milk and I'll slice the bread. And by the end of the morning, you'll know how to make doughnuts too. We need to get my recipes written down for you." The two stood, and by the time Gretchen returned to the kitchen and Arnett set the milk pail in the sink, the platter of toast in the oven let them all eat at the same time.

Mavis drained the syrup pitcher. "That's another recipe you'll need — syrup. I better start making a list."

"What about the cookbook in the pantry?" Gretchen turned to Cassie. "I read it sometimes. It tells all about keeping a house too and even making a garden. I'll get it for you." She darted off to the pantry and, on her flying return, handed Cassie the thick book and headed down the hall.

Mavis got up to fetch the coffeepot and lifted a lid on the stove to check the fire.

Arnett watched her and said, "Don't you worry none. I'll fill up that woodbox. I brought my book here with me. No sense keeping a fire going in the bunkhouse too. Waste of good wood."

"That's so kind of you, Arnett." Mavis sniffed, managing to make it just a small sniff. "Thank you."

Cassie felt like hugging them both. It seemed to her that she was watching Jesus in action.

Gretchen returned, radiant. "Do you realize yesterday was my last day of school this year! Christmas holiday! Are we going to have a Christmas party this year?"

"I'm thinking not. After the wedding, we'll have a big party here." She looked to Cassie. "What day would you like the wedding?"

Cassie shrugged. "I was thinking around the first of the year. Maybe we can let Lucas decide on the date." *A big party. How can we plan a big party so quickly? Do I want a big party all churning around with people I don't even know?*

Mavis brought the calendar from the wall and laid it on the table. Her finger moved down the weeks. "Let's see . . . the party at the church is here, and Christmas is here . . . Do you think the last Saturday in December would be too soon? That's the thirty-first."

"It's fine with me. If it's all right with Lucas." Cassie paused. "We don't have to invite a whole lot of people, do we?" She fought to keep her voice firm, even though her middle was doing its best to spin out of control.

"That's up to you and Lucas. We can do whatever you want."

"But what do people usually do around here? What do they expect?" Cassie strangled her coffee cup. "I thought maybe we could just have a ceremony here, like we did for Micah and Runs Like a Deer." Panic tried to close her throat. Why had she never thought about all those details of a wedding? She'd heard most girls — er, women — dreamed of their wedding day and their groom and . . . Maybe something was wrong with her.

"We'll have to ask Lucas. Maybe he's always wanted to be married at our church. That is what I expected, but Cassie dear, we can do whatever you want. Traditionally, it is ultimately the bride's choice."

"I reckon we need to get my house cleaned out before then," Arnett said. "Why don't we go over there after you make the doughnuts, and we can decide what needs doing. In the meantime, I need to go open the fence to the hay pile that Ransom said we'd start feeding with."

"Oh, I'm sure he has done that already," Mavis put in.

"Well, I better check. I looked out there at first light, and them buffalo was throwing up snow like they was surrounded, like a cloud was sittin' right down on 'em. They don't let a snowfall stop their grazing."

Cassie nodded and smiled. "I saw them do that when we were coming down here. The cattle followed right behind them. Are they wearing a blanket of white?"

"Sure 'nough are. That is some sight." Arnett hustled out the door.

Over the next several hours, Cassie learned what went into making doughnuts. Nothing simple about doughnuts. The ingredients were important, of course. Mavis said only buttermilk should be used. She explained how hot the lard in the kettle needed to be — a bit of bread dropped in it should brown quickly at the right temperature. And then there was how to roll out the dough, cut the doughnuts with a cookie cutter, use a thimble to cut out the center, drop the tender dough into the lard, turn them, and finally lift the golden brown circles out to drain on the slotted rack. Gretchen tossed a few of them in a bag of sugar to frost them, so to speak.

Arnett came in and backed up to the stove, thawing out. Cassie handed him a mug of coffee without being asked.

"Now what are you doing?" Cassie asked when she saw Mavis dropping in the round bits of leftover dough.

"Frying the holes." Mavis kept watch over the bobbing rounds of dough.

"My favorite part." Arnett shook the first batch in the sugar bag and popped one into his mouth. "Ow!"

"Hot?" Mavis asked with a chuckle. "Serves you right."

Boots thumping on the back porch announced the arrival of the boys. Lucas opened the door with a shout. "Doughnuts! I could smell them clear up the hill. Told you so, Ransom." He snatched up one of the sugared ones and ate half in one bite.

Ransom shook his head with a smile. "He nearly drove the horse into the ground, he was in such a hurry."

Cassie watched his face to make sure he was teasing. "Did the smell really go that far?"

"Out to the barn anyway. We did good up there during the night. But after breakfast we decided we had too much to do to spend the day up there. But we could if we had to. We proved that point." A doughnut lasted four bites for him. Lucas devoured his third and then hit the holes.

"You could leave some for the others." Mavis carefully eased the lard kettle over to the top of the reservoir to cool off.

"I'll get the coffee." Cassie had been nibbling on the same doughnut, savoring every morsel. This woman had to be magic the way everything tasted better here than she'd ever before experienced in her life.

"You want to go with us over to my place, look over the house to get it ready for you two young'uns?" Arnett asked as he made two more holes disappear.

"When?"

"Right away."

"Before dinner?" Lucas gave his mother a horrified look.

Mavis rolled her eyes. "Good heavens, can't the doughnuts hold you?" When he shook his head, she pointed to the oven. "The baked beans and ham are ready."

Cassie wanted to go hide somewhere. How would she manage to cook the kind of food Lucas was used to? Her stomach rolled first one way and then the other. What kind of crazy was she to agree to such a hurry-up affair? Why not wait a little longer, take a deep breath, get everything organized? What was the rush? Why, oh why had she said such a thing?

But when she tried to say something about it, her tongue refused to move. She promised herself she would talk to Mavis later.

After dinner Lucas leaned back in his chair. "You still want to go over there?" He glanced around the table to receive nods from all but Ransom, who paused, then shrugged and agreed. He sat up straight. "Although I don't know what you need me along for."

"Your strong back, of course." Mavis clapped him on the shoulder. "We'll leave the dishes. Hitch up the sleigh and let's go."

"Oh my! Everybody hide! The world is coming to an end." Lucas waved his arms wildly in warning. "Mor is leaving dirty dishes in the sink!"

Mavis rolled her eyes and smiled at Cassie's look of confusion. "He's teasing me because I always tell them never to leave unwashed dishes." She smacked him on the shoulder. "Smart aleck."

"There are bells on the harness," Cassie exclaimed a few minutes later as the horses trotted out, the sleigh runners swishing over the snow.

"Ransom always puts the bells on the harness when he brings out the sleigh," Gretchen told her.

"Sleigh bells signify Christmas to me." Mavis raised her voice. "By the way, when are we going to look for a Christmas tree?"

"When do you want to go?" Lucas turned to ask over his shoulder.

Arnett was seated in the back on the other side of Mavis. "I ain't cut a Christmas tree in years."

"The sooner the better. Have you scouted one out? What about those we planted a few years ago?"

"They're up to about six, seven feet. There's a beauty up beyond the aspen bowl, however, that we've been watching. Should we go up after church tomorrow?"

"Good." Mavis turned to Cassie. "Have you ever cut a Christmas tree before?"

"Never. We always bought ours from a lot, if there was one. One year my mother pasted green paper on the wall and we called that our tree. It all depended on where we were wintering."

"I never thought about not having a tree before." Lucas shook his head. "Poor Cassie. We'll have to show you how to really celebrate Christmas."

"I ain't put up a tree since my Hazel died.

Just didn't have the heart for it. If you hadn't invited me for dinner that day, I'd prob'ly forgot what day it was. Sad when ya let things like that happen." He cleared his throat. "Now, about my house. Hazel would have a fit if she saw it and me bringing you all over. Dirt and dust never stood a chance when she got after it. I can just hear her saying, 'Daniel Arnett, what's the matter with you, bringing company home to a house like this?' "

"Arnett, you know we need to get this ownership business settled before Lucas and Cassie move in." It was Ransom's turn to shout over his shoulder.

"Ain't nothin' to settle. I'll just draw up some papers, maybe go see a lawyer — your lawyer's probably as good as any — to make sure it's all right and legal. We sign 'em and that's it."

"But —"

"Ain't no buts about it. I can do what I want with my land, and this is what I want to do. Unless you want me to move back here, that is."

They'd just turned into the long lane that led to his house and farm buildings.

Cassie didn't know what to expect from the way Arnett was talking. Maybe the house was really run down. Not that they couldn't fix it up, like they did the cabin. But to move here with just Lucas? She cut off that line of thinking. *Please, God, make sure I grow into loving him.*

The sight of the little log ranch house nestled between two big trees, their huge branches sheltering the low building, made her smile in delight. The ranch house was similar in design to the Engstrom house. A front porch extended half the length of the house, the hitching rail keeping it company. The snow dressed it all to look like a postcard she once saw. The peak-roofed barn wore a lean-to attached to each side, the two shed roofs sloping away. There was a large door in the middle of the V-shaped peak, through which, she knew, they hoisted hay up into the mow. Corrals spread out in all directions from the lean-tos. Nearby, a windmill spun in the breeze. The stock tank at its feet was also wearing a cape of white.

Arnett looked wistful. "Seems strange not to see columns of smoke rising outta those chimneys. There's a fireplace at the west end there. Ivar helped me build that . . . well, he and all the neighbors raised both the house and the barn. But that rock fireplace — Hazel always thought that pile of rocks was the most beautiful part of our house. Wait'll you see. I carved the mantel under her instructions. I thought stone would be good, but she had her heart set on a wood one. We found a big old oak tree what got blown down by the wind, been lying there for who knows how many years."

Cassie listened to the love in his voice. It was a shame she never got to meet his Hazel. Was she like Mavis?

Ransom drew the horses to a halt and wrapped the reins around the hitching rail. "Hand me those blankets, and the horses'll keep 'em warm for us."

Arnett pointed to the hills to the north of the house. "Not far to the Engstrom land, as the crow flies. We used to ride over that hill all the time, but coming around by the road takes some longer."

With the blankets thrown over the horses, they followed Arnett into his house, Lucas right by Cassie's side. The cold was nearly as penetrating inside as out.

"You two young bucks start the fireplace, and I'll do the kitchen stove. Get this place warmed up right quick."

As the men scattered to do his bidding, Cassie looked around the central room that took up the west end of the building. Windows faced the south, and like he'd said, the fireplace was magnificent. Two oval braided rugs lay in front of two rocking chairs, a cowhide thrown over a davenport that looked real similar to the furniture at the Engstroms'. She crossed the worn wood floor to look at the pictures on the mantel. That oak mantel wore a line of elk carved across the front.

She turned to Mavis. "Arnett carved this?"

"He sure did. The two of them did about everything together, Arnett and Ivar, especially after the children left home. But this Arnett did years ago, as he said. Come, I'll show you the rest. I'm thinking we'll take the bedclothes back with us and wash them at our house. The place doesn't look as bad as he said, so just a day of cleaning should do it."

A huge cookstove dominated the kitchen, with cupboards all around and a pantry with a food safe beside the frost-covered window. The rectangular oak table would seat eight easily and looked like it had for years, decorated with dents and burns from hot pots, the chairs huddling close for company. Arnett had the stove fired up and already fighting to inhale the cold. A window, cut in the wall over the sink, with red-and-white-checked curtains, looked out onto the back porch.

Three bedrooms opened off the hallway, one of them turned into a sewing room.

Cassie stared at the machine. All this was to be hers? She turned to Mavis, who, along with Gretchen, was already collecting linens and rugs that needed washing. "Are you sure Arnett doesn't need to give some of these things to his children?"

Mavis shook her head. "He's not even sure if all of them are still alive. We know two have gone on to heaven. I have a hard time believing they'd never written to him, if they were still alive. At least when their mother died. But the one that went to California to dig for gold, he just disappeared. Mighty hard on Arnett and Hazel."

She glanced around the sewing room. "That Hazel, she did well at everything she set her hand to do. She made quilts for new brides and for new babies too. She was my best friend. Sometimes it is still hard to believe she is gone. But I know she would be thrilled to know that someone else is going to love her house and make a home for a young family." Mavis took Cassie's hand. "I sense the turmoil inside you, and I want you to know you can always ask me anything you want to, and I will give you an honest answer."

"Th-thank you." *I am not ready for this, really I'm not. God above, am I making the mistake of my life, or is this really what you want me to do?*

11

After they'd returned from Dan Arnett's place, the girls had washed up the dinner dishes while Mavis got supper underway. With the stew simmering on the stove, Mavis had finally found some time to sit in her chair. "Lord, we sure need your guidance here." Mavis stared at the Bible in her lap.

"Mor?"

"I'm in here, in my chair."

Ransom ambled in from the kitchen. With a glance at the fire burning down in the fireplace, he added the one hunk of wood that was left in the iron rack at the side of the raised rock hearth. Then without another word, he picked up the canvas sling and headed for the front porch to bring in wood. After three trips that left the rack full and the fire roaring, he sat down on the hearth, facing his mother.

"What's bothering you?" she asked.

"How do you know something is bothering me?"

"I'm your mother, remember. God gives mothers an extra sense for our families. You used to accuse me of having eyes in the back of my head."

"One time when you were taking a rare nap on the couch, I tiptoed up and studied the back of your head, looking for those eyes."

"You didn't."

"I did." He shook his head. "No extra eyes there. That was a real puzzlement, because you said you had them. And I always believed you when you said something. I think that was the beginning of my education."

Mavis smiled, thought a moment, and the smile widened. "Ah, Ransom, you have always been such a truthful boy and now a man. So what is causing that furrow in your forehead?"

"What usually causes me concern?"

She narrowed her eyes. "Usually it is the money situation." She paused and thought again. "Or Lucas."

Ransom rolled his shoulders and leaned into the heat. "Can't do anything about the first at the moment, so it is the latter by default."

Mavis studied her eldest son. Change had never been easy for him. He was the one who took it the hardest when Ivar died, and yet he was the one who remembered the drinking years. Ivar had never been easy on his boys, expecting a great deal from them, both in action and character. As the eldest, Ransom endured more. But of the three sons, Ransom was most like his father — determined, dependable, a deep thinker, and one who always stood by his word.

While Jesse had done his share of the chores, he'd been the studious one. He always preferred reading to hunting or fishing, or ranching, for that matter. Except he loved making animals, and all living things broken, well again. His curiosity had become some of the family's shared memories.

But Lucas now, perhaps they had spoiled him because he made them laugh so much. He loved to make people laugh and have a good time. In her mind she'd often compared him to a butterfly, flitting around the garden, touching down here and there but never staying long.

"So what has Lucas done, or not done, now?"

"Well, he's gone to Hill City to deliver that elk and talk with Porter, but all he needs to do is let one of us know. In advance would be good."

"In other words you planned what you

would do today and were counting on his help."

"Yep, but I should have known better. I just thought he'd take the elk tomorrow. I even thought of going with him."

"Do you need something in Hill City?"

"Well, Porter so admired this furniture Far built that I thought to see if he might be wanting to purchase some. Arnett and I are talking seriously about turning that barn on his place into a woodworking shop. We'd use the steam engine to power tools. He thinks he can pretty much make or collect the basics."

Mavis nodded. "That surely bears thinking about."

"Says he has some downed hardwood trees that might be cured enough to use."

"That Arnett. Like you, he's always thinking." She nibbled on her bottom lip. "What are we going to do about Arnett's land idea? Seems to me there needs to be a provision of some kind in case one of his children shows up."

"Or one of his grandchildren?"

She nodded. Their lives had sure changed when Adam's daughter showed up. This was going to be one of those wonderful kinds of stories to tell the grandchildren. Someday there would be grandchildren running around this house, riding the horses, playing with the baby pigs, planting the garden with her. Ivar would have been a good grandpa.

"You're thinking something special." Ransom turned his head slightly to the side, watching her.

"I was thinking of Ivar and Adam sitting up there in heaven, talking about what they see going on here."

"You think they really can do that? See the world, I mean?"

"Well, there's surely scriptural backing for it."

Ransom's right eyebrow rose. "I guess. Then Far is certainly shaking his head over Lucas's antics." He stared at his hands, clasped between his knees. "Back to the contract thing. We will take it to a lawyer for sure. Maybe he can write in such a provision. But I get the feeling Arnett is not happy with his children, if they are still alive." He closed his eyes and rocked a bit. "That has to be so hard, never knowing."

"It's bad enough knowing."

"I need to talk with Arnett more too. Putting these two ranches together will be a good thing for sure. And his willingness to share his sawmill . . . Mor, sometimes all this just overwhelms me. His generosity, I guess."

"He and your father always worked well together. I think Arnett used to dream about one of you boys marrying one of his daughters, but then two of them died and one of them left. I know Hazel and I thought about that at times. Just seemed like a good thing."

Ransom pushed himself to his feet. "Is Gretchen helping Cassie?"

Daughters. Yes. "Or Cassie helping Gretchen. Those two have been holed up in the bedroom for some time now. I've not seen hide nor hair of them, but I hear them laugh every once in a while. And the sewing machine treadle sings along. What are you going to do?"

"Go talk with Arnett, I guess. I thought he'd be up here at the house."

"We'll have supper in about an hour."

"Think I'll split wood for a while, then."

Mavis nodded. Most wood got split around there when the two sons were squabbling, or when Ransom was working something out. She found making bread accomplished the same for her. One could work out all kinds of feelings when kneading bread. She heard another hoot of laughter from the bedroom. What a gift for Gretchen Cassie had been. What a gift for all of them, even though Ransom was still a bit of a doubter.

She turned the pages in her Bible, seeking the wisdom promised. Her gaze stopped in Joshua. *But as for me and my house, we will serve the Lord.* That made her think of a familiar verse from Jeremiah. She flipped to the right place. *For I know the thoughts that I think toward you, saith the Lord, thoughts of peace, and not of evil, to give you an expected end.*

Nothing happened without His knowledge, and all along she'd believed He had sent Cassie to them. So it always came down to how to plan within His plans, work in the direction He wanted them to go. So was it God's wish for the ranches to merge like this? Arnett had invited the newlyweds to move into his house. What had Lucas said regarding the ranch house? He had seemed pleased with the idea. Well, pretty much so. Why was she doubting him? That bothered her more than anything. He had insisted he would marry Cassie, and now she had agreed and set the date. They would talk with Reverend Brandenburg in the morning. And wasn't this her own unspoken dream come true?

Lord, I ask for peace, beg for peace. My son has grown up, and I have done all that I can.

He is in your hands, another reminder for me because I gave him to you at his birth, when you gave him to me. Ivar was so happy to have sons. The three that have lived bring me such joy. She thought of the ones gone on to heaven — two babies, plus another son far too young. She kept the rocker singing its song, her hands busy knitting and her mind praising her Father for all that was and was to come. Thanking Him in advance was getting easier, the more she reminded herself to do it.

When Lucas drove into the yard later in the evening, Mavis was grateful for the moon so bright it threw dark shadows on the snow.

"I was beginning to think you were going to come home tomorrow," Mavis said, removing the stew she'd kept in the warming oven just in case he made the long cold drive tonight.

Cassie smiled at him, bringing hot coffee at the same time.

Lucas smiled up at her. "Thanks. I think I'm cold clear through. I have good news for all of us. Where's Ransom and Arnett?"

"Arnett just made his way to the bunkhouse, and Ransom decided to go to bed early." Gretchen took the chair by her brother. "You want me to go get them?"

"I guess it can wait until tomorrow."

She scowled. "Do we all have to wait until tomorrow?"

Mavis smiled at her daughter, mentally thanking her for saying what her mother was thinking. "I guess we can all use some training in patience."

"Is the light still on in the bunkhouse?" Gretchen leaped up and went to the window. "Arnett's still up!" She grabbed a shawl as she darted out the door.

Lucas barked a laugh and dug into the food in front of him while Mavis headed down the hall to knock on Ransom's door.

"Important?" Ransom called out.

"Yes." *At least I think so.* Indecision made her pause.

"I'll be right there, but this better be good."

His muttering followed her back down the hall.

"Arnett will be right up." A draft of numbing cold blew in with Gretchen. She shivered and kept the shawl around her shoulders as she rubbed her hands in the heat over the stove.

Mavis emptied the coffee grounds into the chicken bucket and, after rinsing out the coffeepot, filled it with clean water. "Gretchen, would you please bring those leftover cinnamon rolls and gingerbread in here. We'll warm those too. This sounds like more than just a quick announcement."

"You are so right, Mor." Lucas warmed his hands on his coffee cup.

Gretchen slid the two plates into the oven and shut the door again. Returning to the pantry, she put the rolled-up rug back in place at the bottom of the door to keep the cold draft from invading the kitchen.

Mavis heard Arnett stamping his feet on the porch. Even with the path dug to the barn and the bunkhouse, boots picked up more snow than anyone wanted tracked into the house. At the same time, Ransom, wearing his moccasins rather than boots, appeared, smoothing his hair back with both hands.

"Lucas, this better be good."

"Sorry. I got home as fast as I could. I have two letters, one for Cassie and another for all of us. Porter is so excited about the Fourth of July rodeo and Wild West show, he talked nonstop." He looked to Ransom. "Did you see the elk tonight?"

Ransom shook his head. "Not down with the cattle. I didn't go out there."

"Henri wants another as soon as possible. Says his customers rave about the elk. He has found a smoker, and the sausages are really popular. He wondered if we had a hog to butcher to mix with the elk, but I told him sorry on that. He brings in pork on the train. Refrigerator cars sure make a difference in the foods available. Oh, I nearly forgot." He rose and dug in his jacket pockets on the tree. "Oranges for us all." He lined them up in the center of the table.

Cassie brought plates from the cupboard and set them on the table too.

With the food all in place on the table and the people seated around it, Mavis brought over the coffeepot. "You go ahead and start, Lucas. We're ready."

"Fortified enough?" His grin made them all smile.

Ransom rubbed his eyes and scratched the stubble on his chin.

With a nod and a smile, Mavis took her place. "Now we are. Get to the telling."

Lucas drew the two envelopes from his pocket and handed one to Cassie and one to his mother.

Cassie quickly read through hers and told the others about Mr. Porter's ideas for the following summer's Wild West show.

"Now you read, Mor," Lucas prodded.

Only the crackle of moving paper broke the expectant silence. A chunk of wood settled in the stove. Othello, by Cassie's side, snored, snuffled, and snored again.

Mavis nodded as she read, then cleared her throat to read aloud.

"To all of the Engstroms,
I am delighted to tell you of the success of our plans for the show, as I will refer to our ideas from now on. The leaders of Hill City are solidly behind the idea of a combination Wild West show and rodeo. They are pleased with the date, already planning ahead to make it longer next year. I have never seen such solidarity among our merchants and business people. My fear that this would be a hard sell was totally unfounded."

Mavis paused and smiled at those around her table. "Good news is right.

"We are definitely planning on the barbecue, hoping your ranch will be able to supply the steers to be roasted over the coals. How many do you think it will take, and is this a possibility or do we need to look elsewhere also?"

Lucas glanced at his brother. "I told him we do half a steer here and how many we feed. Usually over a hundred, isn't it?"

"And we rarely have anything left over."

"But a whole steer would leave too much." Mavis read ahead. "Listen to this:

"We are trying to come up with more events that will benefit the ranchers around the area. Do you have any ideas that we might incorporate? Is there anyone who might invite city folk to come stay at their ranch a few days? Involve them in the day-to-day ranch work? They could learn to ride, possibly learn to shoot, work a lariat, rope something. Maybe even milk a cow if you have one. Feed animals. You tell me other chores that those with no experience could do."

Mavis stopped and looked around at her family. "What do you think?"

"How about tour a gold mine?" Ransom leaned back in his chair. "You think people would actually pay to take part in our daily life?"

"Cassie could teach them to shoot. Arnett could teach them to ride. He taught lots of others. Here they would even see buffalo up close." Lucas stared at his brother. "That gold mine might pay off after all."

"But where would they stay?" Gretchen

picked at the crumbs of gingerbread.

"The bunkhouse," Arnett threw in. "A whole family could stay there."

"He can have my room, and Mor and I will stay where we are."

"How long would it take us to build another bunkhouse?"

"We could jack up that bunkhouse at my place and bring it over here. It ain't as heavy to move as the steam engine. That would be two cabins."

"How long would it take to build another one or two?" Mavis rose and fetched her tablet and pencil. "We need a name."

"We have a name. The Bar E."

"The Bar E what?"

"Guest Ranch?" Cassie asked.

Lucas squinted his eyes and rocked his chair back on two legs. "What was that word I heard?"

Ransom scowled. "If you break the chair, you have to fix it."

Lucas flinched and the chair legs thumped back down. "Come on. We read it in something."

"It's a term for Easterners." Ransom's inflection on the final word was not complimentary.

"Dude?" Cassie asked, question marks all over her face.

"That's it!" Lucas clapped and pointed a finger at her. "Good girl. Dude. Bar E Dude Ranch. How does that sound?"

"It sounds like a lot of work." Ransom heaved a sigh. "But then it could bring in actual cash money."

"We could have a shooting contest at the end of — Would they stay a week? More? Less?"

"Why would someone come so far for less than a week? Maybe two? If we did this during July, they could help with the haying. If people want to learn about ranching, we sure could teach 'em."

"Maybe overnight camping at the mine?" Ransom started to rock back, glanced around, and sat back quietly.

Mavis tried to keep her grin to herself, but when she looked at Ransom, he winked. "How would we feed ten, twelve people? They would have to understand that we are a working ranch. July would be before the garden needs to be put up — mostly. They could come here after the Hill City celebration or a week before that. Or . . . ?" She nodded as she reread her notes.

Could this be the answer to their prayers to save the ranch? It sure looked like something they could all get excited about. Would anyone have dreamed this up were it not for the letter from Mr. Porter? In the long run, Cassie was at the center of the change. What would Ivar say? She blew out a breath. Would someone really pay to work on the ranch with them?

12

"Lucas, don't we need to talk?"

"Of course." He motioned to the chair across the table.

Cassie caught her bottom lip between her teeth. "I . . . ah . . ." She glanced at the bustle going on around them, with everyone getting ready to leave for church. Why was this so hard? She'd thought they would discuss the wedding yesterday, but he was gone by the time the kitchen was cleaned up, and she'd not realized he was heading to Hill City. But then the others didn't either, the way Ransom had asked about him and then glared. Ransom's glare always made her grateful she was not the one on the receiving end.

She snagged her mind and dragged it back to the moment. "Are we planning on talking with Reverend Brandenburg after church?" She put the emphasis on the *we*. After all, Lucas was the one who had been pushing so hard to marry her. She so much wanted to say, *Look, if you've changed your mind, you just need to let me know.* But she was committed now; she had given her word.

Lucas nodded. "I guess we should, huh?" He exhaled heavily. "Did you choose a date?"

"Isn't that something we should do together?"

Lucas leaned forward. "I'm sorry, Cassie. I got so involved in the plans for our future, our whole family's future, that I guess I figured that whatever you decide is fine with me." He reached for her hand. "Now that you've agreed to the most important question, that is."

Somewhat mollified, Cassie dropped her voice. "Your mother suggested the last Saturday of December, the thirty-first."

"Sounds fine to me."

"Do you want to have it at the church?" she asked. Why was he not offering suggestions? After all, this was a rather momentous event.

"Fine."

"Or here at the house?" She held up a stop hand before he could finish shrugging.

"We have to leave now or we'll be late," Mavis called from near the front door.

"Ransom has the sleigh up."

Lucas pushed back his chair. "Let's go. We can talk about this on the way to town." He lifted her coat from the rack.

"I need to get my hat." Cassie swirled down the hall and lifted her dress hat off the peg on the wall. If she'd had any money she would have bought a real lady's hat, rather than her white felt western show-day hat, but she'd not had money, and one did not go to church without a hat. In fact, most women did not go out of the house without a hat. Back in the kitchen, Lucas held her coat for her, and she shoved her arms into the sleeves. Without even saying thank you, she sailed out of the house and allowed Ransom to help her into the sleigh. Now to just loosen her jaw and . . . She sucked in a deep breath of icy air and turned her head at Lucas's call.

"Too many for the sleigh. I'll catch up with you." He was heading for the barn. How were they supposed to talk this way?

"Sorry, Cassie, I could have ridden," Arnett told her over his shoulder.

"Sorry, nothing. We've had six in the sleigh before, and while it was tight, we did it." Ransom flipped the reins and turned the team in a close circle. They jingled merrily out the long lane.

The sleigh bells singing, the glory of sun on snow, and the warmth of Mavis's shoulder next to hers sent a measure of calm to Cassie's spirit. They would ask Reverend Brandenburg about the date. Assuming he agreed to that, should they do it in the morning or afternoon? Evening would be too hard for them to come out to the ranch.

What did she want to do? "Mavis?"

"Yes, dear."

Cassie stared at the robe tucked around them, then looked to Mavis. "Should we put the wedding off until later in January or . . . ? I mean, there's no real reason to hurry, is there?" *Other than I want to get it over with so I can get on with my life.* Now, that was a rather stupid thing to even think, let alone say.

"That's up to you and Lucas."

Somehow Cassie had known that was what the answer would be. "I don't want something fancy." Not a lot of people around was what she really meant. People she didn't know. She had never had trouble meeting people, but usually she'd had her father to introduce her or after that, Jason Talbot. Here, Mavis had pretty much taken over the responsibility. When she thought about it, maybe she had left all her responsibilities up to Mavis, ever since the night of the shooting. Everyone had shelter — at least she hoped and prayed Chief had a place to live — food enough, and while she wanted to give them more, nothing else was critical.

"How can I help you, Cassie?" Mavis leaned closer to ask.

She shrugged. "I think I just have to work this out." She made sure her mouth smiled. "Thanks."

Once inside the church, Cassie found herself flanked by Mavis on one side and Gretchen on the other. Lucas sat next to Gretchen. Cassie caught the nudge and the frown, but she had also noticed the entire Hudson family in the pew three rows behind them. The daggers to her back were becoming familiar. Would that last forever? Maybe it would be better for them all if she didn't come to church. Maybe it would change after the wedding.

When the organ broke into the opening hymn and the congregation rose to sing, she forgot the eddies swirling around her and lost herself in the waves of the song. " 'Jesus calls us o'er the tumult of our life's wild restless sea. . . .' " She'd seen waves breaking on rocks one time when her father took her to the northern Atlantic coast. The song fit, both with her memory and her present.

When Reverend Brandenburg started his sermon with "Jesus calls us; beloved; let us listen to His call," Cassie almost stopped breathing, the better to hear. "Let us listen closely and carefully so the restless sea around us does not drown out His voice. Our Jesus said to Peter, 'Come to me.' And Peter heard Him over the call of the sea and stepped out of the boat to walk to Jesus on the water — until he took his eyes off Jesus and started to sink. Peter immediately cried out — he did not think of anything else — 'Save me, Jesus.' So if you feel you are sinking, even into a sea of your own making, call out to Jesus. Reach out to Him and He will take your hand and lift you up to safety."

Cassie barely heard the congregation's amen and the blessing that followed. Jesus would hear her cry. When they all stood for the benediction, she heard the words again. "The Lord bless thee, and keep thee . . . and give thee peace."

Peace. As her mother used to say, *"Peace, not pieces."*

The daggers were back as she moved down the aisle. What could she do? Or was this something Lucas had to take care of? *Lord, let Lucas begin to heal this wound so that there can be peace again between these*

175

two families. I do not want to cause dissension and conflict. Peace. I want peace.

When she asked to speak with the reverend, he smiled at her. "Of course. I would love to talk with you. It'll be just a few minutes."

Cassie nodded. She felt Lucas leave her side and turned slightly to find Mavis and Gretchen right behind her, as if they were her watchdogs. As they paused on the top step to let their eyes adjust to the snow glare, she saw Lucas waiting in the shoveled-out area at the bottom of the four steps, staring intently out to the wagons — where his former best friend was helping his sister into the sleigh. Was Lucas looking at Betsy or her brother?

The die is cast. That famous line most assuredly applied to her, to them, as they left town behind and whooshed toward home. So very few days remaining until the wedding, or ceremony, or whatever she wanted to call it. While she would much prefer to think about this in the quiet of her room, the others were already discussing it.

Lucas rode right beside the sleigh so he could take part in the conversation. "Ask Cassie" seemed to be his answer to every question.

"But what do *you* want?" She raised her voice. "Lucas, you have to say what you want."

"Apple pie for the dinner?"

The others sort of laughed, but Mavis shook her head. "Done. Now let's get serious. Besides all of us and the Brandenburgs, who all should be there for the ceremony?"

Lucas thought and shook his head. "If we were having a big party, that would be different. But if Cassie really is serious about keeping this simple, then you needn't worry about it anymore. We'll have the ceremony at noon and dinner after that, and then we'll drive to our new home. I plan to move over there as soon as . . ." He paused and shrugged. "Soon as we have it ready, I guess, and we have signed the papers with Arnett. I don't want to live there until that is finished."

"Won't take much, I keep trying to tell you," Arnett said. "We draw up the papers and go in to see your lawyer. I was hopin' to see him in church, but he wasn't there. Maybe Wednesday or Thursday, whichever is best."

"Thursday." Mavis looked to the others for confirmation. "Good. Then we'll go get the Christmas tree as soon as we've had dinner."

Later that afternoon, all mounted on horses, they rode across the pasture and up toward the cabin, following the trail Micah had created, Benny and Othello bounding along beside them. When Benny announced their arrival, Dog ran out to meet them and Micah and Runs Like a Deer met them on the front step.

"We're going for a Christmas tree," Mavis announced. "Do you and Runs Like a Deer want to come? We can get one for you too, or you can enjoy ours."

Runs Like a Deer peeked out from under his arm, shaking her head. "No tree here."

"But you can come with us. We brought coffee and cookies too."

"Come on, Micah. I never see you anymore." Cassie hoped pleading would work. She missed having her family around.

"Okay. But we don't have horses up here."

"You ride behind me, Runs Like a Deer."

"And you can take my horse, Micah. I'll ride with Mor." Gretchen slid to the snow as she talked.

After shifting riders, the group headed up the hill, Ransom riding in the lead to break a path through the knee-deep snow. While under the pine trees, the snow wasn't as deep, but in the shade, the cold bit harder.

"Are you warm enough?" Cassie asked her friend.

"Always. Micah makes sure the fire is going."

"Micah is a good man," Cassie mused. *For all the years I've known him.*

"Yes. Very good to me."

Cassie smiled over her shoulder. "I'm so happy for you. We set the date today for the wedding — the last Saturday of December."

"You marry Lucas?"

"Yes." Perhaps saying it more often would make it seem real. "Has Lucas told you about Christmas Day at the ranch house?"

"Yes."

"And you'll come?"

"Yes, of course."

Cassie ducked as a shower of snow slid from the branches higher up. Wind Dancer pranced to the side, and Othello barked at the falling snow. She could hear Runs Like a Deer chuckling behind her. She, who had laughed so seldom before, was now enjoying the romping dog and snow showers. Surely that could be called a small miracle.

As they approached the aspen grove, two deer bounded out from the side and on up the hill.

"I knew I should have brought the rifle."

"Not today, Lucas. Let them run free," Mavis chided. "We don't want for meat."

"Ah, but the Hill City Hotel does. I'll come up again later."

Only a few leaves remained on the silvery aspens as the tree-seeking party cut across the middle of the grove to move up the mountain. Cassie saw areas where the deer had bedded down. Had she not learned from Chief, she'd not have known that bit of lore. How was he? She'd forgotten to ask Reverend Brandenburg if he could give her the name of the Indian agent or someone on the reservation. Perhaps they could ask when they went in to sign the papers at the lawyer's office.

"See that one?" Ransom pointed up the hill. A young pine tree stood alone, needles and branches weighted by snow.

"It's a shame we can't keep the snow on it," Mavis said with a nod. "How beautiful."

"The candles will make up for the snow." Gretchen laid her cheek on her mother's back. "This will be the prettiest ever."

A crack like the shot of a rifle had Cassie ducking and staring around. "Where did that come from?"

"That was a tree splitting in the cold," Ransom said. "No one is shooting at us."

"Besides," Lucas added, "we allow no hunting on our land, and this is still part of the ranch."

"No hunting?" Micah asked.

"Other than us," Lucas reassured him. "You can hunt anytime you want."

"Need to move the snares farther out. Not so many rabbits close-by anymore." Runs Like a Deer slid off over Wind Dancer's rump. She plowed through the snow, Dog at her side, her deer-hide leggings, wrapped with thongs, keeping her drier than those with pants and boots. She walked around the tree, nodding as she went. "Beautiful."

The others dismounted and followed her tracks, all inspecting the tree. Lucas untied the saw from his saddlebag while Micah kicked the snow away enough to reach under the tree. After shaking the snow off, the two men dug their way under and started sawing.

Mavis studied a couple of pine trees farther up the hill. "We could take down some of the limbs for decorating the house." She looked to Ransom. "Isn't there a cedar tree near here?" At his nod, she continued. "We could stop there on the way back, right?"

"Good thing we brought lots of rope."

Mavis chuckled. "You always see to that.

Remember when we used to come up looking for trees when your far was alive? He always had a hard time getting into the Christmas spirit."

Ransom nodded. Lucas let out a yelp.

"What's the matter?"

"Got a bucket of snow down my neck. That's all."

Cassie didn't bother to try to hide her delighted cackle, and that set the others off. Micah muttered something unintelligible, and even Runs Like a Deer started to laugh. Othello bounced over and through the snow, sticking his head under the tree and barking at the two men.

"Othello, come here." Cassie could barely get the words past the laughter erupting. Slowly the tree tipped to the side and fell into the snow. Micah and Lucas struggled to their feet.

"You better get the coffee and cookies out, Mor. We earned a break."

Othello put both front paws up on Micah's shoulders and tipped him back in the snow. "Get off me, you mangy mutt."

Cassie tried to call her dog off, but giggles got in the way. "H-he's . . . he's not a m-mangy mutt. Hold him, Othello."

Othello sat down on Micah's chest and gave him a slurp from chin to hat.

"Cassie!"

"Serves you right." She finally quit laughing enough to call her dog again, and this time he yipped and then came to her side.

Micah heaved himself to his feet in time to accept a cup of coffee, that, while no longer hot, was at least warm, and dug two cookies out of the sack. "Thank you."

"You're welcome." She handed a broken piece to the dog. "Good boy."

Cassie caught Lucas and Micah exchanging glances, most likely of pity.

"All this for a Christmas tree."

"That's right. You can be sure we won't forget this tree day." Mavis sipped her coffee. "What an absolutely perfect day."

Cassie agreed. She finished her cookie and tossed the dregs in her coffee cup out on the snow. This was a far cry from any Christmas she'd ever had before. If only her father and mother could be here to join them. Was this more like her mother's days in Norway, with snow and mountains and trees to cut in woods now richer with the smell of pine pitch? And a sky so blue it hurt your eyes and the sparkles between the snow and the sun as they battled for supremacy? Gratitude welled up in her heart and leaked out her eyes. She dashed the tears away and caught Mavis doing the same thing. The two smiled at each other, nodded, and started putting the coffee things back in the saddlebags.

Ransom dragged the tree on a rope behind his horse, and when they'd cut cedar limbs to add to the pine Lucas was pulling, they all made their way back to the cabin.

"Thank you," Runs Like a Deer said as she slid to the ground. "I will come help with preparations if you want."

"Thank you." Mavis leaned over and reached for her hand. "I'll let you know when. I'm so glad you both came with us."

"Me too."

With everyone back on their own horses again, they rode on down to the ranch house.

If this was what family felt like, Cassie was all in favor. It wouldn't be long until she was a real member of the family, not just adopted by contract. The thought didn't bring the excitement she'd dreamed of feeling when preparing for a wedding — her wedding.

Her wedding.

13

While the women were baking up a hurricane in the kitchen over the next couple of days, ranch chores remained pretty much the same. If the weather held, Ransom hoped to get those dried hardwoods milled so he could stash them in the barn, either at the homeplace or over at Arnett's. They'd know more regarding how dry the wood really was after sawing it into usable sizes. Now he not only needed to come up with Christmas gifts, he needed a wedding present for Lucas and Cassie. What could he make for them?

Doubts as to the wisdom of the union still raised their grizzled heads periodically, but he bashed them back down to the murk of confusion. He'd given Lucas his blessing, and that was that. It was time his younger brother stood on his own two feet. Upon thinking on it, the three brothers were so very different. Jesse was committed to becoming a doctor no matter what it took in the way of effort and dedication. Ransom's own dedication was for the ranch — not only keeping it alive but making it prosper. And Lucas? While definitely the most charming of the three, he seemed to lack that stick-to-itiveness that exemplified the Engstrom blood, inherited from both mother and father. Gretchen at age twelve showed more determination than Lucas. Unless one thought about his ability to entertain. Ransom deliberately swung his thoughts away from Lucas.

The community was having a party at the church meeting hall on Friday night. Arnett had agreed to play Santa and was even shaping his beard for the role. While Ransom would just as soon stay home, the entire family would attend. So there he'd be, like it or not, smiling and making small talk and agreeing that the bride-to-be was beautiful.

She certainly was that.

Other than Sundays at church, this would be Cassie's community-wide introduction. If the Hudsons showed up, there would be sparks for sure.

Back to Lucas. The sooner he was married, the better.

Ransom decided he ought to quit thinking and pay closer attention to what he was doing. Eager to reach the barn, the horses had turned into the last gate so sharply, the front sledge corner scraped the upright post. *Come on, Ransom! Wake up! Daydreaming is for children.* And maybe for Lucas.

He turned to the man beside him as they drove toward the barn. "You think you and I and Micah can run that sawmill? Lucas won't be back until late." He didn't add "as usual," but he thought it. Lucas had taken the last of the smoked elk into Hill City. The orders from the hotel were going a long way toward keeping them solvent, or he'd complain more. To whom, he wasn't sure. His complaints didn't seem to faze his younger brother. And Mor certainly disapproved of them.

Arnett nodded sagely. "We could, but that extra set of hands moves things along better. Runs Like a Deer might be willing to keep the fire stoked and keep watch on the boiler. You want me to ask her?"

"Up to the cabin?"

"Nope, I saw her go down to the ranch house."

Ransom stopped the team under the open door of the hayloft. "I'll go on up and fork it down. You spread it?"

On the good days, they fed the cattle out

of the hayloft, and on the bad they opened the fence on one of the haystacks. This way they were able to waste less, although the buffalo cleaned up what the cattle trampled in their desire for the better hay. Spreading hay into the corners of the wagon — now turned sledge with the winter runners — and distributing the hay on the load helped them to pile more on, therefore needing fewer loads. Efficiency. Ransom loved efficiency.

"Sounds good to me." Arnett stepped off the flat bed of the hay wagon, and they each removed the harness from one of the team and hung both on the wall inside the barn. "When's that cow gonna calve?"

"From the look of her, it should be any day."

"Cassie said she wants to learn how to milk a cow."

Ransom raised his eyebrows. "She did?"

"Son, you just don't give her credit. That little heifer has a heart big as this ol' barn. She's gonna make Lucas a fine wife. Just give her some time to catch up. She'd come up there and monitor that ol' boiler."

Ransom didn't bother to answer. He was not going to ask her, and that was all there was to it. "Let's get this wagon loaded again, and then we'll see."

"Good, you're just in time," Mavis said when the two men returned to the house. "We're going over to Arnett's for an afternoon of cleaning, and two more sets of hands will make it happen faster." She paused. "Unless you had something else planned, of course."

Ransom heaved a sigh and shook his head. "It'll wait. But one of these days, I'm telling you, sometime this week I get all the men up at the mill."

Mavis rolled her lips together. "Yes, sir. How about some sweet rolls to sweeten you up some?"

Ransom ignored her sass. Leave it to his mother to have the last word. "Thank you." He took the snail-shaped roll with almond-flavored frosting and made short work of it on his way to the table for dinner. The house smelled good enough to eat, and his stomach rumbled to prove it. Maybe he should just give up and not try to get anything important done until after Christmas. And then the wedding. And then the New Year. One thing after another.

"Your turn to say grace, son."

Ransom bowed his head. "Thank you, Lord, for this food before us and for the loving hands that prepared it. Amen." Short was better than adding complaints, although

189

he knew he needn't voice them for the Lord to see into his heart. And right now, he wished that were not so. No wonder God promised to change them, starting on the inside.

This seemed to be a pondering kind of day, he thought as he dished up the chicken and dumplings his mother set before them. If he spent much more time on it, he'd be back to fighting to come up with new ways to bring some cash money into the ranch. His mother had reminded him just last night how much they had to be thankful for. Leave it to her. She had an unerring instinct about when to push and when to remain silent. She'd called times like these *"serious stew times."*

He jerked his mind back to the table. Who had called his name? Glancing up, he realized most eyes were on him. He could play the dodging game or just come out and ask. Might as well own up. "Sorry, what did I miss?"

"Arnett asked if you wanted to search through his tools at the ranch for anything that might help with the furniture building." His mother gave him her raised-eyebrow look.

"I thought . . ." Arnett paused, mouthing a bit of dumpling. "I thought if we get those

190

trees milled, we can store 'em in my barn and bring in the steam engine to provide power. Seems to me I have a plane and a lathe." He shook his head. "Been so long since I did anything like that, I sorta forget. Hazel wanted to put my tools to right one time, but I scared her off. I didn't tell her what to do in the kitchen and she could right leave my tools alone." He gave Ransom a considering look. "I looked at some of your plans. You got good ideas, son. Take after your pa, you do."

Ransom narrowed his eyes, nodding gently all the while. "We need to go through Far's tools too. Lotta stuff got thrown in the corner. We find real treasures there from time to time. Sounds like both places could use some cleaning up."

"We'll do Arnett's house first." Mavis held up the bowl of chicken and dumplings. "Anyone for more?"

Ransom swapped a man's look with Arnett. The law had spoken.

The crew spent that afternoon and the better part of the following day laboring at Arnett's place. By the time the reluctant work crew needed to be back to the Bar E for chores, Arnett's house nearly sparkled with clean. The bedding had been washed by

Mavis and Cassie, and now both inside and out of every cupboard, drawer, and closet bore the determination of women on the warpath against grime. Ransom and Arnett polished the windows that were no longer scrolled in frost paintings and swept down any cobweb that dared to exist, both inside and on the porches. The stove wore the sheen of vigorous scrubbing, leaving no trace of the rust that cast iron welcomed so warmly.

"Thank you all," Mavis said, raising her voice to be heard above the harness bells as the cleaning crew headed home in the sleigh. She turned to Cassie. "Now you know where everything is, and that mouse family got moved out. You take a cat with you when you move in too. There's nothing more comforting than a cat in front of a stove. It's a good thing Othello tolerates cats. He is one adaptable dog."

Ransom glanced over to his mother and saw Cassie frowning. What burr had gotten under her saddle? One didn't usually see her with a furrow between her brows. Surely she should be pleased at all their hard work. Not every young bride got to move into a house all furnished and ready like Arnett's. And if she was disgusted with Lucas not being there to help, she just better get used to that. Lucas lived by his own clock. And even though they spent the afternoon on Arnett's spread, he and Arnett had nary a chance to get down to the barn and the machinery shop. He clucked the team into a trot. Maybe it was time to give Lucas a real piece of his mind.

The setting sun was dimming the land by the time he let the women off at the house. While Lucas's horse was in the corral and the fires were restoked in the house, there was no sign of Lucas.

Gretchen met them at the door. "You could have left me a note or something. I was beginning to worry."

"You only missed out on cleaning out my ranch house, little girl," Arnett said. "Be glad. Where's Lucas?"

She shrugged. "Don't know." She hung up her mother's coat and scarf while the others put the cleaning supplies away. "I put the leftovers on to heat when I saw you coming."

"Thank you, dear. Did you and Jenna have a good time?"

She bobbed her head. "We're supposed to remind all the families about the party, since it is to raise funds for the school. We need new textbooks."

Ransom left them talking and headed back

out to take the team to the barn. When he opened the barn door, he saw the lit lantern hanging by the box stall, where he could hear Lucas talking. He left the horses stamping against the deepening cold and leaned over the half wall.

The cow was up and Lucas was cleaning off the calf with wisps of hay and a gunnysack. She nosed her baby to get it moving while Lucas stepped back.

"What happened?" Ransom kept his voice low.

"She needed some help. I looped the rope around the front legs and helped it out. One mighty big calf, but he took a little rib pushing to get him breathing. Too long in the birth canal, but he's getting stronger."

They watched as the calf tried to get his back feet under him, but instead of standing, the wobbly newborn collapsed back in the straw. His mother nudged him again and continued licking him dry. He shook his head and tried again, this time getting his rump in the air and his front feet straightened out. As he heaved himself to a shaky standing, the two men silently cheered him on. The cow turned to get her udder closer to him. After another collapse, he bumped her with his nose and finally found the teat.

Ransom was impressed with the baby's

persistence. "That cow is one mighty fine mother. This is what? Her fifth calf?"

Lucas nodded. "I think so. An hour ago I wouldn't have bet on his making it."

"I'm glad you were here."

"Me too. Heard her distress call when I was unsaddling. I think she'd been at it for quite a while already." He breathed a sigh of relief. "I'm going for a bucket of warm water for her. Wish we had some of those oats ground. Warm mash might be just what she needs."

"Put some molasses in it too. I'll get the team put away." Ransom watched his brother heading for the house, a bucket swinging from his gloved hand. He'd done it again. About the time Ransom was ready to light into him, he did something just right. They might have lost the calf and had a dreadfully sick cow had it gone on too long.

He let the horses out into the corral, hung up the harnesses, and after feeding the hogs and checking the chickens that had gone to roost, headed for the house. He saw Arnett out on the porch refilling woodboxes, the warm lamplight through the windows making him pick up his pace. He met bundled-up Cassie and Lucas coming out the back door.

"She wants to see the new calf," Lucas said, then turned as Gretchen closed the door behind her. "You coming too, squirt?"

"You're not supposed to call me that anymore. Mor said."

"Sorry, I forgot." He turned to Ransom, who was scraping his boots off at the boot brush. "Remind me to tell you Porter's latest bright idea. That man has good ones and some not so good."

"And this one?"

"Jury's still out on it." The three headed for the barn, leaving Ransom shaking his head. While curiosity was gnawing at him like a beaver on a poplar tree, he'd not let Lucas know. There had to be some satisfaction in that somewhere.

"So Bess finally had her calf!" Mavis turned from the stove at his gusty entry. The wind was coming up too.

"She has a live one, thanks to Lucas." After hanging up his gear, he crossed to the stove to rub his hands over the heat. He peeked over Arnett's shoulder at the drawings he was studying at the kitchen table. "What smells so good?"

"Applesauce cake. Do you think the pond is frozen enough for skating?"

"That and some. Why? You want to go skating?"

"I do. Cassie is getting better on skis, and now she needs to learn how to skate. If they weren't having the Argus annual Christmas party this week, we could invite some neighbors over for a skating party."

"The ice needs to be swept off first." One more thing to do to keep him from milling.

"Just a thought." She peeked inside the oven and closed its door.

Memories came pouring in. He almost smiled. "Been a long time since we've had a skating party."

"I know, and it makes me wonder why. I used to love to skate."

"Your momma was the picture of grace on skates, boy. And so was my Hazel." Arnett looked up from the drawings. "We get the wood milled tomorrow, and then we can start tinkering with the tools. I got me a couple a good ideas too." He pointed to a drawing of a whatnot table. "Your pa used mostly cottonwood?"

Ransom took the chair across from him. "He did. Said it was plentiful and soft enough to work pretty easy."

"But we're gonna use oak and elm?"

"Got some maple in our barn," Ransom said.

"Seems to me this would be a good starting piece. Sell 'em in lots of two. Is there enough cherry for two?"

"I have no idea. Old man, you got a dreaming head on those shoulders."

"You know my mantel?"

"I do." A picture of that carved mantel flipped through Ransom's mind. "I've always admired that piece."

"Well, what if we did a bit of carving on the front of the drawer on this table? Make that a kind of signature of our work. I know your pa made a statement with his cottonwood pieces in your big room and some in mine. We could copy his or come up with our own. Did you see the light go on for Porter when he saw them pieces?"

Ransom shook his head.

"Well, it did. Bet we can get him to buy some right off. He gets the crowds in from the East for his shooting matches and the Wild West show, and we just might have us a market."

Staring at the old man, Ransom continued shaking his head. Here he'd thought his neighbor to be on his last legs, and look at him now. Not only thriving but dreaming big dreams and figuring ways to get skids under them to bring 'em home. Ransom didn't remember ever seeing the old man with this kind of enthusiasm. But then, maybe he hadn't been looking, or perhaps this was just the right time. As his mother so often said, *"God's timing may just surprise you."* Was this an example of God leading? Of God's timing? Was He closing one door, like the mine, and opening another?

14

Lord, I don't have any idea how to work this all out. Instead of trying any further, I'm putting it all in your hands. Lucas first of all. If my middle son is so in love with Cassie and determined to marry her, why don't I see more signs of that? You'd think he'd want to spend time with her, and while he is out working with the other men, of course he needs to do that. But what about the evenings? They never seem to talk.

She opened the Bible in her lap to the Psalms, where she always went first when things were not clear. *Praise ye the Lord: for it is good to sing praises unto our God; for it is pleasant; and praise is comely,* she read.

She heaved a deep-from-the-heart mother's sigh. *I know that, but I let all this other stuff get in the way. I have trouble praising you when things are muddled, and yet I know that's when I need it the most.*

She leaned her head against the back of

the rocker. She could hear the sewing machine humming away in Cassie's bedroom. The fragrance of cardamom drifted in from the kitchen. Benny and Othello were tussling on the front porch, their happy yips and fake growls showing the friendship that had grown between them. Dog stayed with Runs Like a Deer at the cabin and still acted standoffish when the woman came down to help at the ranch house.

Today she had said she had things to finish up there.

Everyone seemed to be in the normal hurry to finish the gifts race in the days before Christmas. She could bring in the boughs now to decorate the house. The tree was waiting in a bucket of water on the back porch so the sun couldn't dry it out.

Sing, sing, sing songs of praise. Sing praises to my name. The words trickled through her mind. "Lucas is yours and Cassie is yours, and I will sing praises to your name." What was the tune? It seemed so familiar and yet she couldn't place it. She closed her Bible and put her feet up on the hearth, staring into the orange and yellow flames.

In a few minutes, she planted her feet back on the floor and stood, stretching her arms over her head and twisting from side to side. It was amazing how much lighter she felt.

201

Why didn't she start with praise, instead of only seeking it when she was in distress? God had brought Cassie to them, and He had a plan, a good plan, as He promised. She strode into the kitchen to check on the round loaves of julekake, the Norwegian Christmas bread with currants and candied fruit in it. She always used to take a loaf over to Hazel and Arnett. Just a reminder that life changes and goes on.

She pulled the pans from the oven and slid the loaves onto the wooden rack to cool. She'd frost them later. The kitchen was filled with the fragrance of Christmas baking, one of her favorite things about the holidays. Tomorrow when they went into town to sign the ranch papers, she'd take a basket to Molly Beckwith. Maybe they should invite that family out for Christmas Day. That way they would have some children in the house for a change. Just think, maybe by this time next year there would be a baby in the family.

She raised her voice. "Cassie, you about ready for a cup of coffee?"

"I'll be there in a minute. Let me finish this seam." The *kerthunk* of the treadle resumed its beat.

Mavis replenished the stove and pulled the coffeepot to the front to heat. What a

202

pleasure it was to have another woman around to share the coffee. Such a simple thing, so cherished. So many things to be thankful for. She put both gingerbread and sour-cream cookies on a plate and found herself thinking there should be even more. Nonsense. This was ample.

"What smells so heavenly?" Cassie asked as she entered the room.

"The julekake just came out. I'll set the loaves in the window box to freeze. We serve them for breakfast on Christmas Day. I usually give some away too."

"My mother loved both the smell and taste of cardamom. Said it reminded her of home in Norway. How come people use it only at Christmas?"

"Good question. I think they use it more in Norway. For us it is a special treat, like lutefisk and lefse. We'll have that for Christmas Eve supper. Have you ever helped make lefse?"

Cassie shook her head. "I remember my mother trying to teach the cook how to make it, but she was never satisfied. I think she used to wish for home the most at Christmas — home meaning Norway."

They sipped and nibbled in the quiet before Cassie raised her head and looked directly at Mavis. "May I ask you a question?"

"Of course. I'll answer if I can."

"You said that you chose security over love, yet you said you loved Ivar. When did that happen, the . . . uh, the knowing that you loved him?"

Mavis shot a swift prayer for wisdom heavenward. "I think it was a gradual thing. No big bursts of light or anything, just day to day realizing how much he meant to me. One day he brought me some bluebells from down by the barn, and I could see love shining in his eyes as he handed them to me. I knew I had made the right decision, and my heart felt like it might burst from the love inside. I was pregnant with Ransom, and that little gift made me cry. Of course, when you are with child, you cry easily anyway, but I remember sobbing. He wrapped those long arms around me, and I could tell he was confused. But when I could talk, I told him they were tears of joy. Then he kissed me again and went back to work." Mavis realized she was circling the rim of the mug with her forefinger.

"Thank you for telling me that."

Mavis reached across the table and laid her hand over Cassie's. "Learning to live together as husband and wife takes some doing, but when you can talk things over, it helps a lot." Did Cassie notice how Lucas seemed to be avoiding talking things over?

Cassie nodded. "My mother and father talked a lot, about business things and personal things and their dreams. As a little girl, I sometimes felt left out, but then my father would set me on his knee and I'd ride horsey. He had a song he sang to that."

Mavis watched Cassie's face take on a faraway, dreamy look. *Please, O Lord, keep my son from hurting her. She has been hurt enough.*

At dinner when they were gathered around the table, Mavis turned to Lucas. "Didn't you say you had a letter or something from Mr. Porter?"

"Ah, that I did. I forgot all about it. Sorry." He headed for his room, returning with an envelope to hand to his mother. "You read it. I pretty much know what's in it. Told Ransom and Arnett too."

Questioning him with her gaze, she slit it open and pulled out a single sheet of paper.

"Dear friends,

"This is in regard to the idea about opening ranch homes to guests, and I would like to hear your opinions on this. The guests would pay for this privilege, of course, and I know money is tight these days. This could bring in some extra cash and be doing strangers a good deed at the same time. I know that is in the middle of the busy summer season, but the folks could ride and learn about life on a ranch.

"Please let me know if we can count on you and your ranch to take part. I don't think we need a lot of ranches, but if we publicize it, it would be a shame to turn people away. We would have to set up pricing and some guidelines. I suggest we plan a meeting here at the hotel in January.

"If this works out, we could become known for both our show and our western hospitality. I look forward to hearing from you.

"Sincerely,
Josiah Porter"

Mavis looked up from the letter. "We should make a clear decision about this. What do you all think?"

"Besides my bunkhouse, we could also turn my ranch house into a guesthouse real easy, since there are three bedrooms there. So we have the room." Arnett leaned forward. "This sounds like a winning idea to me."

"I vote let's do it." Lucas looked to Ransom, who appeared to be studying his thumbs. "What about you, big brother?"

"You know me. I don't go making quick decisions. What if someone were to get hurt, like falling off a horse or something?"

"Good point, son." Mavis nodded her head slowly, as she sometimes did when she was thinking. "This could have real possibilities, though. Will we have enough to do to keep them busy?"

"They could help build fences. And they could help us with haying; that would be a real experience." Lucas turned toward Cassie. "You could maybe put on a show. A little one."

She nodded. "I could teach adults to shoot, maybe older kids."

"We could take them on rides up into the mountains, camp out." Gretchen leaned against her mother's knees. "Kids could maybe play with the calves if we brought in a couple to be tamed. And baby pigs; I think we'll have piglets by then. I think this could be fun."

The ideas came from all sides of the table, except from Ransom. "Takes some thinking. It could be a lot of hard work. Cooking for the extra people, cleaning and washing. Would we have just one group and would it be before or after the Wild West show? Or on through July and into August?" He wagged his head.

When he did that, he was not very excited about the subject, Mavis knew.

He asked Lucas, "How soon do we have to let him know? His letter seems to be asking for an immediate answer."

Lucas shrugged. "The sooner the better. This should go out with the other publicity. We're actually behind already, since we thought of the show so late. Most community events like this start planning years in advance."

"Don't you want to talk with some of the other ranchers? Who all did he send this out to?"

Lucas shrugged again. "Beats me. But I think we should let him know right away, get in right at the beginning. I mean, we've been trying to come up with cash crops, and here one's dumped right in our laps."

Arnett was still planning. "We could maybe use some of that slab wood to side another bunkhouse. And I could teach someone how to carve wood." He said to no one in particular, "I think this has real possibilities."

"You could do this with your ranch, you know," Ransom suggested.

"Our ranch, you mean. That will no longer be my responsibility, but these two young'uns living there. That still leaves two bedrooms for company."

Mavis watched Cassie a moment. What did she think of these ideas? No indication.

And she found herself getting caught up in the game. "If some want to learn about gardening, we can teach that. I think this could be a real adventure. Let's pray about this tonight and see what God has to say about it. You could mail a letter back to Mr. Porter when we decide."

Lucas was grinning. "Or I could ride into Hill City and tell him."

Mavis caught the glare Ransom sent his brother, and she knew what Ransom was thinking: Lucas would always rather be off somewhere and planning than working on the ranch. A curious thought struck her. What would it be like with Lucas and Cassie living in the other ranch house?

The next morning, as soon as breakfast was finished and the dishes cleaned up, they all loaded in the sleigh and headed for town to talk to their lawyer and sign the papers. The discussion over breakfast had shown agreement but with some reservations. Although any new thing like this could call for all kinds of uncertainties, Ransom had agreed to give it a try. If it didn't work out, they could go back to regular ranching. Arnett signing away his ranch weighed more heavily on Mavis's mind than the possibility of ranch guests next summer.

"You're absolutely sure you want to do this?" She turned to Arnett, sitting beside her. For a change Lucas rode with them instead of on his horse.

"Absolutely. We can do more working together than with me living in that house all by myself. Why, I feel twenty years younger since I moved into your bunkhouse. Mavis, yer actin' like an old dog worrying a bone." He held up his hand when she started to argue. "It is my land, free and clear. I've got no one left to inherit it, no one I want to sell it to, not that anyone would want to buy it, and I spent a lotta time thinkin' this through. We all know how much better I been since I moved into your bunkhouse. I got a new lease on life. Ransom and me makin' furniture, these two making my house a home again, why it all just seems so perfect to me. And if'n we have ranch guests next summer, all the better; I profit and you profit. Mavis, the good

Lord says to live in today. And this way I got the freedom to do just that. I think I'm the one getting all the good outta this deal."

Why did Mavis think she could change his mind? The Engstroms were strong willed, and the Arnetts every bit as strong. That strength was in their blood, in the blood of every family making a living in this country.

Arnett reached over and took Cassie's hand. "And maybe this little girl will bring us all some grandbabies to play with." He chuckled at the red creeping up Cassie's face. "I always thought I'd be a good grandpa."

"You will be, Arnett, and I won't bring this up again. But you know the lawyer is going to ask you a whole heap of questions."

"Let him. I know what I want, and we got the papers that say how we want it. Ain't any of his never mind, other than making sure we have good documents." He sat back in the box and snuggled deeper into his blanket as the sleigh whispered them toward town and the horses' bells jangled merrily.

Daniel Westbrook, their lawyer since forever, was not in, and his office door was locked. Now what?

"I know what. Wait here." Lucas hastened off up the street.

Lucas never could stand still. Mavis could only shake her head.

He returned in a few minutes. "Dan is in Missouri for the holidays. He may stay till spring. There is another lawyer in town, a new one, over beyond the church."

Ransom frowned. "Where did you find all that out?"

"From Sig. Barbers hear everything and know everything."

So they all trooped up the street past the church. Two blocks beyond, Lucas announced, "I think this is it."

A newly carved and painted sign hung on a little iron post by the street. *James Minton Westover.* Someone had neatly shoveled out the brick walkway to a little cottage set back from the street. Mavis was profoundly disappointed. She wanted the lawyer who knew her and knew Arnett just as well. Perhaps he could convince Arnett to abandon this notion.

And she was certainly right about the lawyer asking questions. For an hour they sat in his office doing nothing but answer questions. At one point the lawyer even sent all the Engstroms out so he could talk to Arnett privately. The one-on-one conversation lasted quite a while.

To be fair, the Engstroms and Arnett were

strangers to this man, as was he to them. Of course he must be cautious. He was a youngish fellow from Chicago, said he had practiced with a law firm in Rapid City and now was setting up his own firm. He certainly was upright and sincere. And humorless. But isn't that how it is when strangers deal with strangers?

Mr. Westover was shaking his head as he put his signature to the deed papers. "There. This is legal. It will stand up in any court. But I still don't think you are serving your own best interests, Mr. Arnett."

Arnett leaned forward in his chair. "We been through all this. Let me explain it this way: Say, when you get old, old like me, who's gonna take care of you? Your children — the ones that didn't die young — haven't so much as sent you a letter for years. Everyone you love except the dog has died. There you sit, sick maybe, or crippled. A couple cows, some chickens. What you gonna do then, Mr. Westover? Who cares about you enough to take care of you when you're not young anymore?"

The man nodded grimly. "But you are giving up a great deal."

"And I'm getting more than I'm giving up."

The man sighed. "I hope this is indeed for

213

your best. If one of your children challenges this, I can in good conscience insist to them that you were not being coerced. And will do so."

"Good. That's all we ask of you. Now show me where to sign."

Signing one's name can take a long time. First the lawyer sent Lucas out to fetch Sig and his apprentice. A barber! *Why does this lawyer think he needs a barber now?* Mavis puzzled.

Sig and his boy walked in. He grinned. "Yep, Jim, these are the Engstroms, all right. Hello, Arnett. Haven't seen you for a long time. Lucas, looks like you could do with a little trim." He picked up a pen, bent over, and ran his finger down the papers Mr. Westover had laid out, looking for the right place. "Ah." He signed on the witness line.

Witnesses. Of course. These two were witnesses, and it appeared they did this sort of thing frequently. They left immediately. Mavis had not thought about witnesses.

By the time they had all signed the deed in triplicate — one copy each for the Engstroms and Arnett and one to leave with the lawyer — Mavis was more than ready to quit that stuffy room. Why was she letting Arnett do this? They all said their thanks, everyone shook hands all around, and they filed out to the sleigh.

"Home?" Ransom untied the team.

"No, Brandenburgs first and then I brought a basket for Molly Beckwith and her children."

He climbed into the box. "I'll drop you off and go back to the store. Lucas, you want to take the list and get JD started on it?"

"Will do."

Cassie climbed up onto the box. "And I need more shells if I'm going to start practicing again. My arm is back to better than it was before the match."

"What kind?"

"I need them for all my guns."

"All right." Lucas clambered up into the back. "Anyone need anything else?"

Ransom clucked to the team. "Arnett, how about while Lucas is off and the women are with the Brandenburgs, you and I go over to the lumberyard and look at some of their machinery?" The sleigh whispered forward. The off horse shook his head, giving his bells an extra jangle.

Arnett nodded. "Mighty good idea. You know, I been thinking. Sometimes a piece looks real good with more than one kind of wood in it. Like the cherry could be the top and the front of the drawer and maybe oak for the frame. They got any dry oak here?"

Then each rode in silence, wrapped in thought. When they arrived at the Brandenburgs, Mavis was chuckling to herself as Ransom helped her and Cassie out of the sleigh. How strange the directions their lives were taking! A winter business of furniture building, a summer of hosting city folk who want to learn about ranching, and all the while the ranch work keeps on steady as ever. A couple of months and the beef cows would be calving and the cycle would begin again. While winter was usually a bit of a respite, this year it seemed to be a time of rebirth. Or at least a hatching of ideas. Where in the world was God taking them?

And it all had started with the arrival of Cassie.

15

"So Cassie, how are the wedding plans coming?"

Cassie lay in bed early the next morning, thinking back to Pastor Brandenburg's question. She'd answered by assuring him that the last day of the year, and the last day of her old life, was indeed the day. But when he'd asked a question about Lucas, she'd just smiled and told him that Lucas said he would be happy with whatever they planned. So the wedding was set. That would be her wedding day forever after. Then why wasn't she happy about it? After all, Mavis had assured her that love would come. Lucas was indeed a lovable man. She liked him a whole lot.

But then she liked Micah too and trusted Micah, had for years, but she'd never felt anything more than friendship. Just like with Lucas. She stared at the ceiling, still clothed in the darkness of night. *Lord, if this is what you want, I know it will be a good thing. I am learning to trust you, I know, thanks to Mavis and the Brandenburgs and church and your Word. More and more I find good things in your Word. This is what Lucas believes too; at least I assume so.* How could he not, growing up in this house, with a mother who prays for him all the time?

A thought hit her like the recoil of a shotgun. She'd not been praying for Lucas. She'd prayed about the wedding and about learning all these new things and about Christmas presents and about Betsy Hudson, but she'd not prayed for Lucas. In the still of the sleeping household, Cassie took Lucas to the throne of God and asked the Father what to do. Lucas had vowed to make her love him. *Father, if this marriage is to be, I accept that as your will for us. If it is not, please do like Mavis says and close the door. Help Lucas to truly know his heart. Teach me to love him in all the ways a wife loves her husband and let us become one, as you say in your Word. I want to be a loving woman, a wise woman, the woman you plan for me to be. But I'll need help doing that.* She heaved a sigh and finished with a heartfelt amen. So be it.

Unable to go back to sleep, she bundled into her robe and slippers, lit a lamp, and after setting it beside the bed, brought the last of the men's handkerchiefs she had hemmed to now be monogrammed. The final two were for Lucas. She'd hemmed those for Arnett and Ransom already. The aprons were finished for Mavis and Gretchen, along with a reticule she had found amongst her show things that she thought Gretchen might like. Since Runs Like a Deer did not wear aprons, she'd made her a flannel vest to wear under her clothes to help her keep warm.

When she heard someone else stirring, she dressed and headed for the kitchen to start the stove. Today they were going to be preparing food for the party at the church. The men were going to run the sawmill again. And today she also wanted to go out to see Wind Dancer and George. The snow was crusted deep enough that she could walk on it now, or perhaps she would ski out there. Maybe she and Gretchen could go skiing after Christmas.

With the coffee near to boiling, she hummed as she set water on for the oatmeal and brought in ham to slice. She could at least make breakfasts now. She may have to cook three breakfasts a day, but her husband would not starve. Her kitchen skills were definitely improving.

"You sound cheerful." Mavis tied on her apron as she came through the door.

"I am. Christmas is coming."

"Yes, it is. We'll have a busy weekend. With Christmas falling on a Sunday this year, we'll go to church as usual Sunday morning. And we'll decorate the tree tomorrow, Christmas Eve. But first we've got the party tonight. I plan on taking an elk roast, along with two cakes and probably pickles. I think we'll make a couple loaves of bread and potato salad too. Have you ever made potato salad?"

"No, but I'm always willing to learn."

"I know you are, Cassie dear. That is why I have such a wonderful time teaching you. Do you want to do the bread today?"

"What kind?"

"Regular bread." Mavis measured the oatmeal into the boiling water and threw in several handfuls of raisins. "Lucas went down to the barn?"

"I think so; I think it was he I heard. You know, when spring comes, will we do a garden at the other house too?" Why wasn't she able to say *my house* yet? Surely that would change when she and Lucas moved over there.

"Of course. I was thinking we should plant more potatoes there and other root crops.

That way I won't have to make my garden plot bigger. Especially if we are going to feed Easterners. It would be good if beans and some other things were producing by then, but we'll have to have an early spring for that to happen."

Cassie slapped the largest cast-iron frying pan on the hot part of the stove, then poured them each a cup of coffee and motioned for Mavis to sit.

"Cassie, you spoil me." She sat down and inhaled the steam. "There is nothing like the first cup of coffee in the morning."

"I agree." Transferring a plate of corn bread from the warming oven to the table, she sat down and passed the syrup. "Would you rather have jelly?"

"I'll have jelly later. This is perfect. I feel like I'm loafing." The two smiled at each other and dug into the square of corn bread.

Thank goodness for snow on boots. The stamp of feet on the porch announced the arrival of the men long before Arnett came through the door, with Lucas right behind him.

"Looks like it might snow out there. Nothing like coming into a warm, food-smelling kitchen." Arnett hung up his coat. "Gretchen's Biscuit is saddled but still down in the barn."

Cassie finished her treat and got up to pour more coffee. She turned the ham steaks and set the dish-towel-covered pan of corn bread on the warming shelf.

Just as Cassie heard more boots on the porch, Gretchen wandered into the kitchen and slumped in a chair. "I really don't feel like doing anything today. I want to stay home."

"What's the matter?" Her mother laid the back of her hand against her daughter's forehead. "No fever. Away you go. You told Jenna you would help the Hendersons today, and they're counting on you."

Gretchen grimaced and accepted a mug of hot coffee.

Ransom came stomping in, milk pail in hand, bringing chill air with him. "I opened the fence to that second haystack," he said as he hung up his things. "We won't have to take that load out."

"So we'll finish up the milling?" Arnett asked over his coffee cup.

"And hopefully get the boards hauled down to the barn. Should be a couple of loads."

"I was thinking," Mavis started and stopped when she heard her sons groan. "You could at least let me finish."

Cassie grinned, down inside of course, or

the boys might feel embarrassed.

Lucas snorted. "We could, but every time you use those words, it means more work for us."

"Every time?"

"Sure seems that way." Lucas sat down at the table. "You better get a move on, squirt. You wouldn't want to miss out on any work. I hear they're butchering two hogs. Two! That's gonna be so much fun, right?"

Gretchen rolled her eyes.

Cassie slid half a dozen fried eggs onto a platter, piled the ham on another, and set both platters on the table. "Arnett, it's your turn to say grace." She could feel her eyes growing round. How could she have said that?! What audacity! Downright rude. All of those at the table stared at her, and then the old man burst out laughing.

"Well, I guess I really am part of this family now. Let's pray." He paused. "Dear Lord, thank you for this family and all the love around this table. Thank you for bringing us together, and thank you for the food that you bless us with. I am so grateful. Amen."

Cassie slid into her chair. "I . . . I don't know what got into me."

Mavis chuckled and patted her hand. "God did, Cassie dear, as a good and gentle reminder." She slid a slice of ham onto her plate and then finished the last bit of oatmeal. "Sitting and being served like this makes me feel guilty."

Ransom shook his head. "Don't waste your time with guilt. That's what someone I know well always tells me."

"I wonder who that could be." Mavis raised her eyebrows, obviously trying to look innocent.

With everyone chuckling, Cassie patted Mavis's hand. "Mothers are supposed to say things like that. At least that's what my mother told me."

Gretchen pushed her chair back. "Guess I'm on my way." She rose, kissed her mother's cheek, and headed for the coatrack. "Thanks for getting my horse ready, Mr. Arnett. See you all later. Much later."

Cassie watched the girl bundle up and head out the back door. The thought of riding in this cold did not sound appealing. She turned to Arnett. "Is it really going to snow today?"

"Sure looks and feels like it."

"But how do you know?"

"By the clouds and the wind; snow clouds have a look all their own. You'll come to know that when you been here awhile."

"So there is a difference between rain clouds and snow clouds?"

"Yep. One's in winter with the cold air, but you can smell rain coming too."

"Really?" Cassie glanced around the table to see the others nodding. "More to learn, eh?"

Arnett grinned. "You keep on with the cooking, dear Cassie. You been learning plenty."

Cassie looked up to catch a wink from Lucas. Funny how that little bitty thing made her feel good.

By the time the men were out the door on their way up the hill, Cassie was kneading more flour into the sourdough starter. She'd already added bacon grease, molasses, and the ground-up oatmeal. Who would think you could grind oatmeal fine in a coffee grinder? "So what other things might you add to the regular bread dough, either sourdough or potato starter?" Sometimes they bought yeast now at the store in town, so now there were more ways to do things.

Mavis put the last of the dishes on the rack. "Sometimes I add cornmeal, rye flour when I can find it, eggs, or more sugar or honey for a sweeter dough. Different grains make different kinds of flour. Now those oatmeal bits will make a chewier bread. You know the shelled corn we feed the chickens? We should bring some of that in and run it through the coffee mill. I've not done it, but I heard someone else talking about doing it; might be worth experimenting with."

"But it all uses the same basic recipe?" There was so much to learn, so much to remember!

"Yep. Oh. Currants or raisins make a sweeter bread too. And cinnamon. Oh, how I love a loaf of cinnamon bread. In fact, let's take part of this and do just that. But the dough has to rise and be punched down and then after the second rise, when we shape the loaves, we roll one flat out like cinnamon rolls, add cinnamon and sugar, and then roll it up and shape it into a loaf. We'll have that for breakfast tomorrow morning. Now, if I were going to be really fancy, I could slice that loaf and make it into French toast for something special."

Mavis got started on the cakes for the party while Cassie kept on kneading. Thump and turn and roll the dough in and push it down again. The rhythm now came automatically, just like Mavis had said it would. And her thoughts could drift elsewhere as she worked. There was something special about baking bread, all right.

Far too quickly that day, Gretchen was back and they were all ready to leave for the party at the church meeting hall. Cassie was having a full-blown butterfly attack. This was worse than before any ring performance. In a performance, she knew exactly what she was going to do. And she knew that almost always she could get her audience oohing and aahing and laughing. Not this time.

If only she could stay home . . . but then Gretchen would feel hurt, and there was no need to cause that to happen. They packed the food in baskets and stowed them in the frigid sleigh. With heavy blankets to snuggle in and heated stones as warm footrests for their feet, the sleigh was quite cozy. Lucas chose to ride, since there really wasn't room for one more adult in the sleigh. He tucked the robes around them and swung aboard his horse. He was soon out of sight far ahead.

Cassie wriggled in deeper. She found skiing fun and this new world of snow and cold interesting. But her nose felt very cold already, and they'd not yet left the last gate behind. She was beginning to understand better why the show went south for the winter.

Their sleigh jingled cheerfully into town and up to the large hall behind the church, the horses' bells joining the jangle of other horse bells. Cassie did not feel cheerful. The

Engstrom horses looked dark in the flanks and steam rose off their backs. Ransom and Lucas double-blanketed them against the cold. Cassie scooped up two baskets and, with Gretchen right behind her, followed Mavis inside. Mavis marched over to where the women were putting the food tables together.

An older lady whom Cassie had not met called, "Hello, Mavis! If you have something hot, there is still some room in the oven."

"Not this time. The roast is done." Mavis waved an arm in several directions. "Gretchen, salads there. Cassie, you put the cakes on that table over there. Make sure you cut them in even pieces or the older boys will start arguing over who gets which piece. Make sure there is a pancake turner in each too. We'll eat later this evening but we want it all to be ready now."

Cassie did as she was instructed, smiling at the other women and introducing herself when they did. All the time she was wishing she could go off with the girls like Gretchen did, or better yet, just stay home. She had just finished cutting the second cake, when the musicians quit their discordant tuning and a polka was announced. Lucas appeared at her side.

"Do you know how to polka?" At her nod,

he took her hand and swung her out onto the dance floor to join the others whirling to the music. The movements were too fast to talk much, but the joy of the music made her smile and finally laugh. She kicked her heels high.

"That's my girl," Lucas said in her ear at the finish. He stayed beside her as the music started again, but Arnett tapped his shoulder and swung her away into a waltz.

"You dance mighty good," Arnett said.

"My father taught me. He and my mother loved to dance, but when they did the waltz, all the world stopped to watch them."

"Well, missy, you have their grace, then. You make an old man look good."

She saw Lucas dancing with Gretchen and Ransom with his mother. All ages were on the floor. She watched a father dancing with his daughter, the child young enough to stand on the tops of his shoes as he danced them both around. A mother held her little son in her arms, and they twirled around the room, the little guy giggling and making those around him laugh too. When that dance finished, the announcer called for a square dance, and Cassie went to get a drink of punch.

Lucas found her. "Do you know how to square dance?"

"Sort of. But I'm not very good at it."

"Come on, the caller will tell you what to do." He hustled her back out onto the dance floor, where they joined three other couples to form a square. "Cassie says she's not used to this, so we'll all have to make sure she goes the right way." The others laughed and greeted her.

The caller looked very familiar. Who was he? She realized it was Edgar McDougal, the sheriff. His booming voice rang out with a lilt.

But she immediately forgot about the caller, because keeping up took all her concentration. The allemande left, with which the dance began, was especially vexing. A couple of times one of the men would grab her and guide her into the next step. At the end she wanted nothing more than to simply sit down, for a minute at least.

"You did just fine, Miss Cassie," one of the men said. "You can dance in our square anytime."

That stranger's kind words pleased her more than she would have guessed.

She plopped onto a chair along the wall and just watched. Young and old, good dancers and poor dancers, hefty men and dainty girls, they all danced as if they were the greatest dancers in the world. No, that was not quite it. They were dancing as if making an error did not matter. That was it. Mistakes didn't matter. Is that what life is all about? Do your best, ignore the mistakes, and move on? Might that make a marriage of friends turn into a lifetime of love for two people?

The music paused and Sheriff McDougal announced another waltz. Ransom appeared in front of her and extended his hand. "I won't let Arnett steal you this time." She smiled as he led her out onto the floor. Arnett had led well, but Ransom was even finer.

The piece had scarcely begun when she noticed Ransom looking at something off to the side. She followed his gaze to see Lucas talking with Betsy Hudson. They moved beyond other dancers, and she lost sight of them. Now why had he done that?

"Everyone dances with everyone at these shindigs," Ransom said when the music stopped. "He was most likely just being polite." He'd not said a word the entire dance, but Cassie remembered his mother claiming that Ransom didn't like taking part in social chatter. He was uncomfortable with idle talk. Keeping silent hadn't been hard for Cassie either, for she felt pretty much the same, but keeping her thoughts away from Lucas and Betsy was another matter.

Cassie nodded. "Thank you." But when she looked up at Ransom, she saw that his jaw had that same hard look as when he and his brother went out to chop wood.

When the musicians called for a break, the women put the finishing touches to the tables and asked Pastor Brandenburg to say grace.

After the amen, Gretchen came to stand beside Cassie. "Do you want to eat with me and Jenna and some of the other girls? They have been wanting to meet you."

Cassie nodded, forcing herself to ignore the feeling that Lucas should come to eat with her, but maybe things were different here. She'd been afraid he was going to announce their wedding in spite of her asking him not to, but he didn't. So that was something to be grateful for. But still . . .

When Arnett and Ransom sat down across the table to eat with them too, she wondered again. But then maybe that was the way things were done out here. She put her thoughts aside, for now Mavis brought her plate over, and it became more like at home. Then all the girls began to bombard Cassie with questions.

"How long did you star in the Wild West

Show?" "How old is your horse?" "Did you really raise a bull buffalo?" She added some stories of her show days, but when Gretchen told about her talking horse, that brought down the house. She'd not realized Gretchen was such a good storyteller, but at her description of Wind Dancer flipping Pastor Brandenburg's hat off, they all laughed and giggled.

So when Reverend Brandenburg stopped at their group and said, "You might not want to believe all that you hear," they all burst out laughing again.

"Will you do a show like that again so we can all come?" one of the girls asked.

"I don't know. Maybe Gretchen could have a party and —"

"Of course!" Mavis smiled broadly. "And you could all come. I think that could be arranged as soon as the snow is gone and the land dries up some. The corrals are really slippery sloppy in the early spring. What a fine idea." Mavis smiled at Cassie. "If it is all right with you, Cassie dear."

"I would love to do that. And I know Wind Dancer would love to show off for young ladies. He has a special spot in his heart for girls, you know." At Gretchen's grin, Cassie leaned over and gave her a hug. "We'll have fun for sure."

When the music started again, Cassie looked around for Lucas, but she didn't see him anywhere. She didn't see Betsy either. One of the other men asked her to dance, a youngish fellow, and he apologized for his strangely red nose. He said it had gotten too cold when he was out driving stock in from pasture. He was a very good dancer, and she forgot about the twinges of disquiet deep inside her. When she finally saw Lucas again, he was dancing with his mother.

Sometime later, when the sheriff called out that this was the last waltz of the evening, Lucas stopped at her shoulder. "Will you dance this one with me?"

"Of course." She turned into his arms, and they dipped and swayed with the others. "Is this a typical dance out here?"

"Pretty much, although Santa usually doesn't visit."

"Arnett was a good Santa." Cassie looked at the tree in the corner, now bare of the gifts that had been under it. Every child in the place had received a wrapped present, along with an orange and a candy cane. The little ones were especially delighted and sucked on their candy canes for the rest of the evening.

The music ended and Cassie found herself wishing it would go longer. And to think she hadn't wanted to come!

Everyone clapped their appreciation to the musicians. Then began the exodus for recovering wraps and finding their own kitchen things.

"This was such fun."

Lucas laughed. "Haven't you about danced your shoes out? You only missed one the whole evening."

"Feels that way." She smiled at Mrs. Brandenburg, who was passing by with an empty casserole dish. "The people here are really friendly, aren't they?"

"You are easy to be friendly to."

"Why, thank you."

The hall emptied quickly and the families climbed into their sleighs. One set of sleigh bells, then three, then a cacophony jangled cheerfully in the cold night air, but now Cassie was cheerful too.

"I'll meet you at home," Lucas called as Ransom turned the team toward the ranch.

Snuggled down under the robes, Cassie felt Gretchen slump against her shoulder, sound asleep. She had a hard time keeping her own eyes open. Would they really go back into town Sunday for the Christmas service? Snowflakes started drifting down. And now they were zipping, not drifting. Cassie wanted to shake all this loose snow off the blankets, but that would let cold air in. Better to let it lie. By the time they reached the ranch, the snow on the blankets lay an inch deep and it was snowing hard enough to make seeing the road impossible.

"Good thing the horses know their way," Ransom said at one point. But Lucas was not at the ranch when they climbed out of the sleigh, and he hadn't yet returned by the time Ransom and Arnett put the team away. From her room, Cassie heard Ransom come in. Not long after, the dogs barked, announcing that Lucas was home. All safe. She ought to join the others in the kitchen; instead she crawled into her soft, cold bed and tied herself into a tight knot, waiting for her chilly nest to warm up. She was so tired!

She'd had a good time, most of the time, but some things just didn't seem quite right.

16

Cassie sat staring at the Christmas tree they'd finished decorating. White candles were clipped to the ends of branches to be lit on Christmas Day. The bushy pine tree stood seven feet tall, with a silver star on top that Ivar had made years earlier. Popcorn strings looped the tree and glass icicles hung, glinting back the light from the fireplace. And the ornaments! Hand-carved sleighs, horses, and snowmen, with more stars and crocheted red bells, white angels, and blown-glass balls peeked out from among the fragrant boughs. And candy canes. Not glass, not carved. Actual candy. She'd never seen such a lovely tree. Sure, it was beautiful before they decorated it, but now . . .

"Wait until you see the candles lit." Mavis handed her a cup of cocoa and sat down beside her, a cup in her hand. Gretchen brought in a matching steaming mug and a plate of cookies.

"Are we going to frost cookies this afternoon?" She sat at her mother's feet, joining the others in staring from tree to crackling fire.

Mavis smiled at her daughter. "If you'd like. We need to bake another batch of sour cream cookies too, so you can frost some of them."

"The gingerbread men need faces and buttons. How come you forgot the raisins?"

"You weren't here to remind me."

Gretchen grinned up at Cassie and rolled her eyes. "I told you I needed to stay home from the Hendersons'."

"Are all your Christmases like this?" Cassie made a sweeping gesture that encompassed the room. Arnett had made small wreaths to hang in the windows and a big one for the door. Pine boughs over the doors and windows and lit candles in the windows flanking the front door made the room even more festive.

Mavis nodded as she looked around. "I love it like this. I always hate to put Christmas away."

"Where are the men?"

"Down in the barn working on something secret."

"I wonder what it is." Gretchen grinned

at Cassie. "Maybe we should sneak down there and look in the window."

Her mother nudged her with her knee. "You'll do no such thing. But we could bring in those presents that are wrapped and put them under the tree. Mine are done."

"Mine too." Cassie had raided the brown paper stash to wrap hers, using bright yarn for the ribbon. "My mother used to love wrapping presents. One year she sewed a bunch of bags of calico and muslin and used those to wrap the packages. I think people were as pleased with the bags as the gifts."

Mavis nodded. "That's a very good idea. One can always find a use for a drawstring bag. That would be a good way to use up those scraps too. That and for quilts."

Cassie nodded. "I saw a patchwork skirt one time. I always thought that would be a fun thing to do."

Gretchen propped her chin on her hands and her elbows on her knees. "I'd like that. We could each make one after Christmas while I'm still on vacation."

"Remember, we have a wedding to prepare for."

"Mor, remember when you made my rag doll?" Gretchen looked over her shoulder. "I thought she was the most beautiful doll ever. You even dyed and braided the yarn for her hair."

"Is that the one on your pillow?" Cassie asked.

"Yes. Mor repaired her for me a couple of years ago, and I sewed her a new dress. I'm going to give her to my little girl someday."

"I had a doll once too, but I never was one to play with dolls. I liked the animals in the Wild West Show better. Every spring we'd have calves, and then my father found me a puppy. His name was Fredrick, and I called him Fred. When he grew old and died, we found Othello, who's been with me ever since. Along with George and Wind Dancer, of course. I had a pony for years too. Her name was Miss Jay. I called her Missy. It is so hard because animals grow old much faster than we do. I cried for days after she went lame and my father put her down. He said it was an act of mercy, but I had a hard time forgiving him. I was so sure she would get well again."

Gretchen sniffed. "That makes me sad too. It's bad enough when a wolf gets one in the winter, but that seems more natural. Still, I cried too when a wolf got one of our ponies once. I wanted to go hunt and kill the wolf, but Ransom said no. That was the way of the wild and the wolves were doing what God made them to do. Take care of the old and infirm."

"Remind me not to get old and infirm around here," Cassie said with a shudder that made Gretchen and her mother chuckle. She drained her mug and set it on the low table, eyeing the candle in the center. "Did you make the candles too?"

"I made a bunch of them years ago, and this is one of the last ones left. Used to be we made candles out of melted fat or tallow. One year we found a bees' nest and I used the beeswax. This is one of those."

Cassie shook her head. "Do I need to learn that too?"

Mavis chuckled and patted her hand. "No, Cassie. Now we can buy candles, like we buy kerosene for the lamps. Some places have gaslights and some have electricity now, like they did at the Chicago World's Fair. Someday we'll have electricity and telephones too. Things just come slower to the ranches than to the towns, especially the big towns like Rapid City and Hill City."

Gretchen snorted. "Mr. Porter will have the latest in Hill City — just ask Lucas."

Boots stomped, the kitchen door slammed. "That's the men. Go pull the coffeepot forward, Gretchen, will you please. I'll be right there." When Gretchen left the room, Mavis turned to Cassie. "Is there anything else you would like me to do to get ready for the wedding? What are you wearing?"

"Not that I can think of. I know Lucas wants apple pie instead of a cake. And I have a good dress in the chifforobe at the cabin. I need to get it out and get it pressed. I'd like to take that over to the other house — the chifforobe, I mean."

"Of course. And we'll need to stock the pantry too. Did you look through the kitchen things when we cleaned?"

"No, I didn't take the time to look carefully, but I am learning to use the basic things, at least. I will discover soon enough what I lack." She thought for a moment. "I know there wasn't a lot of firewood there."

"We'll take over a load of that too."

They both stared into the fire for a moment, watching the orange flames slither about, the blue flames hiding among the blackening sticks. *What is it about fire that is so enthralling?*

"Cassie, I cannot begin to tell you how delighted I am that you will soon be my daughter-in-law. That is the best Christmas present ever, far as I'm concerned."

"Thank you. I will do my best."

"I know you will." She squeezed Cassie's

hand. "I suppose I better go see to the men."

Cassie listened to the conversation going on. Lucas was teasing Gretchen, and Arnett cautioned her to stand up for herself. Gretchen said something they couldn't hear, but the laughter from the three men said she was taking Arnett's advice to heart.

Both women stood and headed for the kitchen.

"The lefse! Of course. We must make lefse," Mavis said as they paused in the doorway.

Like little boys, Lucas and Ransom started arguing over who had to peel all the potatoes this year.

Arnett stepped in. "You two go finish hauling the milled wood down and I will peel the potatoes." He didn't have to offer twice before the brothers were out the door, as if fearing he might change his mind.

"I could surely peel the potatoes," Cassie offered.

"No, this is just fine. It's bad cold out there. Let them work off some of that steam. I used to peel the potatoes for my Hazel. She was the best lefse maker in the valley." He grinned at Mavis. "Other than you, of course."

"So many years she and I made lefse together. And usually fried fattigmann the

243

same day. Both jobs that did better with two sets of hands. I know last year you seemed mighty lost."

He nodded. "I only went to church with you 'cause you came and dragged me out, brought me over here. I weren't much caring if I lived or died. And this year, you took me in again." He sniffed.

Mavis wiped her eyes with the handkerchief in her apron pocket. "Seems I remember two neighbors who stood by me after Ivar died. Good thing I had the children, not that the boys were children any longer, but keeping busy makes the grief easier to bear. It's just part of life is all, and God promises to walk beside us. Sometimes I think He does that in the guise of neighbors and friends."

Cassie could certainly understand that. "I was fifteen when my father died, and I thought the light had gone out in the whole world. I kept seeing him reunited with my mother, and I knew they were almighty happy again. That helped but not always. The people around me took care of me."

"Ah, isn't this supposed to be a happy day?" Arnett asked. "Sure doesn't seem like it so far."

"Start peeling."

By the time she'd rolled out the tenth ball

of dough to the thickness Mavis required, Cassie had that part of the process down. So she switched to using the thin, flat lefse stick to turn over the circles of dough, bigger than pie dough, on the top of the range. She used crumbled newspaper to clean the flour off the grill every now and then and stacked the finished lefse in the layers of towels that kept it from drying out.

"I remember my mother doing this on Christmas, but I was too little to help. She took over the kitchen in the cook tent for the afternoon. I loved being there with her. I remember it being a happy party with lots of laughter and some kind of hot drink. They'd raise their cups or goblets and everyone would say 'skål' and take a drink. I was never offered a cup to join them.

"That night for supper, they'd bring out the translucent fish to the table from baking in the oven, potatoes and lots of melted butter, along with the lefse that I thought was the best. I never cared much for lutefisk, but I ate my share to be polite."

She remembered her father whispering in her ear, *"Eat it quick and it goes down easier. We do this for your mother because it really makes her happy."* They'd never had lutefisk and lefse after her mother died. Quickly she shut off the memories. She'd think of them later or any minute she would be bawling like a baby. She glanced up to see Lucas watching her. The look in his eyes made her think perhaps he too knew something of sorrow. Maybe someday they would be able to talk about things like this and begin Christmas traditions in their house too.

Lord, I want a marriage like my mother and father had. I know they might not have started out the way I remember them, but they loved each other so much. Mavis reminds me that nothing is impossible with you. I'll keep telling myself that. After all, look at all the miracles you have done here so far.

"Are you all right?" Gretchen asked quietly.

Cassie nodded. "I will be." She'd never had a sister before either. Surely this was another miracle.

They woke up Christmas morning to wind-driven snow. It not only fell from the lead-gray sky, the wind carried the powdery stuff along the ground. A horizontal snow to go with the vertical snow, drifting against the buildings and fences, piling in a cone up against every tree. The men went to the barn to milk and take care of the animals, and Cassie was downright happy she didn't have to go out there.

Arnett arrived covered in snow. Even his beard had ice in it. "Sure glad we strung them ropes to the barn and bunkhouse. It's so thick out there you can get lost even in that short distance." He hung up his things and then backed up to the woodstove, a moment later turning to face the heat. "What we need is one o' them rotisserie things, toasts all your sides."

When the boys staggered back into the house, Ransom plunked the milk pail down and announced that they'd not be going to town for church, but then everyone knew that anyway. While this was not a true blizzard yet, there was a strong possibility it would turn into one. As they sat down for breakfast, they could hear the wind shrieking at the corners of the house.

Cassie shuddered. "Is it often like this?"

"Usually a couple times a year. Long as we can keep the livestock fed and watered, we hunker down and ride it out." Ransom sounded so casual, so confident when it sounded like the world was going to bury them. He half smiled at Gretchen. "Remember I am the checker champion from last year."

Mavis sighed. "So the Beckwiths will not be able to join us for dinner, but I sure hope Micah and Runs Like a Deer can make it down here. It would be a shame for them to miss out."

"I hope they're smart 'nough not to chance it." Arnett shook his head. "Was bad enough from the barn. Could hardly see the house from the bunkhouse."

Cassie went to stand at the kitchen window. Snow whipped by on the wind, not dancing and swirling but being chased. "I wonder if it was this bad in October. When we were in the wagon, we could feel every gust of wind. Felt like it might pick up the wagon any moment and hurl us across the land. I'd never felt anything like that in my life."

Mavis stood up. "Well, this isn't the first Christmas we've spent snowed in, and I'm sure it won't be the last. The ham is in, and the scalloped potatoes will go in later, as will the squash. We will take our julekake and coffee into the other room and light the candles on the tree and open our presents. The water pail is right by the tree. Lucas, I'd like you to read the Christmas story this year. And no matter how that wind howls, it cannot get in."

The back door blew open and Micah grabbed for it, ushering Runs Like a Deer ahead of him. Cold and snow swirled in around them. "Merry Christmas, everyone!"

" 'Bout scared me out of a year's growth," Arnett muttered. "Merry Christmas, you two. I sure am glad yer safe."

"Followed the tracks down. The fence line is still above snow too." Runs Like a Deer slung the deerskin pack off her shoulder and set it on the floor while Micah hung up their coats.

"Have you had breakfast?" Mavis asked.

"Yes, thank you. Should we put these things under the tree?"

"Of course, and if anyone else hasn't done that, now is a good time. Ransom, bring the dogs in. They won't mind missing the storm either." Once they were all seated in the big room, Ransom and Lucas lit the candles on the tree and sat down. Lucas picked up the Bible and began.

"And it came to pass in those days, that there went out a decree from Caesar Augustus that all the world should be taxed. (And this taxing was first made when Cyrenius was governor of Syria.) And all went to be taxed, every one into his own city. And Joseph also went up from Galilee. . . ."

Cassie put her arm around Gretchen and hugged her close. She had a family, a real family. The love she felt for them made her eyes wet as the ancient words poured into her heart.

"And she brought forth her firstborn son, and wrapped him in swaddling clothes, and laid him in a manger; because there was no room for them in the inn."

Gretchen laid her head on Cassie's shoulder. Runs Like a Deer and Micah were sitting on the floor in front of the fireplace. Othello laid his chin on her knee. She stroked his head with her free hand. Instead of watching Lucas read, she closed her eyes and let his voice roll over her.

"And there were in the same country shepherds abiding in the field, keeping watch over their flock by night. And, lo, the angel of the Lord came upon them. . . ."

What must that have been like? *Fear not.* How could one help but be afraid? She opened her eyes again to watch the candles on the tree. Such beauty! Surely God was in this place.

When Lucas closed the Bible and laid it back on the table, Mavis breathed a contented sigh. "That was beautiful. Thank you.

Can we keep the candles lit for a while more?"

Ransom, sitting close to the tree, nodded. "I think so. Let me just pinch out a couple." He sat back down. "Since Gretchen is the youngest, she has to give out the presents, right?"

"I thought it was the oldest." She grinned at Arnett.

"You wouldn't make this old man get down on the floor, now would you?"

"What old man?"

Arnett cackled and shook his head. "Mavis, you done raised this girl right. But I'd rather you did the handing out, young lady. Your eyes are better than mine for reading the names."

Gretchen left her place at Cassie's side and knelt at the tree. She read the name on the first present, and they passed it around the room to Mavis. She continued reading until everyone had a package and then announced, "Now open them."

"All together?" Cassie asked, eyeing her calico-wrapped gift from Mavis.

"All together."

By the time the only gifts left under the tree were for guests who would not be coming, at least not today, Cassie felt overwhelmed. She had a rabbit-skin vest from

Runs Like a Deer. A card of six buttons from Lucas. Arnett gave her a lovely cameo, saying he thought she could wear that on her wedding day. His Hazel had worn it when they got married.

At that, she fought back the tears. That would have been a good time to wear her mother's locket, the one lost in the fire. "Thank you."

Arnett and Ransom left the room and returned with a small whatnot table. "Sorry this isn't quite finished, but it is the first piece of our new furniture line." They set it in front of Cassie.

Cassie rubbed her hand over the top of the table. The top and front were of a reddish wood, and the rest were of a gray-brown wood with a lovely grain. It was not yet varnished, but the splendid craftsmanship glowed. "It is beautiful. Thank you."

They left the room again and returned with another one to set in front of Lucas.

"We thought your new home could use a matched pair."

"Thank you. How you managed to pull this off without me knowing is hard to believe." He looked at both pieces and nodded. "You ought to be able to sell these real easy, especially if our guests this summer see them in our houses."

"We'll get 'em finished up for you, maybe even by next Saturday. Too cold to varnish out in the barn, but it's nice and warm in the kitchen."

"I like that carving on the front of the drawer. It will make a good signature, I'd think."

Cassie's gifts were a hit. Mavis put her apron on and went to the tree to help pinch out the candles. "This has been the best Christmas ever."

"Mor, you always say that." Gretchen opened her reticule one more time. "I love this. Thank you, Cassie." Gretchen was already wearing the rabbit-skin vest that Runs Like a Deer had made for her. She stroked the vest. "This is the best ever. Every kid in school is going to envy me." She smiled at her friend. "And those belts for the men. They are wonderful."

"Good use for elk hide. Lucas did the design."

Mavis held up her foot to show off her moccasins. "I have always wanted a pair of these for in the house. And they are so warm."

"I'd like a pair of those too." Cassie admired the moccasins. "Runs Like a Deer, you could be making those to sell next summer. And the belts, the mittens, the vests."

She eyed the deerskin vest Micah was wearing. "That is beautiful. They used to sell leather things like this at our show. Maybe we can do that too. I'll help you if you show me how."

"Me too." Gretchen smoothed the fur on her vest. "Do you have enough rabbit skins?"

"We have many yet." Runs Like a Deer smiled impishly. "What do you think we have for supper?"

The rest of the day passed with Ransom still the checkers king, but Gretchen was close behind.

Arnett came in third. "You just wait," he said, his eyes narrowing. "I'll practice more, and I'll be king next time."

When Cassie went to bed, she listened for the storm outside and instead heard a gentle breeze. The window rattled a little, but the wind had died down considerably at some time during the evening. What did it look like out there? She really should bundle up and go look, but she was too weary — happily weary. What a fine day!

When Ransom had come in from the evening milking, he'd said the storm was easing. The near silence now seemed full and waiting. Somewhere out there, very faintly, she heard a coyote yip-yip and howl.

Another joined it. What a chorus for the evening of Christmas, a perfect Christmas.

Cassie was starting the stove the next morning when Ransom came in the back door. "I thought Lucas was down at the barn milking, but he's not. Have you seen him?"

She shook her head. "Not since last night. Maybe he stopped by the bunkhouse to talk with Arnett."

"No, I checked the bunkhouse." Ransom stomped past her to the back of the house, returned immediately. "Get Mor up. Something is wrong."

From the doorway, Mavis said, "I'm right here. What is it?"

"I'm going back down to the barn and check around again."

Mavis asked again, "What is it?"

Gretchen entered the kitchen yawning. "What's wrong?"

Mavis frowned at Cassie but Ransom was already back out the door. "Maybe nothing. I'll be right back," he tossed over his shoulder as he left.

Cassie explained, "Lucas seems to have disappeared."

Mavis wagged her head. "If Ransom doesn't know where everybody is every minute, he gets worried."

But Cassie felt her stomach roiling. She filled the coffeepot with water and set it on the stove. Where could Lucas be? Had something happened to him? Mavis had commented that Lucas had been acting strange lately.

Perhaps the problem was simply that he had never talked about getting married before, and he was having a little trouble dealing with it. She remembered a young man in the show, a good fellow named Jack something some years ago, who wanted to marry a girl he met in one of the towns. But he couldn't say how he felt or what he wanted, and apparently the girl was just as tongue-tied. He even tried to hire Cassie to speak for him.

As it ended up, Cassie's father said, "Well then, you can talk to me." He set Jack and his lady down in front of him. He asked Jack a question, and Jack answered him while the girl listened. Then her father asked the girl a question, and the girl answered him as Jack listened. It was the perfect solution. How Cassie needed her father now, with his wisdom and simple ways of achieving the unachievable.

Ransom came storming back into the house. "The milk pail is hanging on the wall and his horse is gone. There are fresh tracks out the first gate, but by the time they reach the road, they've been wiped out by the wind." He stared at his mother, an angry and perplexed look wrinkling his face. "Where could he be?"

17

"Did he say anything to anyone?" Ransom looked over his shoulder from pacing the kitchen. He stopped in front of Cassie.

She shook her head. "Had he any meat to deliver?"

"Not that I know of," Mavis said. "I'm going to go through his room and see what else is missing." She stopped at the door to Lucas's room. Clothes were hanging on the pegs along the wall, his button-making supplies on a table. Was anything gone? Not that she could tell. His bed was made.

She returned to the kitchen. "Perhaps he went hunting?" Mavis suggested. "Or up to the cabin?"

"No hunting without a rifle." Ransom pointed to the rack on the wall, where both rifles and the shotgun filled their regular places.

Cassie returned to her room to brush her hair; she hadn't done that yet. She rushed back to the kitchen moments later, a folded paper in her hand.

"Mavis?" she said, her voice croaking. Trembling, she handed the note to Mavis, who read it aloud slowly.

"I'm sorry, Cassie. I couldn't face you. You don't have to learn to love me.

L"

Her voice rang strangely in the silence of that room. She stared at Cassie. "He left because he didn't want to get married?"

Cassie wagged her head as she plopped into a chair. "All he had to do was say so. He didn't have to run away." Her face was filled with disbelief.

Ransom muttered something, but no one asked him to repeat it. It was probably what they were all thinking anyway.

Arnett propped his elbows on the table. "I expected better of that young man."

"Didn't we all." Mavis brought the coffeepot to the table and started filling cups. "I'll start breakfast."

Cassie stood. "I'll help."

"I'll go milk and finish the chores." Ransom stomped out the door.

"Me too. Get done quicker that way." Arnett pushed himself to his feet. "Sad day."

Mavis heaved a sigh. "Nothing is making any sense. Why would he just leave like this?"

"Because he didn't want to face Cassie. That's what he said." Gretchen clanged the stove lids. "He was so all fired up to marry Cassie. What changed his mind?"

Mavis stared out the kitchen window. Sun threw flashing splinters on the snow, so bright it hurt your eyes if you didn't look away. The storm of the day before had left over a foot of new snow and moved on, leaving a snow-washed sky of the deepest blue. This would have been a perfect day for a skiing or sledding party on the hill. A day to play and enjoy the spirit of Christmas. What was going through Lucas's mind, wherever he was?

They'd just finished breakfast when the barking dogs announced visitors. A sleigh stopped at the hitching rail.

Mavis met the Hudsons at the door. "Come in, come in. I'll put the coffeepot on again."

Mr. and Mrs. Hudson were not smiling.

"Is Lucas here?" Mr. Hudson asked. Actually, his tone was more of a demand.

"No. He left sometime during the night, and we have no idea where he is. Why?"

"Betsy is gone."

"Betsy is gone?" Mavis stepped back. "Come in where it is warm. What is happening?"

She took their coats and ushered them into the kitchen. "Cassie, refill the coffeepot, please. Gretchen, slice the julekake."

Mr. Hudson held out a note. "This is what we found on the kitchen table this morning."

Mavis took it and read it aloud for the rest of her family.

"Dear Ma and Pa,
  "Don't worry about me. We will be fine. I will write when I can.
                    "Love always,
                        your daughter"

"She took her horse, and two sets of tracks rode out of the yard. One rode in."

"Please be seated. Anywhere you like. *We.* Who does she mean by *we*?" Mavis studied both of her friends.

No one sat.

Mr. Hudson had in no way lost his scowl. "Well, if Lucas is gone too, I am assuming he is the other part of *we.*"

Mavis stared at the table "But Lucas was going to marry Cassie. I thought Betsy hated him now."

Did Mrs. Hudson soften a little? It seemed so. "It's Sarah who hated him, but she was only sticking up for her sister. Harry rode out to look for them, but he lost their tracks by the time he reached the main road."

"Have a seat. Please."

Ransom pulled out chairs for both of them. "So you think Lucas and Betsy ran off."

Mrs. Hudson settled into a chair, looking weary. Very weary.

Mr. Hudson sat down cautiously, as if not trusting anything Engstrom. "If he acts dishonorably with my daughter, I swear I'll shoot him myself."

"Now, Bert. You know better than that." Mavis set out plates and cups. "They were raised right, both of them. I saw them talking at the party the other night, but to my knowledge, they've not spoken since. Did Betsy seem any different? I mean yesterday, Christmas?"

Mrs. Hudson pulled a hankie from her reticule and blew her nose. "Not that I noticed, but she's been mighty quiet for months now, so that wasn't new. She didn't say anything to indicate she was planning on leaving. Nary a word."

"Did she say anything to her sister?"

The two exchanged glances, as if it had

not occurred to them. They shook their heads.

Mrs. Hudson tucked her handkerchief back into her reticule. "I didn't search her room. Just saw that the bed was made and her coat and some of her things were gone. But I didn't really look through the rest of her things. This just doesn't make sense." Her bottom lip quivered and she sniffed again. "What can we do?"

"I'll ride into town to see if anyone there knows anything." Ransom reached for his coat.

"That's where Harry is. He said he'd come find us here. Sarah stayed at home in case Betsy comes back. She is so upset."

Gretchen silently set out the julekake and poured the coffee.

Mrs. Hudson looked crushed. "If this had happened earlier . . . but Betsy has never been one to sneak around. When she saw Lucas escorting Miss Lockwood, she was heartbroken. Naturally. She had always dreamed of marrying Lucas. She said he was the only man she's ever cared for. So then we sent her to my sister's in the hopes that would help her get over this."

Mavis pressed her lips together. "So what can we do? Besides pray, that is?"

Mr. Hudson snarled, "You better pray I

don't kill him."

"Only if I don't get to him first." Ransom propped himself against the sink and crossed his arms. His face had gone granite.

Mavis shook her head. "I think we are overreacting. Maybe there is a simple explanation for this." *Please, Lord, let it be so.* If only she had gone over to see what they were talking about at the party. *Why would you do that, Mavis? You're not an eavesdropper. But why should Lucas get all the blame?* In her mind, it took two. Surely someone would have heard something if he had carried her off against her will. That was not even possible. She held up her hands. "All right, let's stop right now. There is nothing to be gained by threatening and making ourselves angrier." She stopped for a moment. "What if they took the train?"

"To where? Hill City or Rapid City?"

The dogs started barking again, and Gretchen craned her neck looking out the window. "I think it is Harry." She ran to the front room and flung the door open.

Mavis heard Harry's rough baritone. "Hi, Gretchen."

And her urgent "Come in. They're in there." She brought Harry into the kitchen.

He came in stomping across the floor, leaving clumps of snow from his boots. "No one has seen them in Argus. They did not catch the train and Sarah found this in her and Betsy's bedroom." He handed a note to his mother. "I think they went to Hill City, on horseback."

Mrs. Hudson unfolded the paper with trembling fingers and read:

"Don't worry about us, sis. Lucas and I will be married in Hill City. I don't know where we are going from there, but I will write when I can. I'm sorry it had to be this way.

"I love you all.
Betsy"

The paper rattled as she folded it again.

Mavis realized her mouth was hanging open and shut it. She sighed loudly and shook her head, covertly watching Cassie to see how she was doing. "Well, at least we know something."

"Guess we better let Reverend Brandenburg know there won't be a wedding here." Cassie raised her chin and straightened. "Anyone want more coffee?"

No one did. Eventually, the Hudsons broke the painful silence by rising and taking their leave. Harry followed them out. Mavis stood on the porch to see them off and then walked back to the warmth of the kitchen.

Cassie poured more coffee. Although no one said anything about wanting coffee, they all sat around the table sipping from their mugs, each lost in his or her own thoughts.

After her mind went round and round a few times, Mavis sighed and pulled herself back up onto her feet. "I don't know about the rest of you, but I am going skiing. If we saddle one of the horses to drag the toboggan back up the hill, we could all go play on the hill. That is what I had in mind to do today, and I think it's still a good idea. It will help us take our minds off our sorrow."

"Sorrow, my foot. I'd like to take him out to the barn and beat the stuffing out of him." Ransom's granite had not softened.

"And what good would that do besides give you a bloody hand?"

"Beat some sense into him? He obviously could use some."

"You think he will come back — ever?" Gretchen's voice wobbled like her chin. Tears trembled on her lashes. "He didn't have to leave like this."

Cassie reached over and wrapped an arm around the girl. "He'll come back. Once we know where they are, we will write to them and tell them we forgive them and we want them to come home. All Lucas had to do was tell me he changed his mind, and they could have gotten married just fine."

Ransom rumbled, "But he was chicken and ran off instead. Leave it to Lucas to make things hard for himself. And for us."

Mavis asked, "You aren't mad at him, Cassie?"

"I think my feelings are more hurt that he couldn't be honest and just talk with me about it. Remember, I was the one who was hesitating." She looked up at Mavis. "I prayed last night that if our marriage wasn't in God's plans for us, that He would close the door. Just like you told me to." She gave a little half laugh. "I guess that door just slammed."

Mavis half smiled as well. "Yes, I do remember, and I suppose if this is what it took, then . . . then . . ." She used the corner of her apron to wipe her eyes. "Then all is well here. God has made His will known, and Lucas and Betsy will have to learn their own lessons — the hard way." She gathered the plates and cups from the table. "Let's go enjoy this glorious day and be grateful God is indeed in control." She looked to Ransom. "All right?"

"If you say so." But his look said things were not all right at all, and she knew her eldest son well enough to know that he would not forgive his brother so easily. Especially since he had finally come to believe Lucas was sincere in his pursuit of Cassie.

The thought of Lucas being gone from the home and ranch made her feel like crying. Of course, she had known this could happen, but other than threatening to homestead in Montana, Lucas had never talked of living anywhere else. And having him and Cassie on the neighboring ranch had sounded so perfect to her. Why did not God agree to that perfection?

Now nothing would be the same. She forced herself to put a smile on her face and some spring into her step. She'd go skiing whether the others wanted to or not.

"What is a toboggan?" Cassie asked.

"A child who has never seen a toboggan! It's like a long sled with a curled-up front. We can ride three or four at a time, and life is easy if we have a horse to pull it back up the hill. New snow like this will make sliding down the hill really fun. You will come, won't you?"

"Of course." She looked to Ransom. "All of us?"

Arnett waved a hand. "You kids go enjoy

yourselves. I'll keep the home fires burning."

Ransom poked Arnett's arm. "Come on, Arnett. You can ride the horse if you're afraid to ride the toboggan."

"Who said I'm afraid? I just figured you wouldn't want an old man to slow you down."

"Sure wish you would quit calling yourself an old man," Ransom said. "Why, look at all the life and ideas you are bringing to the furniture business."

Arnett swallowed and nodded. "Thanks, Ransom. Your opinion means a lot to me. You've been like the son I dreamed of. My boy just never did take to ranching. Lit out the first chance he got." He lifted a shoulder. "Oh well. Spilled milk and all that. Let's go show Cassie how that toboggan works." And he lurched clumsily to his feet like an old man.

Preparing for the first run, Gretchen sat in front with her knees high, Cassie right behind her, and Ransom sat down behind her and tucked his legs in, gripping the rope to steer. "We're going straight down," he instructed, "so don't go leaning to either side or we could tip over."

"I get to ride the next one." Mavis laughed

at the girls, Gretchen so cheerful and lighthearted, Cassie's eyes as big as skillets. Mavis had left the skis on the porch, since they'd be taking turns on the toboggan.

"Give us a push."

"Hang on tight!" Push she did, and down the hill they swooped, powdery snow flying up on both sides.

She spotted Micah and Runs Like a Deer making their way toward the group. Mavis's heart gave a happy little leap.

Micah was smiling. "Looks like too much fun to just watch through the window."

When the toboggan slid to a stop beyond the bottom of the hill, Cassie let out a whoop that made Micah laugh. Arnett, riding Biscuit, tossed Ransom a rope and started up the hill, dragging the toboggan behind.

It didn't take long for Mavis to tell Micah and Runs Like a Deer about Lucas and Betsy. She watched Micah's face go from happy to still.

Runs Like a Deer frowned, puzzled. "They didn't tell anyone?"

"They each left a note. No one suspected."

Micah asked, "How's Cassie doing?"

"Says she is fine. She wasn't the one who wanted to get married, and she had prayed for God to close the doors if it wasn't right.

He did, and she seems to have accepted that."

Runs Like a Deer studied the snow in front of her thoughtfully. "I never thought of prayer that way. I mean, that God would handle things if you asked. I mean — not like that. I mean —" and she let it go there.

Snorting and puffing, Biscuit arrived with Arnett on top and the toboggan right behind.

Arnett grinned. "Your turn, Mavis."

"Me too." Gretchen took the front again, and her mother settled in behind her.

Othello yipped and danced around Cassie until she threw a handful of snow at him. When he tried to catch it, he had a mouthful of cold. The look on the dog's face made them all laugh. Then Cassie gave the toboggan and riders a shove and down they went, Gretchen shrieking in delight.

It took some doing to talk Micah and Runs Like a Deer into trying it, and Ransom again took up his place in back.

By the end of the day, Arnett was the only holdout. "I had my fun watching and bringing the toboggan back up. I'm thinking we could pull it with Mavis, Cassie, and Gretchen on it all the way back to the house." And they did.

Mavis and Ransom leaned the toboggan

against the wall of the house on the front porch, and she just stood and stared at it. Ivar had made that toboggan so many years earlier. He surely could not in the least bit have guessed how his family would turn out or who would be riding on that toboggan today. She snapped out of her reverie. "We can wax this like we do the skis," Mavis said. "I know your father used to do that."

Ransom snorted. "It didn't go fast enough for you?"

"I'll put the horse away." Arnett chuckled and rode back to the barn.

"Oh, it did. The snow was perfect." Mavis looked out over the valley. "So beautiful. I'm glad we did this or I'd have been down in the dumps all day."

"Don't let it get to you. We'll do fine without him." Ransom took his mother's arm. "Come on, I could eat a bear. That tobogganing was hard work."

"Uh-huh. All that steering wore you out." Gretchen shook her head. "Good thing if you are tired. Then I'll be able to beat you at checkers."

"Ah, probably not. I'll get the fireplace going. What are we going to eat?"

"Leftovers. We have enough to feed an army. Ham and cheese sandwiches sound real good to me."

"Fried in butter?" Gretchen grabbed Cassie's hand. "Come on. You and I can get it started."

Mavis looked out over the valley again. Snow made the scene whiter than white, crystalline, pure, and untouchable. Cold and distant and familiar. Somewhere in the far distance her son was taking a new and unmarked path. *Please, Lord, watch over my son.*

She turned and went back into the house, grateful to hear laughter from the kitchen. Lucas was so often the one to make them laugh. Tomorrow they'd ride into town and talk with Reverend Brandenburg. And God would live up to His promise to not leave her comfortless. She counted on that.

"Gretchen, how would you like to have a room of your own again?" She hung her things on the coatrack. Or maybe she should offer that room to Arnett?

18

"We can ride or take the sleigh," Mavis offered the next morning.

"I'd rather ride," Cassie said. "It feels like months since I've been on Wind Dancer."

"You don't have to go, you know. I could give him the message."

"On second thought, maybe we'd better take the sleigh. I need to get more shells at the store." Cassie tried a smile that didn't work. "Thanks anyway. I need to deal with this situation." When she thought about it, like this, she needed to grit her teeth. If Lucas had been honest, she wouldn't have to go explain to Reverend Brandenburg. When she really thought about it, her heart cried, *What did I do wrong? Am I not good enough? Is it something about me?*

"Can I go too?" Gretchen stood in the doorway.

Mavis said, "If you want and Cassie doesn't mind."

Cassie shrugged, her mind still on the heavy task she must do. The last thing she wanted to do was go tell Reverend Brandenburg that there would be no wedding. On the other hand, she reminded herself, it wasn't her fault. But with Lucas gone, the burden was left on her. Commanding herself to stay calm didn't really help. But at least it helped to look that way, even if inside she felt like exploding. Riding might have helped her calm down, but ten or more boxes of shells didn't fit in saddlebags or hang well in a bag looped over the horn.

"I'll stay home if you'd rather." Gretchen slumped just enough to let Cassie know how she felt.

Cassie felt like slapping herself. Gretchen was entirely too perceptive. "No, I would love to have you come along."

"You want me to beat up Lucas for you?"

That made Cassie smile, and then the picture of it made her laugh. "We could do it together perhaps."

"Well, then there would be three against one. If anyone gets to give Lucas a whack or two, count me in. I thought I raised him better than this." Mavis tucked a cloth around the things she had gathered together. "Let's go hitch up the team." With the men working over at the other place, as they'd taken to calling Arnett's barn, there had been no one there to hitch the team, and Cassie figured it was high time she learned. When she mentioned her thought, Mavis nodded.

"Good idea."

By the time they were on the road, the sun was well on its way to noon, with Cassie driving. The horses were more than willing to pick up a good trot, so the trip to town went faster than with a wagon, by far. And so much smoother. The world around the ranch looked so much different all dressed in white. Fence posts wore white top hats, their shadows dark against the glitter, exclamation points marking the fence lines.

"Do you miss school?" Cassie asked. She glanced at the girl beside her and caught her look of astonishment. "I thought you liked school."

"I do, but I hate missing out on the things happening on the ranch. I wish I could do both."

"When summer comes you'll be looking forward to school starting again because there is too much work in the summer." Mavis smiled at her daughter.

"Cassie said she would teach me some of her riding tricks this summer."

"That's up to Cassie. But I know you'll have fun. We need to talk a whole lot more about the guests coming to our ranch. You might be real busy if they have children along."

"Do you really think people are going to pay to stay with us? I mean we're not real fancy or anything. Just getting enough horses trained for riding is going to take a lot of time. We can't afford to buy well-broke ones. Will we have enough?"

"Good question, Gretchen. Right now we don't have enough to even take four riders out. We need to start making lists. I keep thinking about building another bunkhouse, like Arnett has mentioned before."

"You think Lucas and Betsy will come back to help?"

Mavis said quietly, "I sure don't know. I'd really like to know where they are and how they are."

Cassie had a good idea that while Mavis hadn't mentioned the two much, she was praying for them and thinking about them a lot more than she let on. Had this not happened, in just a few more days she would have become Mrs. Lucas Engstrom. Thoughts of thankfulness welled up and caught her by surprise. Sure she was mad at him, but in the long run, this was better.

For all of them. She'd ask Micah or Ransom to set up targets again and get back to work.

As they entered town, Cassie asked, "Do you want to stop at the store first?"

"Yes, let's. Then JD can be filling our order while we visit the Brandenburgs."

Once they'd entered the store and after the greeting, Cassie said, "I'm sorry I'm not able to pay off my debt yet."

"Not to worry," JD said. "You'll do other shooting matches and you'll be back to winning. I couldn't believe you even competed so soon after being shot in the arm. You are an amazing young woman. We have faith in you."

Cassie swallowed — hard. "Th-thank you. I know we'll be going to one in the spring. I'll need to do lots of practicing."

"I ordered extras just in case, and I can always get more." He turned to Mavis. "What do you need today?"

She handed him her list. "Have you heard anything about this idea of ranches opening their doors for guests during the summer?"

"Let's see. Someone was talking about that. Who was it? Oh, I know, Cal Haggard. He thought it a rather clever idea. Not surprised you were invited, what with Lucas working with Porter on the Wild West show and rodeo." He dropped his voice. "Sorry to hear about him leaving like that."

Mavis's mouth dropped open. "How did you know?"

"Oh, Hudson's been here. He's all hot under the collar about Lucas and Betsy. Wanted McDougal to arrest them, but the sheriff says they're grown-ups. Besides, where are they? Then Bert *really* got mad, thinks the sheriff should go find 'em. Don't worry none about it. He'll cool off."

Cassie wandered off to look at the fabrics and notions. What would it be like to sew a skirt or dress or something for Gretchen? She picked up a bolt, spread out a yard of it, and turned to the girl beside her. "A dress. What do you think?"

"We could do it together before I go back to school. But we were talking about making patchwork skirts the other day. I suppose this might be more practical." She fingered the fabric. "Mor was teaching me how to sew last summer and then we got busy. We never got back to it."

"What would you like?"

Gretchen shrugged. "My skirts are getting too short. I think I'd like a dark skirt like the one you have. Corduroy would be warm and heavy enough that I could ride without it blowing around. I'm outgrowing my dresses and pinafores."

"So what are you two thinking?" Mavis joined them in front of the fabrics.

"Mor, Cassie wants to sew something for me." Gretchen beamed.

Cassie watched the girl and almost felt like crying. Was this what it felt like to have a little sister? If so, she was all in favor of more feelings like this, and considering how she'd been feeling so let down by Lucas, this was wonderful. "I thought maybe that was something we could do before she goes back to school."

"Like the skirt Cassie has," Gretchen said.

"We could use that as a pattern and make it smaller for you. Although you are almost as tall as Cassie right now." Mavis turned to Cassie. "Are you sure you want to do this?"

"Yes. I wouldn't have suggested it if I didn't. I like sewing on your sewing machine, and I'd like to do more."

Mavis nodded. "Then let's choose the fabric. Serge would be good for winter. It has a nice tight weave, or corduroy. They have navy and brown, but not black, I think."

"The navy," Gretchen said, fingering the material. "It would look nice with the sweater you knit for me."

"That it would." They took the fabric up to the counter. "We'd like three yards of this, please, and add it to our account. I'm sure I have buttons at home."

"Or I could use one of Lucas's buttons."

"Is he still making those buttons out of antlers?" DJ asked, looking up from writing a list.

"He has a place back east that buys all he can make."

"Really? Hmm. You know, that might be a product we could sell at the Wild West show. Along with moccasins and some other things like that."

"Runs Like a Deer made some of us deerskin moccasins for Christmas. She does rabbit-skin vests and mittens too." Cassie could feel a bubble of excitement starting.

"And she is . . . ?"

"A friend of mine. She traveled here with us."

"Do you want to talk to her about making some things?" he asked. "I'm thinking maybe some people on the reservation would like to do this too. We need to start thinking about things now, to get enough ready for that big show."

"I'll talk to her. We'll let you know."

Mavis stepped back. "We'll be back on our way home. Thanks, DJ. Good thinking ahead like that. As Mr. Porter said, he hoped plenty of people in our area would profit from the show."

"Do you know anyone who does any woodcarving?"

"Arnett does some."

"Tell him to come talk with me. If you know anyone else . . ."

"We'll send them your way."

As they left the store, Gretchen asked, "Why didn't you mention the furniture Ransom is making?"

"I'm not sure. But I know he'll be right glad to hear about this conversation. I wish Chief were here. He'd know people on the reservation to contact. Didn't Mr. Porter say he'd talk to people there about being in the show?"

Cassie untied the team and climbed into the sleigh. This would be her first time backing them, but she and the horses did fine and stopped again in front of the Brandenburg house.

"Welcome, welcome." Mrs. Brandenburg stepped back and motioned them in. "You're just in time for dinner. Come along. We're both in the kitchen."

"We didn't come for dinner."

"But you are here, and we haven't eaten yet, so you will join us. I have a big pot of soup on the stove that will last forever if we don't have help. We sure missed you Christmas Day, but only the town folk who could walk managed to get to the church for the service."

Cassie inhaled the wonderful fragrances coming from the kitchen. Her stomach grumbled that breakfast had been a long time ago as she and Gretchen hung their things on the tree by the stairs.

"What smells so good?" Mavis asked.

"Oh, the soup, and I baked some apples. I also decided to make fruit soup today. I used up some of the bits and pieces left from other things. I found dried prunes at the store one day, and that makes such good compote. DJ had the large tapioca too. I bought plenty because he rarely has it. He brought some in for Christmas, I guess. If you want some, I will share." She took the basket Mavis handed her. "Just take your places at the table. I think my husband has probably added more plates."

"Merry Christmas, since we didn't get to say that on Christmas Day. That was some snowstorm, was it not?" Reverend Brandenburg set the silverware next to the plates. "What a treat this is."

They all sat and as soon as the food was dished up and grace said, he smiled at his guests. "I can't say that I am surprised to see you. I heard what happened." He turned to Cassie. "And you, my dear, are the wronged party here, and I will have none of your thinking it is your fault."

"But if I had not come —"

"Oh, Cassie, please don't feel that way." Gretchen leaned forward and laid her hand on Cassie's arm. "I have never had a sister before, and if you hadn't come, why . . . why that would be terrible. Lucas . . ." She shook her head. "I just hope Betsy is happy with him, because he sure doesn't live up to his word."

Cassie blew on her spoon of ham and bean soup. Mrs. Brandenburg passed around the platter of corn bread.

"I put cracklings in this. So I hope you like it."

There was another new word. "Cracklings?"

"That's the residue left when you render lard," Mavis explained. "I use them for all kinds of flavoring. The scalloped potatoes had cracklings in it. You know, what we had Christmas Day. Sometimes we eat them hot with salt on them. Crunchy and tasty." Mavis obviously knew all about cracklings.

"I saw you rendering the lard," Cassie said.

"I froze some of it, but it's half gone already, so one of these days I'll render some more."

"When you do, I'd like some, if you don't mind," Mrs. Brandenburg said. "I use them in baked beans too, and with string beans. Soak the dried beans with cracklings before you cook them together."

Cassie cut her square of corn bread and spread butter on it. Gretchen passed her the jelly dish.

"You'll like this too. Apple butter. I use the leftover apple peelings from making pie and cook 'em down in the oven."

Cassie nodded and took a bite. The flavor exploded on her tongue. "I have so much to learn."

"I think you are doing right well," Mavis said. "You try new things all the time. Your bread is getting lighter, and your pancakes are about as good as mine." She turned to the reverend. "Cassie is trying to spoil me by having the stove hot and the coffee ready by the time I get out to the kitchen."

Cassie half smiled. *Tell him. Get it over with.* "So you knew there would not be a wedding on Saturday?"

"I did. Word travels fast in this town, like any small town. And Lucas and Betsy running off like that was big news, set all kinds of jaws to flapping." He scraped the soup out of the bottom of his bowl. "I don't suppose you know where they went?"

"Not really. I'm thinking Hill City because he likes to work with Mr. Porter. But where they are living and what they are doing for clothes and a place to sleep, I don't know. I know Lucas didn't seem to have taken much with him. One change of clothes is all I noticed."

"Serve them right if —"

"Now, Gretchen, we won't have any such talk."

"There is that old saw: They made their bed and now they have to lie in it." Mrs. Brandenburg made a face. "Not a good one for right now, I suspect."

"Will you go look for them?" Reverend Brandenburg asked.

"No. I'm praying Lucas will come to his senses like the Prodigal Son and come home again. But we shall see."

Mrs. Brandenburg picked up the dishes and brought a large bowl of the stewed fruit to the table. "And to think you brought me cream. We can use it right away." She dished up a bowl for each of them and passed the cream pitcher.

Cassie smiled her thanks and wondered if she should pour on the cream first or try it without. She remembered her mother talking about this from her childhood in Nor-

286

way but had never made it. A round stick lay in her bowl. Was she supposed to eat it . . . ?

Mrs. Brandenburg chuckled. "You don't eat that, Cassie. That's a cinnamon stick and it's just for flavoring. We usually suck the pudding off the stick and lay it aside. I'm sure Mavis has some of that in her pantry too."

"I use it in making hot apple cider sometimes. Heat the canned or frozen apple juice with spices and maybe some honey in it. We didn't have any at Christmas this year. Usually we do."

Cassie picked up the stick and tentatively licked the shiny stuff off it. "That's really good." She finished sucking on the stick and laid it aside.

"The cream is really good on this."

Cassie picked up the pitcher and poured some on the edges. No sense in jumping in with both feet when a toe tip would work. Gretchen, who was sitting beside her, giggled.

"Cassie has tried lots of new things since she came to the ranch, like cleaning guts for sausage casings and baking bread and —"

"Cooking anything was new, and now that I've eaten the smoked sausages we made, cleaning the guts was worth the time and stink. I still have so much to learn, but I have good teachers."

"Remember, you can come here anytime, and we'll try some other things." Mrs. Brandenburg patted Cassie's arm. "I would love to share what I know."

"Just so it isn't knitting." Cassie shook her head. "I have not conquered the knitting needles. I have tried and tried, but I never end up with the same number of stitches in a row. I took the yarn out so many times, it shredded."

"But she sure is good at sewing, and the handkerchiefs she made had perfect hems and monograms. She made Gretchen and me aprons and a flannel vest for Runs Like a Deer. Now these two are going to sew a skirt for Gretchen for school. Maybe I won't have to sew all her clothes any longer."

Cassie had a hard time keeping from squirming in her chair. It wasn't like she had done a whole lot for Christmas, but knowing that it was appreciated felt mighty good. Maybe she really could contribute to part of the ranch work. But if she would win some prize money, she could do a whole lot more. The only way to make that happen was to practice a lot and get herself back in shape. That was one good thing about spending winter in the warmer climates of the south, as they had for years. Down there, without the ice and snow and mud in the corral, she could keep riding and working on new routines with Wind Dancer. They had a lot to do to be ready for the coming shooting matches and the show in July. Let alone with guests coming to stay at the ranch. Life was picking up speed.

Would she be able to keep up?

19

How could Lucas do something so selfish as running off with Betsy when he had pushed Cassie to the point of agreeing to marry him? The part that frustrated Ransom the most was that he'd finally thought his brother had grown up a little and knew in his heart that Cassie was the woman he had always dreamed of. He could hear Lucas saying those very words: *a woman I'd dreamed of.*

Well, the fool had made a commitment now and there would be no backing out. Maybe Ransom ought to ride into Hill City and see if Lucas was indeed there. But why? What could he do? Other than deck the brother who'd made him furious so often through the years. There would be no pile of wood that needed splitting there.

All the plans they had made. The furniture building, the mine — well, that was his dream, not Lucas's. But he wouldn't be here for spring calving or roundup or branding or any of the other work that needed doing. Good thing Micah was such a willing worker and that Arnett was enjoying being back to work and planning ahead.

Ransom felt like slamming his fist into a wall . . . or into a face. He was just as angry today as the day he'd discovered Lucas had run off. Maybe he should go talk with Hudson and the two of them could form a posse of sorts and go searching for Lucas. The cow shifted her feet and swished her tail.

"Sorry, Rosy, I'll be more careful." He stripped her until she was dry and shifted the milk pail out to the side. He could have gotten Gretchen up to milk, but right now, keeping really busy was helping him with his temper. Forking hay onto the sledge was another good thing. He patted the cow and hung the three-legged stool up on the post. Arnett said he would gladly milk too. Whoever would have dreamed that the old man would lose ten years off his age just because he now felt he was needed and could still do the work? Age certainly hadn't dimmed his mind. The workshop they were setting up in his barn was proof of that.

Cassie Lockwood did not deserve to be treated the way his brother had treated her.

291

But she didn't sulk or cry or do any of the other things he'd expected. She and Gretchen seemed to be having a great time sewing together. And Mor was glad Cassie hadn't moved out. He never thought he'd see the day that he'd be feeling sorry for her. Not that she seemed to need that, but Lucas was a member of the family, and their mother and father had instilled in them certain principles, not the least of which was Do unto others as you would have them do unto you. Sometime there would be repercussions from Lucas's behavior, and right now, Ransom would not mind being one of those dealing out repercussions.

He poured some milk into the flat pan for the barn cats and some in another bucket for Rosy's calf. After setting the calf bucket in the frame he'd built to hold it, he watched the calf drink the bucket dry, tail twitching like a metronome. Then he scooped up both buckets and headed for the house. Leaving the calf on the cow would have been easier, but they needed the milk too. There was enough cream now to churn butter, and the pigs and chickens always loved the leftovers.

In the house he set the bucket with the milk in the sink and took the other to the stove to dip hot water out of the reservoir to wash the milk bucket. "You want me to strain this?"

"No. I'll get it later." Mavis set the platter of fried eggs on the table. "Come and eat."

Ransom washed his hands and sat down in his place. The sight of the empty chair next to him made his teeth clench. Getting Hudson and going to look for Lucas was an idea that might appreciate a bit of nurturing. However, he knew what his mother's answer would be if he mentioned it, so he kept his mouth shut.

What kind of reason could he give for going to Hill City today? Or perhaps he should be like Lucas and just take off without telling anyone where he was going. The thought made his stomach tighten into a knot. How could he do something like that after all the times he'd railed against Lucas for just such a thing? He spread butter and jam on his biscuit and dipped it into the egg yolk, slightly runny, just the way he liked them. He glanced up to see that the others were all staring at him. Had he been asked a question and not heard it?

"Sorry. My mind is elsewhere. Did I do something wrong?"

"We didn't say grace yet." Gretchen turned her head slightly and gave him a raised-eyebrow look.

"Excuse me." He laid his biscuit down

and stopped chewing, eyes closed.

Gretchen closed her prayer with, "And make my brother pay better attention. Amen."

He gave her back look for look. "I said I was sorry."

"It's not like you to act like that."

Great, another reason to feel guilty. First thinking about finding his miserable, selfish brother, second not paying attention. Perhaps if he had paid attention, he would have realized Lucas was up to something. But that was going over old ground again. He'd spent too much time between going to bed and falling asleep, trying to recall some clue.

Cassie retrieved the coffeepot and went around the table refilling the cups. When she got to Ransom, he shook his head. "I've had enough, thanks." As she refilled Arnett's cup, Ransom asked, "Do you need help with your targets?"

"If you want to. I can set them up."

"I'm sure you can, but how about if Arnett and I get out there and dig them free of the snow? You want them at certain distances?" Why was she looking at him like that? As if she was surprised he offered? Usually Lucas helped, but since he wasn't here, someone else needed to.

"I thought you were going over to Arnett's."

"We are, but we'll take a few minutes to do this. Micah is going with us."

"You want me to fix you something to eat to take along?"

"If you want to make sandwiches, that would be great."

"I'll get those woodboxes filled before we go." Arnett propped his elbows on the table and cradled his coffee cup between his hands. "Sure is easier when the cattle feed off the stacks. Ya know, since I'm not feeding out my hay, we need to bring that over here or take the stock over there."

"The latter would be easier, but I'm not comfortable with them there and no one living in the house. Might be an invitation for problems."

Mor frowned. "But there's not been any rustling since that crew was thrown in jail."

"None that we know of. I haven't asked any of the other ranchers, have you? Or the sheriff?"

Arnett bobbed his head. "Nope. You're right. Let's take the sledge over then, and Micah can fork down a load while you and I work on the shop. I got an old barrel stove somewhere that we can put up to keep it warmer in there. And plenty of firewood."

He let out a sigh. "I sure was lookin' forward to those two young'uns moving into my house. Houses don't do well when they're left empty. Kinda like old people who die from bein' alone. We all need to feel useful."

Ransom looked at Cassie. Was she feeling bad too? If so, she didn't appear to. But then, she'd been a performer all her life. She could probably keep from showing her feelings. But when she raised her head and caught his glance, he could see the darkness of pain in her beautiful eyes. Had she fallen in love with Lucas after all? If so, that made this all the worse. The urge to pound Lucas made him clench his fists. He saw his mother looking at him and sure hoped she couldn't read his mind.

"Well, let's get those targets back in place. Gretchen, you want to ski up to the cabin and tell Micah we'll be ready in about an hour?"

"Sure. Cassie, you want to come with?"

"I'll work with the targets instead. Thanks." They all rose and set their plates and silver in the dishpan heating on the stove and then got into their outer things. Cassie helped clear the remainder of the table before getting into her coat.

The sun made it look warm out, but it

hadn't warmed up a whole lot. Ransom waded through the knee-deep snow and retrieved the stands they had built to hold the targets. The snow crust was strong enough to hold them up, so he set them just to the side of where they had been. He could hear Arnett hauling the wood. A crow flew overhead, scolding them in his scratchy voice. Gretchen buckled her skis over her boots and, using the poles, headed off across the field.

If it weren't for thinking about Lucas's actions this morning, setting him off, he'd be thinking this was about as close to perfect a day as one could have in the winter. The cattle were gathered around the haystack, snow from the last storm still riding the backs of the buffalo. The sky wore the intense blue that made the snow seem even whiter. He heard a horse whinny and saw Wind Dancer loping across the field to see who the skier was. Tossing his head, he trotted along with Gretchen, as if anyone was better than no one. The spinning windmill was refilling the stock tank, so the cattle had been up to drink. And glory be, the pipes hadn't frozen. Ever since they ran the pipe to the house and the hand pump in the sink, he'd taken time to wrap the pipes when the weather turned cold. Sometimes, though, if the cold got very bad, even that was not enough, and the pipes would burst.

"That's great, thanks," Cassie called. "I'll put the targets on them."

"Tell Arnett I'm down hitching up the sledge." He watched her turn and go back in the house. She wasn't really anything like he'd thought she was in the beginning. Much as he hated to admit it, he'd misjudged her. The thought made him pick up his pace. Admiration was not something he'd ever expected to feel for Miss Cassie Lockwood.

He'd harnessed the team by the time Micah joined him in the barn. "Thanks for coming."

Micah nodded, still not one to waste words. Together they hitched the team to the sledge and drove toward the house, where Gretchen was just taking off her skis.

"It's so bright my eyes hurt. I should have worn a cap with a brim."

"Yep, you shoulda." Arnett stopped beside her. "You make sure you get more wood if your mother needs more. Don't let her do that."

Gretchen grinned at him. "Yes, sir."

Yes, Ransom thought, *Arnett is part of the family for sure. Sounds just like a father.*

With the bells still on the horse harnesses,

they set off for the other place. Between the singing sleigh bells and the beauty of the day, it was rather difficult to stay hotly angry at Lucas. But Ransom would try.

"When do you want to bring the steam engine down?" Arnett asked, leaning against the rack part of the hay wagon.

"I thought as soon as we get the shop in order. We're going to need to go to town soon and see if those piston rings you ordered are in."

"He said a week or two. I'm thinkin' we could use a drill press too. Go a lot faster than a brace and bit. Between the tools that run on the donkey engine and what hand tools we have, we can do most anything."

Ransom was feeling better and better about this business of making furniture. Arnett was a fine partner, as opposed to brothers who went kiting off unannounced, leaving you to do everything. "Let's bring home any that are rusty, and we can work on those in the evening. Sharpen blades too. I made a couple of drawings but didn't bring them. I need to go through that pile in our barn again. If Far saw that pile, he'd have a fit." His father. It seemed so long ago, yet he remembered every detail about the man.

Arnett nodded sagely. "He always kept his tools and things in perfect order."

"Micah, you ever do any carving?"

From the back came "Some. Simple things. I'm making a chair now."

The horses were slowing, so Ransom flicked the lines as a reminder. The sleigh bells resumed their usual jingling. "You know you are always welcome to use the tools we have. Did Chief do any carving?"

"Not that I know."

Curious. When they turned into the lane to Arnett's, they saw that a sleigh had been there, pulled by one horse. There were no tracks showing it had come back out.

"Hmm." Arnett looked ahead. "Who could that be?"

"You told people you are living at our place now?"

"Nope. Figured the less that knew it, the less chance there'd be a break-in. Places left vacant can be targets."

A steaming horse harnessed to a four-seat sleigh waited at the hitching post. Tracks led to the front door. Ransom turned the sledge before stopping. "Stay here, Micah." He dropped to the ground. Both Ransom and Arnett headed for the house.

Arnett opened the door. "Who's here?"

"Why, there you are! We came out to check on you, and imagine our surprise when no one was here, and it didn't look like anyone had been for some time." Cal Haggard came hustling out from the kitchen.

His Lucretia loomed in the kitchen doorway behind him. "We were so worried about you, Arnett, I insisted we come to check and make sure you weren't lying on the floor somewhere."

"Also why we came over, I was thinking to talk with you about the guest ranch letter. Thought maybe you got one too. Ransom, good to see you." Cal reached out to shake their hands. " 'Bout scared us out of our wits when there was no indication you'd been outside, and when your dog didn't bark. What have you gone and done?"

"Ah, Mavis and her crew invited me to come stay in their bunkhouse so I'm not here alone all the time. So that's what happened. You want I should start a fire and —"

Ransom interrupted. "Cal, Lucretia, why don't you go on over to our house and talk with Mor. I know she'd love to see you. We're working on setting up some machinery here and getting a load of hay."

"What'd you do? Move all your livestock over there too?"

"Yep. Better for all of us."

Cal nodded and turned to his wife. "Now

you can just quit worryin' about Arnett here. We'll go on over. I take it you got a letter too?"

"We did, and Mor can fill you in on all our decisions." Ransom was rather surprised how cold the inside of this house had become. And for some reason he felt he wanted to leave it. Why would that be? He half grew up there, since the Arnetts and Engstroms were such good friends. "We'll get that load of hay and go straight back. I know Mor is going to insist you stay for dinner, and we do too."

"I hate to keep you from your work."

"Getting the hay is the most of it. Everything else can wait."

"See you over there, then." The couple walked ahead of them out to the sleigh.

Arnett reached high over the door and pulled down a key. "Might's well lock this, it seems." He drew the front door shut and twisted the long key. "So much for workin' here."

He was wagging his head as he walked back toward the sledge. "Never thought someone would come to check up on me. Guess it musta given them a fright, all right. That'd be something, to walk in and find somebody froze solid in their bed."

Ransom grunted. "Yeah, well that's what

302

we wanted to make sure didn't happen to you. Let's load the hay."

With three able hands, loading went fast. Ransom explained to Micah that Cal and Lucretia Haggard owned a fairly large spread in the next valley over. If Micah was going to be living here, he ought to know everyone. They drove back into the Engstrom yard with their load, and Micah volunteered to take it down to the barn and put the team away.

Ransom handed Micah the lines. "You come back up to the house for dinner then, get to know the Haggards, and we'll plan on going back out there to work tomorrow."

Arnett suggested, "Why don't I go through that stack of lumber in the barn? Sort it out to see what we can use?"

"We'll do that after they leave. I want you to hear about the plans for the guest ranches, since you'll be part of our plan for here."

"If you want." But Arnett sure didn't sound real enthusiastic about sitting around the table with the Haggards. Why would that be?

Arnett and Ransom walked on around the house to go in the back door. They could hear laughter as they were brushing the snow off their boots.

"Sounds like ol' Cal is in high entertainment mode," Arnett said with a grin.

"Well, I know Mor is glad to know we weren't the only ones concerned about you being alone over there all winter."

Arnett sobered. "He offered to buy me out after Hazel died — sort of insisted on it even, but I said I wasn't selling."

Ransom looked at him. "And yet you were set on giving us your place for free."

Arnett shrugged. "He's got enough land already. Besides, I like our arrangement far better." And he led the way inside.

"So how many do you think you can host?" Mavis asked after they'd finished eating and were enjoying another cup of coffee.

"Well, like you we got a bunkhouse and a spare bedroom," Cal replied. "A family could stay in the bunkhouse and a couple or a single in the bedroom. You say ten letters went out?"

Ransom explained, as if Lucas had not disappeared, and his anger boiled up all over again. "Lucas is working with Mr. Porter, and that's what he told us. Kind of like a trial run to see if something like this has any chance of success. If people really like it, they'll tell their friends, and next year could be even bigger."

Lucretia didn't look very convinced. "Have you ever heard of anything like this?"

"I guess some folks down in Texas and Oklahoma have tried it."

"With what kind of success?"

Ransom shared more of her reluctance than he would like to admit. "We don't know. But with Porter taking care of the advertising, how can we go wrong?" He leaned forward. "As we see it, it isn't like we'd have a huge outlay in expenses. I don't know about you, but we could always use some extra cash money."

"It would be a lot of work what with all the ranch chores going on. It would be like cooking for a threshing or haying crew." Mrs. Haggard puffed out her cheeks. "Me and the girls have been talking about that part. I mean, what if the guests are real snobby and don't like what we offer?"

Mavis shrugged. "I guess that would be their loss. They could always leave and go back to Hill City to the hotel."

"So you think someone will really pay money to come work on a ranch?" Cal leaned back in his chair. "I can't find enough good hands when I offer to pay them."

"Promise to take 'em fishing on your lake. That'll go over big."

"Sure, if they catch something. Can't tie the fish up to make sure they catch 'em."

Ransom almost laughed at the forlorn look on Cal's face. "Come on, you don't have to do it, you know. It was an invitation, not an order."

"True. You know anyone else that got an invitation? About the guest ranch business, I mean. A letter?"

"Nope." Ransom sat back. "Lucas did agree that if enough ranches say they don't want to try it, it wouldn't be worth the advertising. Porter's whole plan is to get folks here for the rodeo and Wild West show, to fill up his hotel and put Hill City on the map as a place for Easterners to come visit. You got to admit we live in real pretty country. Not that I know what it's like back east, but . . ." *Cassie knows whether it's pretty back east. Her show performed there.* Now, why did that pop into his head?

"Well, we'll give it a try. Same as you." He pushed his chair back. "Come on, Lucretia, we best be heading home. Oh, Arnett, we brought you a basket of things. Guess we should bring it in."

With multiple rounds of good-byes, the Haggards climbed into their sleigh and it glided out the lane.

As soon as they left, Ransom and Arnett

306

went down to the barn with Micah. They lit a couple of lanterns and hung them overhead. Together they sorted through the jumbled stack of lumber and trash and odd things, cleaning off metal pieces and stacking any wood that might be usable. Down at the bottom, Ransom found his old farrier's nippers. "Will you look at this! Been searching for these nippers for years. Wonder how it got thrown in here."

Arnett snorted. "How'd anything get thrown in here? Quite a mess."

Gretchen came in to feed the chickens and gather the eggs. She leaned over the pen wall and called to the calf. "We need to give him a name. Poor baby, all alone in here." He sniffed her hand and then backed away. "I know. I don't have anything to feed you. You gotta wait until we milk. Is he eating grain yet?"

"I mix some rolled oats into the milk once in a while." Ransom looked up from the pile of stuff. "Bring those wood carriers down, and we can use some of this for kindling." He stepped back and looked around. The usable lumber lay in an orderly stack. Small tools, including the nippers, were placed on a nearby shelf. The trash to be discarded waited in a pile by the door. "Well, this sure looks better. Thanks Arnett, Micah."

Micah smiled. "You're welcome. I'll clean that cow's stall and the pen here before I go back up to the cabin. Gretchen, did Cassie do any shooting today?"

"Yes, and she plans to again tomorrow if the weather holds. She sure goes through the shells. Maybe you could load some for her, Ransom."

"I can do that." Arnett set the bow saw blade he'd been working on up on the shelf. "Tell her I'll bring my mold and press back with me tomorrow. And my lead. Might as well put them to use. All I got is black powder, though."

Ransom removed his leather gloves and slapped the dust off them against his thigh. It was amazing how much they could accomplish with three sets of willing hands. Maybe he wouldn't be missing Lucas so much after all. But then, Lucas almost always wangled out of tedious jobs like this. He was rarely willing to take part in work unless it was for hunting. Still, Ransom would like to talk with Hudson, see what he had to say. It might be interesting.

20

"This was supposed to be my wedding day." Cassie stared at the ceiling she could just barely see, thanks to the moon reflecting off the snow outside her frost-painted window. Talking to the darkness like this probably wasn't a big help, but somehow saying the words aloud made them so. Today she was supposed to have become Mrs. Lucas Engstrom. Most people would think she'd be heartbroken. Perhaps if she'd really loved him, like she'd wanted to love the man she would marry, she'd be feeling differently.

So what was she feeling? She let her mind sort through the question. What were some words that might apply? *Anger?* No. *Hurt?* No. *Sad?* Not really. *Relieved?* That was it. What she really felt was relief. Relief that she didn't have to leave this place she'd begun to think of as home and go live in the other house with a man she liked well enough but didn't love. Besides, now she'd have more time to get ready to be married someday to a man she really loved.

She closed her eyes to think about that. Had she met the man yet? A picture of Ransom setting the targets for her the morning before floated into her mind. Her eyes flew open and she shook her head. There was absolutely no chance of that happening. He didn't even like her. But every once in a while he would do something really nice, like setting the targets. Or making her the lovely little table. And a matching one for Lucas. That thought almost made her laugh. Those two tables would not be living in the same house, that was for certain. She looked across the room to the corner where it sat, waiting for Ransom to have time to finish it.

It was far too early to be getting up, but she didn't feel like sleeping anymore. And if she lit a lamp, no matter how quiet she was, Othello out on the front porch would hear her and bark at least once, thus waking either Ransom or Mavis or both. If they saw the light coming from her window, they would come check on her. Mavis had said that when she couldn't sleep, she used that time to pray.

Now, that was an interesting thought. What did she need to pray for? Or probably more important, whom did she need to pray for? God's Word said to praise Him, to come into His presence with thanksgiving and enter His courts with praise. She could thank Him *for* things, but she didn't have enough Bible verses memorized to think on without her Bible open.

Hmm. So I thank you for your Word, for sending Jesus to die for my sins, for raising Him from the dead, for giving me a home here, a place to belong. Thank you for my new family, for Mavis, Ransom, Gretchen, and Arnett. And thank you that I am not marrying Lucas. What would it take to thank God for Lucas and Betsy? She pondered that. Shrugging, she just did it. *Thank you for Lucas and all he has done for me. And for Betsy, and, Lord, I ask that you bless them and heal the hurts that their leaving has caused.*

Where did that come from? But it fit.

More pondering. She had read that the Holy Spirit would pray for us when we didn't know what or how to pray. Was that what just happened? A giggle started down in her middle, and she clamped her hands over her mouth to stifle it. Was she really praising God like He said? What else could she be thankful for? The warm and comfortable bed, the beautiful moon on the snow, the frost on her window, Othello, Wind

Dancer, and George, Micah, and Runs Like a Deer.

And dear Lord, take care of Chief. If you could only bring him back here . . .

Was it good or wise to pray something like that?

Her eyes grew heavy and she caught a yawn. *Thank you for sleep and . . .*

The next thing she knew, the fragrance of frying bacon tickled her nose. "Oh no!" She threw back the covers and dressed as fast as she could pull her clothes on. All the petticoats of winter and the wool stockings and vest were not cooperating, but she finally bundled her hair into a snood and tied on her apron as she strode down the hall.

"I'm sorry. I slept right through . . ."

Mavis and Gretchen smiled at her, Gretchen setting the table and Mavis checking the biscuits in the oven. "We figured you needed some extra sleep after all the folderol around here."

Gretchen handed her a cup. "Go pour yourself some coffee and let us wait on you for a change."

"But, I . . ."

Mavis pointed to a chair. "Sit. The men will be in any minute."

"Can't I do something?"

312

"Sure, you can drink your coffee and enjoy every sip."

Gretchen rolled her eyes. "You know better than to argue with Mor. You never win."

"Then I'm washing the dishes."

"We'll see."

One thing Cassie had learned in this family: *We'll see* quite often meant *No, but I don't want to dash your hopes right away.*

What else about this family? She pondered as she ate. For one thing, she realized she was an odd person here. Most of the time the men, seated around the table at breakfast now, did outside work. And here were the women, who did the inside work. Only very occasionally did they switch roles. But Cassie worked inside and outside both, although she was a bare beginner at women's work. This was the kind of home she wanted to make someday, glued together with love and respect, and with everyone gathered at the table before scattering to their duties.

By the time they'd all finished the bacon, eggs, biscuits, fried potatoes, and applesauce, Cassie had gathered the plates and set them in the dishpan on the reservoir. She returned to the table with the coffeepot and refilled cups.

"I'd sure like some of that julekake if there

is any left," Ransom said.

"Sorry, it's gone," Mavis answered, "but we do have a few doughnuts left. We can warm those up."

"They'll warm up dunked in the coffee."

Gretchen returned from the pantry with a round tin and passed it around.

Ransom grabbed two doughnuts. "We're going back over to the other place again. Micah should be here any time to go over with us. Okay?"

"Of course. Between churning butter and baking bread —"

"And hemming my skirt."

"And target practice."

"We've got plenty to do."

"The elk were down in the pasture. Do you want me to go hunting? I could probably take it in to the hotel." Ransom looked at Cassie. "Unless you and Mor want to go out."

Mavis nodded, obviously in her thinking mode. "When do you want to go to Hill City?"

Ransom heaved a sigh. "What you mean is, do I want to take the chance on seeing Lucas?"

"I guess that is what I do mean. But that cook pays good money for an elk carcass, and I know Runs Like a Deer would like the hide. We have plenty of meat here for us — for now at least."

Ransom slapped his palms on the table and pushed back his chair. "Don't need to decide that right now. Come on, Arnett, the dogs are barking."

Cassie knew he meant that Micah was near. Othello's bark had already told her that. He had a special bark for Micah and other friends, while only Cassie got the wiggle yip. Dogs know far more than people give them credit for.

Cassie mixed and kneaded the bread dough — she was getting pretty good at bread — while Gretchen and Mavis swapped off plunging the wooden churn dasher up and down. Finally the three of them paused for a coffee-and-cookie break before washing the butter in cold water. Once all the liquid was washed away and the thickest buttermilk set in the pantry, the wash water went into the bucket for the pigs. Nothing was wasted. Mavis kept slapping the butter with a wooden paddle until all the liquid had left, then salted it until it was just right and patted it into the two wooden butter molds with a carved flower in the bottom.

"One to sell to the store, the other to keep, although we'll have plenty of butter in the weeks ahead."

Cassie was accustomed to yellow butter. Buttercup yellow. "How come it is so pale?"

"You watch, come spring when the grass is growing again, we'll have golden butter. The egg yolks will be a darker gold too when the chickens can be out on the grass."

"Really?"

Mavis nodded with a smile. "Wait until you've been here a full year and gone through all the seasons. Each is so different."

"And this summer with guests here, it'll be even more different." Gretchen looked up from hemming her skirt. "I wonder if we'll have a family with children."

"I guess we could make a request for that if we want."

Cassie was just shrugging into her coat, her gun bag beside her, when Othello gave an unusually enthusiastic friend bark. She frowned. "Runs Like a Deer must have decided to come down for a visit." But it didn't sound like Othello's Runs-Like-a-Deer bark.

She pulled open the front door, saw who was petting Othello, and was stunned yet again.

Chief.

She meant to laugh with joy, she really

did, but instead came a sob and tears of joy. She leapt down the step and threw her arms around the man who looked like he'd aged ten years. She clung to him. "You came home!" He was home. He was here.

He hugged her in return and stepped back. "If I am still welcome."

Her wits were more or less returning, and it was high time. *Chief.* She took a deep shuddering breath. "You are always welcome. Where have you been? Did you go back to the reservation? Are you all right?" *Stop, Cassie!* She took his arm and led him inside. "Please come in. I'll take care of your horse, then."

Gretchen stood in the kitchen doorway, and Mavis came hustling over as Cassie closed the front door. "John Birdwing, you are indeed a welcome sight! I've thought of you so often, but we never knew if the letter we sent got to you. Come in, come in! How long since you've eaten? You are planning to stay, aren't you? Oh, we have such news for you."

Cassie was finally getting back some composure. *Chief.* She took his elk-hide jacket and hung it on the coat-tree. "How long did it take you to get here?"

"Three days."

"Out there? Where did you sleep?"

He smiled. "Under pine trees. Made a fire. Glad it didn't snow again."

Mavis waved a hand. "Please come into the kitchen. It's warmest there. A cup of coffee?"

"Please."

He took the chair Cassie led him to and smiled at her as he sat down. "You look good. Your arm good again?"

"It's still some weak but I'm working on it. Oh, how I've wondered about you." She wanted to ask how it had been on the reservation, but knowing how reticent he could be, she didn't.

"Were they glad to see you when you got there?" Gretchen asked instead.

Chief took a swallow of his coffee while Mavis sliced bread and, after buttering both sides, laid the pieces in a skillet to brown.

She asked, "Can I heat you some soup now or . . . ?"

"I will wait. This will be enough. The stock looked good out there."

So he was ignoring Gretchen's question. That did not bode well. And he was here. When Cassie thought about it, that did not bode well either. What went wrong at his old home that he would travel through snow for three days to come back here? She grinned. "Plenty of hay, and George is just

318

as testy as ever. I haven't had much chance to ride Wind Dancer, though."

"Micah, Runs Like a Deer, they're all right?"

Cassie had so much to tell him, and she wanted to do it all at once. "Oh yes, we'll have to tell you all about that. The men are over at Arnett's now, setting up a furniture-making shop in his barn. Micah is in on it too."

"And the mine?"

Mavis sat down across from him. "It's pretty much on hold for now. We have some real interesting news. You knew about the Wild West show and rodeo they're planning for this summer in Hill City?"

He nodded and inhaled the fragrance of the toasted bread Mavis served him. "Sure smells good."

Mavis seemed as eager as Cassie to fill the man in on everything all at once. She was talking faster than usual. "Well, Mr. Porter has added another idea. He is calling it guest ranches and sent out a letter asking if some ranches want to host people from the East who come for the show but might like to see what ranch life is like."

He chewed and nodded at the same time, noncommittal.

"He also said he would go talk to the

319

Indians on the reservation and see if some of them wanted to come to the show. Did he write you a letter?"

Chief shrugged. "I never heard."

"Hmm." Mavis frowned. "It probably went to the head of the reservation, I expect. Would that be a chief, or an Indian agent, or what? Anyway, Mr. Porter is wanting Indians to perform in the show."

Cassie went back outside and put Chief's horse up in a stall well bedded with straw and amply supplied with hay and a big scoop of oats. "Don't worry." She gave him a parting pat. "We'll fatten you up. Soon your ribs won't show like this." She hung his saddle on the rail by the front door, checked on the calf, and returned to the house.

When she brushed off her boots and stepped inside, they were sitting around the table talking and eating cookies. As expected, the women did most of the talking, and Chief did lots of nodding.

When dinnertime came, Mavis dragged the kettle of soup to the front of the stove, set out a bowl of applesauce, and made more coffee. They kept on talking as they ate their soup and still didn't get nearly all of it said. Cassie watched Mavis awhile just to make certain. Yes, Mavis was just as glad as she was to have Chief back in her kitchen.

"I need to go practice," Cassie said when they finished eating. "Do you want to help me?"

Chief nodded.

Mavis stood and gathered up dishes. "John, you are welcome to stay in the bunkhouse if you'd like. There's plenty of room. At least you'll have a bed that way and not have to sleep on the floor." Mavis gestured with the coffeepot again, but he shook his head.

He stood also. "I'll talk with Runs Like a Deer and see. Used to a pallet on the floor."

"Better than in a snowbank." Cassie picked up her satchel and headed outside.

She did a round through all the targets and was pleased with her success. It was coming back; she was shooting like the old Cassie. Gretchen came out to watch, so Cassie enlisted Chief and Gretchen to take turns throwing wood chips up in the air. Gretchen's chip sailed high in a lazy arc. With her shot, it instantly exploded in two directions. Chief's chip arced far higher, nearly overhead, and a little twinge darted through her arm as she closed on it and fired. Direct hit.

The next "bird," Gretchen's, was a hit, but when she closed on Chief's, a stab ran up her arm. Another. Another. She was still hitting them, but now her arm quivered whether she was taking aim or not. Her arm felt tired, an ugly sort of tired. This was discouraging. When she missed two in a row, she called a halt. Her arm was visibly vibrating.

She let her shotgun hang at her side. "Thank you. You make great birds flying. I need to do plenty of raising and lowering the shotgun. That wasn't very good at all, but it is getting better, I guess. I'm glad there will be no matches until spring."

"Not very good?" Gretchen practically shouted. "You got all but those last two and one other!"

" 'Good' is when I get them all. Thank you both again."

In a tone of half joking, half not, Gretchen said, "You expect too much from yourself, Cassie," and went back to the house.

Chief held the bag as she put her guns away. "You been working with Wind Dancer?" he asked.

"Not since we've had snow."

"You have what? Three months after it melts out?"

"To get ready?" She nodded. "I know, but maybe we'll have some time in March and

April too." Getting them both back in shape was going to take a lot of work, she knew that, and Chief's curt reminder only made her worried. "I'll just have to do the best I can. If we can't manage the trickier things, they won't be in the act."

What would her father do if he were in this situation? Enough snow lay about to make any show maneuver dangerous. Even when the winter weather let up, from what she understood, the melting snow would turn the ground to slippery muck, and there was no way they could do sharp turns and quick stops in a muddy corral. Maybe out on the open pasture with good grass cover, but then . . . No wonder the Wild West Show had gone south for the winter.

"You did better than you thought." Chief gave her a half smile and began the walk up to Runs Like a Deer and Micah's cabin.

She called after him, "Come down for supper, will you please? And bring them along." She walked up to the house, wandered back to her bedroom, and put her guns away. Maybe they'd better just forget about high shooting. Her arm had felt perfectly fine until this.

What next? Make sure the kitchen was ready for supper preparations. She was entering the kitchen doorway when Othello barked again, this time his warning bark. Not a stranger, but not family or friend. Cassie opened the front door and stepped out on the porch, and when she saw who it was, called Gretchen.

"I brought mail," Jenna called, sliding off her horse. She cast a wary eye toward Othello and then came up the steps. "Pa went to town, and these came in on the train."

Gretchen popped out the door beside Cassie. "Jenna! Can you stay?" she asked eagerly.

Mavis stepped into the doorway drying her hands on a kitchen towel.

"Not today, but if the weather holds, we were wondering about maybe sledding down your hill after church Sunday." Jenna handed the envelopes to Gretchen.

"That would be good fun," Mavis said, her smile as wide as the girls'. "Tell your ma to bring everyone. Do you have a cow milking now?"

"No. She just stands there eating hay and being wide. This wide." She spread her arms. "Pa says she'll likely drop twins."

"Good, then you all won't have to be back for milking. Let's have supper here."

Mavis was always up for a party, Cassie thought.

"Ma will want to know what to bring."

"Let's just potluck it. Tell her I'll be making a roast." Mavis rubbed her hands together. "Oh good! We've not done this for far too long. I haven't seen your mother for months, except in church. Now I wish we had poured a skating rink in the corral. Wait here a minute." She disappeared back in the house.

Gretchen urged, "Bring your skis too. And we have the toboggan."

Cassie hoped Mavis would return soon. She was getting chilled standing out here.

Jenna giggled with Gretchen. "See you at church," she said and walked back out to her horse.

Mavis came hustling out at a fast walk, a canvas bag in each hand. She gave one of them to Jenna. "Some cookies to take back with you. Don't eat them all on the way, hear?"

Jenna giggled again. "Would I do that? Thank you, Mrs. Engstrom." She hung the bag on her saddle, turned her horse aside, and headed out the lane toward the gate.

Cassie heard her call cheerfully, "Hi, Mr. Chief! Glad to see you back."

Here came Chief walking down the hill from the cabin. Cassie saw him wave to Jenna, but she could not hear if he responded. Cassie puffed out a frosty breath.

"Well, that sure is a change in plans. But it will be so nice to see the Hendersons." Mavis looked at the letters. "One from Jesse and one from Mr. Porter. I'll read them to everybody tonight."

Cassie was really getting cold now, but she waited on the porch with Gretchen and Mavis as Chief came through the gate and walked over to them. He waved a hand in the general direction of the barn. "Go get my horse. Stay up at the cabin tonight. Thank you for the dinner."

"Take these with you." Mavis handed him the other bag of cookies. "Micah likes cookies too, and there is no oven up there."

Chief bobbed his head once, a nod, and walked off to the barn.

Cassie led the way inside. Behind her, Gretchen said, "Mor, I thought you'd give both bags to Jenna."

"I intended to, but then I saw Chief coming down the hill."

Gretchen settled into a kitchen chair. "I wish he would talk more. I want to know what it was like for him on the reservation. He hasn't said anything about where he went or what he's been doing."

Cassie parked herself in front of the stove. "I prayed sometime during the night or very early morning that he would be all right and that he would come back. I was hoping if he ever came back, it would perhaps be a visit during the rodeo and show."

She stepped aside, for Mavis was bringing a big iron frying pan to the stove.

Mavis stopped and looked at her. "There is a verse I dearly love where God says, 'Before they call, I will answer.' "

Cassie stared at Mavis. "Are you sure?"

"Of course she is sure. Mor knows everything about the Bible." Gretchen stood up and headed for the doorway. "I want to wear my skirt tomorrow. I didn't think how far around that skirt is."

Cassie smiled. "All that's left is the hem. I'll help. You'll wear it."

"Maybe I should wear my hair up too."

"I don't think so. You are not a young woman yet." Mavis tapped her daughter on the nose. "Besides, if you are a young lady, you might not want to go tobogganing."

"That doesn't work, Mor. Cassie is a young woman, and she likes the toboggan too." Gretchen ducked away from her mother's playful swat and went to fetch her skirt.

"I'll make the bread loaves while you two sew the hem. I think I'll fry some pieces for an afternoon treat." Mavis paused and stared out the window. "I'm glad he's back

327

where we can take care of him. He doesn't look to be in the best health."

Cassie closed her eyes. *Please, Lord, let Chief live here with all of us a long time. And if you want to give me a way to get him talking more, I'd sure be tickled.* In her next thought, she chided herself: *He already answered one of your prayers today. What do you want to be — greedy?*

21

Cassie stared at the calendar. The New Year really had come in with a roaring wind and another foot of snow. Gretchen was supposed to go back to school today, but there was no getting through those drifts. The short, familiar path between the barn and the house had been obscured by swirling, blowing snow, and had those ropes not been strung between house, barn, and bunkhouse, the men could easily have become disoriented and wandered out into the blizzard. But thanks to the ropes, Ransom and Arnett could make sure the cattle were fed, the cow was milked, and the barn animals were cared for, and return in safety to the house.

She thought back to Sunday, when the Hendersons came over to dinner and the afternoon of fun on the hill. She'd even learned to make real turns while on skis, though she fell the first few times. By the time they finished, even the horse Arnett rode looked plumb tuckered out from dragging the toboggan back up the hill. Mavis had set apple juice to heat with some spices to warm everyone up again before the guests waved good-bye from their sleigh.

So far Cassie had won two rounds of the latest checker tournament, but when she played Ransom for the third time, something about him distracted her.

He won by a king.

What had it been? Was it the twinkle she saw in his eyes? Ransom's eyes didn't twinkle much. Or had she just not been paying enough attention? Whatever it was, she lost the tournament and wasn't doing much better on figuring it out.

One of the pleasures of winter, she had learned after Christmas, was Mavis reading aloud every evening with them all gathered in the big room. Cassie was darning wool stockings, Arnett was carving something he wasn't really showing, and Gretchen was knitting herself a pair of stockings with fine yarn they had dyed a gentle yellow using onion skins. Ransom alternated between ranch bookwork and drawing furniture plans.

While Cassie had read *The Adventures of Tom Sawyer* before, she enjoyed it even more this time.

"Read some more," Gretchen pleaded when her mother put the bookmark in place.

"But what if the storm stops and you have to go to school tomorrow?"

"So I'll have a hard time getting up."

Mavis glanced around the room to see the others nodding. "All right. One more chapter."

Being read to like this made Cassie remember some of the times her mother had read to a group of children during school time or she and her father had read in the evenings. Being read to always equaled love in her mind. She wove the darning needle in and out, picking up knitting stitches when she could so the darn would be less obvious, laughing with the others at Tom's antics. Twice when she glanced at Ransom to see if the twinkle had remained, she caught him looking at her. It wasn't a critical sort of looking, or a curious looking, or a vacant staring-into-space looking, and certainly was not ogling. Just looking. Was that a smile when the corner of his mouth lifted oh so slightly?

That he had caught her looking at him made her face and neck feel as if she were sitting right next to the fireplace. *Pay attention to what you are doing,* she ordered herself when she had to loosen a couple of stitches she had pulled too tight.

Gretchen stretched and yawned when her mother closed the book, making Cassie yawn too. The yawn traveled around the room and left them all almost laughing. Almost a twinkle from Ransom's eye too.

What would it take to make him really smile, she wondered, or indeed, laugh out loud? She had never ever heard a genuine, deep-down belly laugh from him.

Ransom closed his ledger and stood, stretched, and wandered over to the window. Swirling blackness out there. Cassie could see it as well as he. He opened the door for a better look, only to let a blast of powdery snow swirl right into the room. He slammed the door shut. Both Benny and Othello raised their heads, looked at him, and settled back down, eyes closed.

Ransom started toward his room. "Guess they don't want to go out in that either. Good thing Chief chose to stay up at the cabin. He'd never have made it back down tonight."

"Good thing that rope goes to the bunk-house too." Arnett brushed the curls and chips from his carving into a basket kept for tinder.

"You could sleep in here if you want," Mavis offered. "It's warmer."

"Naw, my dog is waiting out there. I banked the stove real good, so I only need to throw more wood in when I get out there. Mavis, thank you always for such a perfect evening, good food, good company, and entertainment too." He looked to Cassie. "You shoulda won that, ya know. G'night, all." And he disappeared into the kitchen.

Later, Cassie found herself chuckling again as she slipped her cloth-wrapped hot rock under the covers to warm the bed. That Arnett. A tap on her door caught her attention.

"Come in."

Mavis stuck her head around the door. "How are you holding up with shells?"

"They are about half gone. Why?"

"I've been thinking if this breaks, we might go into town tomorrow. I know Ransom wants to get back to the woodshop. Do you want to go?"

"All right. Yes."

But while the wind had dropped by morning, clouds were still hanging low, hinting at more snow to come. Ransom and Arnett decided to work on repairing two old chairs they'd found in the pile in the barn, mending some harness pieces if they were not too dry to be mended, and sanding rust off the replacement discs they'd discovered so they could be sharpened. Repairing machinery was always a winter chore, one Ransom had neglected this year in favor of shoring up the mine.

As they left for the barn after breakfast, Ransom cautioned, "I'd rather you didn't head to town today, Mor. Looks iffy out there."

"I agree. I wish I had kept Gretchen home." But the sledge had come for her and off they had gone.

"If it gets bad, you know they'll keep the kids in town."

"I know, but . . ." Mavis heaved a sigh. "Maybe I have cabin fever."

"You?"

"I know. I have plenty to do but . . ."

Ransom shut the door. "What is it?" His voice hardened. "Lucas?"

Mavis paused. "Possibly." She thought some more. "Probably. I guess I thought maybe there would be a letter from him."

"Lucas won't write. He's too afraid I'll come and find him. If we ever get an elk, I'll see if he is in Hill City."

Mavis straightened her shoulders. "I'll be fine. Come on, Cassie, let's make cinnamon rolls."

Ransom nodded. "See you for dinner."

Mavis and Ransom had read the clouds well. The storm came roaring back soon after the men returned to the barn. The windows rattled and the kitchen darkened. Cassie decided she didn't want to think about the mournful howling and frigid drafts. She'd think about other things.

"I've been thinking," Cassie announced after they slid the pans of cinnamon rolls into the oven. "Would you like to help me write a bunch of letters? Well, write the first one and then I'll just copy it as soon as I get addresses."

"For shooting matches?"

Cassie nodded. "I need to get started on this."

"Sure. Be glad to." They sat down at the table with a tablet and pencil. "We'll write the body of the letter and leave the address and salutation to be added later."

"Right. It won't look funny, do you think?"

"Not if we do it right."

Cassie tapped her chin with the end of the pencil and started writing.

Greetings.
My name is Cassie Lockwood, and I am the daughter of Adam Lockwood. You might have heard that he passed

away five years ago and I stayed with the Wild West Show of Lockwood and Talbot that is no longer around.

"Change that to *in business,*" Mavis suggested.

"Good." *In business. I am looking for shooting matches to shoot in.*

"How about *to participate in?*"

Cassie made the change. *If you know of any, I would like to . . .*

She looked up to see Mavis squinting hard to think better.

"I know." Cassie jotted quickly, *I would appreciate your assistance in ways to contact them.*

She nodded. "All right. Add our address — *The Engstrom Ranch, Argus, South Dakota* — and then you'll sign them when you have contact information."

Cassie read the letter again. They made one other change, and Mavis went to put more wood in the fireplace and bring good paper and pens back to the kitchen. "Got to get the rolls out."

She pulled the two pans from the oven and immediately tipped each over onto the racks and then lifted the baking pans off. The cinnamon fragrance wafted around the kitchen, and steam rose from the rolls.

"Does anything in the whole world smell better than that?" Cassie inhaled with a blissful sigh.

"*Mm,* lilacs in the spring?" Mavis shook her head. "Maybe not. I expect Ransom will say he could smell them clear to the barn and show up anytime to make sure."

"The way it is storming out there?"

"Maybe not. But either he has a better sense of smell than most dogs, or he has a sixth sense time-wise as to when rolls should be ready." She pulled the coffeepot to the hotter part of the stove. "We can write while that heats."

They each copied one letter and wiped off the pen nibs.

"It's hard to believe it is only three o'clock, dark as it's gotten." Mavis set a plate with rolls on the table and poured them each a cup of coffee. She poured two more mugs as well and set them on the rack above the stove.

"They won't let the kids come home in this, will they?"

"No. Some people in town will take them in. One of these years when the telephone lines come clear out here to Argus, we'll be able to keep in touch. Doesn't that sound amazing?" She turned at the sound of stomping feet on the back porch. "What did

I tell you?"

Arnett came in first, crystalline snow frosting the scarf that covered his face and tied his hat down. "You'll have to sweep us off."

Mavis fetched the broom and had started on him when Ransom entered, the full milk pail over his arm.

He set it in the sink. "I'm next. The milk is already cold." He sniffed. "I knew it."

Mavis swept him off too. "I told Cassie you'd be here, and she didn't believe me." Hearing a bark at the door, she let both dogs in. "Where's your dog, Arnett?"

"Inside the bunkhouse. He didn't figure it was worth going out today. I stopped there and restoked the fire."

The men took their coffee and rolls in to sit by the fireplace, and Cassie and Mavis returned to copying letters.

"Seems a waste to be lighting the lamps in the middle of the afternoon, but . . ." They both paused to listen to the wind tear at the eaves. "Sounds almost like a hungry beast, doesn't it?"

"On a day like this, there's only one thing to do. I think I'll bake some gingerbread." Mavis got out the ingredients and the utensils. "Put some more wood in that stove, would you, please? I need to get that oven hotter."

Cassie did as asked and then went ahead and strained the milk, setting flat pans in the pantry for the cream to rise. She shut the door on the pantry and tucked the rolled rug against the bottom of the door to keep the draft out of the kitchen. "Do you mind if I make cocoa? A cup of that sounds so comfortable."

"Make plenty. You won't be the only one who wants some."

Cassie measured cocoa and sugar into a pan and added enough water to make liquid, then added milk, stirring as she did. She slid the pan away from the hottest part of the stove and went to the big room. "Do either of you want cocoa and possibly another cinnamon roll?"

"Is it snowing outside?" Ransom asked.

Cassie frowned, rather confused. "Well, yes."

Arnett cackled. "He's teasing you, missy. What he means is, 'Why, yes of course, thank you.' And me too."

Cassie glanced at Ransom, who gave a slight shrug, his face impassive. He nodded. "Thank you."

What was happening with her? When he looked directly at her, her heart tripped or something. "I-I'll bring in a plate of rolls."

"You could bring your cocoa in here too

and help us enjoy the fire." Arnett's invitation made her smile.

"Thank you." She stopped at the window on her way back. It was black as night out there but the sun was not down yet, and the wind still clawed at the roof. It seemed strange for Gretchen not to be galloping in about now and the dogs barking their greeting. Instead, both dogs lay curled up on the rugs in front of the fireplace. She turned to the men. "They should be all right up there, shouldn't they? At the cabin?"

Ransom gave a slight nod. "They have plenty of wood and water. Although they could melt snow for water if they needed to. The cattle and horses will be crowding together in the lee of the barn or by the haystack. This is not a terrible storm, just lasting longer than usual. You needn't worry about any of them."

Easier said than done. He might be used to being shut up in the house, but this was all new to her. Her winters had never included a raging beast trying to rip its way into the house and devour the occupants. And when it was cold enough to cool the bucket of milk between the barn and house, it was some cold. If it was this bad from inside the house, what was it like outside for Wind Dancer? George and his kind were well prepared, but her horse had never experienced such weather.

"Do you think Wind Dancer is all right?"

"He's been feeding at the haystack with the rest of the horses and cattle. The buffalo come up sometimes, but I guess they like digging for frozen grass better than sharing."

Cassie nodded. "Thank you. I was hoping to ride him one of these days."

"Once this blows over, we'll have good weather again. That's South Dakota for you."

Cassie went to see if the cocoa was hot enough. Mavis was just sliding the pan of gingerbread into the oven. "There now. That will taste mighty good after supper." She turned to Cassie. "You're worrying about something?"

Cassie felt her shoulders and upper back twitch and her face take on a frown. "I'm not sure it's worry so much, but —"

"But if that wind would stop screaming and shrieking, you'd feel a whole lot better?"

Cassie thought a moment. "How did you know? I didn't."

"Oh, my dear, I've lived here a long time. Others have felt that way too. I read a letter one time from a woman who was homesteading out on the prairie, and she talked about the wind driving people insane. That some actually ran out of their houses and died because they couldn't stand it any longer."

Cassie turned to see that Ransom had come into the kitchen.

He nodded. "I've heard that same thing about wolves howling and prowling around the sod houses and shanties. Life out on the prairie is hard. We have it much easier here." He inhaled the mingled fragrances. "Mor, your kitchen always smells so good. Think I'll have another cinnamon roll if it is long until supper."

"Is fifteen or twenty minutes long?"

"Well, I better have one just in case."

"Just in case?" She cocked an eyebrow.

"Why, just in case the house blows away."

Mavis laughed, and sure enough, there was that twinkle back in his eyes. Matching his mother's.

So that's where he got it, Cassie thought, fighting a grin herself. Is he different since Lucas left, or am I just paying more attention? "I'll fix you one," she told him. "Do you want it heated?"

Sure enough there was a twinkle in his eye.

22

Cassie jerked upright in the middle of the night. What had she heard? She listened hard, not breathing. Nothing. That's what she heard. Nothing. The wind had stopped. She flopped back on her pillows, almost giggling in relief. She drifted back to sleep, feeling the smile her mouth insisted upon.

Surely the storm was no more, because after breakfast and chores, the men all rode out through the new snow to Arnett's place. They would not have done that if there were any chance of more snow pending.

That afternoon when Gretchen came home from school she brought not only stories of the storm but also mail. Mavis smiled at the envelope from her son Jesse. Cassie stared at the two envelopes addressed to her. One was from Tyrone Fuller, the man who'd won the Hill City shoot, and the other was from Mr. Porter.

"So open them." Gretchen returned from

hanging up her things. "Oh, it feels so good to be home."

"Where did you stay?" Mavis asked, slitting an envelope with a table knife and handing it to Cassie.

"With the Brandenburgs. Both me and Jenna. We had the best time, but it was scary, even just walking to their house, the snow and wind was so bad. But our teacher told us all where we would be going and let us out a bit early. Before it turned pitch black. Did you ever see anything like that, Mor? So dark, I mean?"

"I agree, it was bad."

Cassie opened the letter from Mr. Porter first. After a quick skim through, she went back to the beginning and read it aloud.

"Dear Miss Lockwood,

"I'm sure by now you've received your invitation to the shooting match in St. Louis. My wife and I plan to attend, and we hope you would like to travel with us. You could join us on the eastbound train in Argus on February 22. We will provide your ticket and look forward to getting to know you better as we travel the rails. I know trains are not new to you, but we are looking forward to seeing new country.

"Sincerely,
Mr. and Mrs. Josiah Porter"

"That's not far off." Gretchen stared at her in wide-eyed wonder.

So true! Cassie slit open the second. "The shoot is in St. Louis on February 25, and it lasts two days." *Can I be ready by then?* The question knifed her, making her hands shake. Before, her shooting depended on her arm healing. Now her practicing depended both on her arm and on the weather. At least she had shot that morning. Not for long, though, because the cold had seeped right into her hands to the very core, making them stiff in spite of the gloves.

"But you'll go?" Gretchen's brows furrowed.

Cassie nodded. "I guess I better answer them both." She fetched the good paper from Ransom's desk, along with ink and pen. What would it be like to sit at that desk and write her letters? She almost smiled at the thought, how mature and dignified she would be, sitting there and writing.

Once upon a time she'd had no doubts about her shooting ability. Her father pointed her toward the targets, and she took them out. Now she couldn't help wonder what if she wasn't good enough anymore? Mr. Porter would be throwing his money away on her again, as would JD at the store.

"All you can do is your best." The voice of her father came as if he were standing right behind her. If she thought about it, she could feel the warmth of his hand on her shoulder. She nodded, blew out a breath, and headed back to the kitchen. But what if her best wasn't good enough?

"You look worried. About the shoot? We'll be praying for you, Cassie." Mavis turned from the stove. "God says we can do all things through Him, who strengthens us."

"Then I sure hope He makes my arm strong again too. Do you think winning a shooting contest is important to Him?"

"Good question. But somewhere in Psalms, I think, there's a verse that says something along the line that whatever concerns us, concerns Him. I'll have to find that again. That's not it exactly. But He can use your shooting for His glory too. I'm not sure how, but He'll find a way."

Gretchen prompted, "Mor, read the letter from Jesse."

"I will, after supper."

"Since they are all over to Arnett's, I suppose I better go milk." Gretchen peered out the kitchen window. "Sun's down behind the hill. 'Course it was nearly there when I got home." She did not look at all excited by the prospect.

If Mavis noticed, she made no sign. "Take this bucket of scraps for the chickens. Oh, and check to make sure the stock tank didn't freeze over again. I know Ransom took an ax to it this morning."

With a dramatically heavy sigh, Gretchen did as her mother said, even to throwing a look of despair over her shoulder.

"I should learn to milk," Cassie suggested.

"In due time. You're learning new things every day." Mavis fetched a slab of beef from the pantry.

Cassie frowned. "I thought we were having chicken and dumplings tonight."

"We are. I'm cutting this beef up into three or four smaller pieces so that it cooks through better," Mavis explained. "It's the brisket, a pretty tough piece, so it will need extra cooking. I'll let it simmer through the evening, and by tomorrow it should be nice and tender, ready to serve."

Mavis was right, of course. Cassie just learned something else. When you have a tough piece of meat, cook it longer.

One thing Cassie now knew how to do was peel potatoes and scrape carrots. She busied herself preparing the vegetables for supper. Finally Gretchen returned. There seemed to be less milk in the pail than when Ransom milked.

Someone was knocking at the front door. Gretchen hustled out to answer. She called, "Come in! Mor! Chief's here and Runs Like a Deer." Gretchen herded them all into the kitchen.

Runs Like a Deer untied her headscarf and scrunched it together in her hands. "Micah and I thank you for the cookies."

"You're certainly welcome. Please sit! Have some gingerbread. I'm afraid it's from yesterday, but I just put another pan to the oven. We'll have fresh gingerbread soon." Mavis set the plate in the middle of the table and settled down on a chair across from their guests. Leaning forward, her smile was as warm as a summer sun. "Now first, I am so glad to see you. Second, what can we do for you?"

Chief sat for a moment, apparently thinking what to say. "First, make sure I'm welcome. If not, please say and no hard feelings."

"John. Cassie and I and the boys too have been praying that you were safe and that you would come back. We want you to consider this your home. You mean so much to Cassie and to us — you have ever since the beginning."

He considered this a moment and nodded. "Thank you. That's that one. Next, Micah says why don't we use that slab siding up there to build a lean-to onto the cabin. Rock up a second chimney against the first. Depending on weather, we could have it done in a couple months. They have cabin, and I live in lean-to."

Mavis was beaming, just beaming. And Cassie was sure she must be too. Chief was making plans to stay — just what she'd asked God for.

Cassie sat down beside Runs Like a Deer. "Chief, are you sure you're going to be all right? You seem so tired."

The corners of his mouth moved up a bit in an almost smile. "I'm good, Cassie. I'm good."

He didn't look good, but Cassie was not going to say that and contradict her old friend. His cheeks were pinched in, and he appeared almost gaunt, and his hair was thinner.

"No." Mavis was saying no to Chief? "You are welcome here under any circumstance, John. We've made that clear, but I want you to know you are being cruel."

His mouth dropped open. "Cruel?"

"You are loved. You know that. Love also

means *caring about.* You are not well. You know it. We all can see it. And yet you are keeping secrets from the people who care about you most. That is cruel."

He stared at her for long, long moments. His voice then was quiet, nearly a whisper. "Loved." He nodded, paused again. "When I went back, I sought my son. He was gone, no one knew where. The elders, the old people, nearly all dead. No one knew me anymore. No one wanted me to be there, to eat their food. I got sick; no one cared. They said, 'Go somewhere else.' What they meant was, 'Go off and die. We can't feed you.' "

"That's terrible!" Mavis looked aghast.

He shrugged. "That is how it is on reservation. If you are no use, you leave and go die. So I left. Come here. Still sick but not as much. Summer will be good." Suddenly he pointed at Cassie's arm. "Getting better?"

So that was all he would say. It was enough. Cassie said, "You saw when you were throwing birds for me. It still gets tired and trembly real fast, especially when I'm shooting high. I need a lot of practice to strengthen it, but with this weather it's hard to get the time in."

His head bobbed in a sort-of nod. Thoughtfully he stood up and went over to

pick up the broom in the corner. He carefully eyed the hanging lamp over the table
and moved well away, near the front room
door. He held the broom as if it were a rifle,
with the handle end to his shoulder and the
broom-straw end out to where the muzzle
would be.

He swung his makeshift rifle up and said,
"Bang." He lowered the "muzzle" to the
ground, mimicked seeing the next bird high
overhead to his left, and swung the broom
up. "Bang." He grasped a handful of the
broom straw. "Put this heavy end out from
you, more like a gun barrel, practice swinging anytime." He almost smiled again. "Use
less shells that way."

Cassie laughed out loud. "Of course. What
a great idea."

But now boots were stomping on the
porch. The furniture makers had returned.

Mavis hopped to her feet. "Oh good! Here
are the boys. You two will stay for supper, I
hope. Chicken and dumplings, and we
turned out fresh bread this morning." As
the men entered, she grinned. "Very good!
Here's Micah too. Ransom, would you bring
in more wood, please?"

So this was what a real home felt like. Cassie felt a sudden wash of joy. Friends and
family gathered at the table, everyone . . .

No, not quite everyone. She wondered about Lucas. Were he and Betsy doing all right? And how painful this must be for Mavis with her son absent from the family table. Being a family in a real home was far more complex than Cassie had ever imagined.

After supper, when everyone gathered around the fireplace for dessert and coffee, Mavis opened the letter from Jesse. Cassie knew this was her youngest son, and he was in college, hoping to one day become a doctor. That was all she knew. She had never seen a photograph. If Ransom, Lucas, and Gretchen had become like her own brothers and sister, this was Cassie's other brother. What an odd thought.

The young man did write a nice letter and, as Cassie saw over Mavis's shoulder, in a small, neat hand. He was sorry he wouldn't be able to help with guests next summer. He thought it was a fine idea, but he was going to school right on through the summer. He was not happy with Lucas but happy for the union of the two ranches — he wrote fondly of his time spent as a boy at Hudsons' and Arnetts' — and the furniture endeavors. He mentioned how good their father was at furniture building. He sounded just like the kind of man Mavis would have raised.

As soon as their guests-that-were-family left, Cassie hurried to her room with the broom to try Chief's stratagem. She swung the "muzzle" high. Bang. Lowered it to the ground and then swung it high in another direction.

Over the next weeks, Cassie practiced in her room and out on the porch. When she very nearly broke a window on the porch, she went back to practicing in her room. Her arm still got overly tired, still began to tremble after a while, but the while stretched out longer and longer each day.

Chief set up targets for her, made suggestions, and sometimes just sat on the corral rail watching as she worked. He hammered three eight-penny nails halfway into a corral post, and she drove them home with three shots. It began to feel more and more like old times when Adam Lockwood had introduced his daughter to the audience and she'd drawn gasps and murmurs and oohs and aahs with her sharpshooting.

How she wished she could take Micah along to handle her guns. Then it would really be like old times. But she couldn't possibly ask Mr. Porter to buy Micah's ticket also, and she could not afford to bring him along with her own money. She did not have money; she owed money. She *must* win this shoot!

February 22 arrived long before Cassie felt she was truly ready. She packed what she needed in a carpetbag borrowed from Mavis, wrapped her guns, and nestled them in their bag. She was ready. Ransom bundled her and Mavis into the sleigh and drove off to the train station. Mavis and Cassie spent quite a bit of that travel time praying.

It was snowing lightly when Ransom tied their horse up behind the station. He offered his mother a hand, then Cassie. Even through their gloves she felt a jolt go up her arm. Rolling her lips together to stop the sensation, she sucked in a deep breath of icy air. What was going on? Unable to look him in the face lest he read her confusion, she muttered a thank-you as he lifted out her guns and carpetbag. When she reached for them, he shook his head, ignoring her confusion. Carrying her bags, he led the way to the platform.

"It's all right," Mavis whispered in her ear then tucked her arm through Cassie's. Together they followed the man with the rigid back and the purposeful stride.

When Cassie walked out onto the long

wooden platform, it felt like home. Many were the trains that had carried the show south and north again. She saw the engine's puffs of smoke far beyond the trees, gray smoke against gray sky. Since the track curved away between the houses and through the surrounding woods, she could not see or hear the train. It wouldn't be there for ten minutes yet, at least.

Ransom suddenly took her hand. "You'll need this for meals and such." He pressed a roll of something into her hand. A roll of what? She was afraid to look. It was money!

"Oh no! I can't, really." She stared from her hand into his face.

His jaw was set, the way it squared when he was arguing with Lucas. And always won. "You will. Really."

"Please, Cassie," Mavis added.

What could she say? "Thank you." She slipped it into her reticule.

Of course, Ransom would be taciturn, but now not even Mavis had anything to say, it would seem. They stood about, waiting. Cassie shifted from one foot to the other. She tried breathing around the lump in her throat, and when she wet her lips, the cold reminded her of the folly of that.

The engine appeared from beyond the curve, huffing out extra steam as it slowed down approaching the station. It glistened black in the gentle snowfall. Cassie had forgotten how noisy an engine was and how massive. It thundered and loomed, monstrous, past the platform, rattled and screeched to a halt. A blast of steam roared out from under the wheels. Its bell clanged and a conductor in a black uniform swung down to the platform and placed an iron stepping stool in front of the door on the third car.

Josiah Porter came bouncing off the train with a lively step, beaming broadly and obviously delighted to see them. He swept off his top hat and executed a slight bow. "What a pleasure it is to see you all."

Mavis looked just as happy. "Hello, Josiah! Have a safe journey. We'll be praying for you all, that's for sure."

"Thank you, thank you. Here you are, Cassie." Mr. Porter handed her a ticket.

"Thank you, Mr. Porter."

Curious. In all her years of traveling on trains, she had never once seen a railway ticket. Always either her father or Jason Talbot took care of travel arrangements. She simply boarded the train with the rest of the troupe.

"Call me Josiah, please. We're business colleagues here. Oh, and Ransom, Mavis,

Lucas asked me to tell you both hello."

Mavis gasped. "You know where Lucas is?"

"Why yes. He and Betsy work for me at the hotel. He does some handyman repairs now and then but mostly goes out hunting. He's very good at providing elk for the restaurant. Brought in a bear recently too. Henri fumed at first until he tasted it with turnips and cauliflower in a mornay sauce. You have to special-order that dish. And Betsy works the front desk. She's very good at welcoming people and keeping records straight. My former desk clerk couldn't seem to do that consistently. I tell you, Mavis, it's hard to get good help nowadays. Lovely girl, Betsy Engstrom."

Betsy Engstrom. Not Cassie Engstrom. Cassie tried to digest that; her mind would not cooperate. Did she feel sad? She shut her mind on that, something to ponder later.

Mavis wrapped her in a warm hug. "Blessings, dear Cassie." She stepped back.

"Blessings on you, Mavis." The urge to flee back to the sleigh and the safety of the ranch nearly undid her.

Until Ransom pulled off a glove and extended his hand for a shake. "Shoot well."

Shake hands with a woman? That was not done. Cautiously she accepted his hand. It was warm and firm. "Thank you. Blessings on you too."

She reached down to pick up her bags, but Josiah scooped them up. She heard Ransom say, "Take good care of her, Josiah."

Allowing the conductor to assist her, she started to ask where to go but heard instead Josiah's instructions.

"About the middle, on the left." He followed her to the car.

Then she took the extra-long step that carried her from Dakota's good, solid earth onto the train that would bring her, eventually, to the city of St. Louis.

There sat Abigail Porter. She smiled brightly and scooted over to give Cassie room. A little potbelly stove at one end of the car was supposed to be keeping the car fairly warm, but the leather seat crackled with cold as she slid into it. "Cassie, I have not been to St. Louis for ages. This is going to be great fun!"

Josiah gave Cassie's carpetbag an extra little shove into the overhead rack and settled himself across from her. She so wanted to ask about Lucas and Betsy, wanted to know everything about them since they'd eloped, but she kept her questions to herself. As the train pulled out of the station, she ordered herself to stop her woolgathering and attend to her hosts. After all, traveling like this was nothing new, and she had plenty to look forward to. Now if only she could convince her middle.

The Porters picked the subjects of conversation — well, usually Josiah did — often as questions, and she responded. But she longed to know how Lucas and Betsy were really doing and if Lucas harbored any regrets.

Abigail asked, "Have you been to St. Louis before?"

Cassie smiled. "Yes and no. Yes, the show played there several times. No, I only saw the street between the railway station and the field where we set up. That was all. I never actually saw the city."

"Ah!" Josiah looked pleased. "Then I believe you will enjoy walking along the riverfront. A great deal of interesting barge traffic goes up and down out of St. Louis. You can stand on the very spot where Lewis and Clark stood more than a hundred years ago. Amazing how far this country has come since then, the West especially."

During the rest of the long journey, Cassie learned a great deal about politics and the opening of the American West that she really had never thought about, nor did she care to. But Josiah's political monologues filled the hours, and she could listen with half an ear while she enjoyed watching the lovely scenery pass. So many farms. Homes. Each of them was home to someone, just as the ranch was home to the Engstroms. Would that ever truly be Cassie's home?

She did, however, learn some useful things as well, particularly about the business end of shooting matches. One thing, for instance, was that she would have to place at least third in the contest in order to meet expenses.

When they finally reached St. Louis after two long days on the train, she was given another nice surprise. Josiah and his wife took a room at the hotel and provided Cassie with a room of her own. She had never had a room of her own in a hotel before, and she thanked Josiah profusely. It would feel wonderful to sleep in a bed tonight. It had been all but impossible to get comfortable on the train seat last night. Of course, now if she failed to win the shoot, she would owe him more money than ever. She put that thought aside and simply enjoyed for the moment the lovely room and feeling grand.

That night, as she was returning from the bathroom, she saw the housekeeper's closet standing open, with a broom right by the door. Feeling only a little twinge of guilt, she borrowed the broom and practiced in her room for several hours. Swing up, bang, lower the gun to the floor, swing up, bang, point to the floor, swing up, bang . . . She put the broom back and practiced the same movement for a while with her unloaded shotgun, which was much heavier than the broom. Her arm was still not what it once was, but she was pretty certain that it would hold up for the shoot. The boost of confidence that flowed through her felt welcome indeed. *Thank you, Lord,* seemed the only possible response.

The first morning of the meet, they ate a hearty breakfast in the hotel dining room. Josiah sure had a lot to say about how the quality of this meal compared with what his Henri prepared. As they were leaving, Cassie glanced toward the tall, well-draped windows. Wait; that man with the graying beard, sitting at breakfast by the window — he certainly looked like Jason Talbot. She sucked in a calming breath. No, it couldn't be. This fellow was heavier, older, more worn-out looking than she remembered Jason to be. Then Josiah was ushering her out the door into a hansom. They were on their way to the match.

When the actual moment of the shoot arrived, she expected butterflies to be fighting to get out of her clenched stomach. They did not. Why was she not more nervous as she stepped forward to be introduced, the only young woman in the meet? She ought to be terrified. This was a shoot of national ranking with experienced participants from all over, like she used to participate in, not just a local contest in Hill City. She would take her sense of calm as an effect of Mavis's prayer. For surely Mavis was praying this very minute.

Beaming like a new father, Mr. Porter served as her assistant and only made two minor mistakes. How he loved being near the center of attention, if not in it. Ty Fuller and George Sands, who had placed one and two in that shoot of Josiah's, survived the first day, as did Cassie. Nine fellows dropped out, already too far back to place.

The second day of the shoot dawned cloudy and windy, but not windy enough to affect shooting. Cassie did not see the Jason Talbot look-alike in the dining room. She noted that Josiah ate heartily in spite of his opinion that this cuisine was not the equal of Henri's.

As typical of a two-day shoot, the audience today was much larger than yesterday's, and noisier too. Cassie felt herself blooming under their attention, just as she used to. Her father had always said their job as entertainers was to give the audience a good show. She breathed in a calming breath and let herself respond to their clapping and cheering for every good shot.

Many of the contestants remaining were effectively eliminated in the first round. Cassie was still standing, with a perfect score. Tyrone Fuller and George Sands, also with perfect scores, stood beside her. Ty Fuller was the person who had written to tell her of this contest. He turned and beamed at her, as if he were responsible for her being there.

Well, he was. As they prepared for round two, she stepped over to him. "Mr. Fuller, thank you for letting me know about this shoot. We deeply appreciate it."

He nodded enthusiastically. "It's my pleasure. You're a joy to shoot against; you always do your best, and you're very, very good, but you're never nasty. You'd be surprised how many of these fellows have a mean streak. You're a fine challenger but a real lady. We need more women in the sport. You remind me of Annie Oakley."

"That's very nice of you. Thank you." She didn't have time to mention Annie Oakley had always been her hero.

All but five fell away by the end of the second round. Cassie, Mr. Fuller, and Mr. Sands were three of those five. So far she had not missed, including the overhead shooting.

This was it. These people would rank first, second, third, fourth, and fifth. Only the first three would walk away with prize money.

She didn't miss any of the stationary targets. In fact, they were easier to see than her practice targets, because there was no glare from fresh snow. The other four contestants also shot perfect scores. She didn't miss any of the distance targets and scored perfectly on the pendulum targets. Only Ty Fuller equaled that. George Sands missed one and the others missed two each. Now Cassie and Mr. Fuller would have to fail in the overhead shooting to give those two any chance to place.

This was not a shoot where someone tossed wood chips in the air. They released live pigeons, five for each contestant. Cassie was slightly better shooting right-handed, so she took the first three left-handed to save her arm. They tumbled from the sky one by one, with spectators clapping for her with each good shot. She switched to her right hand and fired on the fourth pigeon.

It dropped, as gray feathers floated down behind it. *Please, Lord, one more.* The fifth pigeon fluttered into the air with the tiny *whish-whish* sound that flying pigeons make. She fired. Missed. Quickly fired again. The pigeon dropped. The audience applauded.

Mr. Fuller stepped forward. One. Two. Three. Four. So far he and Cassie were tied. His fifth pigeon flew up and he took it with his first shot. The audience applauded.

Cassie was now second.

The remaining contestants shot, but Cassie did not pay attention to who placed third. The shoot was over, the noisy audience standing up and milling around.

She had not won. Again.

"You did it! Wonderful!" Josiah seized her shoulders, swung her about to face him, and squeezed.

"Josiah, no! I placed second."

"Cassie, second place pays more money than expenses. We made a profit — *you* made us a profit."

"But meals, and the hotel room and train —"

"Paid for and more besides. Congratulations, young lady!"

Ty Fuller seized her hand as if she were a man. "Great shoot, Miss Lockwood! Congratulations."

And now here was Mr. Sands pumping her hand and offering her the best, as if she were an equal. The others congratulated her and Mr. Fuller. All right. Maybe she did do well.

Next time, though, she would place first. No matter what it took, she would be first. *Please, God, let it be so.*

23

He had to admit, calves were pretty cute. Ransom hung his elbows over the top rail of the calving pen, watching their latest little fellow struggle to stand up. His mama, one of their seasoned mothers, was licking him so hard she knocked him over once. Finally he was up on all four knobby little legs, his first time on his feet. Mama turned aside to help him find her teat. He nursed for the first time, his tail wagging metronome style.

Ransom turned aside to complete his chores. Calving gave him an intense feeling of satisfaction, and he never really pondered why. The magic of new birth that Reverend Brandenburg sometimes talked about? Whatever it was, he always looked forward to the end of March, when South Dakota woke up from its long winter sleep. Maybe that was it. Winter had finally passed. No, it was more than that. Calves' gamboling in the pasture was a highlight of the ranching year. He thought back, remembering hanging over the fence like this with his far. Once he had looked up and caught a smile of satisfaction on his father's face. That sight remained with him to this day.

Ransom cleaned out the other calving pen, tossed hay for the new mama, scooped up the milk pail, and headed to the house for breakfast. Most of the snow was gone, leaving sloppy mud and shallow puddles in its wake, but there would be a lot more snowfall yet before spring truly arrived. This was just the first thaw.

Cassie stood at the stove flipping the eggs. She was getting better at breakfasts, but she still wasn't as good as Mor. But then, who was? She flashed him a smile. He nodded in return.

Mor was popping raisin muffins out of the muffin tin. From the aroma, he guessed she had put some molasses in them.

The woodbox was low. Arnett must not be up yet. He'd taken on Lucas's part of the load. He thanked God for Arnett, but that didn't douse the simmering anger he held for his younger brother. Ransom went out back and pulled some sticks from the middle of the woodpile, trying to find the driest to take inside. Like trying to find the driest fish in the creek. He filled the carrier, went back in, dumped it into the box by the stove, and shrugged out of his coat. The wood should have been stacked on the porch, as they used the dry stack there, another one of Lucas's jobs.

Mavis asked, "Hear any geese yet?"

"Not yet." He settled into his chair, and Cassie set a mug of coffee in front of him. He sipped. He could tell who made the coffee from the taste — This wasn't Mor's coffee.

Arnett came sweeping in the back door with a hearty "Good mornin', all!" and took off his coat. He glanced at the woodbox. "Sorry I'm late. You want me to finish filling it now or after breakfast?"

Mavis and Cassie greeting him cheerfully. Ransom grunted. Frankly, he was getting a little bored with Arnett's constant good spirits. *Now and then there's a down day, Arnett. Why don't you admit it?*

"Later," Mavis said.

Arnett carefully lowered himself into his chair. He seemed to be getting stiffer lately. "Looks like you'll have yourself some buffalo babies soon, Cassie. Two of the buffalo cows look ready to pop."

"That would be great. I'll keep a closer eye on them. Should we bring them into that front pasture?" Cassie was looking at

Ransom.

"Wouldn't hurt." Arnett looked at Ransom too. "Should we put the mamas in the calving pens?"

So it was Ransom's choice, eh? "Buffalo cows have been dropping calves for centuries without any calving pens or ranchers to help them. I don't see any need to change that."

He noticed Arnett and Cassie shooting a glance at each other. If they didn't like the answer, they shouldn't have asked the question. Cassie slid the eggs onto a plate and set it on the table. Mor put out the muffins and served the plate of ham. She sat down at her place, and Cassie seated herself as well.

Arnett had just started grace when Gretchen rushed in, wailing, "They're going to be here any minute and I can't find my boots!"

"Did you look under your chair by the fireplace?" Mor asked.

Cassie suggested, "I think I might have seen them by the front door. Look behind the stool."

"Get a little maturity and you won't lose your boots."

Gretchen scowled at her brother. "I'll sure be glad when you finally get rid of that burr

370

under your tail. You're a pain to be around."
She rushed out again. In moments she
called, "They're here!" Was she referring to
her boots or to her ride to school? Mor
snatched up several slices of fried bread and
carried them out to the front room. Mor
babied that kid too much.

A minute later Mor came back to the
kitchen. "Thank you, Cassie. That's where
they were." She sat down.

Arnett resumed saying grace as if everything were just great. It was not great.
Nearly all the spring work hadn't even been
started yet. There was no way they could
build another bunkhouse, or guesthouse,
this close to summer. Maybe next year. But
the rickety fence up by the second gate
couldn't wait until next year. That would
have to be repaired now. The northeast
corner of the barn roof leaked; they needed
to reshingle it before rainwater rotted the
rafters at that end. And there was all the
usual stuff of branding calves — Cassie's
stock all carried brands; did she expect him
to do hers too? — tilling and planting the
garden, pruning the apple trees, which
should have been done two months ago, and
replacing the chicken run that the wind tore
apart last January. Arnett had repaired it
with chicken wire from his place, but that

stuff was old and rusty and was going to start falling apart any minute now. Thank God for Micah, but with the furniture business in full swing, they needed Lucas.

Mor asked, "Are you going over to the other place today?"

"Yep. Got three pieces put together. Got some sanding to do, then we'll fire up the stove to warm the place and varnish 'em all at once. Gonna look real purdy." Arnett scooped the last of his egg yolk with the final bite of muffin and popped it into his mouth.

Cassie stood up. "Mavis, I'll help you with dishes, and then I'm going to go practice. The corral is still pretty sloppy, isn't it?"

Mavis nodded. "Still too slippery to ride safely. But I have an idea. Perhaps you boys could build a temporary corral out on that pasture high spot. A show ring for her to practice."

"Why not? We got nothing else to do." Ransom felt his anger boiling over.

Arnett bobbed his head. "Good idea! Doesn't have to be strong enough to hold cattle, just obvious, so Wind Dancer can follow it around. We can use those split rails behind the barn."

"Those split rails are to fix the fence out by that gate," Ransom reminded him, which was stupid because Arnett already knew what those rails were needed for.

The old man announced, "I'll go hitch up. Ransom, you were talkin' about some brass nails."

"I'll go look for them. I think they're in that drawer in Far's workbench." He drained his mug and stood.

Cassie picked up the strainer of trimmings. "I'll take these scraps out to the chickens and gather the eggs."

"Ransom, wait." Mor stood too. "I want to talk to you a minute. Sit down, please."

Now what? She already knew the state of their finances and all the work that had to be done. Yet another work project, no doubt.

She moved to a chair directly across from him and sat. "You've been snappy and surly ever since Lucas left."

What could he say? He shrugged. "I'll try to act sweeter." That probably wasn't going to mollify her, and Arnett would have the team ready in a few minutes now.

It didn't. "No, acting sweeter won't solve the problem. Forgiveness will solve the problem. Your heart won't rest easy until you have forgiven Lucas for running off."

"Mor . . ." How should he say this? "He messed up his life, he messed up ours, and for sure he messed up Cassie's. We need him here. There's too much to do on this spread. I can't handle it all alone. And he's gone, deliberately. Let him come crawling back begging for forgiveness, not me crawling to him."

" 'Forgive us our debts as we forgive our debtors.' How often does Reverend Brandenburg preach on that? And I know you've been listening. 'As' means 'in the same way as,' and you cannot receive forgiveness without giving it. It's time to do that, Ransom, to ease your own heart and to make life a whole lot more pleasant for the rest of us."

He rubbed his face. He should have known this was coming. "You know Lucas and I never did get along very well. You came out way ahead on the stove wood, we split so much, but it doesn't help now. He has to ask forgiveness and show he's earned it. And so far, he hasn't even written us a postcard. No, Mor. It isn't that easy to just go and forgive that kind of pure, hateful selfishness."

She looked sad. How he hated that, when she didn't yell or scold or complain. Just looked sad. "I see. Please think about it." She stood up and turned her back on him, busying herself with a mixing bowl and flour and a variety of other ingredients.

"We're going over to the other place and take Chief with us. We'll be back for supper." He closed the door without slamming it, but the fury ricocheting in his mind didn't abate. *Forgiveness. Sure, do what you want, don't pay any heed to those you hurt, and . . .*

He climbed into the waiting wagon beside Arnett, took up the lines, and flicked them. They rattled out the lane, picked up Chief and Micah at the gate, and headed toward Arnett's place. He thought about the brass nails about halfway out there. Too late to go back.

He didn't need Mor to tell him something he'd already figured out on his own. But she just didn't understand. Neither did Reverend Brandenburg, when you came right down to it. It's easy when you sit in your study, thumb through some Bibles, and write a sermon about how forgiving is the lofty thing, the right thing to do, and everything is suddenly rosy. You deliver it on Sunday, go back to your study, and think up another subject to preach on. But it's not that way. Real life is different and harder, and the good reverend never had to deal with a slacker like Lucas for a lifetime. Never was betrayed by someone like Lucas. He forced himself to hold the lines easy-like, but his foot nearly ripped through the floorboards.

Ransom was coming to love that wood-shop where they were headed now. It was noisy in a clean way — hammers, saws, the donkey engine. No critics, no harsh voices telling Ransom he had to be a better person. No irritations, just the smell of new-sawn pine and cherry and oak.

They were developing three designs to start with — the end table, a coffee table, and a leather-covered chair with hassock. They would make six pieces of each design and store their inventory in Arnett's old house. Every piece was to carry their signature carving on it.

The workers were all willing too; Ransom appreciated that. Arnett was a fine carver who did excellent carpentry as well. Micah was learning quickly, becoming nearly as skilled as Arnett. He was good at taking orders and even better at learning. Arnett or Ransom could show him something once, and he had it. Chief stoked the stove, made coffee, made their lunches, puttered around sweeping up sawdust or stacking sawn lumber. He showed no interest in actually building something, but Ransom didn't mind. Chief made the day go smoothly for everyone else. Who could complain about that?

They'd completed two pieces they had started the day before. Arnett walked outside, squinted at the sky, and ambled back in. "Ransom, we best get back unless you want your mama breathin' fire. It's goin' on four already and we got a long ride."

"Four!" Where did the time go? A bigger question: How were they going to build up an inventory when the time here passed so quickly? They weren't getting nearly enough done. Maybe they'd made a mistake in setting up shop in a barn they had to travel to. Maybe he should have just moved the plow and things outside and used his own barn.

They set things in order for the next day and boarded the wagon. Fortunately, like horses everywhere, these two moved far more eagerly in the direction of their barn than they moved going away from it, so they'd be home in jig time.

Ransom would drop Micah and Chief off near the gate and — Who was that coming up the lane? He had never seen that little coal-box buggy before. Classy little bay hackney pony too with a high snappy step. Pretty, but of no use on a working ranch. Hackney ponies weren't common in South Dakota, and they cost a body part. In fact the whole rig smacked of high finance.

Micah echoed his thoughts. "Nice rig."

Ransom stopped at the gate. Micah hopped off. Chief carefully, slowly eased his way to the ground.

And the fancy rig's driver pulled to a halt beside them.

Ransom tipped his hat. "Good afternoon, Mr. Porter. Welcome!"

Josiah Porter, as smiley and expansive as ever, tapped the brim of his hat in return. "Just the man I want to talk to!"

Ransom waved an arm. "Let me introduce my furniture-building partners. John Birdwing and Micah . . ." but they were already on their way up the hill. "Up there. And this is Daniel Arnett. Likes to be called Arnett."

"Arnett. Delighted. Ransom, I stopped by to talk to your mother and Cassie, and they showed me that end table you made for her. Fine workmanship, a beautiful piece."

"Thank you."

"I want to set one each of your furniture pieces in the lobby of my hotel. I'll purchase them, of course. Then if people admire them enough to buy, you can take orders for more."

Ransom nearly choked on his appreciation. "Mr. Porter, that's a fine idea. We would be forever grateful. Marketing is the one area of this furniture-making business where we fall short."

"Marketing a product of that quality in a rural area is difficult no matter how you look at it. However, more and more people of means are settling in Hill City, so the demand is only going to grow. I believe you have here the beginning of a highly profitable enterprise, if you can keep up the workmanship."

"Thank you." He glanced at the house. "My mother surely invited you to dinner."

"She did, and I would love to stay, but I have an appointment the next ranch over, and already I am late for that. Another time. In fact, I'll let your mother and Cassie tell you all the news. Have a good evening, Mr. Engstrom."

"And you, sir."

And away he went. Ransom watched him go for a moment. That coal-box buggy and fancy little horse looked good for sure, but the buggy probably wasn't very comfortable to ride in. The springs on his farm wagon here were suppler than that buggy's.

"I'll put the horses up," Arnett announced as they rolled up to the barn door.

Ransom was about to say thanks and head for the house, but he knew what Mor would have to say about that. So instead, he replied, "I'll help, so we can both go to supper."

And with one on each side of the team, it did go faster. They unhooked the tugs and just left the wagon sitting where it had stopped. Ransom, by the off horse, pulled the breeching and crupper free, opened the girth, and lifted the hames away. He dragged the collar forward over the old horse's head.

Old horse. He paused. Here was going to be another major expense before long. These horses would last only a few more years before they'd be too old to handle the ranch work. Cassie's wagon team wasn't much younger than his, so he couldn't even borrow hers. He was going to have to buy new, younger horses, and that meant not only the expense but a lot of time breaking them in, months and months of time that he ought to spend building furniture or something else productive like fencing. Lucas was a good hand with horses, and he liked working with them. He had been the one who broke in the Engstroms' stock. Lucas. The whole thing was just too much misery to think about.

But he couldn't quit thinking about it. Or his mother's words. He knew she was right but . . .

"I'll milk and fork down the hay after supper." He hung the harness and collar. "Let's go eat."

They trudged to the house through slippery slop, the downside of spring.

Gretchen greeted them with, "We were just going to sit down and eat without you."

"Good evening to you too, squirt." Ransom hung his coat up.

Cassie set a mug of coffee in front of him even before he'd completely settled in his chair. My, but they were in a hurry. He didn't think he was *that* late.

Gretchen seemed to talk faster tonight saying grace. Mor plunked the bowls on the table, and Arnett grabbed the nearest one. He was obviously pretty hungry. Why wasn't Ransom hungrier if it was so late?

"Mr. Porter was by a while ago." Mor buttered her bread. "I invited him, but he couldn't stay for supper. He's going around to the various ranches that agreed to host visitors this summer. Two families have already registered for a guest ranch and paid their deposits."

"We taking one of them?"

"Apparently."

Great. It wasn't going to be cheap, setting up guest quarters, even if they already had the bunkhouse to start with. Towels, linens, ewer and basin, all those basics, probably curtains for the windows — women did things like that — and all coming out of money they hadn't seen yet.

Arnett cleared his throat. "Remember we have my ranch house too." He looked at Ransom. "That's all set up."

Ransom started to say something when Cassie interrupted.

"And he says that registrations for the July shooting match are already coming in. It won't be the same as the big one in St. Louis, but it will be pretty impressive."

Gretchen leaped into the conversation. "I told Mr. Porter I'd like us to host a family with children. And in the mail today Cassie got invitations to a couple more shoots."

Had he ever seen Gretchen so excited?

Cassie. It always came back to Cassie. Everything had been fine until she showed up. Now the whole world was topsy-turvy, and Lucas was gone. He would not have left if he hadn't gotten into that muddle about Cassie. Marry Betsy, move into — where? Anyway, marry Betsy without all that Cassie hoopla that drove him away.

After supper Ransom completed the rest of the barn chores with his mind bouncing around in other places. How could he convince Mor that this time her wisdom had failed her? If she had a fault, it was that she forgave too easily. She probably didn't even care if Lucas knew the pain he'd caused, the work he was avoiding.

Hmm. There was a point Ransom hadn't thought of. Lucas knew perfectly well how much there was to do around here, spring being the biggest season for work, and he was cowering in Hill City. Avoiding the spring work. That was it. He knew they wanted to build another bunkhouse. In fact, it was partly his idea. He was all enthusiastic, but his enthusiasm was for the idea, not the work it would take. Ransom's anger burned hotter and brighter than ever.

He slogged up to the house. He should go through their books tonight, see if there was something he could do, or sell, or make, to stretch their money just a little farther. All these expenses were looming with only faint signs of income. If the furniture sold? If they had a good calf crop, which of course did not pay out in cash money. If the guest idea paid off? Ranching was always a big if. But he'd gone over these and all other ideas countless times already. It only made him angrier and more depressed.

So instead, he spent the evening designing a bedstead that would be the centerpiece of a bedroom suite. Turned out to be a pretty elegant piece. And when Mor was reading *Tom Sawyer,* he couldn't concentrate on numbers in a ledger anyway; the words distracted him. When he was drawing a design, he could ignore her voice. Ignore his mother. That wasn't difficult when she was droning her way through a book he'd already read a couple of times.

He went to bed that night very tired, but not at all sleepy. He lay in the darkness staring at the black ceiling. Outside his window the overcast sky hid whatever phase the moon was in just now. Then it brightened out there, darkened, brightened again. Broken cloud cover, gibbous moon rising. His mind registered that without really registering. Moon phase had nothing to do with the fears and worries that plagued his mind.

His thoughts churned. He rolled to his side. To his other side. He had to keep his knees drawn up because the foot of his bed was so cold. Irresponsible Lucas. Strange, unusual Cassie. He could not quiet his whirlwind of thinking.

He started out of an almost doze. Benny was barking. Othello was going crazy. Now what could be going on? Mor shouldn't have let those two mutts stay in the house for the night; their clamor was going to loosen the rafters. He pulled on his trousers and strode to the front room grumbling. He pushed his way through the frantic dogs to the door and threw it open. They tore out into the blackness, barking frenetically.

He stepped out on the porch, trying to see something, anything. The baying dogs were tearing toward the near pasture. His heart kicked into triple time, as he turned back to the house to get his boots, slamming into Cassie.

"No!" Cassie, in her nightgown and bare feet, grabbed his arms to keep her balance and fought to get around him. "What's happening?" She gripped her shotgun at ready, the cold steel slamming against his upper arm.

"Can't see." He stepped around her.

"I know Othello's barks. There's something really bad out there!" She leapt off the porch and tore after the sound of the frenzied dogs.

"Cassie!" All he could think to yell was, "You're barefoot! *Cassie!*" That fool girl! He recognized now that Benny's bark said far more than just "There's a stranger here." Benny had detected something dangerous. The moon cleared just enough to show Cassie climbing the pasture fence already, headed right into the thick of that danger, whatever it was!

Frantic himself now, he ran back inside and snatched his own shotgun off the pegs.

Mor met him at the door, hugging a shawl around her shoulders. "Ransom, what is it?"

"I don't know. That crazy girl!" He charged off the porch and across the lane to the fence, climbed over it, not nearly as agile as Cassie, and ran out into the pasture. He could just barely make out Cassie's nightgown up ahead, a gray ghost bobbing in the darkness of the moon again disappearing behind clouds.

As if on cue, the moon emerged again and he could see a little better. Maybe it was a bear going after the calves. Bears came around now and then, though not lately. What if Cassie shot at a bear? Her puny little twenty-gauge couldn't kill a bear. It would just make the thing roaring angry, furious enough to charge her. Did she know that? Probably not — and that ignorance just might be the death of her!

He ran faster, suddenly winded, gasping for air, stumbling on the wet grass tufts. He slipped and fell, yanked himself back to his feet, kept running.

Another dog was out there yipping. No . . . not a dog. A coyote! He could see the buffaloes and longhorns all bunched together in a knot, and a white flash in the moonlight told him Wind Dancer was in the middle of the bunch. No, it wasn't coyotes. Coyotes ran with their tails angled down. These animals ran with their tails straight out. Wolves!

Wolves, at least four, maybe six, circling the herd, yipping, harrying.

Cassie had stopped within a hundred feet of the buffalo herd, and Ransom pulled up beside her, gulping for air.

She was sobbing. "I can't shoot! Wind Dancer . . . George! And the dogs . . . Othello! I can't fire into that!"

Suddenly, with a pained yelp, a wolf sailed straight up and arced to a plop on the ground. George with his mighty horns shook his head, lowered it, and went after the next one. A wolf foolishly moved in too close, trying to get around behind him. George wheeled and hooked that one and sent it flying as well.

Benny! No! The mutt was running right after a wolf, challenging it. The animal turned on him viciously, twisting, snarling, drove him yelping to the ground. Benny!

The wolves were suddenly breaking off their attack, running toward the hill. George took after them briefly but pulled up short, staying close to his herd. From the other side of the bunch Othello ran after the pack for a few yards and stopped, still barking his head off.

Cassie swung her shotgun up and fired. A wolf went down. She fired again. The lead wolf stumbled, fell, squirmed to its feet again and tried to run, but now it had fallen behind to the rear of the pack. Ransom fired and dropped it.

Breathing heavily, Mor came stumbling up beside them, gripping her rifle.

The wolves were out of shotgun range.

Mor swung her rifle up but then lowered it. "I can't see them well enough for a clean hit."

Benny came limping toward them. Ransom dropped to one knee and greeted his old friend. Benny's shoulder was torn up near his neck, but he seemed to have escaped any other injuries. Ransom gathered his dog close and muttered praise.

Arnett, rifle in hand, came puffing up. "Well, I see I missed the excitement. Is everyone all right?"

Cassie left them and jogged over to George, where she scratched that huge dangerous head, affectionately rubbing the ears of a ton of beast that had just dispatched two wolves.

Ransom patted his dog, but it was Cassie

he watched. Why did he find himself so attracted to her? He certainly didn't want to be. It was probably just a reaction to Lucas's leaving or something. In other words, not really attraction at all. He told himself that, and he agreed.

Kind of.

24

"So it's going to snow again." Cassie watched out the window as Ransom and Arnett drove their wagon out the lane to build more furniture. She could hear the horses slopping through the mud clear into the kitchen. No wonder Mavis had said she couldn't canter a horse in a corral, not with all this muck. "Mavis, it's the first of April!"

"Oh, it'll snow at least two or three times yet," Mavis added cheerily, "but spring snow never lasts long. It melts off quickly." She paused. "Well, rarely lasts more than a few days. You never can be sure about South Dakota weather."

Making still more puddles and mud. But Cassie didn't say that out loud.

In the near pasture, the longhorns and buffalo grazed as casually as if there had never been wolves last night. And there was the first buffalo baby of the season, a light-brown girl. She stood spraddle-legged near her mother, staring off into space. Wind Dancer didn't seem too upset either, as if wolves were just another part of his new pasture experiences. It occurred to Cassie that when he and she lived with the show, he never grazed out on pastures. Grazing itself was a new experience to him.

She turned away from the window and finished clearing the breakfast table. Her mind stayed troubled, and it wasn't just wolves. Micah had taken the wolf carcasses up to the cabin so that Runs Like a Deer could skin them and tan the pelts. She already had a stack of coyote hides with the fur on that she was sewing together into a wonderful blanket. Cassie caught herself wishing for the finished quilt to put on her bed. The softness of the fur always amazed her.

Mavis was examining a basket of apples beside the stove. "We'll make these into applesauce today. They're starting to go." Apparently realizing she was teacher as well as matriarch, she held up an apple in each hand. "See? They're getting a little soft, and two of them have brown spots. They'll rot pretty quickly if we don't use them before they make all the apples around them rot too."

Cassie had made applesauce with Mavis

before. "So first we quarter them and cook them."

"You are so right." Mavis pulled the big pot to the front of the stovetop so that it would heat more quickly. Cassie dipped water from the reservoir to make it about a third full. Together they cut the apples in half and the halves into quarters, cored them, and tossed them into the pot. It was pretty much mindless work, except when they had to pause to cut away a brown spot or flick out a worm.

Presently Mavis said, "I know you pretty well now. You're usually not silent like this. What's wrong?"

Cassie forced a smile. "I'm working on it. What will we do while the apples cook?"

"Start the early seed for the garden. We can plant peas outside directly, as soon as the ground thaws, along with lettuce and spinach; they don't seem to mind snow. But the cabbage and tomatoes and a few others can do with a head start inside." She smiled too, and it wasn't forced. "I know you've been looking forward to planting a garden. This is the first step."

"At the show kitchen, I think a lot of the vegetables came in cans."

"I have always loved the fresh vegetables from my garden, and I think you'll enjoy gardening too. First, we have to make the dirt."

Cassie's mouth dropped open. Make dirt. She thought of all the vegetable gardens she'd seen as trains passed through farmland, and Mavis's own garden here. Make dirt?

While the apples simmered merrily at the back of the stove, the two women put on coats and slipped and skidded their way to the barn. "Bring this bag, if you will, please." Mavis pointed to a large burlap sack of . . . Cassie peeked inside. Dirt. She picked it up and carried it back to the house. Mavis followed with another burlap bag.

"We'll do this part outside." Mavis donned leather gloves, handed a pair to Cassie, and opened her bag. It was dried cow flops. Cassie could feel her jaw drop. But as Mavis began crumbling them, Cassie gritted her teeth and joined in. If she hadn't known where these came from, she'd not have been squeamish at all. They didn't smell bad, they were so dry. Mavis dipped into the barrel of wood ashes for a scoopful. She poured the burlap bag of dirt into the wheelbarrow, dumped the crumbled manure on top, and tossed on the ashes. "Now we mix it up very thoroughly."

Mavis was right about this being rather fun, but it did nothing to ease Cassie's thoughts as she pushed the shovel into the dry pile and turned it over again and again. She'd read a passage in the Bible just that morning about taking every thought captive unto Jesus Christ. How come the Bible would say to do something but not give detailed instructions so one could actually do it? She could no more stop her rampaging thoughts than she'd been able to frighten the wolves away by shouting. Thinking about what could have happened still made her choke up. She jerked herself back to the moment and making dirt.

"We'll keep this out and bag the rest for later." Mavis shoveled their mixed-up soil into a burlap bag as Cassie held it open. She carried in the big bucket of dirt that was made from dirt and set it beside the stove, having no idea where Mavis would want it next.

Mavis began mixing water into her dirt a little at a time. "It should be moist but not muddy."

Cassie sat down and watched. "Mavis, I've been thinking." How should she say this? "Since no one is living in Arnett's house, I thought maybe I could move over there. Gretchen could have her room back, and

394

Arnett would feel better about the house. He says if no one lives there, it tends to deteriorate."

"You might want to think about this a while. You don't have to worry about the house. Apparently Chief is in there every day heating up dinner, and the furniture builders are in and out too. The house isn't going to deteriorate. They're keeping an eye on it." She paused and stared at nothing a moment. "Have you ever lived alone be-fore?"

"No."

"I'm not sure you could handle that yet. I don't think you realize how heavy loneliness can be."

"I'd work Wind Dancer, of course, spend several hours a day putting our act back together. What with shooting practice, I'd have plenty to do."

"Doing doesn't ease loneliness. And it's extremely unwise for a young woman to live alone out on a spread away from everyone and everything."

"Why?"

Mavis licked her lips. "It just is, that's all."

Cassie narrowed her eyes. Memories of screaming and shooting and fire and sear-ing pain made her catch her breath. "Surely —" She cut off her words. Her right arm tingled at the memory.

Mavis abandoned her dirt, pulled a chair around, and sat down right in front of her. Cassie felt trapped and didn't know how to gracefully get away. "Now, Cassie, explain to me exactly what's going on."

Cassie's heart went thud. Mavis knew things about Cassie that not even Cassie knew, when you started talking about relationships, and love, and all the things that tear people apart and put them back together. Mavis probably knew exactly what Cassie was thinking this very minute.

So she took a deep breath and blurted, "Ransom hates me. I want to be someplace where he doesn't have to look at me all the time."

"Why does he hate you?"

"Because it's my fault that Lucas left, and he knows that. He's hated me ever since I showed up. I can feel it. I've always felt it. He's been miserable for months, and I don't want to add to his misery."

Mavis's voice was soft, even. "Why does it bother you so much that he's miserable? Do you care for him? I mean, of course, beyond simple friendship."

Cassie shrugged. "I care about him, yes. I didn't think I would, but I do." Like she had for Lucas, like a brother. The snort started down about her ankle region, but she caught it before it became audible. *Cassie Lockwood, while you have many faults, lying is not one of them. Like a brother? Ha!* She forced herself to study Mavis's lined and caring face.

"Well, dear Cassie, I've been watching you two, and I don't think he hates you at all. There are other things preying on his mind right now."

"Mavis, I know he does. And I want to put some space between us so he's not so troubled."

"Let me think about this a little. There is more here than it appears." She got up and walked out back, returned with two large, deep trays. "I keep these just for starting seeds." She smoothed her special dirt into a tray and began arranging seeds on top. "I'll only start some of my seeds early, save the rest for planting outside directly later. We'll cover these with more dirt and keep the trays warm and moist. When the seeds sprout, we'll put them out during the day and bring them in at night."

Now what should Cassie do? She helped with the trays, of course, but what should she do about these larger questions? She was certain that as wise as Mavis was, she had missed the obvious on this one. Ransom had made his feelings clearly known. Oh, he was polite to Cassie and all that, but she could feel the resentment, the dislike. Why could Mavis not see it? Because Ransom was her son, and mothers don't see that in their sons. But what if Mavis was right?

The perfect answer came home with Gretchen that afternoon when she brought the mail.

"From Mr. Porter." Cassie waved the letter she had just received and beamed. "Mavis, there's a shoot in three weeks down in Louisville, Kentucky, organized by the man who won this last one and the one before, Ty Fuller. Mr. Porter says neither he nor Abigail can make it to this one, but perhaps you or Ransom could take me." She looked up from the letter. "But you don't have to. I've been there four or five times. I know my way around in Louisville. Frankfort too."

"Go alone? That's not wise, Cassie."

"Ransom has far too much to do, and he's finishing up his furniture. You have a lot too. I'm sorry to run off with so much work to be done, but I should be able to bring home some nice winnings."

Mavis shook her head. "Bad idea."

"I could go with her!" Gretchen suggested eagerly.

"Worse idea. Perhaps Elouisa Brandenburg can accompany you. But you shouldn't be traveling alone."

This was not the time to argue. "In any case, I will prepare for this one. It's an excellent opportunity to earn some money." *And maybe, just maybe, Ransom won't think quite so poorly of me if I start bringing in some income.* Cassie folded the letter and put it in her drawer in the bedroom.

Mrs. Brandenburg was out of town assisting a sister who was ill. Mrs. Stevens could not possibly go. She was entertaining guests from Rapid City that week. Mrs. Hudson had the vapors and a peculiar cough, or she would love to accompany Cassie. Runs Like a Deer? Out of the question. She had never been in a city; she'd be more bother than help. Micah was fixing that broken fence.

Just over two weeks later, when Cassie boarded the train for Joplin, Missouri, where she would transfer to the Louisville train, she stepped from the platform to the car alone.

She stuffed her carpetbag into the overhead bin by herself. She laid her guns, her only companions, across the seat in front of her. Why did Mavis think this such a bad idea? Did the woman not forget that Cassie was an adult, for pity's sake, responsible for a herd of livestock and her traveling companions who had accompanied her many miles when they were seeking the Engstroms' place? She reveled in the new freedom of being on her own for the first time ever, responsible for no one but herself.

Mavis had given her a book to keep her occupied, but she enjoyed too much simply watching the countryside go by. Home, what it meant to people, what she saw passing by, occupied her thoughts a great deal.

And try as she might to dispel them, thoughts of Ransom intruded as well. There were all manner of young men about — that Christmas dance had confirmed that — and any of them would make a proper beau. She didn't need a man who so thoroughly disliked her and blamed her for all his troubles.

Ransom.

She didn't sleep well that night on the train, and in Joplin the next evening, she got off the Rapid City train and walked to the other platform. By the time she realized this was the wrong platform, the correct train had left. She took a room in a nearby hotel, an expense she hadn't counted on.

Already she was a day late getting to Louisville, and she had not had a chance to practice at all during the long train ride.

Early the next morning she boarded the train for Louisville, arriving late that afternoon. She walked to the Pride of Kentucky Hotel near the shoot venue, carrying her bags, rather than pay money for a hansom. On the way to her hotel, she passed a very nice little tea room and stopped for a very late lunch. They were within fifteen minutes of closing, but she was too hungry not to be seated. Lunch cost nearly twice what she had counted on.

She was more than ready to set her bags down by the time she entered the hotel lobby and stepped up to the desk. "Good afternoon. I am Cassie Lockwood. I sent in a reservation two weeks ago."

The clerk, a rather snooty-looking fellow in a dark suit, scowled at her and leafed through a box of cards. "Lockwood?"

"Yes, sir."

"I have no reservation here under that name."

"Sir, I sent it in with my deposit. Then may I take a room anyway?"

"No vacancy. I am very sorry." He didn't look sorry at all.

"But —"

"I am sorry, young lady. There is a shooting contest near here this weekend, and all our rooms are taken."

"Sir, I know about the shoot. I am one of the contestants."

He looked at her as if she had just identified herself as the Queen of England. "Of course you are." His tone of voice insisted she was lying. "That does not mean a room suddenly drops out of the sky. We are full, regardless. I'm sorry. You will have to look elsewhere." He took a sideways step and addressed the man beside her. "May I help you, sir?"

His attitude ignited smoldering embers of anger. It was the shooting match that had filled up his hotel, and she was part of that shoot. "Excuse me, sir. Where is 'elsewhere'? Where will I find other accommodations?"

"The nearest is the Hotel Kentucky. Several blocks in that direction." He gestured vaguely toward the front doors.

And so she carried her bags another three blocks up Market Street. There it was. The sign looked dull, and the paint was peeling a little on the arched doorway of the Hotel Kentucky. In the small lobby there was no lovely furniture, and the clerk behind the desk was not dressed fancy. But he smiled. It was not a particularly friendly smile, more a cold smile, but at least it wasn't a sneer.

"May I take a room here for the night, please?"

"Second or third floor?"

"Second, if possible."

"They cost more."

"Then third." She must husband her money carefully, even if it meant carrying her bags up another flight of stairs. Her arm that was no longer sore was getting sore again.

She received her key and carried her bags up to room 27, stopping at each landing to rest for a moment. Once inside, she locked the door — Ransom's instructions — and shook out her good skirt and fancy shirt so the wrinkles would fall out — Mavis's instructions. She flopped down on her bed, weary in body and mind. She awoke with a start; it was dark outside! She was hungry, but she should not go out on the streets after dark — everybody's instructions, even Micah's. What to do?

She walked downstairs, but this hotel had no restaurant, nor was there one on this block, the clerk informed her. She walked back upstairs. To the third floor. She made certain her guns were clean and ready to go, her ammunition sorted and boxed correctly. She was ready.

Except that she'd had no practice.

Just before she curled up in bed, she took the unnecessary precaution of tipping her plain wooden chair and wedging its back up under the doorknob. Ransom had insisted on it, and she said she would, so she would. Her word was good.

She was so weary and restless, she had trouble getting to sleep. Sometime in the night, her door rattled. She raised her head.

It rattled again, as if someone were trying the doorknob. Now the chair wedged against it rattled. Someone *was* trying to come in! She should call out, but she was too terrified to emit more than a squeak. Who would try to enter her room? Perhaps a drunkard on the wrong floor, thinking this was his room. A mistake, surely, but frightening. The person tried once more; the chair rattled . . . and then silence.

What if it was a thief? Or . . . ? Quietly, she got up and opened her gun bag, pulled her shotgun out, and without making any more noise than necessary, carefully loaded it. Then she sat at the foot of her bed and waited, scarcely breathing. And waited. Whoever it was did not try again. He must have realized his error. Despite the reassuring silence, she could not get back to sleep. She was too nervous, her eyes too open to close again.

The next morning, she dressed in her show clothes, packed everything else up, and left that hotel as soon as the streets were light. She now had three blocks further to go to reach her venue, for the second hotel lay in the wrong direction. Now she was passing the Pride of Kentucky Hotel, and their restaurant was almost open; beyond its plate glass doors, she could see the waiters setting up the tables. She plopped her bags down near the interior double doors and sat down in an elegant chair to wait for them to open. She felt herself drifting off, too tired to stay awake.

"Why, here she is!" A man's far-too-cheerful voice woke her instantly. "Miss Lockwood, my lovely nemesis! And all ready to compete." Tyrone Fuller came sweeping up to her. "Did you sleep well?"

Cassie stood up, partly to wake up a little better. She felt foggy. Should she tell him? He had organized this; perhaps she should. "Not well, no. This hotel was full, and I had to go three blocks to a Hotel Kentucky. It was not a restful night."

"Full? What? Why, I set aside a whole block of rooms just for participants. There was one waiting for you."

"The gentleman at the desk insisted otherwise."

"Come with me a moment, please. You may leave your grips there." He waved toward a nearby bellhop. "Watch her bags!" He marched energetically to the desk. "Mr. Howe!"

The desk clerk looked at him, looked at Cassie, looked at him, looked at the gentleman he was waiting upon. "Excuse me a moment, I beg of you." Mr. Howe was frowning as he moved to their end of the desk. "Yes, Mr. Fuller?"

"I understand you refused this young lady a room."

"We were fully occupied, sir."

"I had a room waiting for her in that block!"

"The block of rooms for the shooting contest were not assigned to specific persons in my records here."

"You knew they were for the participants. Did she not say she was participating?" Mr. Fuller's voice was rising, and Cassie did not like the attention they were drawing. She loved being center stage in a show. She hated this conflict.

The man cleared his throat nervously. "She did, ah, mention it, sir."

"And . . . ?"

"I did not take her claim seriously, Mr. Fuller. She's a little girl."

Cassie glanced about briefly and wished she could shrink away, but there was no-

406

where to shrink to. They now had the attention of everyone in the room.

A third fellow joined them, introducing himself as the manager. Why couldn't Mr. Fuller move his complaint to the manager's office or wherever one would complain in private? He was explaining that she was a star, very famous, and to refuse her a room was criminal, but to top it off, "to send her to the Hotel Kentucky? *The Hotel Kentucky!* That nest of thieves and rounders!"

Cassie was mortified, absolutely mortified.

"Send a young girl amongst cads and pickpockets! What if —"

The manager snapped his fingers. Instantly Mr. Howe handed him a white pad and pen.

The manager looked at Cassie. "Miss Lockwood, on behalf of this hotel, I profusely apologize. My man made an innocent mistake, and I am extremely grateful nothing serious resulted. That does not negate the fact that it was a serious error. The dining room is now open." He jotted something on the pad. "You and Mr. Fuller will please accept a complimentary breakfast, anything you wish. Mr. Fuller, rest assured the cost of the unused nights of that room will be fully refunded." He jotted another note and thrust it at Mr. Howe.

Mr. Fuller fumed some more about incompetence, but the storm had apparently passed. He escorted her to the dining room. Her bags. Where were her bags? She saw them over beside the bellhop. The manager was speaking to him. And now the bellhop was taking her carpetbag away, leaving the gun bag. She so hoped peace was restored. But where was he taking her bag?

They were seated by a window. Cassie looked out on Market Street, where she had trudged down and up again. She secretly hoped Mr. Fuller would be riding to the venue, and she could ride too.

Free breakfast. Perhaps her luck was turning for the better. But she was so churned up by the argument out there — not just her stomach but her head and heart and mind — that she could not eat. She ordered ham and eggs and forced a little something down — the ham slice was greasy and quite thin, not slab size like Mavis's. She knew she would be ravenous long before dinner, but she simply could not eat it all. Mr. Fuller plied her with questions the whole while and commented on how dainty and ladylike her appetite was, but her mind couldn't give him her full attention. This day was already terrible, and it had hardly started!

One little wish came true. Mr. Fuller ordered up a hansom, and Cassie and her gun bag both rode in style. They arrived in ample time to set up.

She was convinced that bringing Micah along next time would surely be worth the cost of a train ticket and hotel room. With Micah handling the guns, she would only need to hold her hand out and the correct gun would be plopped into it. Without Micah, after each set she had to go to her table, choose her next gun, reload if necessary, and return to her station. And now it was time.

When the contestants were introduced and Cassie stepped forward, raising an arm high in greeting to the audience, a curious thing happened. The churning feeling disappeared under an onslaught of that old familiar tingle. This was her world, what she had been born to literally, and she wished that Mr. Howe, the hotel clerk, were watching now, seeing how wrong he had been. She was about to give these folks a good show. It was what she knew how to do, and she was among the best of the best. She returned to her table, picked up her rifle, and stepped out to the line.

In the first set — stationary targets — most of the contestants scored well. Cassie and Mr. Fuller were the only two with perfect scores. Next were moving targets with handguns. Cassie could not find her rhythm and missed two. But Mr. Fuller missed one, so it was not a disaster. Not yet. They were still one and two. By the time they had broken for dinner, four participants had dropped out.

The meal for the contestants was set up in a little tent apart from the concessions serving the audience. Trays of sandwich ingredients were set out, and a young woman ladled soup for each person. Cassie built a roast beef sandwich with triple meat and as many pickles and onions as she could pile on. She tasted the horseradish. Very mild. She had to slather it on to get the full effect. Mr. Fuller sat near her and commented that the daintiness of her appetite had fled.

Mavis said that she made her horseradish every fall. Salt and grated root with a bit of alum to retard spoilage. Her horseradish made Cassie's eyes burn and her nose run. Lucas and Ransom ate it by the spoonful and didn't seem to notice its acrid pungency. The Engstroms. She wished she were there now, but she relished this competition too.

That afternoon her arm held up long

enough to shoot two overhead sets, clay birds and, as night approached, some kind of sparkling fireworks balls. The balls screamed and left a smoke trail. If you hit them squarely, they exploded in a spray of sparks. Cassie loved that set! But she had missed three of the clay birds. She was now fourth, with Mr. Fuller in the lead.

She rode back to the hotel with him in his hansom. "Don't fret, Cassie," he assured her. "I missed a few too. You're not out of the running by any means, and tomorrow will go better for you. Not as good as my tomorrow, I hope, but better than today." And he chuckled.

As she walked into the lobby, two people near the fireplace looked her way, smiled, and pointed. They must have been in the audience. She smiled back. The manager was standing by the desk. He smiled at her also. "Good evening, Miss Lockwood. I hear you did well. Mr. Howe will personally escort you to your room. Sleep well." Mr. Howe jogged around the end of his desk, took her gun bag from her hand, and led the way to a lovely private suite. She realized they were trying to make up for their mistake, but she was going to enjoy this. An elegant suite, all for her alone. Her luck was indeed turning for the better.

The next day, she missed one of the stationary targets but none of the moving ones, and Mr. Fuller missed two of those. By noon she was in third place and Mr. Fuller had dropped to second. The leader was a young man from a town nearby who claimed he'd learned to shoot as a market hunter supplying restaurants with squirrels. For the fourth set, they released live birds, and three of Cassie's birds flew off to increase Louisville's pigeon population. Mr. Fuller missed one. The squirrel hunter missed four. In the end, Mr. Fuller was first, the squirrel hunter second, and Cassie third.

She received her winnings in cash. Although the hotel room was supplied by the organizers, her money barely covered her expenses. Had this hotel been added to her costs, she would have lost money.

Arriving back at the Engstroms' some days later, she had exactly seven cents in profit. She would have to do better in the future.

When she told her story, the whole story, that night by the fireplace after supper, Mavis had only one thing to say. "You will never again go to a contest by yourself." Cassie nodded. But who would accompany her?

25

Snow bullets hammered him, driven by a screaming wind. And that was just his face. His toes were cold, his fingers colder, his nose numb. A snowstorm in early May! Ransom could remember only one other May storm this bad, and he was too young that time to go out and help his father. The wind was driving the snow across the hillside horizontally now, turning this freak storm into a true blizzard. Pretty soon he wouldn't be able to see. He was sure glad he had given Mor his strong, dependable horse, because she was out in this weather too.

Up ahead there, huddled under the only trees around, were four mama cows and their calves. He turned Biscuit that way and rode up and behind them. He noted that the trees offered a little protection and these calves were less than a month old. Should he drive them all down to the barn and maybe lose a couple calves that couldn't make it that far in the deepening snow? Or leave them here, probably to starve before the snow melted off enough to uncover the grass? How long would this storm last, and how deep would the snow get before it was done? Already at least a foot blanketed the valley, and who knew how much more was coming. He decided to try driving them down to the barnyard and hay piles.

The boss cow of this bunch was reluctant to leave the trees, and he had trouble getting them moving. Finally she gave up and trudged down the slope, her wobbly calf at her heels. Maybe she knew better than he did. Or maybe she was misjudging the storm.

Ransom should be praying now. But prayer came with difficulty lately, if at all.

The boss cow's calf was the first to flounder and fall exhausted in the snow. She stopped. Ransom dismounted and put the calf on his horse, draped it across the mane just in front of the fork. Biscuit sidestepped and tossed her head. She didn't like the situation any more than the calf did. Ransom climbed aboard again, dismayed at how cold his feet were. The calf bleated once and settled in for the uncomfortable ride.

A second calf went down. Ransom had to drape that one over the back of his neck, its sharp little hooves kicking under his chin. He was past feeling sorry for himself. This was absolute horrible, total misery, for sure. More than misery. Potentially fatal, if he got lost in this mess. At least the cows and horse knew the way to the barn, because right now he wasn't sure where they were.

Was that his name? He heard it again somewhere out on the wind. He called back as loud as he could.

"Ransom!" A very faint voice. A woman. Did Mor come out here? She was supposed to go looking for cows to the north of the barn. Micah and Chief were riding off west, and Arnett had headed south.

Here came Cassie toward him on Wind Dancer! That crazy girl! She urged her horse to a lope and drew in alongside. "Ransom! Mavis found a couple and Micah and Chief came back with two, so they thought the rest ought to be up here. I came out to help." She rode in hard beside him. "Here. Give me that one." She reached for the calf around his neck.

He took off his hat, bent his head forward, and dragged the struggling calf off his shoulders. It squirmed mightily and he almost dropped it handing it across to her, but they got it draped across her saddle. That saddle. It for sure wasn't a roping saddle. No horn. Instead, it had handles here and there that she would hold on to as she did tricks while her horse cantered full tilt around an arena. What a crazy way to make a living! But then, was it any crazier than riding around lost in a May snowstorm? He paused to look at her face. Her nose and cheeks were red, wet, probably burning with pain, but she didn't seem to care. Strange girl.

They started forward again, Ransom in the lead with the boss cow's calf, Cassie falling in at the rear. And it struck him. Not a girl. This was a woman, a strong woman. She had never once traveled alone, yet she went by herself to Louisville, more than a thousand miles away. She claimed the person who tried to enter her hotel room that night was a confused drunkard, but Ransom would bet that it was the desk clerk himself, trying to enter to . . . He couldn't allow himself to think about that, at least not right now. But she'd been sitting there with a loaded shotgun, defending herself when she had no one to do it for her. As furious as he was that she exposed herself to danger over and over, he had to admit that in a pinch, she could handle the situation. That's not a defenseless girl. That's a woman, as strong and dependable and resourceful as his own mother.

"Ransom? Another one is down!"

He turned back. The boss cow continued on thirty feet and stopped, twisted her head around to look at him. *Come on, will you?*

He got off and scooped the calf up, laid it across Wind Dancer's neck just ahead of Cassie's saddle, climbed aboard again, and they continued on. How much farther?

Over a mile, as it turned out. Finally through the driving snow he could see the barn, very faint, a light gray ghost in an ocean of hazy white. The lead cow broke into a trot, her bag swinging with each stride. Why did cows' teats not freeze the way his nose did? They ought to.

The fourth calf, the biggest of the bunch, made it in on his own, which was a blessing, since they were running out of places to carry calves. Blessing. Ransom had seen precious little in the way of blessings lately.

As Ransom dismounted and dragged the calf off his horse's neck, Mor came hustling over. "Oh, thank you, God! Cassie, you found him!" Arnett came limping up behind her.

Cassie slid off Wind Dancer. "I could follow his tracks out until that rise, but there the wind filled them in, and I lost the trail. So I just kept going in that direction holler-

417

ing, and he finally answered." She pulled the calf off her saddle. It bleated and ran to mama.

Ransom lifted off the other calf. "That was foolish!" He felt his anger building again.

"No it wasn't. Wind Dancer would know the way back." She mounted again.

"Looks like she came in pretty handy." Arnett came up beside them, smiling. "Mighta lost a couple calves."

Ransom hated when those two failed to agree with him. Which was usually, it seemed.

Arnett lost his happy smile. "I had to come in before I searched over by the rocks. That old plow horse isn't used to carrying a grown man ten miles."

"How many are missing yet?"

Mor lost her happy look too. "Micah and Chief went out again, but so far we're missing over a dozen. More."

"I'll go out toward the rocks, see what I can find." Wearily Ransom crawled aboard Biscuit again.

As he left the barnyard, Cassie was following him. He stopped. "You stay here."

"Mor said we're missing over a dozen. If you find that many, you'll need me, and Wind Dancer is still doing fine."

Now even Cassie was contradicting him, questioning his judgment! Totally disgusted with life, he twisted Biscuit's head aside fiercely and kicked her into a trot. On the other hand, maybe Cassie would decide to take his advice. He glanced back.

She had Wind Dancer right at Biscuit's heels, and she was watching him, looking stunningly sad.

He wished he hadn't done that. Now he really felt like a heel.

Fortunately, he knew the lay of the land well, because he could not see the rocks and had to follow the slopes. The road wound out across the hill somewhere close by, but it was totally obliterated. He moved upslope a little, nearer the trees. The other cows had been hunkered down in the trees, so maybe these would be too.

And there they were. Another blessing. They were a couple miles this side of the rocks, that much less distance to have to drive them home. He shook his seagrass rope loose, the better to herd them. Waving his lariat, he rode up behind the boss cow and tried to get her moving. She wasn't leaving. Not only did Arnett and Cassie and his own mother say he was wrong, now a stupid cow was contradicting him! All patience lost, he swatted her on the rump with his coiled rope. She bolted, wagged her head, and started moving. Why couldn't people admit Ransom might be right once in a while, like the cow did?

Cassie rode behind the bunch, weaving Wind Dancer back and forth, as if she'd been herding cattle all her life. But then, Ransom thought, she'd been around cattle — and buffalo — all her life. This was an extension of that, in a way. She seemed to have a natural aptitude for this sort of thing.

The bunch moved out onto the slope, and Ransom could pretty much give Biscuit her head. She knew the way, the cows knew the way, and they were headed home. Half a mile along, a cow mooed from somewhere uphill to the left, the wind muffling the sound, the snow clouding his vision. The lead bossy stopped and bawled back. Here came another half dozen mamas out of the wind-driven haze toward them, lowing. Yet another blessing. Ransom would never have spotted them out there.

Cassie broke away and rode up behind them, pushing them down to join the herd. She swung out to turn back a straggler. Wind Dancer had lost his playful prance. The lead bossy continued forward toward safety and hay.

Dark fell earlier with the storm, making

420

visibility even worse when the cows trailed into the barnyard, slogging wearily, heads down. Cassie had two calves draped across her saddle, and Ransom had three. He had been forced for the last two miles to ride behind his saddle so that he could put two calves in the seat.

He slid off Biscuit's rump, as weary as his cattle. His cattle. His responsibility. And he had discharged that responsibility as best he could, just as his father always did. He pulled the calves down and set them on their feet. The mamas buried their heads in the haystack, their babies nursed. As far as he could tell, no calves lost, the mamas all safe. That gave him a small measure of satisfaction. Well, when he thought about it, maybe not so small.

Cassie was out by the rail unsaddling her weary horse. He should go over there right now and thank her. Without her he would not have been able to bring in the whole bunch safely. Then he saw her profile as she turned to drape her saddle over the top rail. She was either angry or sad or both, or could it be something else? He couldn't read her expression, but it certainly wasn't saying anything about satisfaction. Wasn't she happy they'd saved the cattle? Wasn't she pleased to be of such help to him? What should he say to her? He had no idea. He ended up saying nothing.

Supper that night was very quiet, but you could chalk the silence off to exhaustion. Arnett looked so tired he could scarcely lift his fork. The old man wasn't used to riding for miles in a howling storm. Mor, the same. Ransom was totally knackered. Cassie must be as well, for she was silent too, you might even call it grumpy. Probably just weary like everyone else.

The next morning the wind had died and the snowfall had quit, but nothing was melting yet. After a hurried breakfast, Ransom fitted the sledge runners onto the wagon again and drove out to the other place. When Mor suggested he wait a day, he'd shaken his head. He needed to deliver the furniture now. Snow in May! Honestly.

Arnett needed a day of rest to recover, so Ransom didn't even ask him to go along. He heard axes splitting wood long before he started up the hill toward the cabin. Chief and Micah were keeping the home fires burning, literally, so he continued on without getting them. They were obviously busy. It wasn't that big a chore to load the pieces he wanted to take to Mr. Porter. It just took a little more effort. He wasn't satisfied with them, really. The workmanship was not the best that he and his men were capable of, but Mr. Porter wanted them now. They would have to do. They were heavy for sure. Did that count for anything?

His long alone time as he drove his team toward Hill City gave him lots of time to think. But when he pulled up in front of the hotel, his thoughts were just as muddled as ever, and Cassie dominated them. He didn't know what to do about her or about earning some money or about anything else, at least not anything he hadn't already thought about a dozen times, or a hundred. And Lucas fired his anger as much as ever, maybe even more so. He had really needed Lucas yesterday when bringing in the cattle, and Lucas wasn't there. What if they hadn't got them all? What if Cassie or Mor, or Arnett even, had run into trouble or gotten lost? Women and an old man out doing what Lucas should have been doing.

And back when those wolves tried to take a calf, he'd needed Lucas then too. And all the repairs yet to be done. He still hadn't gotten to that leak in the barn roof.

He climbed down out of the box, entered the hotel, and started across the ornate lobby toward the desk. And stopped dead. He had forgotten. Mr. Porter had hired

423

Betsy Hudson — no, Engstrom — as the desk clerk. There she was, his brand-new sister-in-law, looking right at him as surprised as he was. Now what should he say?

Much more firmly than he felt, he continued to the desk. "Hello, Betsy."

"Ransom."

"May I, uh, speak to Mr. Porter please?"

She frowned. "He wasn't expecting you today, the snow and all. But he's here. Just a moment please." She disappeared beyond a doorway behind her. She moved with the same grace he'd always seen in her. Looking at her objectively, you'd say she was a lovely young woman. Had she not lured Lucas away — no, Lucas was at fault. He was the one who did it.

Ransom looked around the room while he waited. Where would Mr. Porter put the furniture? The place was pretty well filled to the walls with furniture already.

"Ah!" Mr. Porter came out beaming. "Welcome, Mr. Engstrom! I admire your dedication, coming in with a foot of snow out there. Some of the old-timers are claiming more is on the way."

"Just what we don't need. I brought the pieces you requested."

Mr. Porter chuckled. "Actually, I like an unexpected snowstorm. We filled at least

424

five rooms last night with people who decided not to go home yesterday. Nasty out there."

"Yes, sir, it was nasty. We had to bring in the calves so they wouldn't starve or freeze. Took us all day."

"My father was a cattleman. Nearly killed him." Mr. Porter rubbed his hands together. "Let's go see," he said and strode out the door.

Out at the hitching rail, Ransom jogged ahead of him and hopped into the back of his wagon. He untied the canvas tarpaulin and uncovered the pieces. He was suddenly ashamed of them. He saw imperfections, a dozen things that should have been done better. Maybe Mr. Porter would reject these. He probably should.

But Mr. Porter was still beaming. "Excellent. Excellent."

"Sir, if they don't meet with your complete approval, I'll gladly change or replace whatever you think is imperfect."

"Imperfect? Hardly, my dear boy! Let's take them in right now."

"Sure you want to do heavy lifting, sir? Let me, please."

And here came Lucas out the door! Ransom's mouth dropped open. Of course. Lucas worked for the hotel here. He was the handyman. He'd do the heavy lifting. Ransom should have expected this. Why hadn't he?

The slacker smiled brightly. "Hello, Ransom!"

He nodded, only because Mr. Porter was watching. "Lucas."

They each took an end and toted the biggest piece, the easy chair, into the lobby. Mr. Porter pointed. "Right there." They set it down. "Now, if you'll move that chair out of the way and replace it with this one, please?" They did so. Ransom couldn't help noticing that Mr. Porter was just as cool and comfortable ordering Ransom around as he was ordering the hired help around. How much did Lucas make here anyway?

They placed the end table and coffee table, moving the existing furniture aside. The furniture that Mr. Porter was replacing was beautiful, similar to a Queen Anne design, in cherry, with solid joinery. Why was Mr. Porter casting aside these fine pieces in favor of Ransom's that were put together in an old barn?

Mr. Porter stepped back to admire. "Good. I like the effect very much. Change out the draperies for beige damask and we'll have the look I want. Mr. Engstrom, come to my office, please. I'll cut you a check.

Lucas, remove those pieces." No *please.* Just do it. At least Mr. Porter used *please* when ordering Ransom around.

Ransom followed Mr. Porter behind the hotel desk and into his office. "Please be seated." Mr. Porter slid his lap drawer open.

Ransom settled into a remarkably comfortable chair, and this wasn't even Mr. Porter's big overstuffed chair. Mr. Porter's must be really, really comfortable. Ransom wished he could get a look at the underside of this chair to see how it was cushioned to make it feel so good.

Mr. Porter handed him a check already made out. "This is for these three pieces."

"This is more than we agreed on, sir."

He waved a hand. "Transportation. Now. How many pieces can you provide?"

"Depends on when you need them."

"By July."

Two months! Ransom did some quick calculating. It took them at least three days for each piece to really get it right, when you added up all the time that each one took. Three days apiece, sixty days: "Twenty pieces, maybe a couple more. And we have five pieces of each design finished, ready for immediate delivery."

"Excellent. Excellent. I'll take all fifteen of what you have now."

"Sir, are you replacing everything in your lobby?"

"Even the vases and lamps. And wait until you see the new rugs. Woven by Indians down south. Marvelous designs. Vivid. And I can get them for fifty cents a pound, delivered."

"But what you have now is beautiful." Ransom still couldn't digest this.

Mr. Porter settled back into what was obviously the most comfortable chair in the whole world and rested his elbows on the chair arms, pressing his fingertips together into a tepee. "Yes, it is pretty. But my lobby looks just like every other hotel lobby east of the Mississippi. We need something different but just as beautiful if we're going to set ourselves apart. The moment Mavis showed me that end table you made for Cassie, I knew I'd found the perfect thing."

"But —"

"You see, I wanted something that says Wild West but also has all the workmanship and finish of the finest furniture, not just sticks pounded together or tied together with twine or sinew, for pity's sake. Your designs are of the best quality, and yet they say, 'You are out west now, Visitor, and this is nothing like back east. Enjoy your stay.'"

Ransom groped for words. "Thank you,

sir" was all he ended up with.

Mr. Porter continued. "Oh, and I'll need two sofas. You know, davenports. Same design as your easy chair but seven or eight feet wide. Long. I'll take measurements and let you know exactly how long."

"We can do that, yes, sir."

Mr. Porter was absolutely glowing. "Excellent! Custom-built furniture to exactly fit the space for it. Couldn't be better! Now. Even after my lobby is remodeled, keep turning it out. We can set up a booth at the Wild West show this summer, you know, a vendor's tent and later maybe even a storefront, if Hal Whittaker retires like he keeps threatening to do and closes his smoke shop. I keep telling him, Don't quit until after the show, because he's bound to make a lot of money with all those people in town. And, of course, we sure don't want a boarded-up storefront for visitors to walk past. Wouldn't look good for the town."

"No. It wouldn't." Ransom's head was practically spinning. Mr. Porter and all these grand ideas — what if they could actually work? He would need a lot more hired help. Skilled carpenters and woodworkers. That meant salaries. It also meant maybe not getting all the work done on the ranch. How could he handle the ranch and this business both?

He needed Lucas.

Another question came to mind. "What will you do with the furniture you're replacing?"

"Lucas and Betsy are in a little apartment that needs furnishing. I'll give them some. Sell the rest." Mr. Porter stood up. "Mr. Engstrom, it's a pleasure doing business with you."

Ransom stood also. "And with you, sir." They shook and Ransom went out the door, the bank check in hand. He would pay Arnett, Micah, and Chief first, of course, not nearly as much as they were worth, but a nice sum for each, and see how much was left. He'd have to start buying lumber; there wasn't nearly enough to handle this kind of volume. And —

Lucas, over by the door, was placing a lamp on the new end table. He stood erect and turned to Ransom, sporting a grin like he'd seen Ransom only the day before. "Congratulations, brother! Your furniture is a real hit. I'm glad."

And then Ransom did what gave him an immense sense of superiority and satisfaction. He walked out the door.

26

Hector Tamworth. Where had she heard that name before? Cassie studied the return address on this envelope.

"Another shoot?" Gretchen asked. "Or another shooter?" She set out the plates for supper.

Cassie tore the envelope open and pulled out the letter. "Another shoot. In early June. I remember now where I heard his name. Ty Fuller talked about him. He does shooting and riding exhibitions at state fairs."

"Ooh!" Gretchen peeked over her shoulder. "You mean, 'On Tuesday, see this fellow's Wild West show in our arena. Tickets on sale now.' "

"That's it. The Talbot and Lockwood show did a couple of state fairs, but we were usually heading south when most of them were running. They're harvest expositions in most states." Cassie glanced at Gretchen.

The girl was grinning wide and goofy.

"Cassie, it's so exciting to know you! You've done so many amazing things."

Mavis snorted. "One thing she's never done was the milking. So that job is all yours. How about milking one cow now and the other after supper?"

Gretchen's voice dripped sarcasm. "Oh, I'd love to. Milking is so much more exciting than riding in a Wild West show." She picked up her jacket and huffed out the door.

Mavis asked, "So this Mr. Tamworth is inviting you to a match?"

Cassie nodded and put the letter aside. She stirred the gravy on the stove. "He says he heard about me through Mr. Fuller, that I'm good now and only going to get better. He's invited me to Denver. They're doing an expo there. That's short for exposition. And a shooting contest is one of the grandstand events."

"Gretchen is right. That's exciting."

Cassie was only half listening because she was already planning. The shoot was less than a month away. This time Cassie must take Micah along to handle the guns. But no. Micah had a new life now, one no longer tied to hers. He was a bridegroom, a furniture builder, an industrious provider for his equally industrious wife. He seemed to relish his new roles, and Ransom praised his work highly. She could not ask him to leave this.

Then Cassie got a grand idea. "School will be out then. Can Gretchen go along and handle my guns for me? I need someone to have the next gun ready. I had a terrible time in Louisville, trying to do it myself."

"I'll have to think about that. Cassie, she isn't thirteen yet."

Cassie smiled. "By thinking about it you mean you'll be praying about it." And they both laughed.

At supper Ransom was his usual quiet self, and Arnett chirped. Arnett was a curious case, Cassie decided. He acted younger and younger in spirit, but his body moved older and older. He had slowed up since she'd first met him. And Chief. Poor Chief was not nearly as fine as he tried to lead them all to believe. He was ill, he admitted that much, but in what way she had no idea.

That evening beside the fireplace, Cassie carefully cleaned and oiled each of her guns. The shotgun needed bluing, but she didn't have the time or the proper chemicals. She would ask about gun blue at the store when next they went into town. She painstakingly removed the tiny flecks of rust that were starting and oiled it well.

Ransom closed the ranch's ledger, laid down his pencil, and stretched mightily. "I'm about ready to call it a day."

He only half rose because Mavis said, "Before you go . . ." He sat down again.

Cassie watched Mavis. Had her prayer borne fruit? Apparently.

Mavis set aside her mending. "I've been thinking about Cassie's next shoot. Ransom, you and I privately agreed that she is not to go alone. Not only is it dangerous for a woman that age, but before this last fiasco, she'd never traveled alone, and that trip was not a good training event. Besides, she cannot do her best when she's distracted."

Cassie had no idea they'd been talking about her.

Mavis went on. "Gretchen will manage the ranch, doing my jobs and taking my responsibilities, and I will go with Cassie to Denver."

"I think that's an excellent idea." Ransom nodded slowly, thoughtfully, as if still considering the idea.

"Well, I don't!" Gretchen snorted.

Arnett was nodding too. "That'd be good for Cassie and good for Gretchen. Only way to learn responsibility is to take on some. Wish I'd done more of that with my kids. And it'll be good for you too, Mavis. Get you away from here for a week or so. A vacation sort of, but with a purpose. When's the last time you took off from working?"

After sending Arnett a rolled-eyes look, Mavis continued. "It seems everyone agrees, so it's settled." She looked pleased. "Gretchen, if you wish, you may invite Jenna over to help you."

"Can I? I mean, I can?" Gretchen brightened.

No one mentioned it, but Cassie figured that if a man accompanied her, she would have to take two hotel rooms. Two women would need only one room, a fifty percent savings. And to travel with Mavis! Two and a half days each way on the train, call it three, two days at the shoot, perhaps a few days to tour around Denver to see the sights, to see the expo — what a great time they would have together! She was more excited than ever about this next shoot coming up.

Life would be perfect if only Ransom didn't hate her.

Getting into show-shape took a lot longer than she expected or wanted. For one thing, she was riding Wind Dancer for several hours each day, polishing their routine, practicing the simpler tricks. Could she trust her arm to support her without collapsing when she tried the harder ones? She couldn't bring herself to try. She had not done a handstand on Wind Dancer's back in over a year. Could she even do it again?

Shooting practice, though, pleased her. She instructed Mavis on how to handle the guns in a shoot and promised to write down exactly which gun she would be using in which order.

When the day came that they stepped from the platform into the railway car, headed for Denver, she felt a deep sense of satisfaction. *Thrilled* fit better. It was the first time she'd truly felt prepared since that night when her wagon burned. A long, long time ago.

And wasn't the journey south fun! They laughed, they watched the land glide by, they marveled at the mountains and talked about the passing farms and ranches. Cassie most enjoyed talking about homes. The whole idea of creating a home was so new to her. Mavis had made a splendid home that produced wonderful men and women — well, Gretchen would be a woman in a few years. Cassie had much to learn.

To no one's surprise, they talked about Ransom. Mavis remained convinced that he liked her. Cassie could not shake the fact that he hadn't wanted her with him when he went out for those missing cattle during the blizzard. Even worse was when they got back to the safety of the barn and he said nothing to her. Not a word. No thanks, not even criticism. Mavis tried to excuse it away. Cassie wasn't buying that, not at all.

Denver at last. Nice as railway travel was, Cassie was glad to get her stiff body off. The letter that came with her registration said to go to the Cattlemen's Hotel and Restaurant. She was pleased about that. With the restaurant and hotel under the same roof, they could eat without leaving the building.

At the railroad station they were about to hail a hansom when the stationmaster said, "You know, the Cattlemen's is right on the trolley line. You can take an electric trolley for two cents and save the price of a hansom cab."

Mavis smiled. "A trolley. That would be a new experience."

The stationmaster pointed. "Down that street a block. It's a short block. Don't forget to pull on the cord to tell the conductor to stop when you want to get off."

Cassie and Mavis looked at each other, thanked the gentleman, and picked up their bags.

Mavis shifted her bags halfway down the block. "A new experience. Actually, if we're trying to keep you away from nasty surprises, we might not want to court new experiences too much."

"Just don't get into a loud argument with desk clerks, and I think we'll be all right."

"When you become a mother, you'll recognize the value of cajoling instead of arguing. Ah. I think we're here; see that little sign on the light pole?"

"And the tracks." Cassie pointed to them, in the middle of the street.

They waited for less than five minutes before it came, rattling worse than their old wagon on a rough trail. Its wheels were set in the tracks, but it was connected to overhead wires by a long bar that stuck out of the roof. The trolley stopped. Cassie led the way aboard, not at all certain a new experience was the thing to do. Hansoms were much less noisy.

Mavis followed. She sat down with her bag on her lap and pointed above the windows. "That cord right there, I presume."

Cassie twisted. Yes, there was a cord on their side as well. "Now. How do we know when to pull it?"

Mavis asked the lady next to her, "We want to stop at the Cattlemen's. How do we know when to pull the cord, please?"

The lady smiled. "I'm going on past it, so I'll let you know."

Why didn't Cassie think to ask someone? It was the sensible thing to do. She was beginning to wonder how many sensible things she simply didn't think of.

The lady beside them reached up without looking and yanked the cord. The trolley rattled to a jerky halt. Cassie followed Mavis off the car. They were standing directly before the Cattlemen's Hotel. Their trolley went rattling away.

The lobby was absolutely cavernous, at least three stories high, with the largest, most lustrous chandelier Cassie had ever seen hanging in the middle of it. They crossed to the desk. She now knew about blocks of rooms set aside, so she whipped out her registration papers for the shoot to assure the desk clerk that indeed, she was a participant. He immediately signed her in. She was learning; lessons were sometimes painful, but she was learning. They were escorted to the second floor and a very nice little room with two beds. The bellhop carried their bags. Thanks to the service, she felt far more secure and perhaps even elegant. The thought made her swallow a chuckle, which made her cough, effectively canceling the idea of elegant.

Mavis shook out her own dress for the next day, and Cassie hung her skirt and blouse. The leg-o'-mutton sleeves looked flat and limp.

"We'll buy a newspaper when we go to supper," Mavis announced.

Cassie had not seen Mavis read newspapers. But then, this was the big city.

Cassie opened the curtains of their small window. It provided a clear view of another small window a hundred feet away in a building as tall as this one. "This is amazing."

Mavis came over beside her and studied the other building. She frowned. "What is so amazing?"

"A few weeks ago I was riding around in a blinding snowstorm driving cattle, not a building for miles, and now I'm in a huge city with thousands of people. It's just . . . strange, I suppose. I never thought about it before. Shall we go to supper?"

"It's early, but I'm certainly hungry enough." Mavis bought a newspaper at the front desk on their way to the restaurant and tucked it under her arm.

The waiter, a stylishly dressed young man, seated them at a small table for two, deftly swept up Mavis's napkin and settled it in her lap, and then did the same for Cassie. He presented them with the menus. "The chef recommends the prime rib with shallots and horseradish and the steamed asparagus. What drinks may I bring you?"

Cassie replied, "Tea. With sugar, please."

"And for me as well. Thank you." Mavis smiled.

He dipped his head and walked off.

Cassie pointed to the menu. "Here's chicken and dumplings and you don't have to kill the chicken."

"Prime rib and I don't have to grate the horseradish." Mavis lowered her menu. "You know? Arnett was right. It's been too long since I went anywhere farther than Hill City. This is a rare treat for me." She laid a hand on Cassie's. "Thank you, Cassie, for coming into my life. In so many ways you make me happy, and this is just one of the ways, opening up my horizons."

Cassie's eyes burned. "How can I thank you for accepting me?" And Ransom popped into her head uninvited. Again.

A booming voice made them both jump. "Mavis! Mavis Jensen! And Cassie Lockwood! Well, I declare!"

Jason Talbot! Surely not! Yes. He stepped up right next to Cassie's elbow. "Cassie, dear, stand up here. Don't you have a hug for your old Uncle Jason?"

Cassie stuttered. She sputtered, totally stunned. Jason Talbot. And he wanted her to —

She finally found her voice. "Mr. Talbot, I don't think that would be appropriate here."

"Eh, you're probably right. Mavis, how are you doing? It's been so long! Say, did you ever marry Ivar? Is it Mavis Engstrom now?"

"It has been Mavis Engstrom for nearly thirty years."

"Thirty years. It's been that long." He nodded. "I suppose so. And how's Ivar? I recall he doesn't have much of a sense of humor but is a sterling gentleman."

"Ivar died."

"I'm sorry."

"Thank you. His sons and daughter are doing well. I'll tell them I saw you."

He waved a hand. "Say, would you two ladies mind if I joined you?"

Again Cassie was speechless. Mavis was not. "It is a table for only two, Jason, quite small. Perhaps another time. We can catch up on old times then."

"You're here for the shoot, Cassie?"

"I am."

"Then I'll see you there. Ladies, my pleasure!" And Jason Talbot walked out of their view as suddenly as he had just stepped in.

Cassie found herself breathing heavily. "That was a — it was more than just a surprise. Jason Talbot." She wagged her head. "After all he . . ."

Mavis looked just as nonplussed. "I realize I'm no spring chicken, but he looks so old."

The waiter arrived with their tea and silently poured.

"He certainly looks older now than he did a year ago. No, it's not even been a year yet." Cassie took a deep breath to try and slow her thundering heart down. "A little less hair, more weight, and, well, wrinkles. As if he's had a hard life since I last saw him."

"*Hmm.* Perhaps he has. I must be careful not to be judgmental."

Cassie stirred sugar into her tea. Jason Talbot. A little less than a year ago, a lifetime ago at least, Jason declared the Lockwood and Talbot Wild West Show bankrupt and closed it without warning. Everyone who worked there was suddenly cast out jobless, with winter coming on. She, Micah, and Chief had set out in the wagon she'd grown up in, seeking the valley her father had always talked and dreamed about. On the way south, she'd discovered the deed that showed she was now half owner of a ranch. They found the land with Chief's help, what turned out to be the Engstroms' Bar E Ranch, and oh so much had happened since then!

She remembered that she had seen a man at the St. Louis shoot who, she thought then, looked rather like Jason Talbot. Now that she saw him here, she realized she'd been right. That had been he. What was he doing there, then here, so far from there? Did he follow shoots now? Perhaps he was looking for talent to build a new show.

It occurred to Cassie that when Jason disbanded the show he was disbanding his own livelihood as well. Her anger and dismay at his brutal lack of interest in his employees gave way, at least a little, to her curiosity. Perhaps she and Mavis ought to dine with him just to learn what he'd been doing for this past year. One thing was sure: Cassie held him responsible for the show's misfortune. That was a wound not easily healed.

The waiter appeared with a pad and pencil.

"I'll have the prime rib, if I may." Cassie handed him her menu.

Mavis told him, "And I would like the

chicken and dumplings, please." She grinned at Cassie. "See if I can learn something about making dumplings."

The waiter, of course, had no idea why they were giggling. "Very good choices. Thank you." And he marched off.

"Jason just commented about your husband's lack of a sense of humor. Ransom is much like his father, isn't he?"

"Very much. But softened, if you will. Ivar did not know how to relax and enjoy life. Ransom can do that when he has to. And yet he has as strong a sense of personal responsibility. I couldn't be more pleased with him."

"And that is why you insist he doesn't hate me."

"Sooner or later, Cassie, you'll learn that I'm right about that."

Cassie was not convinced.

The chicken and dumplings Mavis had ordered were very good — Mavis gave Cassie a taste — but they certainly weren't any better than what Mavis put on the table on a regular basis. Cassie's prime rib was very tasty, but the horseradish was mild, even bland compared to what Mavis made. It did not make her eyes water like Mavis's did. Cassie decided she would spend the rest of her life comparing every food she tasted to

Mavis's cooking.

After dinner they returned to their room, and Mavis read her newspaper. But that, Cassie learned, was not why she had purchased it. "Your sleeves," she explained. She crumpled newspaper and stuffed it up inside the limp leg-o'-mutton sleeves. "Now we let them sit overnight. If it were plain white paper we could dampen them, but we don't dare with newsprint. The ink would run and ruin the blouse."

The next morning the blouse did indeed look much better. Mavis could teach Cassie so much. But now, today, Mavis was going to have to learn from Cassie how to handle a shooter's guns in a major national-level contest. Yes, they had run through a shoot on a practice basis, but in a real shoot, anything could go wrong. *Please, dear Lord, give us success, and while you are at it, keep us safe.* Cassie wasn't sure why she included that last petition, but she knew Mavis would be praying throughout the day. Just that knowledge brought her a degree of comfort. At least for a moment.

27

"And here's MISS CASSIE LOCK-WOOD!" the announcer boomed out through his bullhorn.

Cassie stepped forward smiling and raised her arm high, her greeting to the spectators in the grandstand. People in Denver obviously appreciated shooting contests; the grandstand was about three-fourths full, and that was a lot of folks. Was Jason Talbot one of those people?

As that old tingle raced up her spine, Cassie welcomed it. These spectators came for a show, and they would get a show! She stepped back, turned, and strode to her table.

Mavis consulted her list. "Rifle." And handed it to Cassie. "I'm almost sorry I didn't let Gretchen come. She would so love this!"

From two stations down, Ty Fuller called, "Luck, Cassie!"

"Luck, Mr. Fuller!" *And luck to us, please, God.* "Perhaps next time." She shouldered her rifle and stepped out to the line.

Mr. Fuller and two others shot before she did and came away with perfect scores. One of those others, Cassie noted, was George Sands.

Cassie stepped forward for her turn. One down. Two down. Three down. Four down.

Click. Her fifth shell failed to fire.

Quickly she swung her rifle barrel to the ground, hoping the shell wasn't in there hanging fire. An official stepped in beside her, watching. Carefully, she pulled the bolt. Four empty casings popped out. She broke the breech and peered down the barrel. There had been no fifth shell. Cassie smiled at the official. "Safe."

The official smiled back and nodded. The announcer called it a misfire. The shoot continued.

"I'm terribly sorry, Cassie!" Mavis looked near tears. "That was my fault! I failed to load that fifth round. Oh, Cassie, I'm so sorry!"

"Aren't you the one who is always telling me God is in control? If you want to be forgiven, I forgive you. But it was a simple error. There's really nothing to forgive."

Mavis did not look the least bit convinced.

She handed Cassie her pistol.

Ty Fuller missed his last stationary. Cassie nailed all five of hers. They were now even and in second place.

Mavis took the pistol and handed her the shotgun.

Cassie had never seen a set like this one. Boys on either side of the backstop threw large beanbags up into the air as hard as they could. Beanbags!

"Beanbags?" The fellow next to her looked at her and shrugged.

She shrugged back.

When a beanbag is struck with the shot from a twenty-gauge shotgun, it explodes amazingly. Beans fly in all directions, a spray of many, many beans. It might be an odd target, but Cassie loved the visual effect.

One of the two shooters in the lead missed a beanbag and dropped to second place with Ty and Cassie. Mr. Sands kept his lead. So far he was maintaining a perfect score.

Dinnertime. Cassie led the way to the food tent, an unusual situation; almost always it was Mavis leading the way. But this was Cassie's world, and she reveled in it. Mavis's world, where knitting was an art, Cassie could not master. It was slowly becoming Cassie's as well, but she had a long way to go. She could cook a decent breakfast, make applesauce, clean chickens. She'd never milked. Here she was comfortable. Mavis did not seem to be.

Mavis fit in well, however, and seemed to truly enjoy talking to the people around her.

Back to work. The next-to-last set was stationaries with rifles, then pistols. Cassie and Ty remained tied, neck and neck, but the other two in second place dropped to third.

And now the birds. This first day they were using the clay pigeons. Mr. Sands missed one. One of the third-place fellows dropped to fourth. Ty shot a perfect round.

All those hours of swinging brooms and shotguns paid off right here. When Cassie finished the set with a perfect score, her arm still felt good.

And now everyone was shaking hands with everyone else. "Good shoot!" "Congratulations." "Good job!" "Good shoot!" "Congratulations, Miss Lockwood!"

"Incredible! The day is over, and it's not even four o'clock!" Mavis wagged her head.

Cassie was laughing. "So let's tour around the expo and eat something absolutely terrible."

What Cassie found incredible was the spirit of this shoot compared to that of Louisville. It wasn't the shooters, really. Many of the people shooting there were the same ones that were shooting here, at least in the top echelon. It certainly wasn't Mr. Fuller, who had organized that Louisville shoot, or even Mr. Tamworth, who was orchestrating this one. In part, it was that Cassie did not have a second there, and Mavis filled that role here. But that wasn't all of it.

"Mavis, you were absolutely right again." Cassie paused beside a booth offering a prize if you knocked over milk bottles with a ball. "I really cannot travel to a shoot by myself and expect any measure of success. Thank you again for coming."

"And thank you for recognizing that I was right. Thank Ransom too. When we were discussing this, he and I agreed on that and on the idea that I should come."

Ransom. Very well. When they got back she would thank Ransom. Why did she feel so much stronger and in control at a shoot, so much bolder? Was it that at a shoot, she was treated as an equal, a colleague, and on the ranch she was the new bumbling girl who had never seen a toboggan? Quite likely. Probably when they returned to the ranch, she would lose her nerve as usual and say nothing. She was not bold there.

The next morning they again took a hansom

to the fairgrounds. The driver tipped his hat as they got off. "Good luck, Miss Lockwood!"

"You know me?"

"I watched you yesterday, and I'll watch you again today." He drove off.

"Well, I'll be." Mavis looked a little dazed. "I don't think anyone in all of the Dakotas realizes you're famous."

Cassie laughed. "Chief and Micah, maybe. Let's set up."

They found the fifth shell under the table. It had rolled off when Mavis was loading the rifle, and she hadn't noticed. Today she carefully, laboriously counted each shell, double-checked the loads.

Ty Fuller arrived with his second. "There they are! Good morning, Mrs. Engstrom, Cassie!"

"Good morning," Mavis returned cheerily.

"Good morning! And good luck today," Cassie replied. She even extended her hand without thinking, a very unwomanly thing to do. Boldness, which she totally lacked on the ranch.

And Ty Fuller, master marksman, shook hands, the acceptance of an equal, chuckling. "Next-to-the-best of luck to you too. This is a good shoot. We're all pretty evenly matched. And . . . well, there just seems to be a friendly, lively spirit about it."

"I noticed that too. The spirit of it especially." *Hmm.* Perhaps her traveling alone wasn't completely to blame for Louisville. "Mr. Fuller, I —"

"Ty, please. We're friends and colleagues."

"Ty, I owe you so much. You helped me get back into the game. Thank you! However" — she smiled as she added — "I was looking at the difference in prize money between first and second place, and I've decided I don't owe you enough to let you win."

He roared with laughter, and she thought for a moment he was going to hug her.

They lined up. They were introduced. The crowd was even larger today, but then, the second-day audience was almost always larger. They picked up their pistols for the first round. Everyone shot a perfect set, including the fellows who had no chance of winning.

Mavis handed her the rifle for the next set. "There are five shells in this. I counted them!"

One. Two. Three. Four. Five. Perfect score on the stationaries.

She glanced toward Ty. He looked at her and grinned. Yes, the spirit of this shoot was quite different.

Perfect score on the moving targets.

There were no beanbags today, but the little boys threw fruit or melons of some sort. Very juicy targets, they exploded almost as satisfyingly as had the beanbags.

When the shooters broke for dinner, the crowd seemed quite pleased, with lots of applause both between sets and after. Good. That's what Cassie was there for.

She and Mavis went through the serving line in the dinner tent. Spaghetti was the main dish today. And the sauce was delicious.

"Excuse me a few minutes, Cassie. I'm going to go find out what they put in this sauce," Mavis said. "The flavor is so rich."

So Cassie was not the only one who compared all food to Mavis's cooking. Mavis apparently did too.

What was that commotion behind her? She twisted on the bench to see toward the door. Jason Talbot was standing outside, arguing with a steward or security person of some sort. It appeared he wanted to enter and the security person was preventing him. And now another fellow, an arbiter of some sort, was there talking to Jason.

Cassie asked Ty down the way, "Do you know who that is?"

"Never saw him. The man who ended the ruckus is Hec Tamworth."

"That's the one I meant. The other person is Jason Talbot. He used to co-own the show with my father."

Jason apparently gave up, because he walked off.

"*That* Talbot! Well, I'll be. So that's Jason Talbot." Ty nodded. "Interesting."

"Why?"

"I've never met him. I've only heard the name, and of course there was your Wild West Show. By reputation he's quite a heavy bettor. Even bets on shooting matches."

"I didn't know that. I do know, though, that my father won co-ownership of Mr. Talbot's show in a poker game."

"Sounds like his gambling goes way back."

Then Mavis returned, so Cassie told her all about it. She didn't seem surprised.

When they returned to the shooting line, the remaining participants were introduced all over again, for the grandstand held even more people now than it had that morning.

All but five contestants had dropped out. Cassie and Ty shot perfectly. A gusty breeze picked up that she failed to factor in well enough, and she missed one of the moving mechanical targets. Ty led by one. Cassie glanced at Mavis. The lady was standing quietly, eyes closed, head bowed.

The next round was clay pigeons with rifles. Cassie missed one, Ty missed two, putting them neck and neck again. Mr. Sands missed four. The fourth shooter moved into third place ahead of Mr. Sands, and the fifth dropped out.

Ty called, "Are you certain you can't let me win, just this once?"

"Not a chance." Cassie hefted her shotgun.

The next round was live pigeons, always harder to hit than clay discs. The discs sailed in a smooth, predictable arc, while the pigeons often veered in unexpected directions.

Mr. Sands got them all, but it was too late. He was secure in third place, and unless Ty and Cassie missed several each, he could not win.

Ty missed one bird that flew up, then ducked suddenly aside. That could happen to anyone. To Cassie.

It all hung on this last set. Cassie raised her shotgun. One down. The gray breast feathers floated lazily behind the plummeting bird. Two down. Three down. Four.

Five down!

The crowd erupted with wild clapping and stomping and cheering! Cassie stepped forward, raising her arm and shotgun high to salute the audience, so happy she had tears in her eyes. She had won! She was back! Her arm was good again. She had found her old form, recovered the skill she once had.

She'd won.

She'd won.

Mavis was actually jumping up and down, shouting, "Praise God! Praise God!"

Ty appeared beside her and grasped her hand in both of his, a bear-tight grip. "Cassie, I consider this the best shoot I've had in a long time. You're a splendid competitor!"

"As are you. It was pure chance that sent your pigeon off in the wrong direction. That pigeon could just as easily have been one of mine." *No, it wasn't pure chance, Ty, not with Mavis praying full time.*

"I insist on taking you and your charming second here to dinner. Six o'clock at the Cattlemen's?"

Cassie glanced toward Mavis, who was smiling. "We would be honored. Thank you, Ty."

He moved off, congratulating everyone, not just the top finishers.

She helped Mavis bag the guns. "Make absolutely certain they're all unloaded."

"I still feel bad about that mistake."

"I hope you get over that. God's will prevailed."

"It certainly did."

Here came Mr. Tamworth, extending his hand. "Fine work, Miss Lockwood. Ty was right — you're an up-and-coming star."

"Thank you, Mr. Tamworth. Mavis, may I present Mr. Tamworth. Mr. Tamworth, my second, Mavis Engstrom."

"Delighted! Do you accompany her to all her meets?"

Mavis shook his hand. "I'll probably do so frequently. You can't argue with success."

"Success indeed." Mr. Tamworth handed Cassie the cashier's check. "I trust we'll meet again soon." And he went off to distribute the other checks.

Cassie passed her check to Mavis.

Mavis's eyes grew wide. "Oh my." She picked up Cassie's gun bag. "I think we can afford a hansom back to the hotel, don't you?"

"I think so."

They were giggling like schoolgirls again as they left the arena.

Mavis suddenly lost her happy grin. "Look who's coming."

Cassie turned. Jason Talbot came hustling over, glowing. "Cassie! Now can Uncle Jason have that hug?"

Cassie really was emboldened. She said simply, "No." And she meant it. She didn't even say, "I'm sorry."

He wilted momentarily and then recovered his happy mien. "Your shooting was perfect! Just perfect! Tell me. Are you driving nails into boards, like you used to?"

"Now and then."

"Good afternoon, Jason." Mavis didn't seem particularly thrilled to see him either.

He tipped his hat. "Good afternoon, fair Mavis. Will you two ladies join me for dinner?"

"I'm sorry." Mavis did not sound particularly sorry. "We already have a dinner engagement."

"Oh? Who?"

Cassie replied, "A friend and colleague." And there she stopped. He seemed so like the old days, smiling and glad-handing everyone. She supposed she should trust him. After all, he'd sent her off with the wagon, horses, livestock, even George. He had given her ownership of them all. He had demonstrated that he had her best interests at heart even as his business was collapsing. He'd earned a fair hearing.

She couldn't do it.

"Well then, perhaps drinks afterward.

You're at the Cattlemen's tonight yet. Right?"

"I believe our evening will be booked." Cassie would book it with something. He should know that she and Mavis didn't drink.

Suddenly Jason raised an arm and waved. "George! Over here!"

Out by the gate, George Sands changed direction and came striding up, his gun bag over his shoulder. "My congratulations, Miss Lockwood. It was a delight shooting against you."

"You were doing so well, Mr. Sands, I fully expected you to win. Next time."

He smiled. "Next time. Actually, I usually do win, just not when up against you and Ty."

Jason said expansively, "Cassie and I go way back, since her birth. Her parents and I were close friends." He reached out suddenly, wrapped an arm around her shoulders, and drew her in close in a sideways hug.

She stiffened, rigid. How could he, in public like this? Her face must have betrayed her feelings. George looked at her face, at Jason, and frowned. Jason stepped away.

"See you, Jason. Safe travel returning home, Miss Lockwood." George tipped his hat and walked off.

"Thank you," she said to his departing back.

A hansom pulled up alongside them. It was not the young man who had conveyed them this morning. Cassie almost wished it were.

Jason whipped off his hat and swept it toward the step into the carriage. "Ladies?"

"You go on to the hotel, Mr. Talbot. We're not done looking about downtown yet." Cassie watched his face fall. Well, that was the way she felt.

"Are ye going, sir?" the driver asked.

"Yes. Ladies, I'll see you later. If not here, then in Hill City. I wouldn't miss the show in Hill City for anything." He climbed aboard the hansom and waved over his shoulder, a benign smile still in place.

Cassie turned to Mavis. "I'm sorry, but I just couldn't."

"I'm glad you handled it that way, and I totally agree with you. Say, the trolley line is only three blocks over. Let's repeat our new experience."

"Let's!"

Riding on the trolley was fun. Cassie was beginning to really like Denver.

They arrived at the hotel in nearly no time and strolled across the lobby to the staircase.

As they were climbing the stairs to their room, they saw Jason enter the front door. He looked preoccupied and failed to notice them.

"So the trolley is faster than the hansom." Mavis's smile could definitely be called smug.

"And only costs two cents."

Every time they looked at each other, the chuckles burst forth again. When they reached their room, Cassie got the giggles so bad it took two tries to get the key in the hole and turn it. Once inside, she dropped her gun case and collapsed backward on the bed.

"I haven't laughed like that in a long time."

Mavis sat down in the wing-backed chair. "You know, if I never see Jason Talbot again, it will be too soon."

"He'll be at Hill City."

"I know. I wonder what we can do to discourage him."

Cassie shook her head. Should she trust him or not? What was the right thing to do?

28

Farm wagon? Hansom cab? Wagon, cab?
Cab, wagon? Mavis couldn't decide which
she liked better. The cabs were well sprung,
providing a very comfortable ride. But then,
city streets were so smooth compared to the
rutted track they were rattling along on now.
On the other hand, she could not imagine
using a hansom to haul those dead wolves
up to Runs Like a Deer to skin, or fitting a
cab with runners to handle the snow, or
bringing a big load of melons or apples into
town to sell. For a practical person, and Mavis was certainly practical, this farm wagon
was the way to go. They hit a sudden bump,
and she almost slid off the seat. Make that
usually the way to go.

They rounded the last curve, and her
familiar valley opened out before them, so
green and spacious. Home. They'd had a
lovely and exciting trip, and their time of
sightseeing had been absolutely delightful.

It made her feel as young as Cassie. But now Ransom had picked them up at the train station and she was home, her most favorite place in the world to be.

Squeezed between her and Ransom, Cassie sighed contentedly. "It's so beautiful, everything about it."

Ransom cocked a boot up against the dashboard and let the horses have their heads. "The lettuce and onions survived the snow and are all perked up again. We're eating off 'em. The starts you replanted just before you left are doing fine, and we're going to put them out soon. And I hired three young fellows to help out around here."

"That's wonderful!" Mavis felt so good to be home. "We're gone two weeks and the ranch prospers. I'm going to have to think about that. Maybe I should retire."

"Don't you dare!" But then Ransom obviously realized that she was joking. "You had me going there. The employees are the three oldest brothers from the Stilson place over beyond Argus. Reverend Brandenburg says they're good workers and they can use the money."

"Stilson. They have how many children?"

"Reverend Brandenburg says nine. Used to be eleven but two died. The youngest brother I hired, Zeke, is only fourteen, doesn't have his growth yet, but he's a willing worker and he's real handy for barn chores. Good milker. His hands are so small he has to turn his thumbs under when he milks, but he strips the cows real good. Gretchen is tickled pink."

"I can imagine." Mavis smiled inside and out. All winter Ransom had been so concerned about finances. Now here he was hiring help. Like his father, he was extremely conservative with money. He would never hire if he didn't have the means to do it.

He continued, "The oldest, Isaiah, is a good carpenter, so I have him working at the furniture barn. Oh, and Arnett and Chief are living over at Arnett's house, so they don't have to come and go every day. I figure as long as Chief is there, we don't have to worry about Arnett."

There was a difference here, a profound difference. Mavis could feel it, see it, but what was it?

Ransom rambled on. "Figure we'll hold off branding until our pretend ranchers get here, give 'em something to do. The reverend says Isaiah's father is a good general carpenter if you can keep him off the bottle, so maybe we can hire him to work on the bunkhouse."

"The bunkhouse?" Mavis ought to quit

woolgathering and pay closer attention to Ransom. "You said a couple months ago that we couldn't afford to build another bunkhouse this year."

"We're gonna call it a guesthouse. Same thing. Porter wrote that plenty of people are signing up, and he's assigning them to ranches. Won't be the queen's palace, of course. Sink inside, privy out back. Got the privies dug already, because the men building the bunkhouse will need them."

That was it! Mavis hit on it. Ransom, usually so taciturn, was talking up a storm. And either he had suddenly become loose about spending money or he had money to spend. And that was making all the difference in the world for him. "How are we paying for all this?"

"Mr. Porter bought quite a bit of my furniture. We're working on that order now. And we got part of the deposit that the pretend ranchers put down to stay with us. Cassie? You're going to set up a bank account for your winnings, right?"

"Oh. I never thought about that. I suppose I ought to now that I'm bringing in some money again." She almost sounded worried. "There are so many things I never think of."

"The bank tells me a woman can't have

an account of her own. Don't know if that's true, but it's this bank's policy, so I'll have to sign with you. I hope you'll understand that the money is yours, and I won't have any part in it."

Her voice bobbed a little when they hit another rut. "So you've been looking into it."

"Rearranging finances a little, yeah. I figure we'll keep the guest money separate from the working ranch account and the furniture account, three accounts. Four with yours. Easier to see what's making money and what isn't and easier to keep the books."

Mavis's heart was singing. *Thank you, Lord! This is what Ransom wanted and needed! Thank you! Thank you! Thank you!*

They rattled into the yard. Benny and Othello turned themselves inside out barking their welcome. Ransom hopped down and came around to give her a hand out of the wagon. "Welcome home, Mor."

Was he that happy to see her? Or was he that happy that she'd be back in the kitchen cooking? At the risk of sounding swell-headed, she'd guess the latter.

She would let Ransom and Cassie attend the bags. She immediately walked around to her garden. It was looking in fine shape, considering that just when it went in, a foot of snow got dumped on it. The potatoes were up, already getting bushy and green. The onion patch was looking real good. And the whole plot was well tilled. No weeds, no baked spots.

Gretchen's voice behind her called, "Here she is, back here!" Gretchen came running up and hugged her mightily. "Welcome home, Mor!"

"Thank you. You took fine care of the garden. Thank you."

"Thank Micah. He keeps it tilled. He decided since you give them garden produce so much, it's the least he can do." She giggled. "I had to show him everything. He knew absolutely nothing about gardening. Can you imagine?"

"I can. Denver is a whole city full of people who have probably never seen a garden." Mavis walked back toward the house but stopped. They had already laid out the foundation for the guesthouse under the trees. A pleasant spot, and the barn smells would tend to blow away from it, not toward it. Three outhouses sat behind it, ready for business. Look at the stack of milled timbers! And she was gone only two weeks!

The kitchen looked pretty clean, although tomorrow or the next day she was going to go into the corners and behind the stove with a wet mop. Gretchen had supper cooking. Mavis lifted the lid. Chicken and dumplings! And there was an apple pie in the oven.

Ransom came in with a load of stove wood.

She smiled. "You did a good job, Gretchen. Thank you."

"You're welcome. Jenna helped me."

"Hah." Ransom smirked. "Yesterday she and Jenna were playing Parcheesi, and I said, 'You know, Mor's coming back tomorrow.' She got this horrified look on her face, I mean scared-like. 'Tomorrow!' and they real fast started cleaning up the kitchen. Took 'em some time too. It was pretty messy."

"Ransom! That's not true!" Gretchen glanced at Mavis. "Well, mostly not true."

Mavis sat down at the table. "Is there coffee made?"

"There will be in a minute." Gretchen went to the stove.

There was much to think about here. Much had changed, and Mavis was going to have to ponder what was going on. Later. "Ransom, when do you start the carpentry on the bunkhouse?"

He sat down beside her. Did he look

younger? He did — he actually looked younger. She had never guessed what a burden their finances had been on him.

"We'll put the framing up in the next three days. Oh, and we bought another donkey engine. Arnett's idea, and he's right. We figure his steam engine might give out one of these days, and then we'd be stuck. We use it for the furniture, the bunkhouse construction, for everything. They're ripping siding over at the furniture barn now for the bunkhouse. Both engines are over there. We'll bring one of them over here when we really get going on the carpentry."

There was a lilt to his voice that she'd never heard before.

Cassie came in the back door and sat down beside Mavis. "George and Wind Dancer and the others are doing just fine. We almost have a buffalo factory going with all those buffalo calves."

"I was going to talk to you about that." Ransom accepted a coffee mug from Gretchen. "We're going to have more buffalo than we need, even when you use them in your Wild West show. I was thinking buffalo steak might be a hit with our pretend ranchers, especially when they have live buffalo right outside their window. That is, if you wouldn't mind selling one of them for butchering. I was thinking that two-year bull, before George starts getting worried about him."

"They're guests, Ransom, not pretend ranchers," Gretchen chided.

"I agree, let's butcher that bull before he starts giving George trouble." Even Cassie was smiling. "And the calves will be young enough. Folks will love to see them when we display them at the show. You should have seen the crowds that would gather around the buffalo pen, just oohing and aahing. I bet some of them paid the admission just to see the buffalo calves."

Mavis frowned. "People paid admission to enter the show grounds?"

"Yes." Cassie's voice was hesitant, as if Mavis had asked if rain were wet.

"Mm."

"Do you think there was something wrong with that?"

"No, not at all." Mavis would do her thinking later. It was time to get back into the rhythm of the ranch. "I realize it's a little early, but I'm about ready for supper."

"And supper is almost ready for you." Gretchen pulled the pie out of the oven. "Let me warm up the bread — it's yesterday's."

Everything was rolling along as usual.

They had money to work with, and Ransom, Gretchen, Cassie — they all seemed happy. Mavis herself could not be happier.

Construction on the new bunkhouse ("Not bunkhouse! It's a *guesthouse*!" Gretchen would fume) began the very next day. Furniture making was temporarily halted as Micah, Chief, Ransom, the three Stilson boys, Arnett, Runs Like a Deer, Cassie, and Mavis all went to work putting basic framing together. The sides were laid out beside the foundation. That part was done by dinnertime of the third day.

With a pencil and scratch paper, Arnett explained how they would get the bottom of the framing up on the foundation, raise the top part, and fasten it all together. Mavis watched the Stilson boys as Arnett showed everyone what to do. They were paying close attention — even the youngest, Ezekiel. He might be a bit short, but he worked like any man. Ransom had chosen well.

Friday morning, Mavis and Gretchen were cleaning up the last of breakfast when here came the Hendersons. It was the whole family too, not just Jenna or her mother. They tied up at the front door.

"Oh dear." Mavis looked at them out the

window. "As much as I would love to sit and visit, we have that work to do."

"They're not here to visit. They're going to help raise the guesthouse. Ransom invited them last Sunday." Gretchen hung up her towel. "You know, when we get the sides up vertical and spike them together, like Arnett was explaining."

"Ransom has it planned out in that much detail?"

"Mor!" Gretchen sounded disgusted. "Ransom plans out in detail how he's gonna hold his fork at dinner." She went out to greet their working guests.

An hour later, Mavis and Cassie had abandoned the kitchen to drive spikes when another wagon pulled into the yard. It was JD McKittrick's delivery wagon with JD himself handling the lines. He drove over to their worksite and climbed down.

Mavis put down her hammer and walked over to greet him. "Good to see you, JD."

"I was going to send my boy out, but I wanted to come by and see your new bunkhouse. Besides, it's a beautiful day to take a drive."

"It is that." Ransom stepped in beside her.

"Oh, and Mavis? I'm really happy for Cassie. She was sparkling when she walked into my store, paid off her tab, and bought more shells for cash. Just sparkling! She's a gem, that girl."

Mavis smiled. "She is that. Always wants to pay her own way and then some, just like her father." Adam Lockwood. So long ago.

Ransom pointed. "If you would, JD, I want to unload them over there. Ike? Come help unload, please."

The oldest Stilson boy came hurrying over.

Mavis followed them to the trees. JD swung the back doors of his delivery wagon open and Ransom hopped up inside. He handed a framed window down to Isaiah; the boy propped it aside against a tree and took another. JD strolled over to stand beside Mavis.

"Windows?" Mavis asked.

"Ransom ordered 'em last week." JD stood with arms folded, a smile on his face. "Says he doesn't have time to frame up windows and glaze them with all the other stuff he's doing. So he gave me the measurements. Lotta people in town do that now. Doc Barnett — that new window in his parlor — I framed that one up for him. Say, the word is that quite a few people are signing up for that live-like-a-rancher thing Porter dreamed up. That's what this is for, right?"

"That's right."

"Well, you aren't alone. Fletchers are putting up an extra bunkhouse — they call it guest quarters — and so is Jay Slatfield."

"Would you like to stay for dinner? And coffee? There are still some pecan rolls, and I made cookies."

"Mavis, I'd love to. You're the best cook around. But I have to get back and mind the store. Another time, for sure."

"Well, then at least take along some cookies."

By the time he turned his empty wagon around and pulled up at the house, Mavis had a bag of cookies for him. "Thanks, my friend! Greet the missus for me."

He grinned. "Oh, I will. She's already envious that I came on out here." He raised the bag of cookies. "Thank you!" He clucked his team forward, and dust spiraled behind him as they trotted down the lane.

Mavis checked her ham in the oven, added water, and returned to the guesthouse.

After dinner they put Arnett's plan into action. They lifted the bottom ends of each frame up onto the foundation. It took all of them to lift a frame. This was heavier work than Mavis had anticipated.

Arnett stepped back, the supervisor. "We'll do an end frame first, for practice.

Besides, it's not as heavy as the long ones. Everybody line up along the top of it; you're gonna lift it up. Cassie, Ike, you'll keep the bottom ends from slipping off the foundation as it goes up. Wedge those two-by-fours against the bottom. That's right. All right, everybody, lift her up. Heave ho!"

The top of the frame rose off the ground. Grunting, the lifters raised it further, hand over hand. Ransom and Mr. Henderson snatched up heavy poles. Ransom wedged his up against the top of the frame to keep it from falling back. Mr. Henderson hopped the foundation and swung his pole up on the other side. He held it ready against the frame.

Arnett called, "Go!" One more heave and the frame rose to vertical, propped on one side by Ransom's pole and on the other by Mr. Henderson's.

"Cassie, Ike, wedge a couple more props in there to hold it firm. That's good. Right!"

Mavis stepped back, sweating. "That went smoothly."

Gretchen was sweating, too. "And just think. We only have three more of these monsters to raise."

This was so much like old times. Mavis recalled clearly the house raising and barn raising as all the neighbors helped Ivar and her put up their buildings. And all the times too, when she and Ivar helped raise buildings for their neighbors.

The frame for the other end went up just as smoothly. Everyone paused for coffee, milk, and cookies. The break was more than welcome.

Ransom said, "Well, let's get back to work."

Mavis stood up. "We'll take care of the cookies and things later, Cassie."

The girl nodded and went off to join Gretchen and Jenna. She might be a winning shooter, but Mavis must not forget how young she still was.

Ransom looked concerned. "These next two sides are over twice as long as the two that we just put up. I'm worried we don't have enough people."

"Well, let's try it," Arnett said.

He pointed out to Cassie and Isaiah where to wedge their two-by-fours, holding the bottom of the frame steady. He lined the lifters out along the top, alternating the weakest and strongest. Mavis noted that he considered Chief one of the weaker ones.

"Get your poles ready, gents." Arnett picked up a pole himself. "Ready? Lift."

Rather shaky, the top of the frame rose up. It sagged a bit in the middle, but continued rising. Then Cassie yelped as the bottom end of the frame began sliding inward. She was leaning into her two-by-four, but her feet were sliding backward along the ground. Isaiah was leaning mightily, but his feet couldn't keep traction either. Once one side slid, the other went with it. The whole frame shifted violently and Mavis fell forward on her knees. She scrambled to her feet, holding on to the frame to keep it from tipping back on top of her. Ransom and both Hendersons were shouting. Arnett was bellowing. She could not see what was happening.

Ransom was beside her now, lifting the frame away from her. "Mor! Let it down. Let it down. That's right."

Mavis squirmed out from under, stood erect. Cassie was back on her feet, but her bloody nose was soiling the front of her shirt. Gretchen was wadding up her handkerchief. She handed it to Cassie. Ransom jumped the foundation and hurried to her, stepping over the rafters and beams. He bent down until they were face to face. Why did that tickle Mavis so?

The framing of the whole side looked skewed as it draped over the foundation. Arnett was studying it, thinking, looking dismayed.

Cassie must have gotten her nosebleed stopped. "Let's try this again. We can do it."

"Not enough of us," Ransom replied.

Chief stepped into the middle of the framing. "Maybe enough if we do it different." Amazing! Until this moment he had not said a single word. "Mr. Henderson. You and Ransom are heaviest. You two block the footing. Cassie, Ike, they don't weigh enough; it pushes them around. Cassie, Ike, Jenna, you put poles up to prop it when it's upright. Mavis, you, me, there." He pointed. "Miz Henderson there. Jerry, Zeke, there. No, Gretchen, Zeke, there. Arnett, you too. There. We pick it up, put the footing on foundation, then you four move around to there."

Ransom bobbed his head. "Let's try it like he says."

Struggling, they dragged the lower part of the framing to rest on the foundation. They took their positions. Chief adjusted the distance between Ransom and Mr. Henderson.

Arnett called, "Lift on three. One, two, three." The frame wavered and rose. This was too much for Mavis to hold up; she would drop it for sure. But as it rose, it seemed less heavy. And now they were hand-over-handing it to upright and it hardly weighed anything at all. Cassie, Jenna, and Ike thrust their props against the top beam. Arnett sent people forward with more props.

When Gretchen and Jenna cheered, everyone else joined in. And all could step back.

"Mr. Henderson, Micah, rope the corners together temporarily, so they don't fall." Ransom handed hammers to Ike and Jerry. "We want to toe in the spikes, get those corners squared. Then we'll put up the fourth side."

Mavis sat down in the grass and simply watched. Ransom was a natural leader, like his father before him. He saw what had to be done and knew who could do it. He gave one order at a time, praised frequently. And she watched Cassie too. Cassie was simply sitting on the ground now, gently poking at her cheek. Her nose had quit bleeding, but her cheek and eye were turning purple. Would Ransom blame himself for the accident? Probably.

One more side to raise. They used Chief's arrangement and got it up on the first attempt. Gretchen cheered and the hammers resumed their pounding. The framing for the walls, the hardest part, was done.

Mavis was so bone weary she could barely

stand up. And now she was going to feed all these people. Well, as the ladies in the church circle always said, "Chickens and pigs don't fly into people's mouths by themselves." She trudged toward the house.

Gretchen jogged up the path. "Cassie and Jenna and I have it all set, Mor. You sit on the porch."

"I have a ham in the oven."

"We know, and we have the rest," Gretchen called cheerily over her shoulder. The youngest Stilson boy came running up past her, apparently to help.

By the time Mavis reached the house, the children were setting chairs and both rockers out on the porch. Gretchen put out a big pitcher of water and here came little Zeke with glasses. So the youngsters had orchestrated this part of the house raising as well.

Why not. Mavis flopped into her rocking chair, and Zeke poured a glass of water and put it in her hand, perhaps assuming she was too weary to reach for it. Mrs. Henderson settled herself in the other rocker. Mr. Henderson and Arnett took chairs. Chief settled himself on the porch step and leaned against the post. Mavis happened to know that was his preferred spot. A few minutes later, Ransom came out and took the last chair.

Mavis looked around. "Where's Micah?"

"He and Ike are doing the barn chores." Ransom smiled. He actually smiled! "Mor, it's all covered."

"Apparently so." This left her free to visit with the Hendersons, putting a delightful end to an exhausting but productive day.

But that evening as she lay in bed waiting for sleep, she thought about Ivar, and Adam, and Jason Talbot. She thought of the prize money Cassie brought home. Cassie said it was a typical purse, not overly large or embarrassingly small. She had won shooting contests when she was with the show, garnering prize money, all turned over to Jason Talbot to be kept safe for her. The Talbot and Lockwood show charged for admission. They charged for concessions. They charged for the performances.

So why did they go bankrupt?

29

"Think we should whitewash it?" Arnett was studying their handiwork, the brand-new bunkhouse. It was mid-June — my, how time flew — and it would still look brand-new when their guests arrived in three weeks or so. Eventually, Mavis knew, the pine boards would weather to the gray of the rest of the outbuildings, but not this year. For now, she rather liked the raw pine, and it smelled heavenly.

"It's supposed to be rustic. Besides, it would be the only white building on the property." Mavis watched Arnett a moment. The old man might be slowing down some, but his eyes still twinkled.

"Since Ransom's in town shopping, thought I might borrow his horse and go out to my place a few hours. The boys are doing good out there, but they need watching. I'll send the horse home with Zeke tonight if I stay."

"Certainly." Mavis filled her bushel basket with apples, very nearly the last in the bin. Shame the guests weren't coming in August, when the first of the summer apples would be ripening. A bowl of polished apples in the center of the table would be a lovely way to greet their company. She carried the basket to the kitchen and set it in the sink.

She was checking for brown spots on the apples when she heard the wagon outside. Were Ransom, Gretchen, and Cassie back from town so soon? She looked out the window and took a deep breath. No, it was not the shoppers. She hastened to the front door.

She opened it as Jason Talbot stepped up onto the porch, two men beside him. Jason was nattily dressed, but then Jason always dressed nattily. By rural standards, these men were downright formal, with cravats and black suits and ties.

"Mavis, old friend!" Jason doffed his hat and bowed.

Perplexed, Mavis said, "Jason. Come in, please."

"Delighted!" Jason moved aside. "I present Mr. Smith." One of them dipped his head as he removed his hat.

"And Mr. Jones." The other fellow removed his hat. "Mrs. Engstrom. How do you do?"

So he already knew who she was, since Jason had not said her name. This was getting more curious by the moment. She waved an arm. "Please be seated. I am assuming you are here on business."

No one moved. "True," Jason said, "but our business is with Cassie. Is she available, please?"

"I'm sorry, she's not." She was about to tell them that Cassie was in Argus with Ransom and Gretchen buying supplies and fabric for the guesthouse, but curiosity was fast giving way to wariness. She would give them no more information.

"It is important that we speak with her," Mr. Smith said. "We have pressing business."

Mavis's neck prickled.

She heard Ransom's horse cantering away out of the yard and out the lane, Arnett leaving on his way to the other place. The two men looked at Jason and dashed out the door.

And she put two and two together. "Jason, come into the kitchen, please."

"Certainly." Hat in hand, he followed her through the kitchen doorway.

She turned on him. "What is going on here? They acted just now like they thought

Cassie was trying to escape or sneak away or something. Who are they and what do you want?"

He raised his hand, a pacifying gesture. "They are business associates, Mavis. We want to offer Cassie a contract. A very handsome contract."

That prickle grew. Rarely did she ever get angry, but she was angry now. Furious. "A business contract."

"Exactly." His smile didn't quite reach his eyes.

"We know what kind of business you conduct, Jason. Chief is with us, did you know that? John Birdwing? And Micah. We've heard all about your business dealings. One day your people are all faithfully laboring on your behalf, and the next day they are jobless, homeless. Out on the street with nowhere to go. Without warning. And you didn't even pay them what you owed them!"

"Mavis, that's not true. I paid them what I could. Everyone got at least half their wages."

"That's hardly cause for congratulations." She narrowed her eyes. "And you turned out your own partner's daughter, whom you knew from birth, a naïve young girl whose only world was your show. Who worked for you and brought you a huge amount of money."

"I gave her the Lockwoods' wagon, livestock, and —"

"A dry, rickety old wagon, a team of horses nearly as old, and some buffalo and longhorns. She made you good money for years, Jason Talbot, and you did that to her! If she hadn't accidentally found that deed, she would have had nowhere to go!"

"Mavis, you don't understand. I love Cassie like my own daughter." He moved in closer. "I'm sorry, Mavis, I really am. I am so sorry. I regret all that very deeply. So deeply. Now I have the means to make it up to Cassie, if not the others."

"I don't believe you, Jason."

"That is all in the past. Now is different! If only Cassie will go to work for me again, I will make her a star. A star, Mavis. I can take her to undreamed of heights!"

"She trusted you, and you turned her out! Without the money she, let alone Adam, had put into that show."

"I did the best I could! Now I'm asking for another chance. Better this time."

Mavis took a deep breath, almost a sob. Another. "Jason, you know how I value hospitality. I never guessed that I would ever say this to Adam Lockwood's partner." She needed another deep breath to actually do it. "Leave my property. Now."

"Mavis, please. You're throwing away her future!"

"And you threw away her past!"

He glared at her a long moment, any resemblance to friendship abandoned. He turned and walked out. Instantly, she ran to the back door, reached up to the pegs, and grabbed down the shotgun.

The window was open, and she could hear the men on the porch. Right then she realized that Smith and Jones had heard the whole altercation between Jason and her.

One of them was saying, "You said she was a friend. That didn't sound like it to me."

And the other said, "I checked in all the buildings here, even the new one, and didn't find her. She's not on the property."

"Let's get out of here."

Mavis peeked out the window and watched them climb into their buggy. She saw them yank on the lines, jerk their horse's head around, and bring their whip down across its back. It bolted forward out the lane, and they hit it again.

Like Ivar always claimed, you can know a lot about a person by the way he treated his horses.

Cassie handed the near horse her apple core. Gretchen was already giving the other horse hers. "What do you think?" Cassie asked. "The flowered chintz or the gingham?"

"They're both really pretty." Gretchen hopped up into the wagon to sit on the box. "The chintz is going to be harder to iron after we wash them. Mor used to have some chintz curtains. I hated them. And the gingham isn't going to fade as fast. On the other hand, the chintz flowers are different colors, so it would be easier to match other things, like a rag rug or something."

"In other words, you don't know either."

"Let's go with that green gingham so I don't have to spend so much time ironing."

Cassie bobbed her head. "Good, practical choice." But the chintz was very pretty.

They walked back to Mr. McKittrick's mercantile. Cassie noticed as they entered that a big pile of supplies was still stacked by the door. She saw dozens and dozens of boxes of shells on the pile.

She pointed. "So Ransom isn't back yet?"

JD McKittrick smiled. "You can always tell the Engstroms' order. All those shells.

Say, do you happen to know a Mr. Talbot?"

Cassie frowned. "Yes. Jason Talbot. Talbot and Lockwood."

Mr. McKittrick nodded. "Well, he was in here this morning asking where you lived. You walked in fifteen minutes after he left, so you wouldn't have passed each other on the road."

"We stopped at Brandenburgs first, delivered some stuff from Mavis." Cassie was still confused. "He said he was coming up for the Hill City show, but that's not until next week. Why would he come early?"

"Beats me. Didn't say why and I didn't ask. So did you two decide on the curtains yet?"

Gretchen looked at her scratch paper. "Twenty-six yards of the green gingham, six of those curtain rods, and forty-eight curtain rings."

He nodded. "Twenty yards come on a bolt, that's a bolt and six yards. I'll run out back and get the bolt."

Cassie wandered over to the dry goods. She ran her fingers down the chintz.

Behind her, Gretchen said, "You really like that chintz. Should I tell him we changed our mind?"

"No. I don't like ironing any better than you do. I was thinking an apron for your mother for her birthday."

"Oh, that would be perfect!" Gretchen snatched up another bolt. "And look at this percale." She held it up to the chintz. "It's exactly the same color as those pansies. We could line it, and then splatters wouldn't soak through. They do sometimes."

Perfect for sure! They carried the fabric up to the counter. Cassie watched Mr. McKittrick deftly cut their order, but her mind kept returning to Jason Talbot. She used to love her uncle Jason, but not since he threw out her friends, not to mention her as well. It was a cheap, tawdry way to treat people who respected him and worked hard for him.

Ransom came in. "There you two are. I'm ready to load and leave."

"So are we." Gretchen reached into her reticule for the fabric money.

Cassie picked up a handful of boxes. "Since so much of this is mine, I'd better help, don't you think?"

He almost smiled. "Whatever you wish. Are you sure you have enough shells?"

Did he mean that as sarcasm or was it a sincere question? She would treat it as sincere, since sarcasm and humor went together, and he had very little in the way of a sense of humor, but tons more than his

491

father, Mavis had insisted. "I do. Mr. Mc-Kittrick is reordering for the show."

"You've been working hard with Wind Dancer." He carried out one of the cartons, Cassie right behind him. "Hours every day."

"I'm so afraid I'll mess up, or Wind Dancer will get confused and misstep. Or something else will go wrong. And it's taking so much longer to get back into show form than I thought it would. This show is very important to Mr. Porter, and I want to do well."

They stowed the shells against his carton and went back inside.

Gretchen carried their fabric out.

Cassie picked up another armful of shells. "Did Mr. Hansel have the brackets you need?"

Ransom went out the door with another big box. "He made them for me on the spot. That's why it took me so long. But they're exactly what we want. He made me a couple extras, just in case."

They nested the shells in between the two big boxes. The wagon rattled and vibrated so much, the shell boxes sometimes walked around on the wagon bed if they weren't secured. Ransom shoved the third large box against the other two. The shells were trapped inside now so they wouldn't go

492

dancing around.

Gretchen announced, "I'm putting these lamps on top of the fabric so they don't jiggle so much."

Ransom studied his fine old farm wagon. "Maybe I should talk to Emerson about some new springs for this thing."

"Oh, I wouldn't do that!" Gretchen's voice dripped sarcasm. "It's only thirty or forty years old. Let's wait another decade."

Cassie giggled. "Gretchen, you ride up front with your brother, and I'll ride in back."

"No, I want to hold the lamps. They're so breakable." She hopped over the backboard and settled in amongst their purchases.

So Cassie climbed up the wheel to the box.

"Ransom!" From down the street came a very familiar voice. Lucas!

He broke his horse into a canter, dragged it to a halt in front of them, and swung down.

Ransom climbed up into the box. "I got nothing to say to you." He gathered up the lines to leave, but Lucas grabbed hold of the near rein.

"Well, I have important stuff to tell you, so shut up and listen. Some guy named Talbot — figure it's the Talbot and Lockwood

Talbot — was asking around all over Hill City trying to find Cassie. Has two bruisers with him, dark men. He found out she's down here in Argus and came here. Everybody I talked to says they think they're up to no good, so be careful."

"Cassie's in good hands. You know that."

"I'm telling you, be extra careful."

Ransom nodded toward his near horse. "Let go."

Lucas lifted his hand off the lines and stepped back. As Ransom urged his team forward, Lucas called to them, "Be careful! Hear?"

And Cassie called back, "Thank you, Lucas!" It was the least she could do. He had just ridden clear down from Hill City to tell them that.

Ransom drew the team in from a jog to a walk once they rounded the bend out of town. "Mor said you two met him in Denver. Any idea what he wants?"

"None. But Lucas seemed worried, as if it's worse than it sounds like. No. I have no idea."

Cassie wished now she'd insisted on riding in back. Being so close to Ransom, bumping into him when the wagon lurched, made her feel funny. Not painful of course, or even bad, just a curious sort of funny. And

494

even mulling this turn of events all the way home didn't make anything clearer. Was Jason starting up a new show? He certainly would have mentioned it in Denver. Surely he didn't think she'd go back to him after what he did. Even if he was starting up again, Cassie wouldn't go with him.

She knew that for absolute, ironclad certain.

30

"Knock 'em dead, dumpling!"

Why did Cassie remember that offhanded bit of encouragement so many years later? She hadn't been quite twelve yet when Jason sent her out into the arena with a pat on the shoulder and that casual remark. Well, at last, after all the careful preparation, it was showtime here in Hill City, and Cassie was ready to knock 'em dead!

Mavis had said that no matter what the weather in South Dakota, the Fourth of July was always sunny and hot. She was right. It was sunny and hot but not too hot. Perfect show weather.

Mr. Porter was emphatically yelling her name into the bullhorn. She squeezed her knees and Wind Dancer leapt forward, galloping out into the arena and around its perimeter. She did a full turn, saluting the audience, her arms high. They clapped and cheered enthusiastically. Good! A lively crowd always made their performance better, hers and Wind Dancer's both.

And now she attempted the one trick that truly frightened her. She would do it first, while she was fresh. With a quick little prayer, she gripped the handholds and swung herself up into a handstand on her galloping horse. Her arm held steady! It was all milk and honey from here on!

She swung down on the near side and hit the ground with both feet, giving her the momentum to sail completely over Wind Dancer's back and bounce off the ground on the other side. She settled into the saddle and raised both arms high to the crowd. Her bad arm was doing fine. The nightmare was past.

When she galloped Wind Dancer out of the arena at the close of their act, the crowd was stomping and roaring, and she felt just as good. It had gone off perfectly, even the part where she did that three-sixty on Wind Dancer's rump.

The guest roper from Rapid City tapped his hat brim. "Great performance, Miss Lockwood!" Then he rode into the arena, his seagrass rope swinging, to perform his act. Mr. Porter's voice boomed through the bullhorn, announcing him.

Cassie slid out of the saddle, suddenly

weary from the strain of trying to maintain perfection, but also very happy. Mavis hugged her. "You're better than ever, aren't you! Cassie, that was wonderful!"

"Thank you. Wind Dancer is the trouper. He knows exactly what to do, and he loves doing it." She gave her horse an affectionate scratch under the jaw, one of his favorite places. And now well-wishers on all sides were congratulating her, including Mr. Porter. That pleased her most. She so wanted to give him a good show.

Gretchen came pushing through the crowd, the only person without a happy smile. "Cassie? Is that Jason Talbot about this high" — she indicated with a hand — "gray temples, hair that's thin on top, cheeks that puff out, and all duded up?"

Cassie's chest bumped. "Yes. Why?"

"He's here on the grounds, and there are two men with him. They look menacing, sort of. Not happy. They even kind of scare me."

"Where did you see them?"

"That concessions booth where Ransom is showing his furniture. They saw the *Engstrom* sign and went right there. He's not telling them anything."

Mavis butted in. "That is a thing to worry about sometime later. Cassie, forget him for the moment. You have more important things to do right now."

"You're right, Mavis." Cassie loosened Wind Dancer's girth. She would do her shooting routine as the last act, join the final flag parade in the ring, and the show would be over. Until then, the Engstroms would take care of anything that needed taking care of. She could be sure of that. Well, the Engstroms and God. She said a short prayer anyway.

The shooting act went beautifully as well. Chief handled the targets, and Micah handled her guns, just like old times. She ended with her favorite trick, driving nails into a board. Chief was really good selling this one. He, like she and Micah, was a seasoned performer who enjoyed entertaining, although just to look at him, you'd never guess it. He paraded across the front of the grandstand with the board held high, hooked his fingers in the three nails to show they were only half driven in, then set the board into the framing that Arnett had made. From across the arena, Cassie fired three times. Chief pulled the board from its frame and again showed it to the crowd, hooking his finger over the nails now sticking out the other side. The folks really liked that one! She left the arena to wild applause.

The Stilson boys ran out into the arena, dragged the two-by-six backdrop out of the way, and the roper came out at a gallop with South Dakota's flag flying. Cassie swung aboard Wind Dancer, waited until the other performers passed by, then followed them out with the American flag set in its staff holder on her saddle and flying free above her. They all did a simple chain weave at full gallop, then, a flag at each end, they lined out down the center of the arena and waved their hats. The audience stood up, stomped, and cheered.

This wasn't like old times. This was better than old times!

As the crowd began to break up, Mr. Porter reminded them that this was only the first of what would become an annual event, and he hoped they would return next year and bring their friends. He reminded them of the rodeo and Independence Day ceremony tomorrow, and said that Cassie Lockwood and her magnificent horse, Wind Dancer, would do one more exhibition. "So we'll see you all again tomorrow. Enjoy the other events going on in town and visit all our vendors. Nowhere else will you have so many choices of authentic western products." He waved his hat in the air. "Adios."

Cassie enjoyed watching him in action.

Wearing a fringed leather jacket, a wide-brimmed white felt hat, and a string tie with a turquoise stop, he reminded her slightly of Wild Bill Hickok. Mr. Porter had invited the audience to return and bring their friends next year. Where would they put their friends? The grandstand was nearly full this year!

Eventually the hubbub settled. Micah, like old times, led Wind Dancer away to his celebratory dinner of oats and alfalfa. Cassie strolled over to the Engstrom furniture booth. She stopped beside the ramada. Ransom was talking to Mavis, and they were talking about her.

Ransom was saying, "And now here's more trouble! Mor, they could have hurt you. I'm sure they're capable of that."

Cassie stayed hidden and listened.

"I can't believe Jason would hurt me."

"You were alone in the house. The men were building furniture, and the girls and I were in town. Yes, they could hurt you. You were wise to hang on to the shotgun until we got back."

Hang on to the shotgun? The only time Mavis was alone was when Cassie, Gretchen, and Ransom went to town a couple weeks ago. Jason and his companions must have come out to the ranch then. Why

501

didn't Mavis tell her he'd been there?

Because they didn't want to upset her before the show. What else were they holding back? On the other hand, that was not only very thoughtful of them, but smart. She still remembered all too well that argument in Kentucky and how it must surely have affected her performance.

But Ransom's next comment slammed into her. "Before Cassie came here, we didn't have any of this kind of thing."

She fell back a step. She couldn't hear what else he said or what Mavis replied. He was blaming her that Jason showed up! She turned and hurried away before they saw her. He still hated her! She had just about come around to believing Mavis, that he cared about her, and now this.

That settled it. She would not be burned and rejected again by an Engstrom man. She loved him, she was pretty certain of that now, but he most assuredly did not love her. It was in a way the opposite of Lucas and her. The show was over, her obligation met. She would leave at the first chance. To go where? It didn't matter. Where an Engstrom was not, that's where.

"Why, Cassie! There you are!" Jason Talbot! He broke out from the people milling around the stalls and hurried over to her.

He was carrying a briefcase of some sort, hard-sided, not a carpetbag. "Wait! I want to talk to you. I've been looking for you."

She stuttered something with "I'm sorry" as part of it. He was the last person in the world she wanted to talk to now.

"No, listen a moment, please. I have wonderful news. Look!" He set that little suitcase on a fence rail and popped it open. He brought out a businesslike sheet of paper. "This is a contract, a very handsome contract guaranteeing you an annual salary. I have been looking all over for you to provide you with this opportunity." He reached into his breast pocket and brought out a fountain pen.

Where were the two dark companions Gretchen and Lucas were talking about? They weren't with him. Oh, there they were, over by the fried waffles tent. Gretchen was right. They looked unsavory.

"Jason, I'm sorry, but right now I —"

"Just listen to this!" He pointed to a paragraph. "An annual income, a very comfortable income, and between shows you will be provided with a nice apartment in Atlanta, Georgia. Lovely part of the country, Georgia, but then, you know that. The show has been through there many times." He pointed to another paragraph.

"You have right of first refusal on any contests and exhibitions in which you may be asked to participate. And here . . ."

Atlanta. This gave her food for thought. She could hardly go any farther to get away from Ransom Engstrom, and Georgia certainly had a nice climate. Perhaps if she read this contract very carefully, no doubt to insist on a few changes, she could sign this safely.

She sighed. "All right. Give it to me and I'll read it later. Right now —"

"Just a simple contract, but it will make you a star." He closed his case, laid the paper on it, and offered her his pen.

"I'll take it along and read it through carefully, later."

"Cassie! You know I've always had your best interests at heart your whole life. It's a simple contract — standard, nothing unusual. Go ahead and sign it, and we can get started planning your career as a star."

She reached for the pen, hesitated, and drew her hand back. She must think. And she was too upset to think. She licked her lips. "I did poorly at the shoot here last year."

"I heard all about that from Ty Fuller. That's when he first met you. He has had nothing but praise for you. You had a severe injury, and yet you came through like the champion you are."

"And when we went to Kansas City —"

"A fine showing."

Things were becoming clearer. "Not in Louisville."

"Extenuating circumstances, I'm sure. Now if you'll —"

"Well," she had to admit, "there was a harsh argument the morning of the first day, and I think it upset me more than I realized, but still, I should have —"

"I cannot imagine anyone arguing with a cute little girl like you. Now, if you'll just sign here."

And now she saw clearly — at least, she believed she did. She raised her voice. "Jason, that's not my point! My point is, I was not shooting at my best, and yet I earned enough money to cover expenses and then some. And do you realize how much the winners walked home with?"

"Of course I do. I organize shoots, as it explains right here. Here's the pen."

She raised her voice. "Where did all that money go, Jason? I earned an immense amount of money for you at shoots, not even counting the Wild West Show, and I never saw a penny of it. I was a child. I didn't even know I was winning any money.

Where did it all go?"

"Expenses. It takes a lot of money to field a show that big."

"I was small and not paying much attention. The business end was grown-up matters. But I do remember lying in my bunk at night, hearing my father telling my mother that we ought to be making more money. And after she died, he said more than once that the show was so successful, yet we were always in the red. I remember, vague as it was, that he thought admission and concessions should have covered expenses, even without the rest of it."

Jason's head bowed. He looked very sad. "I'm sorry, Cassie, to be the one to tell you this. You see, your father was a gambler. It's called a compulsive gambler. He just had to. You know, I'm sure, that's how he became my partner. He won half the show in a card game. His gambling problem was severe in that he lost more than he won. I hate to have to be the one to tell you, but . . . well, there it is. That's why the show lost money."

How could he say such a thing? For a moment, Cassie stood speechless. And suddenly, it all came crystal clear. "Jason! He *won* half the show. *You* lost it! No, he was not a losing gambler, you are. He stayed home in his wagon with his family every night. With my mother and me. You were the one who left the grounds and stayed away most of the night. You lost the show with your gambling."

"Now, Cassie, stop and think —"

Those two dark men came over. One was smiling, but it was the coldest smile Cassie had ever seen. "Good afternoon, Miss Lockwood. You put on a splendid show today. You are amazingly talented."

"Thank you."

"Let me explain why we came with Mr. Talbot today. My name is John Smith, and this is my associate, Mr. Jones. We are business associates of Mr. Talbot's. You see, he knows how to put together a financially successful show, but he lacks the capital to get it started. We can supply the capital, but we have none of his expertise. Thus, the partnership."

"I see."

Mr. Jones stepped in quietly behind Jason.

Mr. Smith continued, "It is we who asked for a contract. We need some surety if we are going to back his enterprise financially. The deal shows excellent potential, but we need some sort of evidence to show our own associates that the idea is viable. We are agreed that they will readily accept a gesture of good faith on your part as that evidence. You will not be bound by the contract, we promise you, but we do have to have the signed paper to go through with the project." He ripped the pen out of Jason's hand and extended it to her.

She crossed her arms across her chest, gripping her elbows with her hands. "I remember something else my father said, more than once. 'Trust your gut. If you don't like the look of a thing, back off until you're happy with it.' Frankly, Mr. Smith, the idea of living in Atlanta is very appealing right now. But I have serious doubts about any enterprise Jason Talbot is involved with. I want to read the contract carefully, perhaps let a lawyer look it over. We have a good one here in town. It will only take a day or two."

The man's cold smile disappeared. His face hardened. "You don't understand, Miss Lockwood. This paper is far more important than you realize, and I'm afraid I really must insist that you sign."

A knife of cold fear cut into her. The man oozed such menace, she suddenly felt afraid. But she was angry too. What a frightening mix of emotions!

"Your interview is over, gentlemen, and

508

the lady has spoken her mind. You'll please leave now." Ransom! There he stood behind them, and never had he looked taller and more forbidding than he looked that moment. Cassie's heart leapt, and it wasn't all love. Hope makes your heart jump too.

Mr. Smith did not move. "This is not your concern."

Ransom took a step closer. "Cassie is family. That makes it my concern."

Cassie is family! His words rang in her head and heart.

Suddenly, Mr. Jones wheeled and slugged Ransom in the belly! Ransom buckled forward, and Jones struck him in the face. He flew backward and landed on his back.

NO! Cassie was so stunned she couldn't move, couldn't speak.

Mr. Smith was saying, "Let's go. Take her with us." He stepped forward and grabbed Cassie's arm.

"Whoa, gents!" Lucas! There he was, over behind Jason. Cassie had not seen him approach. He just stood there quite casually, his thumbs hooked in his belt. "That's my brother down there, gentlemen. Like he says, she's family. We look out for each other. May I suggest very, very strongly that you help him to his feet and dust him off, real friendly-like." His tone of voice would make a rattlesnake think twice about striking. "Now."

Cassie tried to move away, but Mr. Smith was still gripping her firmly.

Like Lucas, Mr. Smith could make his tone of voice strike fear. "We're taking her with us. If you're smart, you won't cause us any trouble, and she'll stay safe. You might want to dust your brother off yourself."

Cassie looked at Lucas, at Jason. On the ground behind Mr. Jones, Ransom was slowly curling up. Perhaps her best bet would be to grab the fence rail beside her and just hang on to it. So swiftly it startled Cassie, Ransom tucked his head, gained his feet, and without standing up slammed forward, shoulders first, into the back of Mr. Jones's knees. The man's knees buckled and he fell backward, tumbling over Ransom, hitting the ground with a satisfying thud.

There was Jason's briefcase! Cassie snatched it up and swung it at Mr. Smith. It caught him in the ear and he let go of her, so she hit him with it again, gripping it in both hands. He crumpled.

Jason bolted forward, started running. Lucas raced after him and quickly outran him. He grabbed him around the waist and carried him to the ground facedown. Jason emitted an "Oof" as Lucas landed on top of him. He didn't move, so Lucas sat down on Jason's rear end.

"Over there! Over there!" From out by the tents came Mavis at a run, shouting.

Sheriff McDougal came behind her at a hard run. He stopped in the middle of them as Ransom stood erect, and Mr. Jones, after making it to his knees, flopped around to sitting. He was still having trouble catching his breath.

The sheriff looked around, rather sternly. "Well, let's see." He pointed to Mr. Jones. "We have that one for sure, unprovoked assault. I saw him do it. And you," he said, looking at Mr. Smith, "were trying to drag Cassie away, and she didn't want to go. That's assault too, you know. Or attempted kidnapping. We'll work out the details later. Lucas, let that fellow up. He's an abettor to assault."

Cheerfully Lucas hopped to his feet. Jason moaned. Lucas grinned. "He says he wants to stay down awhile."

Mavis searched from face to face, looking as though she didn't know whom to hug first.

Ransom picked his hat up out of the dust. "Let's go home."

"Aren't you entered in the rodeo tomorrow?" Cassie realized her knees were so weak she needed to lean against the fence. Had one of those men really planned to haul her away? It was a shame she hadn't brought Othello along. He would have enjoyed joining this little powwow too. Somehow the thought of one or all of the men with dog bites on their legs or someplace else seemed especially fitting. Or perhaps throwing them in with George.

"True, and you are part of the show tomorrow too. We'll escort you, Mor, and Gretchen to the hotel and join you for supper after we get the animals settled down." Ransom shoved his hat firmly on his head. "Do you need help with these scums, Sheriff?"

"That would be right neighborly, Ransom, Lucas. Perhaps we better truss 'em up some. They might try to escape, you know." The look he sent their prisoners made Cassie shiver.

What a strange end to a spectacular day. She let Mavis wrap an arm around her shoulders and Gretchen attach herself to her other side. A strange end for sure, but more than a little satisfying too. What would tomorrow bring?

31

"Mama! Mama!" Jimmy Prewsky came running in the back door. "I got to slop the hogs! It's so fun!"

Behind him, his sister Ella burst in yelling, "And a baby pig got out of the pen, and I helped Gretchen catch it and put it back in! It's only this long!" She held her hands apart to show the size. "Did you hear it squealing? The mama charged right into the fence!"

Grinning, Gretchen came in with an armload of wood and rolled it into the woodbox. "Okay, you two, the woodbox needs filling."

Cassie was laughing with everyone else. "Gretchen, I never heard you get that excited about slopping the hogs. In fact, you're usually a little grumpy."

More laughter.

"I must have been doing something wrong." Gretchen was laughing too. "Come on, let's get more wood or Mor won't be able to cook dinner." The two followed after her, carrying the canvas sling. When they returned, they each had a handle and groaned as they lifted the load into the woodbox. They peered down into the wooden box by the stove and stared at Gretchen.

"Do we have to fill it all up?"

"Not right now." Mavis saved them with a smile. "Did you all wash your hands?"

Jimmy sniffed. "Now you sound like Mama."

"I am a mama. Breakfast time."

Cassie settled with the others at the table. Ransom and Arnett had built a table extension, but it was still crowded. Besides Cassie, Gretchen, Ransom, Arnett, and Mavis, there sat Mr. and Mrs. Prewsky and their three children, Jimmy, Ella, and Jan. Mr. Prewsky was rightly proud that his father had come from Poland as a young man and still pronounced their name the Polish way: Prev-sky. Jan, pronounced Yon, had been the father's name. Cassie noted that Gretchen was having a high old time with the three children and even had them enthusiastic about weeding the garden, while hauling wood was fast losing its shine.

Mavis had once asked how the time went

so fast. Cassie agreed. First the show, then the rodeo on the fourth, then the Prewskys here for a week of adventuring, and five days of that week were gone already. Where *did* the time go?

Mrs. Prewsky — Evelyn, that is — paused, her mouth working, savoring. "This corn bread is delicious. My grandmother cooked on a woodstove, but we've always used gas. Once you get used to it, a woodstove does a wonderful job."

Mr. Prewsky nodded. "Especially on slow roasts, like this ham."

Jimmy announced, "After breakfast, Ransom and I are going to shoe Biscuit."

Mr. Prewsky frowned. "Don't you have a farrier in town?"

"Only one, and he has three apprentices," Ransom replied. "But thousands of horses. So most people here do their own shoeing and just take problems to him. If your horse develops a sand crack or toes in or strikes, he'll build a shoe to correct it. He loves to do that. Sets a very fine scotch toe too."

Gretchen turned her head to listen. "Someone's coming in."

Mavis stood. "You folks take your time finishing up." She headed for the front door.

Why was the back of Cassie's neck prickling again? She followed Mavis out. She could feel Ransom right behind her, a re-assuring feeling.

Sheriff McDougal drew his horse to a halt and dismounted. "Morning, Mavis. How's your guest ranch doing?"

"So far, wonderful. Good morning, Ed."

Beyond him a high-wheel buggy rattled into the yard, with those two dark men driving! Jason's business associates! Where was Jason? Cassie's chest tightened. But then, the sheriff was here. She was safe. The two got out of their buggy and stepped in behind the sheriff.

"You all met Mr. Smith and Mr. Jones here. Just to let you know, they're out on bail. The judge set it kind of high since he decided they're at risk for leaving town. But they said they were coming out here on business, so after that last altercation, I decided it best if I came along."

"Welcome." Mavis's voice had never in Cassie's memory sounded so cold.

The sheriff lost his look of business and narrowed his eyes, a frown creasing his forehead. "I'm sorry, Mavis. I have some bad news. That Talbot fellow admitted he owes these people a lot of money, so he drew up a list of all his assets for them to take to partly satisfy his debt. I stood there watching while he was doing it so there'd be no coercion. He had it notarized. Mr. Talbot says Cassie was taking care of some of the things on it for him. He swears they're his but she's been keeping them for him."

"What things? A list. Show me." Ransom stepped up beside his mother.

Sheriff McDougal handed it to him. "I told him that wagon he listed burned, but he was thinking there might be two and this is the other one."

Cassie realized Arnett had stepped in between her and Ransom. He took the list from Ransom's hand and studied it. Cassie caught her breath and swallowed the words she'd been about to utter. Somehow, the rickety old Arnett looked and acted powerful. That was the only word she could think of. Powerful, and he radiated wisdom. That was it! Cassie suddenly felt more confident herself. Apparently Ransom did too, because he was letting Arnett take over.

Arnett nodded, rubbing his chin. "This says two, but there was only one wagon. Like we said, that burned last winter when those hellions decided to play vigilante. All that's left of that wagon is the springs. You're welcome to take the springs, Mr. Smith. I'm supposing the heat destroyed their temper, so we're right glad to get rid

517

of 'em. And I'll watch while you cross the wagon off the list so it don't come up again. The springs are behind that cabin right up the hill there."

Scowling, Mr. Smith borrowed a pen from the sheriff and scratched out the wagon.

"Hmm." Arnett pointed. "And it says here three buffalo." He waved toward the near pasture. "There they are. There's more than three now, because they reproduce themselves, you know. So pick any three you wish. They're all available. Ransom, give this Mr. Jones a rope so he can go get his buffalo."

Cassie realized what was about to happen. Keeping her face straight took a real burst of effort.

"No need," said Mr. Jones. "We brought our own rope." He pulled a knot of ropes out of the back of the buggy and strode over to the fence. "Uh, how do you get in?"

Equally sober, Ransom opened the gate for him.

He stepped inside and stopped. "Here." He thrust his wad of rope toward Ransom. "You go get 'em."

Ransom stepped back, both hands held up. "It's your buffalo, you get 'em."

Mr. Jones waved to Cassie. "Then you come help me. Herd them into a corner."

518

"If you wish." Cassie walked into the pasture, and Ransom closed the gate behind her.

She did not have to tell George what to do. The massive defender of the herd moved forward, his head low, and stopped.

From behind the fence, Mr. Smith shouted, "We want that big one for sure. It's the only one that looks like a real buffalo."

"The big one," Mr. Jones muttered. "Right." He fought to untangle his mess of rope.

Mr. Smith called, "You! Miss Lockwood! Help him!"

"Yes, sir." Cassie obediently started toward George, being careful to stay well aside.

Mr. Jones stepped toward George, a rope finally draped at the ready in his hands.

George stepped toward Mr. Jones.

Mr. Jones hesitated.

With a snort the huge buffalo lowered his head and lunged forward.

Mr. Jones dropped his rope, wheeled, and raced for the fence. They both arrived at the rails at about the same time.

As the man scrambled over the top rail, George's curved horn hooked his pant leg. George swung his head high, and Mr. Jones sailed into the air well above the top rail.

He landed heavily near Ransom's feet. The attacker dispatched, George trotted back to his herd, tail twitching.

Mr. Smith scowled at his prostrate business colleague. "Not worth taking the buffaloes. And we don't want those wagon horses. They're at least fourteen years old. With automobiles coming in, old horses aren't worth the expense of taking them to a horse sale. But we want that paint horse out there. Get a good price for that one."

Cassie gasped. "You can't have him. My father gave him to me when he was a colt."

"Prove it."

She felt the tears burning. "I had registration papers on him, in my name, but they burned with the wagon. I swear, he was never Jason's. He's always been mine!"

"Not according to this inventory list." Mr. Smith waved it for emphasis. "Talbot swore it's his."

"Well now, you know," Arnett drawled, "talk about old horses. This here is the daddy of that horse you saw in the show yesterday. We keep the trick horse stabled elsewhere 'cause those two don't get along so good."

Mr. Smith looked at him suspiciously. "Well, I'm taking this one anyway."

Sheriff McDougal wagged his head. "I'm

sorry about this, Cassie. I really am. You can send away, get your registration papers replaced, and then challenge his ownership in court. But as of now, his list is legal, at least as far as we know. Go get your horse, please."

No! Oh, God, please, no! God, her prayers shot heavenward. Behind her, Ransom was arguing vehemently with Sheriff McDougal, but she knew it would do no good. The men had that list, the list Jason had given them. Jason had willingly lied about Wind Dancer and the buffalo, just to forgive a few dollars more of his debt. To think she gave even a second of thought to signing Jason's contract! And that was before she knew these two were involved.

Now Ransom was offering to buy Wind Dancer, but Smith refused.

Cassie paused. Why wasn't Mavis saying anything? Cassie turned so she could see Mavis, who had her head lowered, eyes closed. *Please, Lord, hear her prayer! Are you listening?*

Cassie shifted her gaze to plead with Sheriff McDougall, but he shook his head, his eyes sad. No! Please, no! She picked up the lead line Mr. Jones had dropped and walked out to Wind Dancer. He stood there, his ears twitching as if he too were trying to understand what was happening. Always aware of her feelings, he stretched his neck and sniffed the rope, then nuzzled her chest. *No, God!* She tied the rope around his neck in a bowline and flipped a twist over his nose. It was all he ever needed in the way of a halter, not that he even needed that. He'd follow her anywhere. Get on, ride him out! Away! But where? They would always come find them.

She sobbed into his mane. *Oh, please, dear Lord, don't let them take Wind Dancer!* She wiped her tears. Maybe she ought to pray differently. God already knew she didn't want to lose her horse. How? What to do? She stroked his neck. *Please, Lord, show me how to save Wind Dancer from these people. Please help me!*

From the corral rail, Mr. Smith snarled, "Hurry up!"

She called back, "I can't!" She needed more time for God to answer. She knew Mavis was praying mightily, probably the others were too. *"Slow and easy."* The words her father always used when working with animals. *"Slow and easy."* She started the long walk back toward the group, slowly putting one foot in front of the other.

A wicked, intriguing thought popped into her head, part of an old show routine, a really old routine. She and Wind Dancer had not performed it for years. Would he even remember the voice command? She must try!

Again the fellow called, "I said, Hurry up! We don't have all day."

Quietly, she murmured, "Oh, drop dead."

Obediently Wind Dancer buckled his knees and rolled to his side on the ground, playing dead. He waited, all relaxed, for her command to rise.

She called to the men, "There, see? I told you I can't hurry. When he tries to hurry, this always happens. Now we have to wait till he wakes up."

A whole lot of arguing broke out over at the rail. Mr. Jones was back on his feet and holding his belly. The two dark men barked at each other, at the sheriff, at Ransom. Cassie watched, her eyes widening as Sheriff McDougal handed Mr. Smith a pen. They were making some adjustment to that inventory list. Scratching out the paint horse? Oh, she hoped so!

The two men climbed into their buggy, twisted their horse's head aside roughly, and sent it at a fast trot out the lane.

"Well, I'll be. Guess their list wasn't so important after all." He turned to watch Cassie, who was just closing the gate on

Wind Dancer. Her beautiful, clever, wonderful horse, which had dramatically regained his health or lost his excess years, tossed his head and nickered. The sheriff smiled. "He is one beautiful animal, Cassie, and I can't begin to tell you how glad I am I didn't have to haul him away." He went back to watching the spiral of dust departing out the lane. "How'd you get him to do that?"

Cassie grinned back at him. "I'll never tell. Guess he just got tired."

McDougal turned to Mavis and rubbed his hands together. "Now! That invitation to coffee still open?"

Mavis felt so relieved she could dance. Or sing. Or something. *Thank you, God!* She led the way toward the house. "It is, but I have a question. You think Smith and Jones were their real names?"

"I'm sure they weren't, but I didn't bother to try to find out more. They'll run out on their bail, and I'm fine with that." Ed lifted his hat and tipped it toward Cassie. "I know it sounds hackneyed, little lady, but my hat is off to you." He looked at Arnett. "When did you get to be so wise? I woulda thought you were a lawyer or some such the way you studied those papers."

But Arnett was frowning. "Somethin's

bothering me over that, Sheriff. Why'd you believe liars and thieves like that over us, folks you've known and trusted for all these years?"

Mavis opened the front door and ushered them inside.

"They had a legal piece of paper is all I can say, and any judge would have said I had to enforce it. That's one side of my job that I'd gladly give away. I'm just grateful it all ended well."

"Thanks be to God." Mavis led the way to the kitchen to find the table cleared, the dishes washed and put away, and their guest family out weeding and hoeing the garden. "Well, I'll be . . ." She rattled the grate and, after inserting a couple of small hunks of wood, carried the coffeepot to the sink to wash and refill. "Cassie, would you please bring the applesauce cake from the pantry, and Gretchen, a pitcher of cream."

"I promised that young man we'd shoe Biscuit, so I'll pass on the coffee." Ransom headed out back. Mavis heard him call, "Come on, Jimmy, and anyone else who wants to come too. We'll shoe Biscuit, and when we finish, Gretchen can give you kids another riding lesson."

When Cassie picked up the cake pan, she caught her breath and fought the tears that threatened. She'd almost lost Wind Dancer. She locked her knees to keep them from buckling and grabbed on to the counter. How could a man who claimed to be her friend, even to being called Uncle Jason, act like that? How could she ever have trusted him? He even lied about her father.

"Are you all right?" Gretchen asked, standing right at her shoulder. "Should I get Mor?"

Cassie shook her head. "I'll talk with her later." She picked up the cake pan again. "We have company, so on with the show." She could keep it all together till evening, couldn't she?

32

Two days later, they all helped the Prewsky family get loaded into the wagon and waved good-bye as Ransom clucked the team forward to take them to the train in Argus. At the last minute, Gretchen climbed in back with the children to comfort the two younger ones, who had tears streaming down their faces.

"See you next year, I hope. A week's vacation was not nearly enough," Evelyn called. "Maybe we'll be able to stay two weeks, if you don't mind."

"Our door is always open for you. It was our pleasure!" Mavis and Cassie waved until the dust obliterated the departing wagon.

"I hate to see them leave," Cassie said with a sniff. "You know, it's a shame Lucas couldn't enjoy this week with all of us. If the other ranches had as great a time as we did —"

"I know," Mavis said. "Guess it is back to

our real world. Good thing we got the calves branded, even though I thought those kids were going to fly to pieces. Jimmy and the mister sure pitched right in."

"And the family stayin' at my house left me a note, or rather *us* a note, thanking us for the perfect place to visit," Arnett said. "They said they didn't take part in a lot of the events, but they treasured the time to just relax. Exactly their word, *treasure.* Said they sure appreciated living in the quiet of the country." Arnett smiled a little. "But then, I can understand that, 'cause so do I."

He held out the note. "Lookee here. They even enjoyed using the cookstove to warm up the meals you sent over." He read a line: " 'And the barbecued beef was so great, we'll return next year just for that.'

"Can you beat that? And here we were concerned about their meals." Arnett slowly wagged his head. "Thank the good Lord all this worked out so well."

The three turned back toward the house. Cassie thought about the children riding Biscuit, riding Wind Dancer. If she had children — no, *when* she had children — they would learn to ride at a younger age than these. As soon as they could walk, like Cassie did. Children. Whose children? And immediately, Ransom leapt again into her mind, for the thousandth time.

She smiled. "You really have patience with children, Arnett. I was watching you with Jimmy."

"Funny." He gazed off toward the barn. "I like kids a whole lot better now than when I was a father. See ways I shoulda done the job different. Like give them a better sense of home."

A better sense of home. What a curious turn of phrase. Cassie mulled it over and over. Ransom had a powerful sense of home. So did Gretchen. Lucas? In a different way, perhaps. And yet the youngest, Jesse, had moved far away from home to go to medical school. Would that sense of home pull Jesse back here one day? Her father had left home, and for the rest of his life dreamt of returning. How do you instill that in a child, and what did Arnett do differently that he thought he should not have? Or should have.

Arnett heaved a sigh. "Guess Micah and I better finish up repairing that corner of the barn roof. Since the Prewskys helped us get the fencing done, we can cross that off Ransom's list. Maybe the roof too. Gonna seem mighty quiet around here without them kids. Maybe next year we could do this longer, like Mrs. Prewsky asked, that is if you all enjoyed it as much as I did. That Jimmy has a real knack for wood carving. I hope he keeps it up."

"You be careful out there," Mavis warned. "Don't climb up on the roof."

Arnett rolled his eyes. "Yes, my friend, I'll be careful. I won't go up on the roof. I'll let Micah do the roof work, and I'll hand him supplies. Chief will prob'ly be there too."

"Well, we certainly don't need any broken bones. I think when you men go back to the furniture building again, Cassie and Gretchen and I will come clean your house."

Cassie followed her into the kitchen. Mavis watched through the kitchen window as Arnett ambled off to the barn to join Micah and Chief. Ransom was planning on stopping off at the Stilsons' to tell the boys to come back to work, Cassie knew. She could not imagine Ransom and Lucas, without Arnett and the Stilson boys, handling this spread alone, and not to mention Arnett's ranch.

How should she go about this? Cassie sucked in a deep breath. "Can we talk?"

"Of course. Inside or out? Either way, the tone of your voice says we need coffee." Mavis checked the coffeepot and pulled it to the hot part of the stove. "I miss those folks already. Guess I shouldn't be surprised.

When God orchestrates something, it always turns out better than I could have dreamed. Get us a plate of cookies too, please. Might as well enjoy our break."

I don't think you're going to enjoy this, no matter how I say it. Cassie fought to control her mind. If she truly trusted God, like Mavis kept trying to teach her, the fear of what's ahead would not be gnawing on her stomach. *Lord God, how can I do this?*

When they were situated on the back porch overlooking the growing garden and the oak trees on the rise behind the ranch house, Cassie rolled her lips together. "Mavis, I cannot stay here." There, she had said it.

"Oh." Mavis nodded slightly.

"I know Ransom dislikes me, intensely. You said he does not hate me, but I know he blames me for all the problems around here."

Mavis held her coffee cup in both hands and tipped her head against the back of the rocking chair they had moved outside. "And how do you know that?"

She sounded peaceful, as if they were discussing what to serve for dinner. Cassie laid a hand on her middle, trying to keep the rest of her from shaking. "I heard him say that."

The rocking chair sang its rocking song. Two birds up in the oak tree were having a rather heated discussion. Othello came and lay at Cassie's feet and then sat up to rest his chin on her knees. His eyes implored her not to be upset. She stroked his head. "At the furniture booth last week."

"I see." Mavis took a sip of her coffee and moved her head from side to side, small motions that told Cassie she was thinking hard. And most likely praying. "And what did you do when you heard him say that?"

"I left." *I couldn't stand to hear any more.*

"Then you didn't hear him say how grateful he was that you came into our lives. That since you came, the furniture business is bringing in the needed cash money. George saved the calves from the wolves. How much you contributed to the success of the Hill City Wild West show and rodeo, and he figures you are the reason for our success."

Cassie stared at her. "You're making that up."

"Dearest Cassie, have you ever heard me speak an untruth? At least knowingly?"

Cassie shook her head and hid behind her coffee cup. "Then why doesn't he talk to me? Why does he act like I'm not here?"

"Because he's afraid."

"Hah! Ransom is not afraid of anything.

When I was in trouble, he stood up to three grown men." *And he said, "Cassie is family."* It still rang in her heart.

"Oh, when it comes to manly things, like defending a lady, he's fearless. It's emotions he fears, especially his own. He's afraid he's fallen in love with you and that you declared Engstrom men could not be trusted. That was when you were so angry with Lucas."

"But it's my fault Lucas left."

"No, no. Lucas left because he finally realized he was making a mistake. Then he made a bigger mistake by not talking his feelings over with any of us. Betsy is the right woman for him. In that he did not make a mistake." She half smiled. "You were wise when you said you loved him like a brother. He just had some growing up to do yet."

Cassie stared at the garden rail fence, seeing but not seeing the targets Chief had lined up for her there. Ransom was afraid of loving her? The tingle she first felt in her middle warmed to a glow. Cassie opened her mouth to say something and then shut it again. Finally she screwed up the courage to ask, "Why?"

"Why what?"

"Why is he afraid?"

Mavis shrugged and shook her head at the

same time. "Why anything. Because he's a man. Because he sees himself as slow of speech. Because he is Ransom, and he can't bear the thought of rejection."

"He sure manages to say a lot for someone who thinks he is slow of speech."

"Compared to his brother?"

"Who is glib and speaks before he thinks?" Cassie smiled.

"Well, that too." Mavis reached for a cookie. "So what are you going to do about this?"

"What do you mean, me? He's the man. He makes the decisions."

"Bottom line question: Do you love him?"

Cassie answered without a pause. "Yes."

"Then we'll keep praying about this and see how God works it out."

Othello leaped to his feet and raced off around the house to join Benny in announcing someone was coming.

Mavis frowned. "Too soon for Ransom to return. So now who?"

The dogs quit barking, and no one knocked at the front door. The murmur of a male voice arrived before Lucas appeared around the corner of the house. No *Hello!* No *I'm back.* Just "What is Arnett doing up on that ladder?"

Curiously, Mavis did not greet him.

So Cassie started right in. "The three of them are doing a job you promised to do several months ago."

"He could slip and fall."

"True." She could feel anger building, or at least righteous indignation.

Mavis asked, "Is he on the roof or on the ladder?"

"On the ladder with his belt buckle pushed up against the eave. He's nailing down all the shingles he can reach, leaning way out."

Cassie almost had to smile. *Well, he promised not to climb up on the roof, didn't he?*

Lucas asked, almost like demanding, "Where's Ransom?"

"Taking our guests to the train, if it is any of your business. And hello to you too."

Lucas had the grace to look sheepish. "Sorry. Hello, Cassie, Mor." He glanced over his shoulder. "That just scared me. He's too old to be doing things like that."

Cassie snorted. "I wouldn't mention that to him if I were you. Where's Betsy?"

"With her folks. We took a few days off at the hotel so we could come visit." He looked at the small stack of split wood. "No one has time to split wood even?"

"Been a bit busy here," Mavis drastically understated. "Our guests thought splitting and stacking wood, though necessary, was hard work. They cook with gas back home. I'm not worried. The Stilson boys will set to that when they come tomorrow."

"Stilson boys? Ransom has the money to hire help?" Lucas was frowning.

So here was Lucas, gone for how long, and now he thought he could evaluate and criticize. That irritated Cassie immensely. "There's a lot of work to do here. He had no choice, and they are good workers." She held out the plate of cookies. "You plan to stay for dinner?"

He took one. "Not sure I'd be welcome." He slumped down on the top step and leaned against one of the posts holding up the porch, sat up, and then dropped forward again, his elbows on his knees. "Mor, I've come to ask your forgiveness, and yours too, Cassie. I sure made a mess of things."

Why couldn't she be more gentle and charitable, like Mavis? "You did, when all you had to do was have the guts to talk to us. Sure, we'd have been hurt and probably angry, but we could have worked it out. Better than you running out on us."

His voice choked. "Mor, please, can you forgive me?"

"Of course I can, and I already have."

"Cassie, I know I treated you shamefully."

"I was hurt and then angry and then I got over it. And yes, I forgive you too." Did she really? Yes, she could honestly say she did.

"And Ransom?"

Mavis wagged her head. "Cassie and I cannot speak for him. The two of you will have to work that out."

"He wouldn't even talk to me in Hill City. Until that dustup. I heard Talbot and his two friends hightailed it out of here. Bet they forfeited bond."

"Long story, but all is taken care of." Mavis pushed to her feet. "Come, Cassie. We better get dinner ready. And of course you are welcome to stay, Lucas. Ransom and Gretchen should be home in a couple of hours."

He grimaced. "Maybe I'd better start splitting some wood."

"Go take care of your horse first."

Cassie watched Lucas rise and go back around the corner. Obviously, a married man is still his mama's son, to do as he was told. She noted too that no longer did he walk with that cocky stride he used to. It looked almost like life had taken him down a peg or three.

She followed Mavis into the house. What a day this was turning into. And she'd not even brought up the contract she'd been offered, and not the one from Talbot either.

The ring of ax on wood nearly drowned out the arrival of Ransom and Gretchen, especially since the dogs didn't bark. Gretchen came popping into the kitchen. "The Prewskys are on their way home, and Ransom's putting the team away. Mor, is that Lucas's horse in the small field?" She paused at her mother's nod. "And he's splitting wood?" Another nod. "Oh boy, are we in for it now."

33

"What do you think you're doing?" Rage ate at the back of Ransom's throat. Here he was, just like all their growing-up years. Splitting wood as if nothing more than a simple schoolboy disagreement had happened.

"Chopping wood. What does it look like?" Lucas split another round, slamming in the wedge with the maul and then setting up the halves to split again.

"What do you want?" Ransom tested the blade on the other ax with his fingers.

"I want to set things right. I'm sorry, Ransom."

"You think you can come waltzing in here, say you're sorry, and everything will be all right again?" Ransom balanced a round on the other block and slammed the ax down so hard the two split pieces flew into the air and thudded some ways away.

"No, I don't think that." *Slam, thud.* Set

up another chunk. "But I am admitting that I made a mistake."

"A mistake? A mistake is forgetting to close the barn door. Mistakes aren't deliberate. You left all of us in the lurch, including Cassie. *Especially* Cassie, the woman you had decided you would marry. Remember, Lucas? Remember?" Ransom peeled off his shirt. "In the middle of the night you took off without telling any of us. Betsy's folks were frantic. They were over here early, thinking we were in on it. No one knew where you were. If I could've caught you, I swear I —"

Slam, split, screeching wood, and whistling axes. Grunts and mutterings.

"I know. I was there, remember? And I've regretted how I ran every day since. But I did it, and now I'm asking for your forgiveness for doing it. Ransom, I want to come home. I know you need me."

Ransom leaned on his ax handle. "That's another mistake to your credit, Lucas. We do not need you. We did need you, but we survived, that storm in May and all, with all of us working beyond our strength. Thank the good Lord, we survived, and while there's always work to do, thanks to the furniture line, we can hire help. Dependable help."

He picked up his ax again and buried the head firmly in the quarter round he'd set in place. Usually splitting wood helped him think better. Right now all it did was paint a red rage across the back of his eyes.

Lucas rammed a splitting wedge in next to Ransom's buried ax head and struck it with the maul. It dropped through and the split wood went flying. "We could live in Arnett's house."

"Already taken."

"The guesthouse."

"You'll have to ask Mor. The guest ranching is her side."

"I don't even have to live here, you know. I have a good job in Hill City, and Betsy's father already said I can come to work for him anytime."

"Then go do it."

"God help you, Ransom, if you ever make a mistake."

"As I said —"

"I know, a mistake is forgetting to close the gate." Three more chunks flew after the others. "I can't undo the past. What do I have to do to make it right with you?"

Ransom tossed two more pieces onto the growing woodpile. He stared at the chopping block in front of him, unable to think of an answer that hadn't been said already.

Thwack! Lucas settled another round on his block. "I told Betsy you'd never forgive me. I told her I know you, but she said I had to try. She says we're brothers, and that's what brothers do." He thunked the front corner of his ax blade into the chopping block and picked up his shirt. Shoving his sweaty arms into the sleeves of his shirt, he settled his hat on his head. "Good-bye, Ransom." He tossed a couple more pieces on the pile and strode toward the back door.

"Where are you going?"

"To say good-bye to Mor and the others."

"Running off again."

"No, Ransom. This time I am not running. I am leaving like a man. I have done what I can, and I have no idea what else to say to you."

Chuck. Thud. Ransom balanced another round on the block. The memory of picking himself out of the dirt after that Jones henchman caught him with a punch to the belly — and Lucas standing there solid, right beside him. *Whack!* Lucas hauling over the steam engine so they could turn those pine trees into supports for the mine. Another round. *Chuck.* Was the mine a mistake of his own that God kept him from taking further? Lucas skipping out of work by going hunting, true, but then he'd bring home money from the game he sold to the hotel. His mother during one of her forgiveness pitches mentioning the elder brother in the story of the Prodigal Son: *"this thy brother was dead, and is alive again; and was lost, and is found."* And what if something happened to Lucas, and Ransom never saw his brother again?

"Lucas!" Ransom roared out the name. His brother was nowhere in sight. He tore into the house. "Where is he?"

"Gone down to saddle his horse." Mavis wore a weary look that added one more crack to his breaking heart.

"God forgive me, Mor. God forgive me." He stormed out the front door and down to the barn, where Lucas was just mounting. He sensed the women somewhere behind him, but he didn't look. They melted away as Ransom hollered his brother's name again. There, down by the barn.

Lucas was half in the saddle, swinging his leg up over the saddle roll. He paused, watched Ransom approach, and swung back down. Reins in his hand, he turned to face his brother.

"Lucas, I'm sorry. We can't part this way. You asked for forgiveness and I — well, I couldn't. Now it is my turn. Will you forget what has just gone on? And we can start again? Forgive your hardhearted brother and come home." Ransom flung his arms around his brother and pounded him on the back. For the first time in his life, he was not ashamed of tears.

Lucas didn't bother to wipe the tears from his face either. He nodded and hugged his brother back. "I can't promise we won't ever end up splitting wood again."

"How could Mor do all her cooking if we agreed all the time?" Ransom stepped back and, with a lightning move he'd not even considered, landed a sucker punch right into Lucas's diaphragm.

Lucas flew backward and hit the ground with another "oof." He shook his head and grinned up at his brother.

"I know. I deserved that."

Reaching out a hand, Ransom first helped him to his feet and then helped him dust off. "I didn't plan that."

"I know." Lucas rubbed his middle. "You do pack a powerful punch. Let's hope this is the last time we need fists."

"The woodpile is better. I can't say I'm sorry."

"Not necessary."

Ransom heaved a sigh and shook his head, flexing his fist. "Do you need to return to Hill City?"

"Yes, to finish up some things there. We can be back in a week or so."

"The guesthouse will be ready for you. Or we'll talk about Arnett's house. He and Chief have been living there some so they don't have to come and go every day."

"Betsy and I will be back. We just need to spend a little time with her folks too."

"Good. I have one other thing to clear up, and we can make some plans for another house."

Lucas opened his mouth, closed it again, and rode away.

The women were stepping close behind him. Ransom waited until Lucas was out the lane before turning to them. "Let's go eat. We've got lots to do." *God, you got me through that one, now comes the real challenge.*

Mavis gave him a pat on the shoulder as they returned to the house.

What is happening now? Every time Cassie looked up, Ransom was staring at her. Well, not staring exactly, just looking. Studying. He even smiled. After all that chopping and yelling, how could he be smiling? She glanced at Mavis. She looked more like a cat that had just cleaned up the cream. She and Gretchen stared at each other and shrugged. Obviously someone else in this room was as confused as Cassie.

Chief, Micah, and Arnett ate fast and then excused themselves, saying they had to finish the barn roof. They nearly ran over each other getting out the door, as if escaping. And no one mentioned Lucas! Things were getting stranger and stranger. Good thing she could spend the afternoon shooting and working with Wind Dancer. At least he didn't confuse her. And trying to make a decision on that show contract. Shooting events was one thing, but this was for the show season, to finish in the fall. Did she want to take Wind Dancer and Othello and go on the road? This show was on the up and up and promised her a hefty sum of money. Enough to buy cattle and maybe even a couple of Appaloosa horses. Continuing her father's dream, as well as Ransom's. He had mentioned Appaloosas once.

She'd not shown the contract to anyone yet, instead praying for wisdom and God's will. Did He want her to go back on the show circuit? So far she had no answers.

"Something is bothering you," Mavis said at the end of the meal.

Cassie wasn't even sure what she'd eaten. How to bring this up? She should have mentioned it three days ago, when it came in the mail. So much had gone on already, perhaps she should just wait until tomorrow.

"I repeat, something is bothering you." Mavis didn't ask a question; she stated a fact.

Cassie tried to brush her off with a shrug and a headshake but instead had to blink back tears. This should be a happy event. She was being offered a chance to earn enough money in a couple of months to really make a difference around here. Not that they were in as difficult times as last fall, but perhaps she could begin to make her father's dream come true. Where did one buy Appaloosa horses?

Just get this over with. The prompting voice sounded a bit peeved, as if tired of her vacillating. She pulled the envelope out of her apron pocket and laid it on the table. "I have been offered a contract to star in a well-known Wild West show, one of the few that is still in production. The contract includes my shooting act and trick riding, so Wind Dancer would go with me."

"I see." Mavis put on her *no comment* face.

Cassie hesitated to look at Ransom, but when she did, she discovered him staring out the window. Had he not heard her?

Gretchen abandoned her job washing dishes and plunked back down in her chair.

"Have you signed it yet?" Ransom asked.

Cassie shook her head. "You can read it if you want to."

Mavis rubbed her chin. "That's for how many months?" she asked as she picked up the contract.

"Two and a half or three — till the end of the season."

"They will provide your housing and travel, care for Wind Dancer, and someone to assist you during your acts?" A frown wrinkled her forehead. "It sounds like you'd need more than one person."

"In our show, everyone pitched in to help the others. Micah helped me a lot and Chief. Then I had Joe, who sometimes assisted me in my shooting act. Everybody took on two or three jobs as the need arose, even the animals. Wind Dancer hates it, but he can haul equipment wagons if he has to." She stole a look at Ransom. What was he thinking?

When he turned around and slapped his hands on the table, she jumped. "I think you and I need to go for a walk."

"A walk?" She stared down at the contract.

"Excuse us, Mor, Gretchen. Cassie and I have some things to discuss."

The frown left his mother's forehead, and a smile broke out instead. "Well, that sounds like a very good idea."

Cassie reached for the contract, but Ransom beat her to it and stuffed it inside his shirt. Perplexed, she chided, "Ransom!"

"How about we head out to the pasture and bring Wind Dancer in for your practice?"

"All I have to do is whistle."

"True." He led her out the door into the bright sun.

They strolled out toward the three-rail fence of the near pasture.

"You know, uh, I'm not good at stringing words together. I can plan a piece of furniture and run a ranch, but saying what's inside me, not real good at that."

"Mavis says that, yes. She calls you taciturn."

The corners of his mouth crinkled up. "She knows us kids better than we know ourselves."

"She understands me too. It's comforting."

"Comforting? Not always, not when it's your mother."

They reached the fence and leaned against it, shoulder almost touching shoulder. She started to whistle, but he raised a hand.

"I have some questions for you."

Had he moved even closer? Her shoulder felt hot, as if sunburned. That lovely tingly feeling was whipping up and down her arm. How easy it would be to lean her head against his shoulder. *Cassie Lockwood, think about brazen!* She heaved a sigh and stared out at the animals. A thick, sweet warmth rose off the trampled grass. The buffalo were scattered around, calves lying sleeping in the sunshine. The cattle the same. The other horses continued grazing, but Wind Dancer made his way toward them, stopping to snatch an extra-good-tasting mouthful of the rich summer pasture here and there.

"Cassie, I know you said you never wanted to love an Engstrom man, but I sure do hope you've changed your mind." She started to say something, but he held up his hand. "You know I have trouble coming up with the right or the best words at times, so please, just let me get this out."

"I — Sure. All right." The thought of looking at him kicked her heart from a jog to a lope.

"I never dreamed I would be saying these words to you . . . well, to any woman really, but Cassie, you have stolen my heart right out of my chest. I'm pretty sure I love you, and I want to marry you, and I'm double-sure I don't want you going off to shows and shoots all by yourself, but only with me, and being gone for the rest of this summer would be really difficult for me with all the work to do on the ranch, but if you have your heart set on joining this show, we will have to go see Reverend Brandenburg so we can get married, 'cause Mor would never let us travel together if we weren't married, but I'd really rather stay home here on our ranch, but — please say that you love me."

"Yes." She finally managed to get a word in when he paused to suck in a breath.

"But if you want to go, I understand. You —" He stopped and turned to face her. "You just said yes."

"Yes."

"Is that a yes, you want to go on the show? Yes, you love me? Yes, you will marry me? Yes what?"

She almost chuckled at the perplexed look on his rugged face. "All right, I have a question."

He nodded.

"You said you love me?"

"With all my heart."

'Well, you have certainly done a good job of hiding that."

"I know. I was so afraid you'd meant what you said and you'd turn me down. Reject me. And I couldn't understand why you took it so calmly when Lucas rejected you for —" He quit.

"*Which* what I said?" She needed to shake her head to clarify her thoughts. She held up a hand. Wind Dancer stuck his head over the fence and thrust his nose against her hand to be petted. She pushed him away. "Let's start again."

This time he blew in her face and nosed Ransom off to the side.

"I've had it." He grabbed Cassie's hand. "I am not going to compete with a horse."

Cassie hung back. "Let me finish."

"All right."

"Yes, I love you. I think I've loved you since when I got here. Yes, I'll marry you, if you promise to go through with it and won't run out on me."

His look answered that question.

"And . . ." Her heart was bouncing around so wildly, she could hardly think what to say or how to say it.

He waited.

"I only want to join that show for the rest of the summer so I can have money to buy you more cattle and maybe some Appaloosa horses."

"I don't care about those things. I'd much rather have you right here." He pulled her up to his chest, gently pushed Wind Dancer's head away, and kissed her. It flooded her with happiness. It was the kind of kiss her parents used to do when they didn't know she was watching — soft and lingering. It was the most amazing thing she'd ever done.

She melted against him, almost dizzy but not really, some other feeling similar to being dizzy or off balance. She breathed a happy sigh and smiled up at him.

"Do you think we can do that again?" she asked. "Just to make sure?"

"Make sure what?"

"That — Wind Dancer! Bring his hat back!"

But then Ransom kissed her again, just to make sure, and for a moment she forgot Wind Dancer and hats and everything. *So this is what happiness feels like.* He lifted away. "When can we get married?"

"Uh . . ." Her brain had long since ceased working. "How about October?"

"That's three months away. How about next week?"

After a few deep breaths, she was recovering. Mostly. She smiled and suddenly, impulsively, kissed his chin. "Can't we discuss that later? Wind Dancer, bring that hat back!" Secure in the circle of his arm, she watched her horse toss the well-worn hat in the air, and when it landed, he stomped right on it. "I think I owe you a new hat."

"That's the least of my worries. But the biggest one is taken away." He lifted his face heavenward and shouted, "Thank you, heavenly Father! She loves me."

Laughter broke out from the corner of the barn, where a ladder still leaned against it. Micah, Chief, and Arnett were clapping enthusiastically, grinning.

Ransom scowled. "We have an audience."

"Guess we'd better get used to it. Have you ever thought of doing trick riding in a Wild West show?"

EPILOGUE

With the oak and maple trees troubadouring a celebration, Cassie lay in bed and watched a sunbeam peek in the window and tiptoe across to the braided rug by the bed. She'd heard Mavis in the kitchen some time ago but was under strict orders not to make breakfast this morning. After all, the bride was not to see the groom on her wedding day until the ceremony, and right after breakfast, Ransom was heading over to Arnett's house until the time came.

Her wedding day. While she had wanted a small ceremony here at the ranch house, somehow it had turned into a community-wide celebration. She did have her way with only family and close friends for the actual ceremony, and that would be here at the ranch in the big room she so dearly loved. At eleven o'clock she would become Mrs. Ransom Engstrom.

She tried to stay away from the *if only*s,

but thoughts of her mother and father persisted. *Father, I know they are there in heaven with you, and I do hope they can see and rejoice with me, with all of us. I know they would think Ransom a good man who will make a wonderful husband.* She rolled her lips together to keep from laughing out loud in absolute delight.

At a tap at the door, she called, "Come in," and Gretchen nudged the door open with her foot, since she was carrying a breakfast tray. Mavis entered right behind her.

"Oh, what a nice surprise! Is this why I've been confined to my room?" Cassie stacked her pillows in place and pushed herself up against them. "Surely I am not to eat alone?"

"Never fear, we brought for three. Getting Ransom out of here was like trying to lead George. Talk about stubborn males." Mavis set her tray with steaming coffee cups on the dresser while Gretchen settled hers over Cassie's legs.

The sunbeam hit the leaves in a vase on the tray and set the colors radiating fire.

"I prayed for a glorious day and look at this one." Gretchen climbed up on the bed and sat cross-legged at the foot. Mavis handed each of them a plate with two pancakes rolled around sausages, apple-sauce, and thick cream. She pulled the chair closer to the bed and, sitting, leaned back with a sigh.

"You know, when you and Ransom decided that Lucas and Betsy should live in Arnett's house, I wasn't sure that was best, but now I know it is. This way I am not losing my new daughter, even to a few miles. Halfway up the slope behind this house is such an ideal place to build your house. The path is already worn enough to be visible."

Cassie nodded. "Today I think I want to say our grace. Is that all right?"

Mavis nodded.

"Heavenly Father, I thank you for my home and family here. You have showered us with blessings, including this delightful breakfast and a good harvest, and you are rebuilding the love and trust that nearly drove us apart. Thank you for your Son and your Word and your great love for each of us. I dreamed of a home and family, and you made that happen far beyond what I had dreamed, as only you can do. In Jesus' name I pray, amen."

Mavis was the first to sniff and seek a handkerchief in her apron pocket. "Thank you."

The click of claws on the planked floor

announced that Othello was joining the party. He lay down on the rug of many colors, his tail thumping and his tongue hanging out the side of his grinning mouth.

"See? When you are happy, he is happy." Mavis cut into her pancakes. "Lucas and Arnett have been up since well before dawn building the fires in the pit. He said they are about to hang the carcass." Cooking half a steer over coals took hours, and the party was to start late afternoon.

"Lucas said the apple cider was just right." Gretchen grinned at her mother. Lucas had been teasing her about the bubbles rising in the jugs. They'd all spent hours at the cider press to make sure there was plenty for everyone. Good thing the apple harvest had been a good one.

Cassie finished her breakfast and sipped her coffee. Her dress hanging on the chifforobe door made her smile. She, Mavis, and Gretchen had sewn it together. As Mavis said, every stitch was made with love. They'd made sure that Ransom hadn't seen that yet either. Oh, that dress! Shimmery, soft turquoise satin! Pin tucks fitted the bodice and the lower portion of the leg-o'-mutton sleeves to Cassie perfectly, and narrow ruching around the heart-shaped neckline complemented the whole look. Cassie felt regal when wearing it. The ruching circling the skirt ten inches above the hem caught the light in a different shade and looked almost like a string of jewels.

Gretchen and Mavis turned to see where she was looking.

Mavis nodded, her face showing obvious pleasure. "I must say, we did a fine job on that dress. I had no idea you were a clothing designer too."

Cassie shrugged. "Neither did I. Far as I remember we all contributed."

"Someday, when I get married, I want a dress just like that." Gretchen sighed dreamily.

"Don't go getting in a hurry." Mavis tapped her daughter on the knee. "You know that Ransom and Lucas will be real careful who gets to court their little sister."

Gretchen made a face. "Poor guy, having to face them."

"It's hard to believe we have the food all ready," Mavis said as the clock bonged in the front room. "We'd better get a move on. Eleven will be here before we know it."

A couple of hours later, Cassie and Gretchen, all dressed, waited in the bedroom. They could hear Reverend Brandenburg teasing Ransom, and Lucas joining in.

"Are you frightened?" Gretchen asked.

"Should I be?" Cassie turned from staring up the hill toward the half-built house. For now, she and Ransom would live in the new bunkhouse, where he had placed the bed and dresser he and the others had made. The oak set was a work of art, and Mr. Porter already had placed orders for two more sets. Arnett had carved their names and the wedding date on both pieces as part of the decoration he was getting famous for adding.

Gretchen shrugged. "I don't know, but a book I read said the heroine was afraid."

Cassie caught her breath. That was the signal, the guitar playing.

A rap sounded on the door, and Arnett asked, "Are you ready?"

"I am." Cassie took her bouquet of fall leaves and flowers from Gretchen's hands. "You ready?"

"I am." As maid of honor Gretchen took her job very seriously. She walked out the door, kissed Arnett on the cheek, and went to stand by her mother in the doorway.

Arnett held his arm out for Cassie to take. "You look absolutely lovely, my dear."

"Thank you." She touched the flattened lump of gold that Chief had found when the snow melted, the remains of her Mother's beloved locket. He had drilled a hole in it and strung it on a narrow ribbon. She did have one piece of her former life.

"Shall we?" Arnett said.

"We shall."

Cassie stopped in the doorway so Mavis could step to her other side. The fireplace and mantel were nearly hidden by jars and buckets of riotously colored fall leaves. Reverend Brandenburg stood in front of the display, his Bible open, and smiled at the gathering. Gretchen stopped in front of the reverend and turned as they had rehearsed. Ransom, wearing the leather vest Runs like a Deer had made for him over the shirt Cassie had sewn, waited with Lucas as best man. The guitar played an arpeggio, and Ransom turned to face her. His smile had a bit of a wobble on it, probably due to the moisture gathering in his eyes.

Cassie raised her chin slightly. *Thank you, Lord,* was her prayer as she walked forward. At the front she kissed first Mavis and then Arnett and smiled at Lucas, who looked about as nervous as Ransom. But her gaze locked on Ransom's face. This was the man God had given her, had planned for her. She knew that with all her heart.

"Dearly beloved . . ." The words rolled across the room.

Dearly beloved. That was so true for all of

them. Beloved of God and one another.

She lost herself in the beauty of the moment, the hush of the room but for the gentle fingering of the guitar strings. Gathered before God. *Lord, let us always be gathered before you.*

She fought the tears as Ransom looked into her eyes and repeated the words. His eyes shimmered but his voice held strong and true, just like the man.

When her turn came to vow to love and honor her husband, she spoke with absolute conviction. "Till death do us part." *Lord, please let that be many years away.*

When Reverend Brandenburg lifted his hands and voice in the benediction, she heard more than one sniff from those gathered. "And give thee His peace."

The guitar flowed into an old hymn that spoke of peace like a river.

"Ransom Engstrom, you may kiss your bride."

Cassie felt his strong arms go around her and his lips settle on hers. She kissed him in return and then leaned back enough to smile up into his face. "I do love you, Mr. Engstrom," she whispered.

Ransom caught her around the waist and whirled her around to stand in the curve of his arm. Their laughter harmonized as they faced those gathered around them.

"Where are you going, Lucas?" Ransom called as his brother rushed out the front door.

"To check the meat. We have company coming, remember?"

Later, after hours of feasting and celebrating, just as the sun slipped behind the western hills, Cassie and Ransom stood leaning against the corral railing. Wind Dancer waited for his treat, nosing Cassie's hand in Ransom's. Cassie looked up at her husband. "That hat looks mighty good on you."

"It should — you picked it out." But this time he was quicker than the horse. He snatched his fawn-colored felt hat off his head and hid it behind him. "Not this one, Dancer. If you don't like it, too bad. I like it and it is going to stay in one piece." Wind Dancer tossed his head, and Cassie could have sworn she saw him wink.

"Did you set him up for that?"

She shook her head. "Neither time. I tell you, he's the smartest horse I've seen anywhere."

The musicians were tuning up, announcing that the dancing was about to start. Cassie patted her horse one more time, locked her arm in Ransom's, and together they strolled over to the flat area where the folks were gathered. Her father's dreams of his valley had come true for her, the home she'd never had and a family who took her in. Cassie Lockwood Engstrom now had a place to belong and perhaps to dream even grander dreams. She raised her face to catch the evening breeze just starting up. If she listened hard, would she hear the whispers on the wind or had Mavis made that up? Whispers of love and belonging.

"Shall we dance, Mrs. Engstrom?"

"Indeed we shall. For the rest of our lives, Mr. Engstrom."

ABOUT THE AUTHOR

Lauraine Snelling is the award-winning author of over 70 books, fiction and nonfiction, for adults and young adults. Her books have sold over 2 million copies. Besides writing books and articles, she teaches at writers' conferences across the country. She and her husband make their home in Tehachapi, California.